**"The only tin
alive was that
came to my o**

"The opening line of James Grady's new novel is the stuff of good old-fashioned hard-boiled detective fiction. [It] tips us off that *RUNNER IN THE STREET* aims to more, much more, than just another mystery novel. . . . The depiction of how members of Congress can be seduced and sometimes corrupted by 'the taste of power' is realistic and convincing. . . . SUCCESSFULLY DEVELOPED AND WRITTEN."

—*Washington Times*

"*RUNNER IN THE STREET* is filled with interesting and sometimes frightening, information about the functionings of prostitutes, politicians and policemen . . . much worthwhile here."

—*The New York Times Book Review*

"Grady knows how Washington works . . . the grid where prostitutes ply their trade, the clubs where lobbyists and lawyers cut their deals, the Senate offices where compromise is never more than a wink or a handshake away. . . . FASCINATING."

—*Washington Post*

James Grady

RUNNER IN THE STREET

PUBLISHED BY POCKET BOOKS NEW YORK

The author is grateful to the following for their permission to
quote:
  The Washington Post, for use of the excerpt on page 259 from the
October 19, 1980, issue.
  Time, for use of the excerpt on pages 339–40 from the December
22, 1980, issue.
  Bruce Springsteen, for use of the excerpt on page 340 from
"Born to Run," © 1975 Bruce Springsteen, used by permission.

POCKET BOOKS, a division of Simon & Schuster, Inc.
1230 Avenue of the Americas, New York, N.Y. 10020

Copyright © 1984 by James Grady
Cover artwork copyright © 1986 Don Brautigam

Published by arrangement with Macmillan Publishing Company
Library of Congress Catalog Card Number: 84-7953

ISBN: 0-671-55174-4

First Pocket Books printing May, 1986

10 9 8 7 6 5 4 3 2 1

POCKET and colophon are registered trademarks
of Simon & Schuster, Inc.

Printed in the U.S.A.

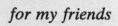

for my friends

RUNNER IN THE STREET

1

The only time I saw Eddie Hampton alive was that Monday morning when he came to my office to lie to me: May 19, 1980. I woke at dawn, aware that that day would be grim even though I didn't know Eddie Hampton or how his murder would mirror an American era and finally lead me to Tara.

I wasn't even there when Eddie Hampton showed up. He came while I was out on an early run—past the Capitol six blocks away from my third-floor combination apartment and office on Congress's chunk of Pennsylvania Avenue, down the Hill, over the Mall's sandy footpaths to the Washington Monument along the Reflecting Pool to the Lincoln Memorial, then back again as the morning commuter traffic soured the cool spring air with the stench of bus and car exhaust.

The first floor of my building is a shop, The Eclectic. My landlord Rich waved to me through its front window as I staggered to a stop on the sidewalk.

"Are you going to live?" Rich asked when he brought me the *Washington Post* and the *New York Times*.

"Probably," I wheezed, "if my heart doesn't beat itself to death."

"That's good, because I think you've got a client."

The horseshoe ring of hair around Rich's shiny dome and his brown beard are heavily flecked with gray. Laugh wrinkles and crow's-feet surround his eyes. He's pudgy, an inverted exclamation point.

"What are you talking about?" I asked.

"Some guy came in a few minutes ago, wanted to know if you were around; if not, when you'd be in."

"What did you tell him?"

"That you were out jogging—right? Unless Maggie is stashed somewhere close by and you ran over there for exercise."

"We don't have Maggie to kick around anymore."

His face stretched to a long, curious frown. My shoulders answered with a *c'est la vie* shrug.

"What about this client?" I said.

"I took him upstairs. He's there now, waiting."

"You what?!"

"You need business, he's got some."

"Rich, if he's some street freak like Radio Woman . . ."

"Trust me. He's got real trouble."

"Even better! You left him in my office, *in my home*, alone . . ."

"The door between your office and apartment is locked. What's he going to do? Pee on your floor? I'll clean it up. Your files and desk are locked. Your answering machine shows zero so he can't snoop on phone messages. I forgot your stack of business cards. God forbid he should take a card, promote your business around town. When I left he was sitting in the chair in front of your desk, just like a client should until you come to help him."

"Looking like this?"

"He drops by at seven in the morning without an appointment, what should he expect?"

"Who is he?"

"He didn't say and I didn't ask. He looks like a guy with trouble. Now get up there and take care of it. Earn money so you can pay your rent."

"If you hear me scream," I said, "call the cavalry."

"I don't want horseshit all over my sidewalk."

2

A trimmed business card serves as the sign on my door and the label for the mailbox downstairs:

JOHN RANKIN
Investigations

I stared at the card taped to my office door, tried to imagine who was beyond it. The chair inside creaked. I didn't want to scare him, so I thought about knocking. That's stupid, I realized: it's my office.

"Sorry I wasn't here when you arrived," I said as I entered. He started to get out of the visitor's chair but I waved him down.

"No, no," he insisted, "I'm sorry. I should have . . . should have waited. I'm . . . I'm sorry."

Sorry summed him up. He was a sheepish, late middle aged blur with wispy gray hair. Florid face, saggy jowls, droopy ears and a too-big nose. Small bloodshot eyes. His timid mouth never quite closed and never completely opened. From his teeth's greenish hue and the brown stains on his thumb and first two right fingers I guessed he was a heavy smoker. Cobwebs of booze-broken blood vessels along each side of his nose implied that nicotine wasn't his only drug habit. He wore a blue three-piece suit like a cheap tent draped over scrawny poles. His white shirt and dated black tie added neither glamor nor fashion to his scarecrow appearance. His fingernails needed to be clipped. They trembled as he readjusted himself in my old wooden chair. Close up he smelled of dried whiskey and dead dreams. I guessed it had been one of those nights, then expanded that judgment to include one of those lives.

"Can I get you anything?" I asked. "Coffee?"

"No, no, I'm fine."

The patter gave me time to get situated behind my desk— and to check the office for any signs of disturbance. I keep the three file cabinets locked to reassure clients, but today I was glad of that cosmetic precaution. Maybe he'd glanced at my framed license on the wall. Perhaps he'd rummaged through the small bathroom behind me, or the closet where I keep my winter coats. The door between those two cubicles separates my apartment from my office, and Rich had made sure it was secure. My desk chair tips like a rocker. I hooked my feet under a drawer, leaned back to stare at my drop-in.

"I feel peculiar sitting in my office with a stranger."

"I'm . . . I'm not sure I want to tell you my name."

"Then there's not much point in you being here."

"Oh," he said with a crippled smile he'd repeat, "there's a point. There's a point."

"Suppose you tell it to me. We'll worry about your name later."

"First . . . You're a private detective, aren't you?"

I sighed. "I doubt that my job means what you think."

"But you've got a card! Your name is in the Yellow Pages!"

"The card says 'Investigations.' I don't do divorce work, domestic snooping, child custody fights, most criminal work. I work some white collar crime stuff, civil litigation, government oversight investigation. I used to be an investigative reporter. Now I investigate for private clients—and I'm picky about who they are. There's a good chance I'm not who you think I am."

"I thought you might be the kind of guy who could help."

"Why?"

"You're the only private investigator with a Capitol Hill address."

"I take political work, but nothing shady. I don't do campaign security, but I can refer you."

"It's an election year, but . . . this isn't like that."

4

"What is 'it' like?"

"Can I . . . Can I tell you in confidence?"

"I wish you'd tell me anything."

"I mean, I can tell you things *confidentially,* right?"

"You can trust me not to blab your stuff outside my office, but there's no legal bond of secrecy. Maybe if I were hired by your attorney I'd be covered under his client confidentiality privilege, but as we are, it's just you and me."

"I'm not sure that's good enough."

"Look," I said, "as long as you don't jab my conscience with something I can't ignore, you've got my word I won't repeat what you tell me." I pushed to the limit. "As long as I don't commit a crime by hearing what you say, I won't tell a soul."

Those tired, sad and sorry eyes looked at me, looked away. The crippled smile came back.

"I think you keep your word," he said. "People probably trust you. They trust me too, because they think they know what I'm worth."

All I could do was shrug. I didn't want to play philosophical Frisbee with this poor schnook. He sensed I'd reached my limit.

"I need to know what a congressional committee might be doing, might be going to do."

"I need to know what the weather might be doing next week so I can plan my running. I've got a better chance at finding that out than predicting what a congressional committee might do."

"But this is serious!"

"So is the weather. Sounds like you want a political spy, and Mister, that's not my game."

"Please! . . . The truth is this really isn't my problem. It's . . . a friend's. And what I want to know isn't illegal. In fact . . . maybe there's some bad going on this could stop."

He knew I didn't believe him so he jumped ahead as far as he dared.

"Suppose there was this congressional committee, and in an investigation they took advantage, rather one guy took advantage, of a personal relationship to . . . to spy on someone else. On someone very important who's done no wrong

5

—but someone who was vulnerable to spying and the kind of . . . stuff it can cause."

"A whole cast of no-named people," I said. "You. Plus Anonymous Mr. Vulnerable. And Innocent Mr. Somebody Else, who is being tricked by Mysterious Mr. Evil—maybe so Mr. Evil can target Mr. Vulnerable via a congressional investigation. And it's wrong, but not criminal or political. Do I have that mess straight?"

"I think so. It's complicated."

"I'm a simple man."

"But you sound like you don't like the idea of a congressional committee abusing the law!"

"You haven't told me anything solid to like or dislike: What congressional committee? There are around a hundred. What law? Laws Congress writes? The Constitution? Federal regulations? State statutes? Municipal codes? I could come up with a dozen examples of a congressional committee 'doing wrong' and not mention Joe McCarthy."

"What would it take for you to help me?"

"A lot more facts, a lot more truth, a lot clearer direction, and a good argument why I should spend my time chasing phantoms."

"What about money?"

"Yes, but that's not first on the list."

"How much money?"

"My standard fee is $30 an hour plus expenses. If you were a nonprofit organization, if this were a long-term contract like hotshot on-call research for a magazine, I might drop the fee a bit. Even if you quit spinning nonsense, give me something to chase . . ." Make it outrageous, I thought. "I'd want a flat $200 retainer fee, expenses, and, on top of the $200 retainer fee, $50 per hour with four hours' work guaranteed, so the least this would cost you . . ."

"Four hundred dollars." Not even a blink. Not even the crippled smile. "For that you'd take my case. Help my friend out."

"That amount of money would make it harder to say no."

"But you're saying no now."

"Flat out."

6

He thought for a moment. "You're saying no to what I've told you. But if I told you more . . . then you might say yes."

"It might rain tomorrow."

"I understand you. But I'm not sure what to do."

"No wonder, with your . . . your *friend's* troubles."

He stood, didn't offer to shake hands, which was fine with me. "Thank you," he said.

"All you took was my time."

That smile. And a last look from his sad eyes. "That's the unrepayable debt. I'm sorry. If I decide you can help, I'll get back to you."

Then he was gone, through the door, his footsteps clumping down the stairs, the faint clicking of the street door. I didn't bother to watch him from my bay window: no matter which way he went, he was obviously lost.

3

By 9:15 I'd showered, dressed and drained my first cup of coffee. I walked back into the office, which meant I was open for business. A stranger named Thomas Armstrong wasn't due to call me from Oregon for more than an hour. I wasn't expecting any other clients, but then I hadn't expected the man who'd come after dawn. Things happen. I sat behind my desk, flipped open the *Washington Post,* and discovered the world had blown up.

The headline atop the far left column read, 8 ARE DEAD IN VOLCANO ERUPTION, while the headline over the far right column read, MIAMI RIOT CONTINUES; 18 KILLED. A massive photograph of a squat mountain billowing black smoke marred by patches of white fire separated those two stories while photographs of utter chaos stretched downward from where their prose ended: overturned trucks, smoking buildings, people running in the streets. Looking at the two smaller pictures I couldn't tell which chaos belonged to which story. There was more.

The European Common Market was limiting its curbs on Iran, where 52 Americans were being held hostage in a political system that teetered between anarchy and religious hysteria. The only constant agreed upon by all sides was televised coverage of the sport.

Inside the borders of our ally South Korea, where 33,629 Americans once died fighting for freedom, May 19, 1980's headline announced that the TRY AT LIBERALIZATION COMES TO A HALT, with the military taking over, dissidents being rounded up, and all civil rights being suspended.

In Florida, 14 Cubans fleeing Communist dictatorship drowned when their boat caught fire, capsized.

In the Middle East, the Israelis and Arabs were fighting—over the alleged military deeds of children.

And finally, only six blocks from my desk, Congress had routinely authorized a five-year military "buildup" for America that would cost $1 trillion. One trillion dollars. World War II only cost the U.S. about $241 billion. Even allowing for inflation, peace was becoming an expensive proposition.

Some years carve their numbers deep into history's heart. There were the shouts of social revolution in 1968, the rolling thunder from a third-rate burglary at the Watergate complex in 1972. Now the tremors of 1980 were shaking society, and this was only May. Seven congressmen and senators plus an assortment of small-fry public servants had been secretly videotaped in an undercover FBI operation called ABSCAM. Fifteen of 19 public officials agreed to take bribes from a phony Arab sheik, giving America a formal corruption factor of 77 percent.

In 1980 the Soviet Union invaded Afghanistan. Consequently, no Americans competed in the Olympic Games held that summer in Moscow, but in the Winter Olympics held before the invasion the USA achieved the impossible and defeated the Soviet hockey team. In the spring of 1980, the Soviet bear squeezed woeful Poland (again).

In the midst of 1980's global crises, student activism on America's college campuses, according to the *Post*, meant cutthroat grade grubbing and two crazes: being tucked into bed and playing a mock murder game called "Assassination."

The phone rang.

"Hello, John Rankin."

"Dog here." *Mad Dog* Saul Lazarian: He'd been my reporting partner for three years at Ned Johnson's muckraking newspaper column.

"Dog, what are you doing up before ten?"

He laughed, his pitch rose a couple notes. "Did you . . . What did you think of her?"

"Who?"

"Of Katie! At the party! Don't you remember?!"

I remembered two dozen people gathered in Joey Mal-

9

letta's backyard court, a barbecue burning in one corner more for form than food. The coal's glow and two porch lights cut the cool Saturday night darkness. Joey's Rolling Stones *Greatest Hits* tape blared from a stereo inside his apartment. "Satisfaction." "Under My Thumb." "Tumbling Dice." "Jumping Jack Flash." "Let's Spend the Night Together." No one was dancing, but we all felt the rhythm of songs we knew. I had my eyes on a joint slowly making the rounds of a four-friend cluster an arm's length away and my mind on better days when Saul leaned close to me.

"That's her," Mad Dog whispered: "There."

A bright-eyed, snow white blond woman walked through the narrow, ivy-lined pathway from the street to the court-yard.

"That's who?" I asked.

"Her. Katie. Isn't she neat?!"

Neat?! She'd wandered our general direction, joined us when Saul called her name: Katie. I talked with her for maybe two minutes while Saul shuffled from foot to foot. She drifted from the party without me noticing her exit. As I talked to Saul that morning I remembered how subdued he'd been after she disappeared. I should have paid more attention to her. It's not always easy to tell who counts.

"How far gone are you on this, Saul?" I asked him.

"Just . . . Just . . ."

"Just remember: romance is a rough racket."

He laughed nervously. "You ought to know."

"What else is new?" I said.

"I'm going after the ABSCAM tapes." A professional blockbuster, but for the first time his work was in second place.

"No hit on you, Saul, but you're trying to bag the hottest shit since the Watergate grand jury reports."

"That's why it's worth going after."

"You could be wasting a lot of time."

"Do you know anybody who'd be a source for it?"

"No, but I'll ask around."

"There's gotta be a way. There's always a way. You just do it. Like everything else—*everything* else. You OK with Maggie yet?"

"Not quite. Are *you* OK?"

"Yeah." A soft, quiet *yeah*. We hung up.

I glanced back at the open *Post*, the folded *Times*, but I wasn't in the mood for contemporary reality. Armstrong was due to call in 45 minutes. I unlocked my desk, took out the manila envelope our mutual friend on the Oregon senator's staff had given me, reread the newspaper clippings.

If I'd read the first story when it originally appeared, the words hadn't marked my memory. Two paragraphs on the fourth page of the C section of the September 28, 1979, *Washington Post* tucked beneath a story on the mayor's optimistic plan for leaf removal:

NORTHWEST WOMAN, 21

DIES AFTER ATTACK

A 21-year-old woman was found beaten and stabbed in the chest and abdomen yesterday in an alley beside a Northwest Washington apartment building, D.C. police said.

The woman was identified as Janet Deborah Armstrong of 1694 Church St., N.W. A friend found her injured in the alley beside that building about 4 A.M. yesterday and took her to George Washington University Hospital where she died two hours later, police said.

That was all. One Janet Deborah Armstrong, race unknown, age 21, occupation unknown, family unmentioned, cut down in a neighborhood that was (a) rough inner city, (b) marginal or (c) up-and-coming chic, all depending on who was characterizing the 1600 block of Church Street. She died just before dawn, the worst time for Washington media: the TV news crews are in bed, at most on call; she fell between deadlines and press runs at the two newspapers. In essence the *Post* story was three working days late. But better late than never, better two paragraphs than nothing. Washingtonians who read this story in 1979 probably assumed that Janet Deborah Armstrong was black like most D.C. homicide victims, probably the end result of a domestic quarrel or a rape or robbery, some ordinary conflict escalated to the limit. Most readers never gave Janet Armstrong a second thought.

Until the second story. Second time around, Janet Armstrong's murder made page 1 of October 4th's *Post,* complete with pictures and a runover to page 3.

> *Dark Passage:*
> THE LIFE AND DEATH OF JANET ARMSTRONG
> by
> Cliff Palefsky
> *Washington Post* Staff Writer

When Janet Deborah Armstrong gave her high school salutatorian speech in Oregon four years ago her bright future included a scholarship to Harvard, a possible career in opera and the support of loyal friends and family members. Last Thursday morning this 21-year-old woman was murdered in the streets of Washington where she worked as a prostitute.

Armstrong was born and raised in Eugene, Oregon. Her father is a respected assistant director of a state social service agency. Her mother teaches at the University of Oregon. The family, according to sources in Oregon, is solidly middle class in a liberal university-logging-agricultural town.

During her Eugene high school years, Armstrong distinguished herself with both academic and musical talent, ranking second in her class of 513. She won state honors for her singing, was in several school choral groups, and during her last two years of high school played major parts in the university's operatic productions. She was in National Honor Society, class plays and a science club.

The mystery is why such a bright, talented, young woman scorned her promising future to become a prostitute. The first sign that she'd chosen what a friend called "an alternative lifestyle" was probably when she left Harvard during 1976's fall term.

"She didn't go because of her grades," said one Harvard friend who, like most of Armstrong's friends, wished not to be identified. "It was the whole scene: she didn't want to put up with the Ivy League."

Armstrong once complained that women in her dorm "didn't even play backgammon for fun."

After dropping out of Harvard, Armstrong returned to Eugene, lived in a small apartment close to the university where she'd once been a musical protégée, worked odd jobs around town. One summer night in 1977, in a chic Eugene bar, she met a man who eventually persuaded her to accompany him to Washington.

Sources in Eugene say this man came to town driving a black Cadillac. They claim, as do Washington police, that he was in Eugene recruiting prostitutes, a charge he denies.

He sometimes shared a two-bedroom apartment in a newly renovated Church Street townhouse with Armstrong. He found her bleeding in the alley beside the apartment building and brought her in his Cadillac to the hospital where she died. He, claim Washington police, was Armstrong's pimp, a charge he denies.

In the streets of Washington, Janet Armstrong was known as "Kristina Campbell," sometimes calling herself "Kris" or "Crystal." She wore "almost conservative, almost classy dresses and skirts," not the hot pants and halter-top type of flamboyance associated with most streetwalkers.

When she died, she was wearing a fake rabbit's skin parka of the kind commonly worn by prostitutes on "the Stroll," as the red-light district of 14th Street is known. Beneath the parka was a simple dress, torn in her struggle. The leather shoes she wore in her final steps are little different from those worn by most women—noteworthy only for their bright red color.

According to several women interviewed at 15th Street and Vermont Avenue—the corner where Armstrong worked—she was "OK" and "sweet to the customers." She allegedly charged the going rate of $50 and, unlike most prostitutes, kept detailed business records.

At a Washington cocktail party where she casually talked of her prostitution profession, she passionately discussed the nuances of *Carmen,* finally deciding that a 1972 version of the opera performed by the New York Metropolitan Opera under Leonard Bernstein was the best.

She'd been convicted of solicitation here and perhaps elsewhere. Police officers who knew her considered her "intelligent, not your average hooker."

"She was nice," said a D.C. policeman who once arrested her. "I told her she didn't seem like the type to be working the streets. She giggled."

Homicide detectives said robbery was apparently not a motive for her murder, and that they have no suspects.

And the girl from Eugene, Oregon, who loved opera, went to Harvard, worked as one of hundreds of Washington prostitutes, who was sweet and giggled, is dead.

Two photos of Janet Armstrong flanked her story in the page 1 box. The cutline for the picture on the left read, "Janet Armstrong at Harvard . . ."

The picture could have come from any American high school or college yearbook, a young white woman's three-quarter, black-and-white profile, eyes raised to the left as bidden by the assembly-line photographer, the posed, angelic smile he asked for curling her lips upward. Her light hued hair was wavy, brushed up at the shoulders, obviously set and sprayed firm for the photograph. I wondered what color it was. She had a handsome rather than pretty face.

The cutline for the second picture continued the ellipses like a cheap ad's *before and after* logo: ". . . and in a recent photograph." The same woman, but this picture was candid and the nuances of her face had changed. The smoothness seemed lost. Her eyes and her mouth were more defined (by makeup, time or the camera? I wondered). Her hair hung naturally, free, with more bounce than in the posed shot. She smiled at the photographer, not at his instruction. As I studied the second picture I realized that characterization wasn't quite right: a grin, not a smile, the wide, happy grin of a woman who could be called sweet and who could giggle at her arresting officer.

Usually when I look through old newspaper clippings I remember what I was doing at the time of the story: we bend history around our personal mirror. As I looked at the Janet Armstrong clips I remembered only how stunned I'd been by her saga. Then had come absolute fascination. The newspaperman in me recognized a great story while the reader in me rose to the high drama spelled out for my edification. Next came a rage that somebody should have died *this way*. Finally I felt guilty: guilty for the entertainment somebody else's grisly murder gave me, guilty because I wondered if some night when driving through that part of town I hadn't perhaps seen Janet Armstrong standing on the street corner, ogled her myth-cloaked female form with that ugly sea we all harbor and try to hide—especially from ourselves. Perhaps I'd done that, then driven by. While she lived she'd been both less and more than a person to me. Now, when it was too late to touch her substance, her shadow fell on my life.

I shook my head, picked up the third clipping:

MAN CHARGED IN MURDER
OF YOUNG OREGON WOMAN.

The story ran on page C1 of the February 4, 1980, Metro section: off the front page but still big news. The *Post* gave Cliff Palefsky his second by-line on the story.

Herbert Jerome "Magic" Murphy, 33, has been charged with murder as a result of the September 27 death of Janet Armstrong, an Oregon woman who dropped out of Harvard and subsequently came to Washington to work as a prostitute. Murphy has also been charged with assaulting Armstrong and a second woman, also allegedly a prostitute, and various pimping and pandering charges.

Armstrong's murder last fall and the bizarre story of her life created a major controversy in Washington, in Boston where she once attended Harvard, and in her hometown where she'd been a star high school student. The *Post* and the Eugene paper which published the *Post*'s story on her life came under severe attack for sensationalism from Oregon residents because of their coverage of Armstrong's death.

The police claim Murphy and Armstrong had a quarrel that turned into a violent brawl, and that she fled the building. Murphy allegedly chased her and attacked her in the alley, finally stabbing her repeatedly with a jagged pane of glass from a window broken in the fight. Allegedly, Murphy then briefly left the scene, returned, loaded Armstrong into his black Cadillac, and took her to George Washington University Hospital, where she died.

After entering pleas of not guilty, Murphy was released from custody on bond. He then left the jurisdiction of the court, was arrested as a fugitive in Ilinois 14 hours later, and extradited back to Washington the same day. He listed his occupation as "unemployed musician and salesman." He is being held in jail. No trial date has been set.

I hadn't read that story when it ran. Maybe I'd been out of town. Right then, out of town was where I wanted to be. I didn't want to talk to a father whose daughter had her life spread over my desk as so much clipped newsprint.

But my phone rang at 10:40. "Mr. Rankin? This is Tom Armstrong in Eugene, Oregon."

I pictured him in a cozy breakfast nook, yellow refrigerator and stove behind him in the spotless kitchen, sitting at a solid blond wooden table holding the phone. There'd be a thick file on the table, a pencil, a yellow page tablet with my name and phone number scrawled on the top sheet. An older man, graying, maybe bald. He'd be well dressed, tie and shirt, suit jacket waiting for him on a nearby chair, preparing to face the world at work. I thought of him sitting there, and I thought of Eugene—cool, gray rain clouds rolling benignly over low

16

mountains, emerald dampness everywhere. Healthy. A river runs gently through the town. Everywhere there is clean, crisp.

"Call me John. When somebody says 'Mr. Rankin,' I think of my father. I'm not him."

"And I'm Tom."

Expensive silence filled the telephone line between us.

"Look," I finally said, "I got your packet."

"Then you know why I'm calling."

"No, not really." I swallowed. "I know what the stories say about your daughter, and God am I sorry . . ."

"Thank you." His interruption was by now probably automatic—yet no less sincere for being a reflex.

". . . but there doesn't seem to be anything to be done. The police have charged that guy. Besides, I rarely handle criminal work."

"I know that the police have charged . . . that man. When I talked with our mutual friend about what I wanted, he said it might be your kind of thing. You're a detective, you're from the West. You know what it's like out here, you're closer to her generation than . . . You probably know about things that maybe other people . . .

"I don't want you to investigate who killed my daughter. The police have done a wonderful job of that. But I must know *why!*"

"Why what?"

"Why . . . Why my Janet died like she did. I carried her home from the hospital after she was born and went to her first singing recital and taught her how to ride a bike and signed her report cards and she died in that goddamned alley as a . . ." His control came back. "I buried her last fall. I want to know *why*. You're the only chance I've got left of finding out. Please, please help me!"

"Finding out why somebody does anything, especially after they're . . . gone, I don't think anybody can do it. Maybe a psychiatrist could tell you . . ."

"I've seen them—about me, about my wife, about Jan. All they do is throw silly words at me about *negative feelings*, about *letting go*. They only know what they can twist around their philosophies and spit back as jargon."

"Tom, I wish . . . I'm just an investigator. I might look for a missing person, but you want me to track a lost soul."

"Look," he said, desperately shifting arguments, "maybe you can find out something, some goddamned hard facts . . . so maybe some other Jan won't end up dead in an alley. So maybe some other father won't end up holding the far end of a phone line, feeling like a fool with only ache inside him. I don't think we can stop all evil in the world. But maybe we can help on one. Just one. Somewhere, somehow.

"All my life, John, I've believed in reason and knowledge. Logic. If you just have enough facts, then you can understand something. *Do* something. Now I've got a dead daughter and nothing makes sense."

"Tom, if I did this . . ."

"We've got the money to pay."

"That's not what . . ."

"But it's what you need to come to sooner or later. Don't worry. We've got money. We've got plenty of money.

"Want to know why? When Jan was a baby I bought a family life insurance policy for the three of us. If it had been suicide, nothing. But murder pays a profit."

"Tom, money wasn't . . . What I might find may hurt you more."

"What could you discover that I haven't already imagined and suffered for without knowing if it were real or not?"

"How does your wife . . ."

"Since the funeral my wife wakes up a little less dead every morning. But I'm afraid time will catch up with her before she comes back to life."

"What will me doing this do to her?"

"You can't hurt the dead. Maybe my wife is one of the dead you can help. You've got to help, help both of us."

I'd set myself up for a Janet Armstrong, for someone like her father, taped my card on my mailbox saying what I did and who I was. They took me at my word. I could tell this man *no,* argue there was nothing I could do. I could be honest and admit I didn't want any of his anguish. Or I could say *yes.* Play at being God passing out judgment. I doubted I'd find solace for this voice from Oregon.

But if I merely walked away, the echo of his pleas and a ghost from newspaper clippings would haunt my footsteps.

"Tom, I can't promise anything. But I'll try to figure out something to do."

"Thank you!" he said and I heard him start to cry. "Thank you! What can I . . . Is there anything . . . anything you want . . ."

Neither of us could take much more, but I knew he had to get up from this phone call having done more than get another promise from another stranger. I asked the only question I could think of:

"What color was Janet's hair?"

"Not any solid color. Call it auburn. Most like brown, but . . . but with red touches all through, red like copper or rust."

4

Washington's subway system was rudimentary in 1980, barely one-third completed after 12 years of construction, just two crosstown lines connecting central parts of the city to each other and to too few suburban commuting centers in this metropolitan capital of a country suffering a transportation crisis. The subway's limitations are not all accidents of incompetence. For years, the parking lot, highway and car lobbies stymied subway legislation, a quaint and quiet historical war that eventually helped swell Metro's massive tax-supported cost overruns and increase the inordinate construction delays. Such is life in this city.

Metro works: the sleek cars are graffiti-free, litter seldom seen, crime uncommon. The Blue Line Eastern Market subway stop is half a block from my office. I rode that line to Metro Center, transferred to the Red Line, got off at Farragut North. I spent most of the 20-minute trip waiting for trains in dank concrete tunnels, carefully clutching the rectangle paper fare card D.C.'s Metro uses instead of coin tokens.

The escalator brought me up from darkness to the sunny bustle of K Street and Connecticut Avenue. A steady stream of well-dressed *professionals* flowed over the sidewalks. The eight-story office buildings along K Street house legal factories of 100-plus-member law firms, hundreds of lobbying groups, and national associations' headquarters. Connecticut Avenue and 16th Street are boulevards of major hotels with fashionable shops for those who don't make it to Georgetown's boutiques. America was groaning under hard times. In Washington, new construction was everywhere, with entire blocks of downtown D.C. being leveled, classic and functional office buildings crumbling before the wrecking crane's ball so newer but no more functional office buildings could rise in their places. As the trucks hauled away the rubble, I'd remember how a foreman on my college summer construction job sang an off-key ditty about "it all makes work for the working man." And money for the man who owns the crane.

Art Dillon's offices were further up Connecticut Avenue on N Street, one of the most beautiful blocks anywhere: trees, wonderously restored townhouses converted to offices, tastefully designed modern structures. Neither he nor his 12-member firm was famous even among law-firm-oriented Washingtonians in 1980. For Art Dillon, this anonymity may be fleeting. I've got a bet with one of his partners that Art will someday leave his big-time legal battles and move back to South Carolina to run for Congress.

Washington is supposed to be a city of law. It is a city of lawyers. In 1980 there were 25,903 active members of the D.C. Bar besides Art Dillon. Only about 11,000 of those attorneys actually "practiced law," the rest being in government or business or some other "nonlegal" endeavor. Probably no more than 2,000 of all those legal eagles ever set foot in a courtroom, with most of those who do participating in civil affairs. Most of the 11,000 practicing attorneys harvest their wealth from paper shuffling or guiding clients through our government. They write wills, settle real estate deals. The government guides "intervene" for their clients through administrative law proceedings—paper wars in which the attorneys try to beat a bureaucracy, perhaps finagle a bureaucracy into beating their client's opponents or the public (who may be one and the same). The big-name legal factories with limousines for senior partners have legions of such lawyers in their fold, hotshots who never make the newspapers while making millions for their clients and rules for the rest of us.

Lawyers who do make the papers as minor Washington celebrities are rarely working attorneys. Their proper label is *lobbyist*. They deny that identity. They claim a lobbyist is a slightly greasy someone who registers with the government to woo a congressman for a client interested in a particular bill.

21

The big-name lawyers see the same congressman, woo him on the same bill, but as lofty guardians of the law they "represent the legal interests of the client" and consequently need not register as lobbyists.

Mixed with the lobbyists, the administrative lawyers, the real estate and divorce lawyers, are a small core of criminal attorneys ranging from Fifth Streeters (so named for the location of several such dubious firms) who solicit anyone wandering through the halls of justice to the crack legal minds who could waltz Satan safely through those same corridors. There are public interest lawyers, idealists following the footprints of Ralph Nader for fewer dollars than a legal secretary makes. There are fakes, fools and finds beyond worth for a man in legal trouble. There is only one Art Dillon.

"What do you know about legacy?" he asked as he strode into the small law library where I waited. Art was always in the middle of something else, squeezing what he was doing *now* out of what he was scheduled to be doing *then*. Art loved the tension his pace dictated, loved the mountains made out of molehills of time. His miracles were his curse as well as his blessing: he was afraid that if he slowed down, he'd lose the luck that let him go so fast so far.

"If you mean life insurance, I've already had one lesson this morning," I said as he flopped into a chair at the conference table.

"You working insurance claim cases without me?"

"It's not like that."

"What's it like?"

"That's why they call us *private* detectives."

He laughed. "Is this other case going to take all your time or can you earn some money from me?"

"I'll make time for your stuff. That discrimination suit you steered me to turned out real well."

"So I heard. Nice firm. Is Cheryl Johansen still gorgeous?"

"As far as I know."

"I hear that's pretty far. I hear that as soon as Maggie is history, you and Cheryl will be more than strictly lawyer-investigator—don't protest! When you can't sell your innocence, ignore the charges. What else do you have going?"

"Odds and ends. Eight Freedom of Information cases."

"Plus this new client we don't get to talk about."

"And now estates."

"*Legacy.* You're stuck with what you're given and you pass on what you did. Life's not clean and free. Everybody leaves a legacy. We're carving a case out of that truth. Remember Jonestown?"

"Jonestown? I'm not sure . . ."

"Reverend Jim Jones and his . . ."

". . . his electric Kool-Aid acid test, yeah, I remember."

"Sick joke, Rankin."

"Sick scene. What are you doing with it?"

"Trying to help some people who got stuck with that legacy. I've got 24 clients, kin of cult members. When Jones and his faithful died in Guyana, they killed their church for all practical purposes, but for legal purposes it and they exist in estate form. Big bucks poured into that jungle. There's property, personal and church, both in Guyana and America. God knows where all."

"Maybe some insurance policies."

"From what my clients tell me, Jones hoodwinked those away. 'Course, if there are some policies in force, suicide would invalidate them. But there was some talk about whether all those 900-some people committed voluntary suicide."

"There's such a thing as involuntary suicide?"

Art grinned. "Damned if I know. And damned if I want to create a legal quagmire raising the question. But maybe we could claim he defrauded his congregation."

"Whatever happened to free will?"

"It's a cloudy concept these days, John. The bureaucracy inherited the J-town mess. Can you pull shit out of the government that might help us determine what legacy the clients can expect?"

"If you think it's worth a shot, I'll do it."

"Then no more sick jokes."

"Why are we doing this, Art? This mess could take years, net our clients zip."

"*Legacy.* I keep telling you, it's all about legacy. Jones scammed those people who died with him. They let Jones con them into thinking he was their only responsibility. They gave him all their worries and all their worth, figured that bought them heaven and the hell with everything else. Their man could walk on water, so they were absolved from the ripples of their own lives. That's always bullshit, so that's what they left behind them. But there's treasure hidden under all that bullshit: buildings, cash, church pews, maybe some of your insurance policies. If nobody fights, then all that treasure will siphon off into the system, go to Jim Jones's buddies or just plain evaporate. I say fuck such nonsense, so I better back up *my* bullshit. Is that OK with you?"

"That's great with me."

5

Maggie had the knives out that night. When I got to the bar she was sitting at a table for two, her back against the mirrored wall. She wore her most expensive suit. There was a drink in front of her, and a wispy snake of smoke curled up to the shadows from the ember in her hand. She knew I hated cigarettes. She wanted blood, as if somehow blood would wash away her hurt. The sultry hostess with waist-length blond hair met me with a professional smile on her lips, maybe more in her eyes, but when I nodded toward Maggie she saved her breath. She looked at that smoldering figure, looked at me, then walked away. She'd seen this scene before too.

"They're bringing you a drink," Maggie announced as I sat down. I put her bulging blue Swissair shoulder bag on the floor as nonchalantly as I could. "And I'm paying for it."

"What am I having?"

"Gin and tonic. It's summer. No, *excuse me:* it's spring. *Please* forgive my sloppy mistake."

I didn't reply.

"Tonight I'm facing the door. I know you love that spot. I used to think that was so cute. Exotically appropriate. But tonight you get to watch nothing but me and the wall."

Behind her in the mirror the hostess led another couple to a table. The woman was pretty in a kinky-haired, petite way. Her suit-and-tied, balding companion looked nervous. The hostess glanced our way, obviously remembered my drink.

I'd come because it was the right thing to do. The shoulder bag belonged to Maggie, odds and ends she hadn't scooped up when she stalked out. She didn't want them as much as she wanted to make a proud exit rather than a tearful retreat be the last time she said good-bye to John Rankin. That was fine with me, that was fair. All that didn't matter, as long as she left. But there were limits.

"I won't fight with you, Maggie."

She stubbed out the cigarette, paused while the hostess set my drink on the table. "I'll have another," Maggie said, "and bring him one too. He drinks fast." Strands of Maggie's short brown hair fell across her forehead. She brushed them back, lit another cigarette. "You know why we never fought?"

"It's a stupid waste of time."

"Un-unh. You've got nothing against combat. But with women, you don't put anything out there you care enough to fight over. Control, John, that's your biggest thing."

"Somebody is always in control," I told her. "Trying to be that somebody doesn't make you bad."

"It makes you safe, John. How have you pulled this shit off for 31 years?"

"It does me no good to show you where you're wrong, Maggie."

"But it does *me* good." She sipped her drink, looked away. Started again in a softer voice.

"You loved me too, didn't . . . Don't do that! Don't turn your eyes cold and dead! Just because I mention love. God, how you must hate that word!"

"You're wrong, Maggie."

"Am I? I remember the first time you said it. You'd been so damned careful all those months, every word measured and weighed, spun out so deliberately . . ."

"I never lied to you, Maggie. I never, ever lied."

"Not in words. You're careful with words."

"It's not the words I'm careful with. It's what they mean."

"Like love. I bet you totaled everything up: 'Well, I like her a lot, more than equals *like*, so therefore I must love her. Somehow.' I can hear you tacking 'somehow' on that. Then you hit me with the big I-love-you. Only it wasn't so big, was it John?"

"I tried, Maggie."

"Yes, you did. I can't complain about that."

26

"You can't complain about anything."

"What you mean is no complaints are *justified*. So what am I *justified* in feeling?"

"I doubt we'd agree on that."

"Me either, John. We sure didn't agree on what love is or what to do with it. Not when we had it.

"Were the others like this too, John? Nice tight script—with you in full control. I'm sure they loved you. If they didn't, I'm betting you walked away from them damn quick. Wouldn't want to be on the losing end, would we Johnny-boy?"

"Nobody likes losing." Ridiculous to need to point that out. I wanted to check my watch, see how much time I'd wasted here.

"Especially you, right John? And you never have! That dawned on me today. It always ends for you first. Then you set them up so they say good-bye, free you of responsibility. And let you stay safe. I bet you always make sure you're safe—and comfortable. Have you got someone already lined up now, some safe replacement, somebody you've been fucking while you were setting me up to walk out?"

"I didn't sleep with anybody after I gave you that promise. Still haven't."

"Maybe not in the flesh. But where's your spirit been sleeping?"

"Your concern with that ended last week, Maggie."

"No, my . . . my *rights,* they ended last week. But I'm still concerned. Maybe I'm a fool or nostalgic or . . . For a while I thought I still loved you. *But I don't!*" She started to cry, stopped herself with three hard sniffles. "I really, really don't, damn you! I . . . part of me hates you but part of me still likes you and worries about you and . . ."

"I still like you too, Maggie, still worry about you too."

"Don't you do that to me!! Don't worry about me, don't make me feel guilty for . . . God you're such a shit! You don't lie to people, you just structure your truth so well the fine lines get missed. You can take a person in faster and farther than anybody I've ever met, but *that wall* is always there. You tell them so with words and what you don't say, but all they see is . . . Oh Johnny!"

She couldn't stop the tears that time. To comfort her would have been cruel, so I sat there while she sobbed, feeling terribly wrong for dumping my private mess in public. I watched her, the reflections in the mirror. Eventually the cigarette she'd left burning in her ashtray went out. The last wisp of smoke brought her back.

"I'm sorry about . . . Jesus, look at me! I come here to . . . And *I* end up apologizing. You always win, don't you? But what do you get? You want love more than anybody I've ever met. That's what hooks the Angelas and Saras and . . . and the Maggies. We think we'll be the one to fill that hole and it will all be wonderful. But we can't. Because you stay behind your wall, nice and safe and sound.

"What do you want, Johnny? What have you been waiting for all these years? Come on. You can tell me. Pretend I'm just a friend." She laughed. "No, I guess you won't do that. Or you'll just use words. Just words. You want it all, don't you, Johnny?"

"If you don't want it all, you don't get what's real, what's worth . . ."

"What's *real?!* What do you think love is, Johnny? Something from one of your damn movies? You want to get hit by a rocket, don't you? What do you think I did to you? You started panting the moment you saw me. What were you supposed to do, *die?!*"

"But there was . . ."

"There was no way I could clear the wall, right?"

"It's nobody's fault, Maggie. And even for the pain . . ."

"What *pain* did you feel, Johnny? Awkward, yes. But what *pain?*"

"Even for all this shit, I'm not sorry we happened."

She smiled, shook her head. Picked up her shoulder bag. Her other hand dropped $15 on the table, and I wondered how many drinks she'd had before I got there. "So you're not sorry we happened. That's damn noble of you, John. Damn generous and damn noble. Me, I kind of think I am sorry." She stood, pushed through the space between tables. She turned and I bet even odds she'd rehearsed the good-bye line.

"But you know what I'm sorry for? For you, Johnny. You want it all so damn bad but you won't be able to get it."

She turned away. As she did I thought: *Not with you.*

"I guess this means you won't want the next round," said the hostess. She'd waited until after I'd seen the reflection in the mirror of the door swinging closed on Maggie.

"Is that enough to cover our bill?" I nodded to the $15.

The hostess glanced at the tab on her tray. "You owe for the one at the bar," she said. "It's been ready for a while, but it didn't seem . . . appropriate to interrupt."

I smiled at her, dropped two ones on the table. "You did right and you did good." I stood, walked toward the door.

"How 'bout you?" she called after me. "How did you do?"

I shook my head at the twinkle in her eye. But smiled.

My battered blue Datsun started on the third try. I cursed it silently and without sincerity. I called it New Car, though I'd bought it used, and loved it not enough to give it a proper name. It got me home. I'd switched both my personal and professional lines into the answering machine. There were half a dozen no-message calls that left whirring gaps on my tape. I wondered if they were calls looking for the investigator or the man, or somebody who wasn't particular.

Cheryl had called: *"I'm . . . I'm not pressuring you,"* her taped voice said, *"just worried, John! Worried about you. If you . . . If you want, call me and I'll come over. I just want to help."*

She'd worry too much if I didn't return her call: "Hi kid."

"Oh John!" I imagined her sitting on her bed as she answered the phone. "How did . . . Was it bad?"

"It was OK."

"That's not what I'm hearing."

"Maybe you listen too hard."

"John, I understand. Really. If you want, I'll come over. We don't have to . . . to do anything. I'll even sleep on your couch."

"Let's wait until tomorrow, all right? Better then. Right then. Bright and early."

"Really?"

"Really."

"That's a promise, isn't it?"

"Always. Now we better get some sleep."

"How can I sleep thinking about what's for breakfast?"

I laughed. "I hope you're as incorrigible as you sound."

"Better," she said. "Better."

After she hung up I yawned, wandered around the office, looked down from my tower window to Pennsylvania Avenue. People shuffled by on the sidewalk. I turned off lights as I walked through my apartment, set my alarm for 5:30. Dawn would wake me when it came through the skylight over the bed, but I wanted to be sure I was ready for Cheryl.

I glanced around my bedroom: change and pocket paraphernalia scattered on the mirrored bureau, laundry spilling out of the pile in the closet, paperback books stacked beside the unmade bed, but nothing incriminating or insulting in view.

As I lay in bed that night I heard the faint sounds of the city. The skylight shade was open, but I saw no stars: clouds, pollution, neon glare, perhaps all three hid those diamonds in darkness. I thought of the gone, good women who'd loved me, of Angela, of Sara, of Maggie, of the others for whom love was definitely not the right word. Of Cheryl.

And then, just for a moment before I slept, I thought about the man who'd visited me that morning, the man who hadn't told me his name was Eddie Hampton. I didn't know his name then. Just as I didn't know that his shadow lay beside me in darkness.

6

The next day, the day Eddie Hampton was murdered, I made love with Cheryl four times, twice in the morning before work and twice in the evening after work. We had dinner, then she went home.

"You sure you don't want me to spend the night?" she said in the morning as we stood in my hallway planning the evening.

"I'd rather . . . I want to be alone." My halting tone implied tender indecision, but the only thing I was unsure about was how to keep my privacy without hurting her feelings.

"I understand," she said, though I doubted she did. "But I won't be just a drop-in."

"I don't want you for that." I kissed her good-bye again.

She waltzed down the stairs lazy and slow and lush, thick brown hair, heavy breasted, taut bell-bottomed, the frenzy of her dawn arrival spent. Somehow she was more sultry now than before. I went back to my office to work.

What I do is like a child's game. Washington is a mound of strange-shaped, well-mixed sticks. In the child's game the trick is to pick the sticks off the mound without shaking the pile. The mound gets smaller with time and play. In Washington, time and play add more sticks to the pile. What I do is learn the sticks, how and why they touch, so that I might know what shakes the pile. The sticks of this city stretch everywhere, from the Capitol to cornfields in Iowa, citadels in Moscow, churches in California and exile camps in Guyana's jungles.

I dialed a phone number I knew well.

"Good morning, Senator Neiberg's office."

"David Henderson, please," I said.

"Hi, this is David Henderson."

"I'm representing a wealthy Arab sheik, and I was wondering if for several million dollars the senator would help the sheik with some immigration problems. I was told you're the man to talk to."

"Absolutely. In fact, why bother the senator with this? He's such a busy man. We don't need him to know what he does. You just get me the money . . ."

"We could get the money," I said, echoing the classic Washington joke mimicked from the Watergate tapes.

"We could get it in cash . . ."

"But . . ."

". . . it would be wrong," said David. "I want diamonds. Dollars are no good anymore."

"Actually, I'm not calling to offer you a bribe."

"That's right, Rankin, disappoint me! You don't call for weeks, then you disappoint me. Makes me angry!"

"So angry you won't help me with a favor?"

"What fun is a favor without a bribe?"

"Could you have the Congressional Research Service run a computer printout of all the federal reports and investigations of the Jonestown affair? That was where . . ."

"I know what Jonestown was, fool! What do you think, that the Library of Congress has nothing better to do than help you? That with my position of power and importance . . ."

"When did your medication wear off, David?" I joked.

". . . that I have nothing better to do than your errands?"

"How many high school term papers did you guys research this week?"

"And those kids can't even vote, right? 'Course, their parents can, and you can't, at least not in our state. What are you doing in Jonestown—looking for God? He left."

"Just a case."

"Oh, you're *working!* That makes a *big* difference. When do you need it?"

"When can I get it?"

"This afternoon. I can bust an intern's ass. Wednesday or Thursday would be better, though."

My second call took less time.

"Good morning, Washington Post."

"I'm calling for a reporter named Cliff Palefsky."

"I'll see if he's in."

The line hummed while the operator hunted our quarry. I imagined buttons lighting up, bells ringing on half a dozen phones scattered around the crowded football-field office of the *Post*'s fifth-floor newsroom.

"I'm sorry, Mr. Palefsky doesn't seem to be here."

"Would you have him call John Rankin, please?" I gave her my number, added, "It's about a story he worked on."

To get the next number I called the main bureaucracy's switchboard, then hung up and dialed directly.

"Homicide, Detective Bechtel."

"Could I talk to the officer who handled the Armstrong case?"

"The who?"

"Janet Armstrong. A prostitute, college girl who . . ."

"Oh yeah, hold on: Hey Sarge! Who handled that hooker who got killed? . . . No, last year, the one with the Harvard shit?"

A voice mumbled in the background.

Bechtel talked to me again. "You want Detective Nick Sherman. He's in court . . . Hey! Wait a minute. Sherman! Call on 3-5."

"This is Nick Sherman. Can I help you?" A pleasant tenor.

"My name is John Rankin. I'm a private investigator . . ."

"Really." Sherman's tenor turned hard and flat.

"Janet Armstrong's father has hired me . . ."

"I wasn't aware he was dissatisfied with our performance."

"It's not like that. I wonder if we could talk about it?"

"Well, Mr. Rankin, I'm due in court now. After that I go on three-to-midnight. But I'm certainly interested in anything having to do with a murder I've handled, especially when a stranger I've never heard of calls me about it."

"Look, if you want to check me out, that's fine . . ."

"Thanks."

Our rapport slid from bad to worse. "I should have a letter from Mr. Armstrong authorizing me to look into this as soon as he can get it here from Oregon. The man who referred Armstrong to me works for an Oregon senator, and he'll vouch for me."

"Good for him."

"I guess this is a bad time, so why don't I call you later?"

"I look forward to it."

"And I'll give you my phone number, in case you get a free moment." I rattled off the digits. "Thanks for your time," I said, polite and friendly as could be.

"Always happy to serve a member of the public."

While waiting out the rest of the day I worked my way through the forest of paper that borders all our lives: power bills, checking accounts, credit card bills. I traded nonsense over the phone with Saul, found no one who could help him with ABSCAM. No one I needed to hear from called me. I checked over a draft of the brief containing my depositions that Cheryl's law firm was going to file. She came by at 5:30. We left for dinner at 8:00. I'd wanted to see Hitchcock's *North by Northwest* at the Biograph, but juggling her and my privacy afterward would have been awkward, so I skipped the suggestion. She dropped me off at 10:00. I read for an hour, listened to the *No Nukes Concert* album, was in bed by 11:30, asleep by midnight. I remember rain tapping on my skylight. The phone beside my bed rang at 20 minutes to three. As I groped in darkness, picked up the receiver, I noticed the call came in on my business line. Too late to ignore it, too late to have rigged that line into the answering machine.

"Yeah?"

"Is this John Rankin?" The perky male voice sounded familiar.

"Yeah."

"This is Detective Nick Sherman. We spoke earlier today. Did I wake you? Were you in bed?"

"That's OK."

"I just came across your number and I thought I better call."

"It's pretty late to notice my number and pick up the phone."

"Oh I didn't get your number out of my notebook. I got it off one of your business cards."

"Where did you get one of my cards?"

"From the vest pocket of a dead man."

A straight razor slid through my bowels. "Who . . . Who is it?"

"That's what we were hoping you'd tell us. I thought you wouldn't mind coming down to the crime scene to take a look before we send the body to the morgue."

"Where are you?"

"Don't worry about finding us. There's a cruiser waiting outside your building to give you a ride. You will come, won't you?"

7

Rain made the roads a black mirror. The rain had stopped, but water still covered the streets. The tires on the blue and white police car *whooshed* as we made our way through the sleeping city. The two uniformed cops made sure who I was, then said no more. We cruised past Union Station, past the House of Ruth where homeless women seek temporary shelter, past the closed Italian restaurant on Massachusetts Avenue with the white marble heroic male statue caged in a black iron picket fence in the parking lot. By then I'd decided these two cops were bored. One black man, one white, color them blue and call them bored, or maybe so tired nothing mattered. I rode in the backseat, listening to the radio squawk. Scout 17 called the dispatcher for a wagon to pick up a wino passed out in a park and scouts 21 and 32 were sent to a possible burglary in Southeast. Scout car 28 was ferrying some fool to look at a corpse. Boring. We drove past blocks of boarded-up townhouses that realtors had been unable to flip into the stagnant renovation market. A decrepit black man sitting on a sagging iron porch watched us pass. His blank expression didn't change.

"Where" turned out to be an alley off 15th Street between O and P streets. The neighborhood was an architectural blur, near downtown but not part of it, mostly old three-story townhouses, some still inhabited slums, some renovated by pioneers. A parking lot took up a corner of the block, but my ferry pulled to the curb where the lot ended and the buildings began. Fifty feet up the street two unmarked cruisers, another scout car and a police station wagon with the words

36

"Medical Examiner" blocked the mouth of the alley. We were close to where Janet Armstrong died. I wondered if her last night had been like this: slowly whirling red lights coloring the darkness, surreal smudged reflections on a black mirror street. Eerie quiet. The damp air that would be muggy at dawn was now cool, heavy with the stench of rotten garbage as we neared three men in suits and two men in police uniforms waiting at the mouth of the alley.

The men in the shadows turned as we approached, one of my uniformed escorts leading the way, one watching me from behind. The tallest of the suits—six-two, six-three—took a cowboy-boot step toward me, stopped. A dim streetlight gave him an outline, the pulsating flashes of the scout cars' rotating red lights gave him solid, rough-faced substance, eyes bright in the night as he waited for me.

"I bet you're John Rankin." Tenor voice. Smooth. Tired, but smooth. He smiled wide and I saw one chipped upper tooth glisten in the corner of his grin. His face was a jumble of flat planes layered and bent around his bones. Not a handsome face, but one which could be many things: pleasant, pleasing, always purposeful and powerful, at times no doubt even terrifying. That face looked down at me, grinned its chipped-tooth grin, and drew me in like a hand curling around a warm cup of coffee. "Sorry as hell to wake you. I'm Nick Sherman."

His handshake could have crushed my fingers.

"What we got is a murdered man in an alley. Somebody hit him a bunch of times in the head, probably with a pipe or iron bar. Lots of those laying around the neighborhood. No wallet, no watch, no money, no keys, no papers, no nothing. Except your business card in his vest pocket where a fast search might have missed it. Would you mind taking a look and telling us who he is?"

"I'll try."

"Good. I hope I didn't disturb your wife when I called."

"I'm not married."

He touched my elbow ever so lightly to guide me toward the alley. "A man doesn't need to be married to avoid sleeping by himself."

I saw the chipped-tooth smile again as he spoke. A benign

smile. A second suit-coated man fell in step behind us. Halfway down the alley ahead of us a uniformed figure stood beside a lump of clothes sprawled over the bricks. Flashlights propped on garbage cans lit the scene. We ducked under a rope strung between two doorways, walked toward what waited there. "I was alone," I said.

"Too bad," said Sherman. "Guy can't always be lucky." His tone implied innocent sexual humor. "Oh," said Sherman, jerking his head, "that's my partner, Arnie Gustafson."

"Nice to meet you," grumbled the man behind me.

"Sure," I said. "Sure."

The dead man spread-eagled on his back in that alley seemed not like a man at all, and the death that was his was not the death I'd met at funerals. At funerals, death is a sorrowful aurora centered on a wooden box containing a wax dummy dressed with memories who once breathed importance in your life. In that alley death's aurora was one of inconvenience, even absurdity: Why did this cloth-clad thing have to be a dead man here and now? How silly it looked, limp, cumbersome. Maybe if there'd been more blood, I would have felt repulsion. I stared at that face, that once florid, now pale, big-nosed face with its sorry eyes closed, its slack-jaw mouth open enough to show those pitiful green teeth. A thick brown line creased the forehead. No one spoke, and I felt gravely out of my time and place.

"This is how we found him," Sherman finally said. He bent, rolled the corpse over to its stomach. The left arm flopped in the air then slapped down to the pavement with a dull *smack*. Dead. Gray hair on the back of his head was matted, stained brown.

"The rain washed away most of the blood," said Sherman. "He got at least one across the forehead, probably first, then a few more across the back and side of his head while he lay there."

"Excuse me, guys!"

White light exploded in my face, burned my vision.

"Sorry to hit you like that!" called a man's voice as my eyes shimmered back into focus. His form receded in the alley, taking the camera with him. "Didn't realize you were in the way."

"Evidence technician," said Sherman. He nodded to the cold flesh on the ground. "Does that guy mean anything to you?"

"He came to my office yesterday, probably got my card there."

"Who was he?"

"I don't know his name."

Sherman turned those bright eyes on me again. I wondered what color they'd be in the light. "I think," he said, "I think you might want to come down to headquarters."

8

"Do you have anything you wish to add to this statement that has not already been covered?"

Detective Gustafson watched the keyboard of the old manual typewriter while he waited for my answer. His partner Sherman watched me while he leaned on the hard edge of the metal desk; while he leaned on my patience, my pride and my paranoia.

I'd told them all about that corpse who visited me, all about his vague story with its cast of anonymous ghosts. They led me through it frontward and backward. Then Gustafson wheeled a typewriter down the corridor between the two rows of desks and led me through it as he typed our questions and answers "one time for the record."

"Nothing I can think of," I replied to his last formal question. I wanted to protest my life's total innocence. But didn't.

"Would you mind waiting while we check it over for typos?" Sherman angled his head toward the front of the squad room. I wandered to one of the six tall windows while he bent to talk with his partner.

False dawn colored the outside world gray. Eleven Japanese maple trees stood in a line in the narrow park separating Washington's municipal building from the federal Department of Labor. The trees were carefully trimmed, their delicate leaves crimson with spring.

The Homicide squad room felt like a long, moldy box walled off behind locked doors from the rest of the city's stone bureaucracy. Two rows of maybe 50 old metal desks and creaky chairs stretched back to the stockroom where the cops kept a coffee maker made famous by an aging baseball hero. A hall led through the back wall, past three interrogation cubicles where the desks were fitted with an iron ring for handcuffing suspects, back to a dead end and another locked door. From Sherman's comments, I'd gathered that a third detective was sleeping in one of those rooms. A fourth sat up front, listening to the police radio, waiting for the phone to ring, waiting for his shift to end. One aqua green wall had a blackboard with pistol-range schedules and an indecipherable note chalked on its surface. Clipboards of wanted posters hung beneath printed notices, artists' composite sketches. The clock in the squad room had stopped at 9:08. Someone had taped a Mack Truck poster between two tall windows, while the opposite wall held a cheap, colored cardboard movie poster still sheathed in protective plastic: *Casablanca*. Humphrey Bogart didn't look happy.

"I'll give you a ride home," said Sherman. Color his eyes black—bloodshot, but the true rare black of romance.

"Who killed him?" I asked.

"We'll know more when we find out who he was."

"Any guesses?"

He shrugged. "Could have been somebody who didn't like him, could have been somebody who didn't care. He could have been mugged too hard. That neighborhood. At night. Maybe he was shopping for some sweet-time company from the whores two blocks away. We'll see. What we do is eliminate the possibilities, take what's left as far as we can."

"That's what I am? A possibility to eliminate?"

"You're a citizen assisting the police in their inquiries."

"Like a witness—or a suspect."

That chipped-tooth grin. "Not the way you tell it."

I looked over to where Gustafson was separating the three copies of my statement. "I suppose this would be a bad time to talk about Janet Armstrong."

"You got that right," Sherman said. "I had five hours of court time today, plus this 14-hour shift. I'm on through Friday. Hiding Saturday and Sunday. Graveyard shift next week. I got a new homicide yesterday, another one tonight. I'm too wore down to handle her now."

41

"What I'm doing with her is no big deal," I said. "I mainly couldn't slam my door in her father's face. I don't know what I can do for him. Hell, I don't think there's really much to it, not since you got the guy who killed her."

"Oh we got him," said the cop. "But that don't matter for you. I talked to Mr. Armstrong after you called. He told me why he hired you."

"Yeah. *Why.* Seems simple to me. She walked into a combat zone, got zapped. Too bad, but what can you expect?"

Those black eyes peeled me down to my core. "Being able to sum something up nice and neat and simple doesn't mean you know what you're talking about."

We didn't speak during the ride home. He barely said good-bye when he let me out. But he watched. He waited until I let myself in the lower door, and he watched.

I stayed in my apartment long enough to decide I was too tired to run, too keyed up to go to bed. My watch said 7:30—too early for action in a just-waking world. I picked up my newspapers from Rich, dawdled down Pennsylvania Avenue to a café that was more like a truck stop than a Capitol Hill eatery, consumed a breakfast more important for filling my time than my stomach. The man who died last night hadn't made the morning *Post.* Neither had Janet Armstrong, at first.

By the time I left the café one of the Hill bookstores was open. I found two paperback books on Jim Jones and his cult. Back at the office, I flipped through their pages of black-and-white photographs: a profile of Congressman Leo Ryan (D-Ca.) and the casket his work won him being carried by marines; Jim Jones, big, swarthy; aerial shots of bodies sprawled through Utopia; close-ups of the washtub of poisonous *electric* Kool-Aid; a dead dog; Jones's throne, empty beneath a biblically lettered sign—THOSE WHO DO NOT REMEMBER THE PAST ARE CONDEMNED TO REPEAT IT; close-ups of corpses, of the dead messiah sprawled on his back, shirt open.

I wrote to Tom Armstrong, asked for a list of Janet's friends. I bet he already had such a list, bet he'd already used it.

I called Cheryl, told her my story. She gave some free legal advice I didn't need, then switched to the personal.

"You sure you're OK?"

"Positive."

"I could take off, come see you . . ."

"If you do, make sure it's not to give me sympathy."

She laughed. "That suburban divorce can only meet me after work. By the time I could drive back into the city . . ."

"Don't worry about it," I said. "You know I want to see you, but I understand." That was very true, but I didn't tell her I was glad for the night alone. "Maybe tomorrow."

The rest of the day dragged through me. I called Saul, told him, heard about Katie and his hunt for ABSCAM stories. More about Katie than anything else. I called a few other friends, chatted about nothing for no reason other than they were alive and so was I.

And the whole time I watched the chair where he'd sat. As the day dragged on, the memory of him there grew harder to find. The memory of him in the alley grew harder to avoid. About 3:00 I ate some leftovers, went to bed. Sunlight glowed around the skylight shade as I lay between my sheets. Just before I drifted into troubled sleep I rolled on my back and my left arm flopped on the bed.

9

"You were awful quiet yesterday," said Rich the next morning as he handed me my newspapers. He pulled a handful of envelopes and two magazines from under the counter, pushed them across to me. "You didn't even pick up your mail."

"I had a hard day."

"Me too." He nodded to two customers browsing by the X-rated card rack. "That's as busy as it got. Business is terrible. I had plenty of time to read your magazines. The guy's not that smart."

I sighed. "What guy?"

"The guy who wrote the lead story in this." He thumped one of America's last general cultural comment monthly magazines with his forefinger. "Big cover story. Big deal. The New Right Evangelists. Suddenly he discovers fundamentalist preachers pushing conservative politics. Been going on for years. So it's slicker and more organized and on TV, so maybe this year more people are scared so they're playing sheep for those shepherds. He acts like it's *new* news. Before World War II, we had Father Coughlin and his Silver Shirts. When I was a kid we had this guy on the radio who praised God and pushed politics. Maybe this year it's significant again, but it's not new."

"Somebody is always trying to save your soul for their sake."

"With these guys, anybody who tells them no is a sinner. All sinners should be shot. Good people with good intentions end up on the firing squad. Nobody ever quite makes it to heaven—because first we need to go through the Inquisition or a crusade or to Auschwitz or a Siberian labor camp."

"Or to the jungles of Guyana."

"They got those jungles in Iowa. It's just harder to see the bush. And the bodies."

"You're a cheery son of a bitch first thing in the morning."

"These are cheery times."

I carried my mail and newspapers upstairs, glanced at headlines as I went. The president had designated a place called Love Canal where chemical firms secretly buried killer garbage as an official disaster. The only mail I couldn't have predicted was an envelope with my name scrawled on it in handwriting I didn't recognize. No return address. I opened the envelope as I sat down, shook it over my desk.

Good thing I was sitting down. The letter fell out, and as it unfolded, ten $100 bills spilled across my desk. Ten of the biggest denomination bill most Americans ever see, lying before my eyes. Philadelphia's Independence Hall decorated one side, a portrait of Benjamin Franklin—rebel, kite flyer, father of two illegitimate children—graced the other. I unfolded the letter:

> *Dear Mr. Rankin:*
>
> *Although I understand your reluctance, I think you are the best man for my job and the only man I can trust. I've enclosed $1,000—twice your estimate plus a $200 bonus. This is a delicate matter. I will not burden you with the names of my principals. Nor will I explain to you what wrong might be involved. I can evaluate the situation after you discover some simple information. The congressional committee involved is the House General Oversight and Special Investigations Subcommittee. I will be able to solve my principals' problems if you can tell me what a staff member named Scott Oliff is working on and plans to work on. I doubt any legal or ethical problems exist in that chore. It is imperative that you do not tell Mr. Oliff or anyone what you are doing. You need not concern yourself with how his activities might affect the personal relationship mentioned to you. I'll know that when I get your report. Do not inquire beyond that. Do not generate disaster by being indiscreet. I'll call you in a few days regarding your results.*

No he wouldn't. No signature, but I knew that shaky scrawled letter came from the sorry man who'd sat in my chair, taken one of my cards, walked down an alley and was sorry no more. I thought I'd seen the last of him when he left my office. I thought I was through with him when I signed my statement for the police. Now this dead man I never knew had sent me more money than I'd asked for, hired me for a case I hadn't wanted, and left me with no clean choice.

I could call the cops, summon Sherman's hard black eyes, but what more could I tell him? Sherman would take the letter, maybe the cash. He'd ask people questions that would point back to me. What I do is supposed to be confidential. This is a small town of small-town politics. Cops bringing up my name because of a set of circumstances I don't choose is like hanging a leper's bell around my neck.

Then there was what the letter could do. My no-name client was right. Indiscretion breeds trouble for innocent people. The man he named, Scott Oliff: he didn't need to be dragged into a homicide he might know nothing about.

There was more. The man who'd written that letter had been a sorry son of a bitch who'd brought me only trouble. But he'd been decent about it. He'd trusted me, paid me. I owed him $1,000 worth of something.

A thousand dollars! God could I use that cash! I could take it off the books and away from the eyes of the tax man. The underground economy, the American hustle of the 1980s. I'd never nickel-and-dime cheated my tax reports. Stealing from my own government didn't make a lot of sense. But $1,000 tax free was half that again in real spending power. Besides, if I reported it, hadn't been square with Sherman, if the government asked . . . the ripple rolled on and on, the ifs, the buts, the maybes.

If I kept it, did nothing, I'd be defrauding a corpse who couldn't complain. But I'd be defrauding. Keeping secrets from cops who care is crazy, but making trouble for innocent people might be worse.

But maybe, just maybe.

Detective Sherman had been jerking me around. Maybe I could do more than give him new information in Mr. No Name's case. Maybe I could save him some time, put fresh facts into perspective, show that letter, the cash and I had nothing to do with the murder. Maybe he'd be grateful. I had the Armstrong case, so did he. I needed his help, so maybe if I gave him some . . .

Maybe I could satisfy the dead man too. Maybe I could find out what congressional staffer Scott Oliff was doing that would make anybody worry. Maybe I could identify the dead man's "principals"—if any existed—working backward from that. Maybe I could approach them—discreetly—satisfy their interests and my self-respect without making waves. Earn that cash, or at least keep my conscience clean by trying.

Maybe, just maybe.

My business isn't the only one making money because of our government maze. Each year private enterprise sells dozens of different guidebooks to Americans looking for a path through their public-service bureaucracies. One of the best maps is the annual *Congressional Staff Directory* I keep on my shelf.

The thick, color-coded directory listed the House General Oversight and Special Investigations Subcommittee as a child of the House Government Operations Committee and printed a polite but vacuous description of its duties. The subcommittee was a toy its reform-minded chairman used to raise hell and grab headlines. Such candor seldom makes it into reference books.

The directory listed Scott Oliff as one of the subcommittee's two investigators. The other investigator was Bill Welch, an old source of mine from my Ned Johnson muckraking days. I found another name I knew on the staff list, Gloria Trang, the office manager. She was a tall woman, slender, with jet black hair stretching all the way down to the curve of her taut bottom. Long legs and high breasts and a smooth, sly face. I'd always wanted to know her much better than the casual banter we'd established over two years.

The directory prints biographies of most congressional staffers:

OLIFF, Scott L. Bn. Sept. 3, 1948, Madison, Ws.; Un. of Wis., 1966–70, B.A. economics; Un. of Chic., 1970–72, M.A. poli. sci.; Leg. Ass. Rep. Joseph Van

Buskirk, 1973–76; Leg. Aide (then Senator) Van Buskirk 1977–78; joined House SbCom. on Overs. & Spec. Invst. as Investigator, Feb., 1978.

And there he was, OLIFF, Scott, Midwestern boy to my Western, only a year older than me, former senate aide like me, investigator type like me, longtime Washington hack. Like me. Easily enough to foster conversation, with the right introduction.

My watch said 10:30. I could "drop by" the subcommittee offices just before lunch hours began. There was work to do on Art Dillon's Jonestown case. There were calls I should make on Janet Armstrong. But ten pictures of Ben Franklin stared at me from my desk top and a sorry face/cold meat ghost stared at me from my memory. I hesitated a moment, swept the money and letter in a desk drawer, locked it and left.

10

"I thought you were my partner when I heard the door open."

Bill Welch smiled warily, nodded to the chair beside his desk. Piles of paper filled this "private office" plastic partitions carved out of a larger room in the Rayburn building.

"I don't think I know him," I said, sitting down.

"Scott Oliff. Good guy."

"He at lunch now? Gloria too?"

"Ah: you would know Gloria. She and the receptionist just left for a long lunch with an ex-intern of ours. Scott is definitely not with them. He's probably storming around the building."

"He got a problem?"

"That intern—a she, young and dangerous. Westerner, just like you. Just as tough in the clinches. She worked here last winter. They played for a while. She took him to the hoop, then walked away. Nothing nasty, but nothing nice. And Scott, well, he'd rather not be around when she drops by to do the clever thing and renew old contacts."

"Scott is our age, right?" I hoped he wouldn't question my guess. "He should know better. Never mess with your heart where you work and beware the young: they don't even know how dangerous they are. Juliet was only 14, and look what happened to Romeo."

"Good sense is easier to have than use."

"Why are you here, Rankin?" he asked. "Glad to see you, but you aren't reporting anymore, so . . ."

"I missed your trusting face. Besides, maybe someday I'll

49

have a client, public interest group, somebody like that, who'll hire me to do something my old sources know something about. I'm going back, seeing everybody I can. Keeping in touch, keeping my hand in."

I didn't lie.

We talked for 20 minutes. Just as I began worrying how I could string our casual conversation out longer we heard the door open.

"Can I help you?" called Bill, starting to rise.

"It's me." Deep baritone. Terse.

The man who walked around the partition had prematurely gray hair, nervous eyes, an expensive suit and a tenuous hold on himself. "Any messages?"

"Nobody called." Bill paused, made it deliberate. *"Everybody* has gone to lunch for a couple hours."

The man grunted.

"Scott Oliff, this is an old friend of mine, John Rankin. He used to be a reporter for Ned Johnson."

"Nice to meet you," I said as we shook hands. "So you help Bill keep in trouble."

"I'm real good at that."

The edge in his words told me subtlety wouldn't work. Either I'd jerk exactly what I wanted out of him with a quick, hard snag or my hook would be lost in his anger. "What are you guys doing these days?" I asked—a casual, innocent question.

Scott wasn't so far gone he was stupid. Good for you, I thought, as he glanced at Bill.

"Rankin isn't reporting anymore."

"Makes no difference," muttered Scott. "If you were a reporter I could play shuffle ball with my answers.

"On the record, as reporters say, our committee last week promised to update its review of the General Services Administration scandals. You remember them—the GSA mess, the big one before ABSCAM but after Koreagate and Watergate. Bureaucrats and contractors stealing a few measly millions from the taxpayers. Maybe half a billion bucks. No big deal. *On the record* that's what I'd tell you we're doing, 'reviewing the investigations to date.'

"On background, with me identified in print only as 'a

congressional aide' or 'a source close to the investigation,' I'd tell you we were still getting our ducks lined up.

"On deep background, where you couldn't attribute what you were saying to anybody, where the reader had no choice but to take your word for it, I'd tell you all that was a bunch of crap, we ain't doing shit, and we won't do shit.

"Man, it's 1980: an election year. We're lackeys for a Democratic House that's running scared. On the line are all our bosses and our Democratic president, the preacher who quoted Bob Dylan and came to town four years ago to clean the shit out of the swamp. So what happens? Up pops the GSA scandal, he starts his crusade. A biggie bureaucrat over at GSA gets canned in the housecleaning. Now this big bureaucrat is a buddy of our Democratic Speaker of this here House of Representatives. The Speaker is pissed off at these new boys in town in general, pissed off about his buddy's problems in specific. So big buddy bureaucrat gets a new job—in the White House of the president who is supposed to be cleaning up the mess the bureaucrat left behind him in his last job.

"Nobody says so to us lackeys, but we can read the writing on the wall. If we rock the boat, it'll get shot out from under us, probably by the people we're rocking it to save.

"Off the record, so you as a reporter couldn't even use my wisdom to phrase questions for other people, I'd say I'm only filling up my fuckin' time. You know what I'm going to do now? I'm going to take a long walk around this goddamned marble museum. Go outside. Maybe lie in the grass and wonder what I'm doing here and how people can not say what they really mean and still not lie but still leave you catching the shaft. That's what I'm going to do."

Bill looked at me a few seconds after the echo of the slammed door. "It really isn't that bad. It's just how he is today."

I nodded, showed him I understood. "Time for me to go." I left Bill sitting in his plastic box where it really wasn't that bad.

11

A steady stream of anonymous faces flowed past my smile as I walked down Pennsylvania Avenue. Sunshine warmed the street. I moved through the crowd feeling as cool as could be. I'd gotten square with my dead client, stayed clean doing so. I could call Sherman, get square by him with the letter and probably keep the cash. I could tell the cop about my run on Scott Oliff, maybe stop Sherman from having to do the same. I had it made, solid and sweet. Then I saw them.

The only one I recognized was Gloria Trang, jet black hair tumbling down a sultry frame. She and two other women, laughing as they emerged from a restaurant. I could see one of the other women clearly, a wholesome, all-American brown haired type. She and the exotic Gloria blocked a good view of their companion, though I saw the third woman wore burnt-orange walking shorts and had slim, long legs. Wore running shoes. Her blond hair made a fuzzy halo behind Gloria's ebony tresses.

Why the hell not? I told myself. There was Cheryl, but even though she wasn't completely colored in, I sensed she fit within predictable borders. The three women strolled along the avenue's rainbow wall of shops, liquor stores, bars and restaurants. I quickened my pace, sure I could "accidentally" encounter them before they reached any destination.

"Gloria!" I called a few moments later as I casually turned into their path. "I was just at your office. How are you?"

"John! I'm fine. I . . . Do you know . . ." Her question broke off as she gestured to her companions.

"We're all strangers," I said.

"John Rankin, this is Bonnie Colden, our secretary." Brown Haired Woman nodded, smiled. Pretty, but only that. "And this is Tara Woodson. Tara used to be an intern in our office."

It wasn't so much the way she looked as the way she took in my gaze and looked *back*. She was long and lean, too supple and strong to be skinny, about five-foot-seven. I remembered poor Scott Oliff, remembered she was too young, dangerous and supposedly a lot like me. She was a strawberry blond, that brazen mixture of red and gold which catches the sun in a thousand subtle, ever-changing shades. That hair held a natural frizz, swept up and out, cut just above her shoulders. Her heart-shaped face curved out to high cheekbones, a small nose and a slightly dimpled, tucked-in chin. Her skin was smooth. She had a lush, swollen-lipped mouth and widely spaced eyes with clear whites, thick robin's egg blue rings around black onyx brilliance. Those eyes didn't flinch.

"Hello," said Tara, her voice husky, low and deep for her slight frame. She wore a white cotton knit shirt that had to be a girl's size to fit so snugly. If she'd been less muscular, she'd have been totally flat chested. She wasn't wearing a bra, and I noticed her nipples were tiny dots.

My eyes marched back to Gloria. "Where are you three going?"

"Celebration lunch," she answered. "Long weekend, Tara's visit, her graduation, her moving down here soon. Good excuses to go outside. So far, every place is crowded."

"Mind some company?" Before Gloria finished her *of course not* smile, I looked back to Tara. "Ever been to the Tune Inn?"

"Where's that?" she said.

"Just down the street. Do you mind?" I asked Gloria, but split my gaze between her and Tara.

"Why not?" said Gloria.

I magnanimously gestured for Bonnie and her to lead the way while I fell in behind them—and beside Tara.

"Last time I heard the name Tara I was at a Clark Gable–Vivien Leigh movie," I told her.

"My mother liked the book." She shrugged and I worried I'd blown it.

"I liked the movie." I grinned. "I've never read the book."

"Me either," she said. Smiled back and everything was fine.

"What school did you go to?" In my life it had been years since that bit of trivia was a common conversational bridge with a stranger. I felt peculiar needing to use it again now, but I was straining so hard to hear her answer I didn't care.

"Bryant College. Small liberal arts school in Rhode Island. I studied in Europe, interned here. Do you work on the Hill?"

"Sort of."

"That's specific."

I laughed. "What I am isn't what it sounds like. I'm a private investigator, private detective." I threw in *detective* to jazz up my legend.

She cocked her head, smiled. "Sounds interesting."

"Mostly I spend my time asking questions."

"I've always liked asking questions."

"I've always liked finding answers."

We laughed as we followed our two companions into the Tune Inn, a Small-Town Anywhere, America, joint with country and western songs on the jukebox, stuffed animal heads on the wall, deer rumps mounted over the bathroom doors, grizzled blue collar boozers mixed in with congressional stuffed shirts at the long mirrored bar, a dozen booths stretching back to the kitchen's swinging half door. We got lucky, found an empty booth.

"This is more my kind of place than the coat-and-tie joints," I said to Tara as we sat down. She and Gloria sat on one side, Bonnie and I the other. "Reminds me of home."

"Where you from?" asked Tara.

"Not here," I said. "Nobody is really from Washington. We just all end up here. I came from Montana. How about you?"

"Washington—*State*. You from Butte?"

"Yup. You're not from Seattle or Spokane, are you? Or anyplace big?"

"No." She looked around—at the rifles on the wall; the carnival-huge, plastic-sheathed, gold-embroidered black sombrero hanging above us; the stuffed owl mounted above the bar. "I like this."

"Not as much young-professional patter in here as other places," I said. "The classic Washington question is, 'What do you do?' In California, they ask, 'What are you into?'"

"How about psycho babble?" Tara asked. "I'm OK, you're not? Or . . ."

But I interrupted her: "I hear what you're saying and I know where you're coming from and I've been through that space before."

"Zodiac signs!" she countered.

"I always lie about that," I confessed. "Say I'm a Virgo, wait for the person to say, 'I just knew it!' Then when they ask about lisps and cusps, I tell them my birthday is May 1st. You should see their faces when they realize I'm not the sign they described."

"I say I'm a sun child with the moon rising over Cincinnati," said Tara.

She and I laughed. Gloria and Bonnie smiled.

"You know," Gloria said sweetly, "you can even hear hustle lines in here."

"Gloria," I argued, "who could suggest anything about visiting their etchings in a place like . . ."

"No, no!" interrupted Tara. "It's not etchings anymore! It's stereo component systems!"

Everyone laughed.

Lunch was beer and burgers and explanations of what I do.

"Look," I said, "why don't the three of you stop by my office on the way back to yours? Sounds like you've got nothing better to do. Maybe my business will make more sense then."

I cajoled them into accepting that absurd logic. Most of lunchtime's banter passed between me and Tara. Which meant nothing, I told myself. Except that we had the most in common.

"There's not much to see actually," I said as I led them first through my office, then through my apartment. Tara cocked her head, read the titles of the books on my shelves. I always do that, too.

"What kind of job are you looking for when you move here?" I asked her as the four of us reentered my office.

"Something that probably doesn't exist. Some kind of blend of politics, writing and . . . Well, I love film."

"You mean movies?" I asked.

"Uh . . . yes."

"Where are you going to stay until you get settled?"

"I've got a couple possibilities."

"But nothing concrete until you get a job so you can afford to live."

She shrugged *so what:* Just like me when I first hit town.

"Why not stay here?" The words walked right out of my mouth.

Gloria showed more surprise than Tara.

"No, really," I continued, growing more insistent the longer the idea lived, "that couch folds out into a bed. You've got that shower bathroom to yourself. I don't turn this into an office until mid-morning. It's better than the sleeping bag you've been using at Gloria's."

"That's . . . I don't know if I . . ."

"Look, it's no big deal," I said and believed it. "I don't mind the company. You'll have a base to work the Hill from."

"I . . . I don't know."

"Don't worry about it now. Tell you what: send me your resumes or leave them with Gloria. We'll figure out where you'll stay when you land in D.C. I know people in journalism, politics. I'll ask around. Maybe I can open a door."

She smiled so softly. "Thank you."

"I think two of us should get back to work," said Gloria. "Would you like to come, Tara?"

"Uh . . . yeah." She walked to the door, trailing them. "This is so nice of you."

"No big deal," I hesitated, but had to know. "This sounds silly, but there's something else familiar about your name."

"Senator Woodson is my father." Even, flat, noncommitted. "Does that make any difference?"

"Not to me," I said. Evenly, steadily, firmly. She took my words in, nodded, smiled again and walked after our friends.

But I lied. All through the smiles and laughter and burgers and beer my mind had gnawed at me. Tara Woodson. Tara

Woodson. Who'd "taken Scott Oliff to the hoop." A special, intimate relationship. That was easy to understand. *So what.* So it was Scott Oliff, investigator for the House Subcommittee on Oversight and Special Investigations she'd played that game with. How was it that doomed man put it? Someone on a congressional committee, someone he later identified as Scott Oliff, a someone who might be taking advantage of an innocent person and their "special relationship" to harm a third party, a vulnerable third party linked to the innocent person. Tara could be an innocent person. Tara *was* an innocent person. As for a vulnerable third party linked to her, she had this father who just happened to be a United States senator from the state of Washington.

If all this were coincidence, it cut too close and too deep. As I stood in my bay windowed tower watching strangers pass on the sidewalk below, all the trouble I thought I'd beaten back with my clever scam just two hours earlier loomed before me again. But even larger than that old trouble was a new crisis hidden in the eyes of Tara Woodson who was . . . I groped for a phrase to capture her: a good person—an innocent person. If there were justice in this world, she wouldn't be dragged into whatever slime oozed from that sorry man's rotting corpse. All the reasons I'd feared that stranger's ghost before now seemed puny beside the simple axiom that I couldn't let anything bad happen to her. I stood by a pit as deep and dark as the core of her eyes; even as I wondered how I got there I was stepping off the edge.

12

"Good afternoon, Senator Woodson's office. May I help you?"

"Could I speak to the senator's personal secretary, please?"

"Who may I say is calling?"

"My name wouldn't mean anything to her."

The woman's voice on the other end of the phone turned chilly as she put me on hold. "One moment."

My watch said 2:34. He could be on the Floor, in a committee hearing, huddled with his staff or constituents, working on his own. But the flag flew over the Senate Chamber, which meant they were in session, and the odds were he was in town.

"This is Sue Harris, Senator Woodson's personal secretary. Our receptionist said you wouldn't tell her your name. Is this my fabled secret admirer?"

"Actually, I didn't refuse to tell her my name: I just said it wouldn't mean anything to you."

"Most people would interpret that as a refusal." Charm closed its bag and stomped out of her words.

"I'm John Rankin. I'm a private investigator and I need to meet with Senator Woodson. Now normally . . ."

"I can't imagine why or how Senator Woodson could help you with your . . . endeavors, Mr. Rankin. Does he know you?"

"No. And it's not a matter of him helping me."

"What is it a matter of, then, Mr. Rankin? I'm his personal secretary. Perhaps if you told me . . ."

"*Ms*. Harris," I said, "I know senators don't casually set up appointments with strangers, especially strangers who sound like they've got a fishy job and who won't specify their business. I don't mind if he tells you about our meeting afterward, nor do I care if he has you there. Because I want him to have that choice, I won't tell you what this is about. You have my word that this is important."

"I don't know anything about your word, Mr. Rankin. Or you."

"I spent more than a year on Senator Applegate's staff. I know he and your boss are friends," I said (a safe gamble). "Senator Applegate will vouch for me. I can give you other names, but the less fuss this raises, the better." I didn't want to spook her or her boss by mentioning my ties to Ned Johnson: few politicians invite a muckraker or even an ex-muckraker into their parlor.

"Does this 'important' matter involve Senator Applegate?"

"He knows nothing about it, doesn't even know I'm telling you to check me out with him. But he'll vouch for me."

"I'll pass that along. You're aware, of course, that the Senate is in session and the campaign is on. To say nothing of the volcano disaster in our home state. Senator Woodson is terribly busy. Perhaps he could telephone you."

"The telephone isn't appropriate for this."

"You make this sound like a life or death matter."

"When can I know about the appointment?"

"I'm not sure when today I'll see the senator," she lied. "If you give me your number, I'll call you."

I gave it to her, then said, "I'll be here until I hear from him. I'll check in later, just in case my line is busy when you call."

"I'm assuming you want to do this soon."

"The sooner this is over, the better for everybody."

Two hours later my phone rang.

"Mr. Rankin? This is Sue Harris with Senator Woodson. Could you see the senator at his home, 8:00 tonight?"

I said of course, she told me how to get there.

Senator Robert Woodson, D-Wash. The "D" should have stood for "divided," not "Democrat." Woodson was a fence sitter known for his "safe" votes, a tendency to back (never lead) easy issues, his silver hair, and a sincere smile. He served on three committees: Banking, Housing and Urban Affairs; Environment and Public Works; and Appropriations, where he chaired the do-nothing District of Columbia Subcommittee. He had the best Senate attendance record of the last eight years. One reference book called him "stoic," which (given everything else) implied the authors were reaching for a tactful way to say "silent."

He was born February 12, 1926, Tacoma, Washington. Native son. I smiled, wondered what his zodiac sign was. State university, Army in Korea (Purple Heart, Bronze Star). Law school in Seattle, served as a small-town county attorney, then a few terms in the state legislature before winning his first of two terms in the U.S. House of Representatives (1964-1968). Elected to the U.S. Senate in 1968, the era of the big Vietnam buildup, King-Bobby Kennedy assassinations, domestic turmoil. Woodson once had a wife, Ann. She died in spring, 1974, just before his reelection in the year President Nixon resigned. I wondered if the sympathy vote helped Woodson. Two kids. I smiled when I read Tara's name: born June 7, 1957. There'd been a son, James, born August 1, 1951—KIA, September 3, 1971, Vietnam. Dead son, dead wife. As I drove to his home that evening I decided maybe Senator Woodson had a lot to be silent about.

Washington wasn't a city where the affluent often lived until the mid-1970s. Before that, if you had the bucks and could crack the color line, you probably lived in Virginia or Maryland, in tiny towns that quickly became exits on the commuter highway, acres of tract housing or high-rise apartments. When gas for commuting stopped being cheap, the middle class (especially young whites) "rediscovered" the joys of city life. Hence the renovation boom that was shuffling many poor blacks from their inner city exile to the edge of the city's circle and post-World War II suburban shelters that were beginning to sag in 1980. Woodson probably didn't care to "rediscover" the city. Few people who had the good fortune to live in his parklike Virginia suburb wanted to trade its splendid serenity for the joys of city life.

Call Woodson's residence a house and you'd be conservative. Most of his constituents would label it a mansion, but then few ordinary Americans ever see the palaces the truly rich and powerful call home. My 25-minute drive took me across the Potomac River to Virginia, west along the George Washington Memorial Parkway, up Georgetown Pike, right down a small, private lane, up a sloping paved road to a well-lit, dozen car capable parking lot in front of a tasteful three-story red brick barn Scarlett O'Hara could have used as a summer place. Three other cars waited in front of the house: a white German Mercedes-Benz, a blue German BMW, and a fire-engine red Italian Maserati. I parked my poor little Japanese Datsun at the far end of that line. Maybe World War II's Axis powers won after all. As I walked up the sidewalk I noticed a kidney-shaped pool off to my left. The diving board stuck silent and still into the darkness.

The silver haired man himself answered the door. I'd expected a butler or maybe a maid, but instead there he was, two inches taller than me and twice as elegant in a tailored sport shirt and slacks. He was handsome as hell. He had Tara's eyes, deep blue, centered black with the politician's tunnel gaze that makes you feel you are staring smack into sincerity. He had the male version of her husky voice—deep, resonant, firm.

"Nice of you to come, Mr. Rankin," he said. The twist he gave my request made me feel even more grateful. His handshake was firm, dignified. I wondered how much of his presence was purposeful, and how much was the person. That's one of the most intriguing puzzles of successful politicians: sometimes the calculated pose and the person's true posture become so intertwined the blend takes on a new personality that's undeniable yet equally undefinable.

"It's a fluke I am able to be here," continued my host as he led me down a thickly carpeted hall to a set of mahogany doors. The paintings on the walls didn't look like museum copies. "I'm attending a memorial service at Arlington cemetery on Sunday, then Monday my daughter graduates from college in New England. If not for those two events, I'd be back home. I was there yesterday, a quick turn around inspecting that volcano. Terrible, just terrible. I wish I could spend more time working on it and less on my campaign."

"You shouldn't have much trouble, should you, sir?" Something about the man elicited deference. "None of the political hit groups have targeted you, have they?"

He smiled as he opened the double doors. "You're always someone's target, Mr. Rankin."

The two men waiting for us inside that book-lined study were standing when we came through the doors. One was off to the left in front of the antique couch. He was portly, wispy white haired, well dressed. He had a stupid smile on his face that I bet didn't belong there. His hands hung by his side; they kept flexing. The second man stood in front of the ornate flattop desk in the center of the room. His clothes cost big bucks too, but they were rumpled, his tie loose. He was shorter than me, stocky. He kept his chin tucked down over his throat as he stared at me with beady brown eyes. No question but that the Maserati out front was his.

Mr. Nervous and Mr. Nasty, I thought.

"This is my attorney, Fred Thomas," said the senator, leading me over to Mr. Nervous. Mr. Nervous/Fred Thomas had a clammy grip. He probably spent most of his time safe and snug in some opulent office, grumbling orders for ambitious minions to sweat out.

"And this is my administrative assistant, Mr. Martin Mercer." The senator gestured toward Mr. Nasty, who leaned back on the desk instead of shaking my hand. Mr. Nasty/Martin Mercer's motion revealed a large reel-to-reel tape recorder waiting on the desk. This senator's number one boy flipped the switch that started the reels rolling.

"Mind if we have this on the record?" said Mercer.

Senator Woodson smiled apologetically. "These days one can't be too careful. Especially with strangers."

ABSCAM paranoia, I thought. These guys don't want to be trapped. If I were secretly taping them, they'd be able to prove what they said even if I doctored my tape.

"That's fine with me," I said.

"Just for the record," repeated Mercer, "do you mind identifying yourself before you explain why you insisted out of the blue that Senator Woodson meet with you?"

"My name is John Rankin. I'm a licensed private investigator in the District of Columbia with applications in process for

Virginia and Maryland." Those applications were "in process" in my desk drawer, untouched by my pen. But at least my fudge kept "the record" clean regarding my work permits. "I came here to Senator Woodson's house at his instructions so we might have the meeting I requested."

I went them one better, dug my license out of my wallet and passed it to Mr. Nervous, the lawyer. "That's my license and ID so you know it's me. Since we're making a record, would you mind identifying yourselves for the tape?"

They did so—lawyer Thomas haltingly, A. A. Mercer cockily. The senator spoke clearly and precisely, as if he were used to bizarre taping sessions every night. At his nod, the four of us huddled in a semicircle of chairs in front of the desk and the propped-up microphone.

"Now that we've concluded those formalities, Mr. Rankin," said the senator, "would you mind telling us why you wanted this meeting?"

"It's one of those long stories, sir."

"We've only got 90 minutes of tape," drawled his A. A.

"It's not that long," I said, and began at the beginning, when the dead man was a surprise waiting for me in my office. I dwelled on how I ran the scam on Scott Oliff to protect *anybody* who might be involved, and how I concluded that the letter reflected a dead man's delusions.

"Then I met your daughter, senator."

"Tara?!" There was concern, shock in his tone. "But why . . . That's right! That was the committee she interned with. I wasn't aware that you two had met. She stayed with friends and we didn't get a chance to talk before she left for Rhode Island."

"As we became friends," I said, stressing the last word, "I realized the two of you fit the criteria in the letter."

"That's idle conjecture and speculation on your part," said the lawyer.

"Wrong," I said: "Tara and the senator unquestionably fit the criteria; whether they are the ones the man referred to is the matter for conjecture and speculation. I'm trying to be sure where I am and what I got, to protect Tara—and the senator. If I dump this in the cops' laps, there is a good chance a fuzzy story will hit the papers. Innocence gets

63

ignored in this town. And it's dangerous for a campaigning senator to need to deny he's guilty of anything, idle speculation or not."

"Who was this dead man?" asked Mercer.

"I don't know," I said. "But we can answer the crucial question without knowing his name." I looked at Woodson. "Did you have anybody approach me about your professional or personal problems?"

"Absolutely not!" insisted the senator, and I exhaled. "Why should I? The bills I'm on, my committee work . . . There's nothing that remotely affects anything that House subcommittee handles. It's an oversight group, not a parallel substantive committee. What interest could they have in my work? What could that young man Tara knows possibly . . . What connection could he have to me other than we work in the same institution and both know Tara?"

"The House staffer couldn't jam the senator even if he wanted to," added A. A. Mercer. "That's an investigatory committee, right? Let's say he had some sort of twisted vendetta against the senator. Maybe . . . Well, Tara has always been a difficult girl. Let's say he wanted to strike at her for something she said or did or didn't do." I disliked his coy tone. "He couldn't use his official position to manufacture trouble for the senator without blantantly abusing it. Congressional staffers, committees, even the Library of Congress are all prohibited from investigating a member in any fashion —unless they're given a special assignment by at least a committee vote, like the Adam Clayton Powell probe."

"That keeps us from using our official powers to cut each other's partisan political throats," explained the senator.

"So you see, my daughter and I may fit the theory, but we can't be what you deduced. If Scott Oliff is guilty of something, then someone else is his victim.

"If you want my opinion, your stranger was a classic Capitol Hill nut. You know the kind: they're the daughter of the czar and want help with their claim, or the FBI has implanted microphones in their teeth to spy on them, or they're the only ones who know to save the world from Martians hiding among us. Their delusion is the only way they can believe their own importance in this vast, impersonal world. More remarkable than their stories is how well some of these people function in every other aspect of their lives. They work hard, hold good jobs, are respected members of the community, dress correctly and are absolutely insane. They don't hide that fact, it just seldom gets recognized during the ordinary relationships most of us make of our lives. But Congress is an extraordinary place, so craziness pops out all over Capitol Hill. Sometimes it's impossible to tell the kooks from the constituents. Sometimes they're one and the same.

"It's unfortunate that man was murdered, but, if you look at the big picture, perhaps that was an extension of his insanity—or proof of it. Walking down a dark alley in America is not the act of a rational man.

"I do want you to know, however, how very much I appreciate your concern—not only for me, but for my daughter."

"I'm glad I have nothing to worry about," I said.

The four of us smiled at each other while the tape reels whirled. A job jolly well done. Martin Mercer finally reached behind him, flipped the switch. We stood. The senator walked at my elbow while the other two shuffled behind us.

"Will you be seeing my daughter again?"

"I'm helping her with a few things."

"You sound like a good friend for her to have." He smiled.

"What are you going to do about the letter?" asked Martin Mercer. "Should we expect more nonsense?"

"If that guy was nuts, I hate seeing Scott Oliff smeared," I spoke to the senator as we stood at the front door, ignored his minions. "I'll probably take a few days, try to quietly nail down if the letter makes sense. I'll need to cough it up for the police sooner or later, but later sounds best to me.

"And don't worry: when I do, I'll make sure the police know my error regarding you and Tara, senator. I'll let you know when I give it to them so you can be prepared."

"I appreciate that," Woodson said, "but as you can see, I'm adequately prepared at any time since this has nothing to do with us."

We shook hands. I skipped such amenities with lawyer Thomas and aide Mercer.

The front door boomed shut behind me, scaring the crickets into silence. They started up again before I climbed behind my steering wheel. I listened to them for a few moments, savoring my relief. Roller coaster day, I thought as I cranked up New Car's tired engine. I glanced back at the house in time to see a folded curtain fall back into place, closed.

13

Cheryl whispers, *"Please!"* and her hands press against my ears, pull me up. She moans softly as I kiss her trembling stomach. Her sunlit bedroom is drenched by the tangy smell of sex and sweat. I slide my hands up from her soft curved bottom, along damp skin, ribs, cup each heavy breast as they lay sprawled separate along her sides. My hands overflow with their warmth. They roll in my grasp, stiff blood-swollen nipples tickling my palms. Squeeze softly. She moans again, pulls my face to her left breast, my mouth to the bud: my tongue flicks circles round its long wrinkled satin. How quiet would we need to be at my place once Tara moves in? Cheryl groans, reaches under my armpits, urges me higher. Kiss her neck, kiss *that spot* & she moans, kisses my temples, hands in my hair, pressing my back, hard fingernails, her thighs strong & sweaty squeezing my hips, her pubic hair scratches as she rubs up, moans. We lurch full onto the bed, *roll,* her heavy on top then quick—*over,* pressing down on her, raise up like a panther; her arms hugged tight to her body push her breasts together. I spread my hands wide—thumb on one nipple & barely just barely my little finger reaches to her other. They rub beneath my touch, marbles so big; push hard & *she moans* nipples big better than small like other women. She presses my hand hard, shaping me around her full breast. Her fingers glide over my chest, snake through my body hair down to my stomach down over my hipbone down inside my thighs, fingernails plowing closer until she holds me holds me guides me bump pullpush: tight, but she's slick, so slick and wet and

in! warm wet hot and easy, easy. *Ahh,* she moans, *Ahh.* Back
and forth, back and forth, back and forth, easy, and where
will I meet Nick Sherman have to tell him back and forth. She
raises her knees, spreads wider and I'm deeper, deeper back
and forth, back and forth. Her legs stretch straight, curl to
contain me like parentheses. *"Yes!"* Her hips shudder with
the grab. *"Yes!"* Faster, and don't giggle as the bed creaks
bumps the wall her neighbors wondering? *"Yes!"* Faster and
faster and fasterfaster faster her hips shudder fire grab surging
AND! And. and.

Easy.

Calm/*jerk shudder!*

Stop, stopped.

Quiet. Minute, no more.

"Oh Jesus," she says as I slide away, roll off, lie beside her.
She rests her head on my calming chest. "Oh Jesus."

"Happy Memorial Day," I say, shifting slightly for comfort.

"I'm crazy about you," she sighed. "Did you know that?"

"Yes."

She hadn't been so crazy about me all weekend: *"What do
you mean she's probably going to be 'sort of a roommate?!'"*

That had been Saturday. I'd waited until then, weighed
phrases, finally ended several Tara stories with the classic,
"Oh, by the way . . ."

"The kid needed a place to stay. She's a friend of good
friends," I'd argued. "What was I supposed to do?"

"What have you *done* is the question," snapped Cheryl.

"What's right." No arguing with that logic, but her look
disagreed.

"What does this 'kid' look like?"

I frowned, wrinkled my brow in obvious concentration.
"Tall, lanky, blond."

"And pretty."

Shrugged my shoulders. "Yeah, I guess so."

"Whatever happened to your precious privacy?"

"It isn't the only priority. Promise ranks up there too."

"What did we promise Miss Tara?"

"Right now, I've only made the offer. If she takes me up on
it, then we'll settle details."

"Un-hun."

"You're not . . . worried, are you?"

"No," she lied.

That was Saturday, cool all day, even the weather. Saturday night we watched *Citizen Kane* at the Biograph with pretended poise. Sunday morning at my place Cheryl woke up calmer, but still touchy enough for me to alternate coaxing her into good humor and avoiding her by puzzling out my next professional moves.

Friday had been business (mostly). Tara had left her resumes at the subcommittee offices. I dropped by to pick them up, chatted with Gloria about Tara and life in general, conned my way into seeing the schedule of all hearings and planned reports. Scott Oliff hadn't lied when he said there was nothing going on and nothing in the works. The subcommittee's last interest had been the GSA scandals, and that was a farce dying from benign neglect. So much for the dead man's paranoia. Scott and I nodded to each other when he drifted through the office. His eyes were full of yesterdays.

The subway connecting the House office buildings to the Capitol and the Capitol to the Senate office buildings took me to David Henderson's office in the Russell building where the decor is stately and somber, high ceilinged, marble arched hallways and ten-foot mahogany doors. I ignored the office door bearing the senator's nameplate, strolled past alphabet entrances A, B and C to enter D. Inside—electric pink shirt, gray slacks, mustached bright-eyed grin and all—sat David beneath his colored posters of distant mountain lakes.

"Don't you know about reception desks, asshole?"

"I'm a back door man."

"Hmph." He tilted his chair forward, cocked his head. Chatter from coworkers at nearby desks, ringing phones, bustling secretaries precluded privacy. "Come on." He grabbed a manila envelope, led me outside to the hall, leaned against a wall. The people hustling past us were too engrossed in their own importance to pay us any mind.

"This is for you," he said, handing me the envelope. "The government's Jim Jones bibliography."

"Want to trade?" I handed him a folded piece of paper.

"What's that?"

"A resume."

"Rankin! You rejoining the straight world?"

"Not mine, a friend's. Named Tara Woodson."

"Woodson? As in . . ."

"As in."

"And?" he asked, raising his eyebrows.

"As in friend."

"Un-huh. And what exactly is it that this *friend* wants?"

"You know: fresh out of college, wants work in exciting areas. Only this one really is smart, has good experience."

"Does she now."

"Come on, David. She's just a kid. Reminds me of us then."

"So you thought you'd give her a helping hand. Or two." He held up his own hand against my glare. "OK, OK, just one friend talking with another and hey: I'm sure my boss would gladly do anything he could to help out the daughter of one of his colleagues."

"Senator Woodson isn't in this. Just her, who she is on that paper. No strings, no backlog favors from Daddy."

"Just her. And maybe you—as in friend."

I shrugged, smiled.

"Should I hear of anything, find anything, where can I reach Miss Woodson?"

"Try my number. If she's not staying there, I can find her."

"I bet you already have," he said.

He disappeared into his office before I could fire back.

The manila envelope held a computer printout sheet as long as I am tall. Typed lines showed "DESCRIPTORS"— cross-reference points: Cults—U.S.; Religious liberty—U.S.; Brainwashing—U.S.; Church membership—U.S.; Peoples Temple; Unification Church; Communal settlements— Guyana; Suicide—Guyana; Murder—Guyana. The printout listed reports by the Library of Congress, congressional hearing reports, General Accounting Office reports. Cross-referenced agencies included the GAO and the State Department. Later that day half a dozen phone calls netted me the name of a State Department official who "had a handle" on the affair, but the man wasn't in when I called.

Friday afternoon I walked to the bottom of Capitol Hill to track Janet Armstrong's post-Harvard history through the halls of Superior Court. All manner of men and women shuffle over that courthouse floor where hallways of hearing chambers stretch out to each side. Rich men, poor men, beggarmen and thieves; families, friends and functionaries. The defiant, the damned and the destined-for-better-or-worse things. Half a dozen Fifth Streeters lurk these halls of justice, approach strangers who have trouble on their faces or a summons in their hands: "Hi, you going to court? Need a lawyer?" These wizards excel at plea bargaining for whatever fee they can get. The most notorious of them was disbarred in 1980 for defecating in a court stairwell not 20 feet from a public restroom. Conduct unbecoming his profession. I rode the escalators to the fourth-floor criminal records division, a tan room crowded with clerks, computer terminals, bound volumes of printout sheets, and a steady stream of lawyers, defendants and worried relatives.

Janet Armstrong left tracks there. I found her in the 1979 alphabetized court disposition book: arrested, tried, convicted of misdemeanor solicitation for prostitution. I gave a clerk behind the counter the case number and disposition data as well as two names: Janet Armstrong and Crystal-Kristina Campbell, her street name. As he disappeared in the aisles of record files behind the counter, I caught a couple other customers staring my way. The black man in the flashy white suit and hat was about 40, with the thick body of a high school fullback who'd gained fat without losing muscle. The balding white man in the three-piece blue suit had a hooked nose, a nervous facial tic and almost colorless eyes behind wire-rim glasses. An old briefcase gaped open at his feet. Definitely a lawyer, probably Jewish. They both took my measure, then stared back toward the canyons of files. Five minutes later the clerk brought me the manila file with legal form sheets clipped inside it.

Both of Janet's identities adorned the jacket, sometimes side by side. Initially she'd pled not guilty and retained an attorney. I wrote his name and all her numbers, the name of her arresting officer and judge in my notebook. She'd switched her plea between her arrest and her appearance before the judge: Guilty. According to what the clerk could interpret from the scrawled notations on the case jacket, the judge met defendant and counsel in chambers—no transcript. The judge fined her $200 and imposed a 30-day curfew which forbade her to be within ten blocks of Vermont Avenue and K Street, the site of her arrest, between midnight and 6 A.M.

So much for the official record. When I got home I found a letter from the dead woman's father with a list of her friends, their addresses and phone numbers. He said he'd write them, asking for their cooperation, send a second list soon. And he asked what I'd learned.

"She got caught," I said, but he wasn't there to hear. I called Cliff Palefsky, *Washington Post* reporter, and once again he was out. This time in my message I included Janet Armstrong's name.

That was Friday, that and dinner at Cheryl's. Saturday was the cool day, Sunday the thaw. Now it was Memorial Day Monday and I lay in Cheryl's well-furnished, comfortable bedroom watching sunset's shadow grow on her wall.

"You want to shower with me?" I said.

"No!" she whined. "You're going to go *now!?*"

"Got to."

"No you don't!"

"You're taking an extra day off, staying up late, sleeping late tomorrow. I'm going to bed early, getting up early to run and earn my living. No way we'd rest well together tonight."

"Feed and fuck, that's your game."

I swung off the bed. She crawled to the edge, propped herself up off her stomach on her elbows, brown eyes looking at me, a soft frown. I stroked her cheek, dropped my hand down her chest, cupped one postpassion red splotched breast and rubbed her nipple with my thumb. I felt it stiffen and saw her smile.

"If that's true, counselor, then we're both guilty."

She stuck out her tongue.

"It'll be awful lonely in the shower."

"Maybe your fucking logic will keep you company."

"Probably," I said.

72

Pause. "Will you at least scrub my back?" she asked. "Just your back?"

My route from Cheryl's apartment usually skirted the edge of the city via Rock Creek Parkway, but that night I drove home through town. I navigated around Dupont Circle, took a right down 16th Street toward the glow of the White House eight blocks away. At K Street I turned left. Two blocks behind me during the day was the lawyers' boulevard; a block ahead of me at night was the prostitutes' strip.

Fifteenth Street, then Vermont and K, the corner where Janet Armstrong had been busted. Boxlike glass and white-washed concrete office buildings, banks, the U.S. Passport Office, a McDonald's hamburger franchise at the corner of 14th and K. Parked cars lined the far side of K Street, the sidewalk border of hooker country. Two gaudily dressed women sauntered up Vermont's angle away from K, and in the middle of K Street's block one followed another. Two more women waited on the corner of Vermont and K: one white, short with long brown hair, heavy makeup and a tan trenchcoat wrapped around bare legs; one black, long and lean, purple stretch pants, crushed velvet scarlet waistjacket, lacquered page-cut hair and slick, crimson lips. Their dead eyes watched me as I slowed New Car, rode past them. Spiders of the night, I thought, and drove on.

New Car carried me to Massachusetts Avenue, through the still-scarred riot corridor to Capitol Hill. As I drove up 1st Street between the Supreme Court and the Capitol, I remembered calling Mad Dog at Ned Johnson's office to tell him still no luck finding anyone who had a pipeline into ABSCAM. Dog was out to lunch. On a hunch, I asked for his adored intern, Katie. She was out too. Un-huh, I thought, reminded myself to tell him the similar but sad story of Scott Oliff—killed that thought fast, hard and unquestioningly. Maybe Mad Dog knew of work for Tara. I'd sent him her resume, just in case.

I slowed New Car at the stop light by my corner of Pennsylvania and 7th Street. There were no parking places to the right down 7th, so I flipped my left turn signal. I didn't pay much attention to the three black men lounging in front of the closed Kresge's dime store. They moved away as I turned. One block up I made another left before the red barnlike Eastern Market, found a parking spot alongside the indoor municipal swimming pool. No lights shown in any houses to my right. The lit bank parking lot to my left held a dozen deserted cars. I could see Pennsylvania Avenue through the 50-foot parking lot driveway gap between the bank and the bicycle repair shop. My landlord Rich was talking to someone in front of the McDonald's on the far side of Pennsylvania. Maybe Rich knew somebody to give Tara's resume to. I remember giggling about astrological fate as I rummaged through the crap scattered in my car, bundled up a couple books with my dirty clothes from the weekend with Cheryl.

They got me as I bent over to lock my car door. Weakness flowed through me, then my wind went, blown away by the shock-pain burning in my kidney where I'd been sucker-punched. I heard their scuffling shoes. *"Get him, man!"* Hands whirled me around. I flung my laundry bundle at a faceless monster: brown nylon stocking pulled over his features. My dirty jeans wrapped his face for too-few moments. A second stocking capped masked monster held my left wrist, forcing me back to the wall of parked cars: he'd sucker-punched me, I thought, and adrenaline hit my system with regained breath. I jerked free, which pulled him closer to me, startled him. My right jab was weak, but it smacked him back. He touched his mask more in shock than pain. Before I could run from the first man who by now had defeated my laundry I discovered I was wrong about who sucker-punched me: it wasn't the second man, the man I'd slugged. It was the third man, the man behind me. He hit me again, this time in the other kidney. My arms flew wide as I fought the new burst of pain. My knees wobbled. The third man grabbed me in a full nelson, his hands locked behind my neck, my arms pried wide from my sides. I know how to break this hold, I thought. But my body was too blurred and weak a concept for action. The second man, the one I'd punched, kicked me in the groin. My knees buckled, I retched, retched again. Acid poured through my veins. I heard their distant voices, felt their alien touch: *"Here!"* My watch left my wrist. *"Hey! Hey! I'm going to do his car!"* My wallet floated out of my back pocket. My vision cleared, I saw my dirty T-shirt snake along the road, crawl up the side of New Car, disappear down a hole. What was that smell? *"Hurry up, man! Give him to me!"* The monster on my back jerked me upright, threw me stumbling across the street toward a form in a blue jacket, black gloves, no face, no face, I saw no face as I tried to stand straight, tried to bring my arms up in front of me. His black-gloved fists snapped to a boxer's guard, his feet shuffled with a delighted dance. He hummed some mindless theme song, feinted twice with his left. I could only lean away from his right jab as his glove smashed into my cheek, spun me around and down to the pavement. I slammed into the concrete with my chin, blew it open, splattered nearby cars. A warm, crimson, sticky stain spread out from my face. The boxer seemed disappointed I wouldn't stand up to play. *"Come on, let's go!"* hissed one of his friends. *"Finish it!"* ordered the monster by the car. He fumbled with his hands. The boxer slammed his sneaker under my stomach, curling & crumpling me up to my knees, my face jerking out of a lake of blood. *"Mind your own fuckin' business, Rankin!"* I turned my face from the next kick. He clipped the side of my neck, flipped me over and I was gone, still there but going, spread-eagled in the road all but gone. My eyes rolled to one side, saw three shadows melt into darkness, saw a burning snake dangling from New Car's side. *WaWhump!!* The gas tank exploded, a ball of fire mushroomed through New Car, billowed out of shattered windows as acrid black smoke rushed to hide the stars. Heat drenched me. Couldn't move for my life, I thought. Don't giggle. Not funny. Footsteps— joggers? Hands dragging me over hardness.

"Oh Jesus!" cried Rich as he pulled me away from the inferno. Sirens. I remember his shirt being stained with blood. I wanted to apologize, offer to wash it, but I couldn't talk. He cradled me, rocked and cried, his tears tapping my face. "Oh Jesus, John! It's going to be OK! You're going to be OK! You're OK, OK, OK!!"

Then I was gone.

14

Of all the visitors to my hospital room the most dangerous to me was Nick Sherman. He wasn't the most universally dangerous person to come through my sickroom door, but he was bad enough news for me.

Good news came in copious quantity. Cheryl met Rich at the emergency room, spent part of the night and came by for breakfast. Rich finally left the hospital at midnight, still apologizing for not rescuing me from danger he hadn't seen. The only way he'd accept my thanks was when I told him we were now even for the time I spoiled the stickup man's fun at The Eclectic. Saul showed up before lunch, Saul and the flaxen-haired Katie. He couldn't keep his eyes off the bandage around my chin or his hands off her. I don't know which one scared him more. Joey Malletta and two other of my ex-muckraking colleagues from Ned Johnson's dropped by; Ned called me from East Jesus, Oklahoma, or some such place where he was giving a speech: "It's good to hear your voice," he said. He always says that. But he called. So did Senate aide David Henderson who sounded more stunned by my fate than I was. Art Dillon wanted to know who to sue. My ex-boss Senator Applegate phoned, asked what he could do. Even Maggie called: I'd made the papers. Maggie sounded worse than me.

But then came Homicide detective Nick Sherman. He sauntered into the white room as I finished with Maggie, leaned on the window sill. He sat his black, hand-held radio on the covered radiator. "Your doctor says the concussion is gone."

"Wasn't bad to begin with."

"How about the rest of you?"

"Twenty-one stitches in my chin, three layers. They think the kidneys are bruised. No big deal." I felt silly propped up on that inclined hospital bed. At least I'd changed from the ridiculous gown to fresh clothes Cheryl'd brought me.

"What the hell am I going to do with you? You're up past your ass in death and destruction. First I got you messing around in the Janet Armstrong stuff . . ."

"You know that's legitimate."

". . . then you pop up in the vest pocket of Eddie Hampton."

"Who the hell is Eddie Hampton?"

"A dead-in-an-alley accountant you once met. A veteran of WWII with fingerprints to prove it. Quartermaster Corps, no overseas service, spotless record then, spotless record since. He ran his small accounting and bookkeeping business out of his basement in suburban Maryland. No records of any Congress-related business. His neighbors barely knew him, though they thought he drank, and neither they nor folks who hang around that alley recognize your picture."

"What picture?"

"We got a nice eight-by-ten glossy of you we've been showing around."

The "careless" evidence technician. "My mother would love a copy."

"Maybe we should take another one now. A before-and-after series."

I didn't smile.

"Just when I figure you're square, Homicide gets a radio report: robbery with violence, arson, victim critically injured, rushed to George Washington hospital. One of our guys rolled on the call—just in case, you un'erstand. He ID'd said victim over the radio and guess what: it's John Rankin. Again. Gustafson and I had to leave a TV rerun of *African Queen,* drive all the way to GW, and then you didn't die on us."

"Sorry."

He shrugged. "Since you're going to live, the First District detectives in your neighborhood have your case now. Sort of."

"Sort of?"

"I've taken a special interest in your well-being. What happened to it?"

"I got mugged."

"So you told the officers who interviewed you last night. Three black males. Young. Masks. Who just happened to know your name."

"They grabbed my wallet before they said it."

"Yeah, your wallet: it was scattered all over that street and down one more. Maybe they saw your driver's license. Maybe they're speedreaders."

"Maybe they set me up, knew my house. My name is on the door. They could have pegged me, figured I had bucks or a gun to steal."

"What other explanation could there be?"

I stared back at his black eyes. "None that I can think of."

"Could they be friends of Eddie Hampton's?"

"You know all I do about that. You know more."

"Yeah, sure I do. I'm a *po*-lice. Knowing more is my job. What have you been doing in your job, Mr. Private Investigator?"

God I was stuck! I wanted to know why I landed in this hospital bed more than he did. But I couldn't trust him. Beyond protecting the privacy of my business, this was neither the time nor the place to justify the letter, the money, my scam; to explain how and why Tara (and her father) weren't involved. Sherman was locked into coincidences, and I didn't want to give him a key to doors I couldn't control. This wasn't the time or the place, yet it nagged at me that such a time or place seemed to be drifting further from my grasp. Sherman's chipped-tooth grin left me little room to maneuver. I couldn't tell all the truth and I couldn't tell any hard and fast lies.

"I've been doing what I should," I said.

"Doing anything you shouldn't?"

I shrugged. "Doubt it."

"Don't play the strong, silent bit for me."

"I've been poking around court in Janet Armstrong's stuff. A couple guys might have overheard me there, but so what? I got a probate case I'm helping a lawyer research, nothing routine but nothing dangerous—as far as I know. Some paper-pushing odds and ends. Sure, I've been thinking about . . . What was his name? Eddie Hampton? Trying to puzzle that one out. Doing nothing to piss anybody off. Certainly nothing to piss off three street punks."

"Sometimes you can't tell how and you don't know who and you aren't sure why, but somebody gets pissed off enough to do something. Unless you're an asshole, you try not to piss off the wrong people."

I heard the squawk of his turned-low radio, the slap of nurses' shoes in the corridor, the *ding-dong* of the hospital bells. An ammonia medicine smell tingled my nose. I wonder how long we'd have stared at each other if *he* hadn't come in.

"How you doing, bro?" That voice born in a mountain cave.

A myth filled the doorway of my room, a myth who was a man—who was a myth. He was absolutely the most dangerous man in that or most other rooms. Sherman rose from his perch, held his hands steady and ready by his sides, aimed his black eyes on that hulk in the doorway. Sherman was taller, though not as heavy in the arms or as barrel-chested. My man's cashmere blazer had to be tailor-made. The straining sports shirt worn open at the collar came off some rack, the thick gold chain necklace came from Thailand, the blue jeans from Levi Strauss and the cowboy boots were once some now probably extinct animal. He carried an electric blue bag in his left hand made of fancy knapsack material that was the shape of an oversized purse. This day his hair was reddish brown, cut short and wild with curls. He let Sherman's form fill his fire-blue eyes, then he walked into the room, leaned against the far wall so Sherman was to his right, the door to his left. He swayed as he moved, a deliberate, rhythmic progress. I'd seen that walk before, in gyms called dojos, in guys who wore funny white pajamas tied shut with long black cloth belts. I hoped he was smiling under that walrus mustache. I felt like a piece of meat waiting to be won or lost.

"Where did you come from?!" I said, then regained my composure. "Detective Nick Sherman, this is a friend of mine . . ."

"Mark Augustine," lied my man-myth. At least I think he lied. At least that wasn't one of the names he'd used with me before.

The two men nodded to each other but moved no closer.

"Are you here to see our beat-up buddy?" asked Sherman.

"Yeah. How about you?"

"That and more. He's a crime victim. I'm a cop."

"No kidding."

"You live around here?"

"I travel."

"We are old friends," I said. "We go back a long way."

"Then I'd be leaving you in good hands," said Sherman.

"Sure," I said.

The cop got a smile from the walrus mustache. Both men seemed to shrink slightly, and the ease in the air let me breathe again.

"Well," said Sherman as he carefully picked up his radio, casually turned the crackling volume up, nonchalantly walked between my man and the door, "in that case, I'll get back to the bricks." He turned to the image leaning on the wall, memorized each and every detail. And flashed that chipped-tooth grin: "Nice to meet you, Mr. Mark Augustine." Back to me: "I'll be seeing you soon."

We listened to the crackling radio recede down the hall. My man walked to the door, looked down the corridor. Satisfied, he turned back to me.

"How you doing, Paul?" I said.

"Better than you. Better than Mark Augustine."

"Who's he?"

"He's dead. Long time gone. Got cute, got in over his head, got dead. You promised me this private eye shit was a no-risk deal."

"It isn't my life: it's the city, the times."

"You sure about that?"

"As sure as I can be."

He heard her first, whirled: Tara stood in my doorway. Her face was tense—fear maybe, nerves. Worry. I felt terrific.

80

"My father read in the paper . . . he told me . . ."

"You must be Maggie," said Paul, a grin lifting his mustache as he offered Tara his massive hand. She gave him hers, but I spoke before she could reply.

"Ah, no, this is Tara Woodson."

"My mistake," Paul said without blushing. "I'm an old friend of John's: Paul Burke."

She turned to me. "Are you all right?" She wore a plaid shirt, blue jeans, sneakers, a sweater tied around her shoulders.

"When they take this bandage off I'll have a souvenir scar, but nothing else. How was graduation?"

"What happened? My father said you asked about Scott . . ."

"It's a long story I'll tell you soon."

"I can't stay, bro," said Paul. "I'll give you a ride home."

"How did you get here?" I asked Tara.

"My father gave me a car for graduation. I've lost my license but . . . It's in the parking lot."

"Busy for the next couple hours?"

She shook her head.

"Remember where I live?" As she nodded I dug my keys out of my jeans. "Let yourself in. Listen to the stereo while you wait. I'll be there soon. Tell you everything then. OK?"

She shrugged. "OK." To Paul: "Nice to meet you."

Again he made sure my visitor was out of earshot before he spoke.

"Sorry about that Maggie slip, but the last time I called you, that was her name."

"Maggie's gone. And Tara . . . She's different."

"So I see. You gave her your keys."

"She may move in."

"I didn't think you were going to do that again, buddy."

"It's not that way with us. I mean, hell: my woman of the moment is named Cheryl. Tara is just a good friend who needs some shelter. Special thing."

"It's hard to keep names straight around you. Does . . . *Cheryl* know about that blonde?"

I nodded.

Paul sighed. "You live too dangerously for me, buddy."

The hospital released me after I signed a pile of forms I didn't read. Paul picked me up at the door in an American sedan whose make and license plate I ignored. He slid into traffic around Washington Circle, drove east on Pennsylvania Avenue. We passed the gray castlelike Old Executive Office Building with its thousands of columns, passed the cake-box White House next door. Paul had served time inside that bleached center of politics, but I never completely knew how or why.

"This still turn you on?" he asked, his gesture taking the city and all it stood for. "This power stuff?"

"Biggest sport around," I said.

"You know who the most powerful man in our lifetime has been?" he asked. "The single most powerful man? The guy who was more influential than all those kiss-ass congressmen you know?"

I shook my head: he wanted to give me the answer.

"Lee Harvey Oswald," he said, then smiled: "The men who were Lee Harvey Oswald. They—*he* sat in that Texas book tower and in one moment he shook the earth more than any of these fools." We turned right, past the Treasury building, waited at the light on 15th Street to turn left, head toward the Hill.

"It's not the man who gives the orders who's truly powerful," he continued. "It's the man who makes the orders happen, the guy out there on the line. Without him, orders and ideas are all just words. You got to learn how to accept that power, then use it. Guys who do are the ones who count, who get what they want."

"I wonder if Lee Harvey Oswald got what he wanted."

"If he didn't, it wasn't for lack of trying."

"Are you OK?" I asked after a block of silence. "I don't know what you're doing now . . ."

"Did you ever?" he grinned.

"Not completely, but . . ."

"But I gave you great stories for Ned Johnson, didn't I?"

"That's not all that's important."

Sentiment makes him uncomfortable. "Those guys who did you, were they professionals?"

"They got my money. If you get paid, you're a pro."

His look told me he didn't appreciate my humor.

"I don't know, Paul. I doubt it. Three hoods versus one sucker."

"You into anything in the life—in my type world?"

"No."

"I checked around. Nobody had you done because of me."

"I didn't figure they did. How did you know about this?"

"I keep my eyes on you.

"Look, you find out who did it, we'll do them. Call that go-between number, ask for me under that other name. And it's done. *Done*. If you need anything else, money, couple guys to watch your back . . ."

"Don't think so," I said as we passed the House office buildings. "But thanks."

"You gotta find out who did this. You know that, don't you?"

I said nothing.

"Your business, you can't afford not to."

"Yeah," I agreed quietly. "I know my business."

"It's more than that. It's life. Somebody rips you, you gotta rip them back twice as hard, because if somebody gets away with taking a bite out of your ass, then everybody will try. That's how you get eaten up."

"There's lots of ways you get eaten up," I told him.

"Don't bother with abstract bullshit," he said. "Worry about *this* one."

"I don't know this one."

"Find out. When you know . . ."

"Then I'll decide what I can do."

"You *can* do *anything!*"

I shook my head. "I've got my limits."

"They're just lines to cross," he said. "Don't let them box you in."

I shrugged. "I've got to handle this my way, Paul."

"Don't be dumb," he said. "And don't decide what you can't do until you get there." He grinned. "You might be surprised.

"Got any cases this might have come from?" he asked, fishing.

"I'm not sure." I didn't dare tell him about Janet Arm-

83

strong or Jonestown. He wouldn't be content until he'd "helped" all he could. No way could I control him once he got rolling. His intentions were basically good; his actions knew no boundaries.

He knew I was holding back, knew not to push.

"That cop is no chump. Is he a friend?"

"I don't know yet."

"Watch him." We slowed for a traffic light. "And watch that Tara girl you got moving in. She's got iceberg eyes. Even if she didn't . . . One inside and one outside can be rough."

"You ought to know."

He grinned, pulled behind The Eclectic, and double-parked.

"Can you stick around?"

"Got to go."

"When will I see you again?"

"You didn't see me now." He handed me the blue bag. It weighed about ten pounds. "Got you a little present."

"Come on! You didn't have to . . ."

"For this I do."

"What is it?"

"Two things. The first is a .357 Magnum revolver. I prefer a doubled 9-millimeter or a .45 automatic, but they take a sophistication you don't have, so I applied the KISS principle. You know what the KISS principle is, don't you?"

I shook my head *no*.

"Keep It Simple, Stupid!" He laughed, tapped me lightly—considering his strength—with the back of his hand.

"I put a box of bullets in there. Packs six, two for each of those creeps. Hell, the goddamn roar will probably scare them to death! I don't want you getting eaten by this fucking town."

"Paul, I . . ." I could only whisper. A key to a door I didn't understand, a door that troubled me, weighed down my hands. I didn't want to offend him, but . . . "I don't think it's legal for me to have this in D.C."

"So? Half this town isn't legal. That's the problem you make it. As far as the law, the Magnum is nothing compared to what else is in there."

I didn't want to ask and he knew it.

"A half ounce of cocaine.

"Pure stuff, medical coke. I know you've tried that street shit a couple times, you fool. Consider this a little diversion from your accident. Friends of yours who heard you took it on the chin passed it along. Don't go dealing it, don't use much at once."

"Paul . . ."

"Watch the lines you push, Bro. Watch what you ask. Your First Amendment rights on knowing things are shaky now that you've quit writing. And remember: those fancy words protect only possession of *knowledge.*"

"What do I say?"

"Say, 'I'll be careful.' And don't lie."

As the car drove away I again didn't look at the license plate. I felt like the whole world was watching as I turned the corner, the blue bag tight in my hand.

I heard history as I slowly climbed my steps, history captured on tape and blaring through my stereo.

December 14, 1978. Winterland: a cramped, marijuana-smoke-filled auditorium in San Francisco. A couple thousand hard core fans. The recording is scratchy, a bootleg taped and retaped before it reached me, but you can hear those thousands of voices chanting, *"Bruce! Bruce! Bruce!"* Then comes the solid tone of Bill Graham welcoming the crowd to the concert. Graham was the impresario of the Fillmore, San Francisco's premier rock palace, the sound stage of the 1960s. Fillmore concerts were the rumble of a cultural wave, the theater a Mecca just up the street from where Jim Jones would establish his Peoples Temple before fleeing to Guyana. Same street, same time. That Fillmore and Jones were gone in 1980, but Graham still lived, at least on the tape of that night in 1978 when he introduced history.

At my door I felt the drum roll more than heard it. I walked into my office as the piano and guitars jumped, music charged hard and Bruce Springsteen tore into "Badlands."

Tara saw me. She turned, fumbled until she found the volume knob to turn the music down.

"Best welcome home I could have had," I said as the music faded.

85

She gestured to the stereo: "Rock 'n' roll and a private detective?"

"It's my life." Suddenly I needed to justify that to her. "I remember when Elvis blew rock 'n' roll out of black rhythm and blues . . ."

"That was about when I was born, wasn't it?" she said.

". . . when Bob Dylan jumped folk into electric rock, Buddy Holly, the Beatles on Ed Sullivan, Motown, Woodstock. Our folks have World War II and Frank Sinatra. We have Vietnam and rock 'n' roll. Power and poetry . . ."

"Power and poetry?!"

"President Carter quoted Bob Dylan in his best speech. Rich downstairs said some Scottish philosopher once claimed he could control any kingdom if he could control its balladeers. Our ballads are rock 'n' roll and country and western music. More people hear those words than read the *New York Times*. More money was raised for antinuclear politics through rock benefits than any other single way. For better or worse, more people take rock seriously than the *New York Times* or political conventions."

"At least you do."

I grinned, moved behind the desk, casually dropped the blue bag of contraband into a drawer. If she heard the *thunk,* she didn't show it. "Only sometimes," I replied. "And always Springsteen."

"He's not somebody I know much . . ." She stopped the diversionary conversation, drew a deep breath. "My father told me about that guy who gave you money and died, about the letter, you conning Scott . . ."

"I'll tell you everything," I interrupted, "but know this first: you're not part of it. Not you. I didn't know about any possible link to that dead guy until after you told me who your father was. Wouldn't have made any difference if I had. I'd still . . . Hell, Tara, we're friends. No scams, no games. There was this shadow that might have touched you, so I threw some light on it, found out it didn't, and that's that. Finished."

Believe that, I silently begged. Because it *must* be true!

"You got beat up."

"Rough town. Sometimes I run pretty close to the

edges . . ." I hastened to stop her concern. "Not too close, though. And nothing you need to worry about. Ever."

"I push it a little too," she said. Almost grinned.

I bet you do, I thought. "You're safe around me."

"Sure?" She didn't stop her smile that time.

"Sure," I insisted. "Hell, I got mugged, pure, simple and clean. Cause and effect, circumstance and coincidence. You and me, we're not part of that bullshit. Now, are we friends?"

For a moment I was afraid, then she smiled, sat down. "What choice do I have?"

"None. You're moving in." She hesitated, so I raced ahead. "It's probably better for me. You'll come in handy."

Her forehead wrinkled.

"Dumb stuff," I said, raising my arms more slowly than their stiffness demanded. "I'm not quite a cripple, but I can use help."

She shrugged, grinned. "Who is Maggie?"

"Maggie is gone. Now her name is Cheryl. You'll meet her. She'll insist on staying over a few nights a week."

"Who's your friend Paul?" Quieter, colder, craftier.

"Let's play make-believe," I said. "Just a story between us.

"Once upon a time Japan believed in a particular kind of empire so they believed in samurais as a way of life. Then another day came, and they didn't believe in that kind of empire anymore—but they were stuck with all these samurais who knew no other existence. They called them Ronin, and Japan bled from Ronin hacking their way through history for a couple decades. The Ronin bled too. Once upon a time America believed in a particular kind of empire. Now, after Vietnam, we don't. Maybe because, like Japan, we can't. Now we have our own Ronin, and they're hacking their way through our history."

"And that's what your friend Paul is?"

"That's too simple for him. He's the most unusual and dangerous man you'll ever meet. You couldn't ask for a better friend."

"Or a worse enemy."

"You got it."

"I got a small warning there, didn't I?"

"Smart kid."

"I'm not a kid."

"In my family, if we like you, we call you kid."

"Did you meet many people like him reporting for Ned Johnson?"

"You don't meet many people like him anywhere. When you do, you better be ready."

"I think you're ready enough to handle about anything."

My ears tingled as we smiled at each other.

I thought about it, I'd been thinking about it since I climbed the stairs. She'd done great so far. Besides, I thought, as close as she's getting, there's really no choice.

"Look," I said, "you're going to be living here. I figure . . . When I met you I knew I could trust you."

"Thank you." A soft whisper. She *must* understand.

"No, thank *you*. Not many people you can trust, not all the way. I, ah . . . There are things I do you can't repeat. Ned Johnson things. Client things. I mean, I am a *private* detective. Personal things too."

Her thumb rubbed back and forth along her forefinger, back and forth, as she nervously waited for me to throw open some ugly closet door. There was no way to do it smoothly. "Look, I'm from the sixties, and . . . Do you get stoned?"

She laughed. "Sure. Not everything. I don't do psychedelics anymore, that was just a phase."

"Never have, never will."

"And nothing bad like PCP . . ."

"Angel *death*."

"When I was younger, I smoked a lot of grass and hash."

"Of course."

"Maybe some other stuff." Cautious, fishing, knowing she hadn't hit the right key.

"I do cocaine every now and then," I said.

"So do I." Relief flowed between us. "But who can afford it?"

"Not me, but I got lucky."

This time her unasked question wasn't defensive.

"You, ah . . ." I said. "You want to try some coke. Now?"

She spread her hands. "Turning it down would be silly."

According to the Drug Enforcement Administration, in

1980 cocaine for the first time surpassed marijuana as the illegal "drug of choice" among Americans and outgrossed that illegal green herb's $11 billion market with $35 billion worth of street sales.

Cocaine. We'd barely heard of it in the 1960s. Sherlock Holmes, Sigmund Freud, other mythical creatures we read about used it. Cocaine was like heroin, wasn't it? And morphine. Addictive. Dangerous. Deadly. Who even knew what it looked like back in 1968?

Back in 1980, 20 million Americans knew very well what cocaine looked like. Hospitals treated 40,000 patients suffering cocaine overdoses. The government began keeping statistics on cocaine deaths. But, as with the prohibited deadly alcohol of the Roaring '20s, Americans obeyed their appetites, not their intelligence. From an esoteric drug of the rich cocaine moved through the country like a blizzard, covering blue and white collar segments alike, most common in usage by the white baby boom, middle-income groups who could afford its average $100 a many-times-cut gram street price. A hundred dollars for about a thimble of magic. Cocaine.

Of all the dangerous drugs used by Americans in 1980— including alcohol, nicotine, amphetamines and barbiturates, hallucinogens and heroin (which frighteningly became ultra-chic later that year), hashish and marijuana, Valium, caffeine —cocaine was the most dangerous because it is the most seductive. If it was not (as it often was) cut with speed or some other horror, cocaine seemed to hand you reality, not twist it away. White crystalline powder, usually snorted through the nose, it numbed sinuses, maybe teeth. But instead of feeling bleary, rounded, dull, you felt sharp . . . *best*. You felt special. You felt elite. Fatigue vanished. Indians in the Andes chew coca leaves to carry them across the high peaks. I played the best game of basketball in my life the first night I tried cocaine—and that coke was low quality. Used in sane amounts, there was no troubling hangover—a mild depression, some coming-down palpitations of the heart, slight nausea, all of which passed quickly. Cocaine made you stronger, made you better, with no evil side effects.

Or so it seemed. Forget that there might be long-range health problems, forget coke-hyped nights without sleep, forget that continued excessive use led to paranoia and perception problems, forget what the experts call "psychological addiction," in which coke becomes the reason for living, forget the cost in dollars and the subversion coke users inflict on their laws and society. Know most that the world cocaine shows is *controlled*—and the real world is not that way. Cocaine makes you seem more than you are, but the world knows different, and when you push reality, reality pushes back twice as hard. Pushes you, not the coke.

But the crystal illusion is so sweet its price is easy to ignore.

When I opened the desk drawer I was careful not to let Tara see the blue knapsack. A paper bag inside the knapsack felt cold and heavy—the gun and ammo. A manila envelope lay beside the gun sack, and from it I lifted a plastic bag with maybe a cupful of tannish, flakelike crystal powder. Pure, unadulterated magic crystal control.

"Paul gave me this once," I said, taking a small buck folding knife from the desk. "We might as well use it." I handed her one of Eddie Hampton's $100 bills. Tara's eyes widened as she took the bill, though she said nothing. So often she said nothing.

"Might as well do it chic," I said. She shrugged, rolled the bill into a tube while I opened the bag. Alkaline, chalk dust filled my nostrils. I used the knife blade to put a quarter-sized mound on a gray paperback I pulled from my shelf: *The Age of Reason,* by Jean-Paul Sartre. Father of existentialism, Sartre died that year of 1980. I still haven't read any of his books.

"That's an awful lot," she whispered.

"We got a lot." I carefully chopped the knife through the mound, flattening it out, then drawing it into eight separate inch-long lines on the book cover's gray photos of bridges over a river running through a city I assumed was Paris.

"I've never seen so much in my life," she said, and I silently thanked Paul: such a cool scene he let me stage.

"I'll go first," I said, taking the money tube from her. I bent to the lines holding one end of the rolled-up bill in my right nostril and pushing the other end along a white crystal track. I snorted one line in quickly, then shifted to the other nostril and snorted a second.

"Here," I pushed the book to her. "Do two, see how they hit."

Oh Jesus did they hit! My right nostril burned as I snorted through the left. My first rush hit by the time I pushed the book to Tara. A forceful tingle roared through my face, between my ears, danced in my brain. My throat tightened slightly, my teeth went numb, the aches of my body faded, my heart raced, and the world . . . the world seemed solid and tight and fine and I was damn, damn good. I watched her spread the lines out, no shyness thank God, take four snorts to do two lines, lean back. I saw it hit her too, saw the black wells of her eyes expanded as her pupils dilated, saw that wide-mouth smile. As she knew it. As we knew it. As the cocaine took us away.

"That's . . ."

"Amazing," I said. She nodded.

"Do you like coffee?" I asked after a second. We talked rapid fire: coherent, but far from *straight*. I wanted to talk with her, hear all she thought, tell her all I had to say. Talk with this new friend. That's who she was. A new friend. I let myself admit the sleek way she filled her blue jeans, noted her taut high bottom. A runner's body? Hair so golden, so fine; mouth so soft, so large. *Later for that,* I heard something deep inside me whisper, something I ignored. I said, "I mean, I've got lots of coffee."

"I love coffee. I'm practically . . ."

". . . a caffeine junkie. Me too." We wandered into the kitchen, paced the floor together. "We might as well make some. It goes great with coke. That . . . Cheryl will be here in about two hours." Tara smiled. "Until then . . ." I nodded toward the coke. "I mean, what else can we do?"

15

Dear Mr. Rankin:

My uncle Tom Armstrong asked me to write you about Janet. I hope you can help him put this terrible thing behind him.

I'm Janet's older cousin—17 years older. I live in Eugene, teach music in the grade schools and piano at home. My husband works for a logging company, but we may have to move because of the economy. I wish I knew where we could move to. I knew Janet all her life.

What I remember best about Janet are her piano lesson days, from age 7 until she was about 12 and too good for me to teach anymore (then she went to a lady at the university here). I wish I could forget those awful months after she went to Washington to do what she did. We all still have a hard time saying that word— prostitution. Janet used to call me from D.C., and she laughed once when I told her that, said back there they call it whore. Only she pronounced it funny, more like "hoe." Made me practice it, repeat it with her, till I started crying and she changed the subject to how her folks were doing. Janet was an only child, and I was as close to being her sister as she ever had. Maybe if I'd really been that, she'd be alive today.

Those piano lesson days. It rains almost every afternoon here in Eugene. By the time I got home from teaching elementary school the rain would have let up some, maybe stopped completely. She was my special *student, and she knew it. I'd watch out the window, see her running through the sunshine, across the wet grass, to get to my house. Sometimes we'd look for the rainbow. We'd laugh and joke, but she worked hard and had real talent. That's why she took lessons twice a week instead of once. She'd take all the teaching she could get. And she'd practice. A little Miss Perfectionist, I used to tell her folks. So polite. Every day, when the lesson was over, I'd leave her sitting there on the bench against the wall underneath the bowl of fruit painting in my living room, all prim and proper in her little dresses or those kiddie coveralls little girls used to wear then. I'd go get a glass of milk for her treat, maybe a cookie or piece of leftover cake, bring it back in. Without fail she'd have cleaned up all the music books, put them in neat little stacks under the lid of the bench where they belonged. She'd be sitting there, hands folded in her lap, waiting to be told she'd done good. I'd say thank you. She'd say, "That's OK, Cousin Beth, that's what I'm supposed to do." And we'd smile.*

I'm sorry, Mr. Rankin. I had to stop for a while.

Janet grew up healthy and good. The only way to describe her as a teenager is to say she was a star. About age 12 they discovered she could sing. That's when her opera stuff started. She got lucky being in Eugene, because we are such a good opera town. She did great in school—top grades, always winning awards. Never any real trouble to her folks—oh, some teenage things, but not bad stuff. Always ran with the good crowd. Got that scholarship to Harvard.

As I look back on it, maybe there were some things funny about her. Maybe she was a little troubled. These days I don't know what crazy is anymore. All the TV shows keep telling me as long as I honestly feel crazy, then I'm OK and that's good. I don't understand. Maybe the funny things in Janet started coming out when she went to Harvard, or maybe we just didn't notice them until then. Whenever she did something that I thought was weird and I asked her about it, maybe told her to snap out of it and grow up or quit acting goofy, she'd get real huffy, belligerent, then not talk to me for a while. So I quit noticing and quit mentioning.

When she took off with that man, none of us knew about him. Finally one of her friends and one of her old boyfriends came by and told her folks where and what and why. As they left—and believe me, her parents were NOT believing them—Janet called from Chicago. I think she told them then. Flat out, no lies. Damn near killed them.

We went to the police, but there was nothing they could do. "Free, white and 21" used to be the phrase. I don't know what to call it now. Her parents tried to "keep communications open" like they say in all the books. Janet would call them from time to time, call me every few weeks or so. It was hard to talk with her. I had to swallow a lot of tears and a lot of yelling: How's Washington, Janet? Do you want to hear a new cake recipe? How's your work?

She was very concerned for our safety for some reason, and that we'd do something "silly," or that we'd worry. She kept saying, "I can get out if I want to. I can leave if I want to." She had a deep view of what she was doing, a very conscious sense of justice. She believed that anyone who's a deep-thinking person should be able to survive both the good and the bad in life through a karma (I think I know what that word means) kind of way. I think maybe some of this was connected with the idea of "I'm going to purify myself or bring to life in me some new, more understanding universal spirit because I've been through this." But she never intended to be a prostitute. She thought she was going to help that guy with the books or something. She told me they talked about opening a jazz club where she could sing, mix opera and rock and pop and jazz and make lots of money to retire, not be a burden to her folks or anyone, maybe go back to school. She didn't talk much like that toward the end, but that's how it started.

She told me once that when she got picked up for prostitution in Chicago it might have been a setup, part *of that guy's plan. She had to work, she said, because of some kind of emergency, got "busted." The Chicago police, according to her, were corrupt—or at least some of them. The girls would be set up to be picked up and then the whole vice squad would catch them and beat them up, which would make them terribly afraid to be caught again, as well as breaking their spirit. I know that her "boyfriend" beat one of the girls who was with them pretty bad when she got busted, but I don't know if he beat Janet.*

Sometimes she kind of bragged about her work, about how she wasn't just a street girl but had phone-in clients too. Important people, she said. A guy who worked for the CIA, a guy who guarded the president: she told her mother to watch for him on TV and described him. She told me she had the class corner and was real picky.

Toward the end she began to worry about getting out. She always said she'd have to leave her things and just go. She came home once for a visit, but then she went back of her own free will despite everything we said. That second time she left hurt even more, because there were no pretenses we could cling to then.

You don't know what her death did to this town. Maybe not so much her death as the publicity. The local paper reprinted that big story the Washington Post did and people here went wild. How could they do that in her hometown! How could they do it to her family! How cruel of the papers! We'd been quiet about the details of her death, even after the huge funeral before the stories. We'd told everyone except family and the local police that she had a job in Washington, let everybody think it was with the government, which is what everybody does in Washington (except maybe you). Then those stories.

You always love those stories when they're about some stranger in some other town, printed in some other paper, like the ones in the supermarket. You say it's different when it's someone in your life, but it isn't. We finally all decided that maybe the stories were good. The rumors would have hit Eugene anyhow. Rumors probably would have been worse because they'd be dirtier, smirked. At least this was in the open. Maybe some girl here won't do it now. And besides, rumor or newspaper story, she is still dead.

We've all talked about why it happened for hours. Lot of the people here have this thing about the pimp being black. You know all those myths. I don't know if that affected Janet. If it did, it was probably a rebellion against racism. But maybe the right creep at the right time could have destroyed her that way, black or white or green.

Her folks don't want to believe the black part because they're good people, but it lurks underneath some of what they say. Her mother is convinced it was drugs, that that guy got her hooked on something like cocaine or heroin, and that made her do it. I was too old for all that hippie stuff, but this is Eugene, and I know a lot more about that stuff than them. I don't think drugs had anything to do with it. But what do I know? I'm just a music teacher from Eugene.

I guess if I had to come up with a reason, what I'd come up with is something like hypnotism or brainwashing like those religious cults do. Maybe Janet had more trouble than we knew, more problems. That would have made all that easier for that man. Maybe it was just the times, maybe instead of being a hippie or a beatnik or a sit-inner she became what she did. I don't think so, but maybe. I know she did wrong, maybe even some bad. I don't care. I loved her. Nothing will ever make me believe she was an evil person. I only pray that when I die God will make me understand why. And let me see my Janet again.

Sincerely yours,
Beth Yates

During the 12 days between my mugging and June 9, when that letter arrived, reading my mail was the only work I'd done besides wondering who my enemies were. I called Nick Sherman and told him about the two men who could have overheard me asking for Janet's files. He said their descriptions meant nothing to him, but he'd think about it. And he

sounded friendlier. Tara moved in the day after I got home—
under Cheryl's accommodating gaze. Those two women
practiced hollow conversations. I'd sneak a wise smile to Tara
when Cheryl wasn't looking. In my bed that Cheryl insisted
on sharing every night I'd tease her into accepting the gawky
"kid" who'd come to stay. Mornings I'd make coffee for the
three of us, distribute the newspapers, joke about the ragged
beard growing around my stitches. We were all so mature.

Cheryl left at 9:30 weekday mornings. Then Tara and I
drank more coffee, laughed. She'd listen while I rambled on
for as long as I thought she would stay at the table. She was a
magnet pulling at my mind. We were so much alike. By the
third day she found evening waitress work. She canvassed the
Hill and other centers of acceptable employment. I sent her
resume to anyone I thought would help.

"I got the perfect job!" she yelled as she walked into my
office on Tuesday, June 3. "The *American Media Review,* a
new monthly magazine. I'm a gofer, proofreader now, not
much money, but an assistant editorship opens up soon
and . . ."

"And who else could they give it to?" I said, proud that
she'd won, disappointed I hadn't helped.

Even Cheryl seemed excited by Tara's job, though not as
excited as she was the next day when Tara announced she'd
found an apartment four blocks away on E Street. Cheryl was
most excited about the man Tara met.

"He's nice," Tara told me. I smiled through her whole
story. "He covers arts for *Time* magazine. When I waited on
him we joked about how he wasn't going to pick me up."

We both laughed as she continued. "It's *just* nice: he
understands that. He won't take any of the time I need for
myself."

"Sounds great to me," I said. During hours of antiseptic
and oh-so-adult reviews of our lives I'd told Tara about
Maggie and the others. About Cheryl. Told her secrets you
share with such a good friend. She alluded to several men in
her past, asked me if, like her, I'd always found too much
missing and too little to share with yesterday's heartbeats. Of
course I had. We marveled at the coincidence. I smiled when
she told me about The Man From Time.

Cheryl laughed when I told her: "She's hooked some sucker! And she's leaving here! Wonderful! You don't plan on helping little Tara move out, do you?"

"Why not?"

"After all you've done for her, that too?"

"All I did was help a friend. And if we were keeping score, then what about the car?"

Even Cheryl couldn't deny that car, a gift from Tara's father the daughter couldn't drive because too much speeding cost her her driver's license for a year.

"I don't mind risking it," she said, "but . . . Well, he is up for reelection." She never used the senator's name, seldom said "father," never something as mild as "Dad." "Besides, I don't need it. The magazine is only an eight-minute walk from my apartment. And without you, coming down here would have been rough, so . . ."

"I doubt it," I argued.

"Until you get squared away, though, why don't you keep it? It will rust away if you don't. If I need it, I'll take it.

"I didn't even want it," she explained as we walked to "meet" the car, "but a graduation sports car must be good form, so that's what he did—or had his lawyer and Martin Mercer do, if I know him.

"It's a 1978," she said as she steered me to the curb, "used. Here's a key—I have one too. Is it OK?"

"OK" insulted that car. I'd assumed some cheap, dented midget convertible green MG with a patched black canvas top. What waited at the curb was a mint condition, black-leather interior, silver Porsche 911 coupe with a speedometer ending at 150 mph.

"It'll do," I said. The rear engine fired up immediately, growled as it idled in the sun. Faces turned, saw the silver dream machine, the beautiful blonde, the scruffy-bearded fool lucky enough to be with them. "It'll do."

That scruffy beard came off the day the letter from Janet's cousin arrived. My stitches were only two days gone, the scab still ugly, but the hobo look was totally inappropriate for my destination.

"He," as Tara called her father the senator, had his personal secretary make the arrangements. She'd been charming when she called: anyone her boss met twice must be worthy of respect. She and I agreed on lunch that Monday, 12:30, at the private Senate dining room in the Capitol. No, she didn't know why. Neither did Tara when I asked her. Tara looked worried, said little, asked nothing.

The telephone rang as I finished shaving.

"I asked around about you," policeman Sherman told me after I answered. "Friends on the Hill, plus a reporter I know who knows about Ned Johnson's staff."

"Biographical data to go with your photo collection?"

"You and I started out bad. We don't need to stay that way."

"Not as far as I'm concerned."

"Then I got a proposition for you, Mr. Private Detective. You're investigating a murder, no matter how you define what Armstrong wants or how far you decide to go with it. I bet you don't know much about murder or investigating one."

"You win."

"Then I want to do you a favor. You don't need to worry about why or what favor I'll ask in return."

"You sure I don't need to worry?"

"You got to trust me."

He laughed when I didn't respond, then said. "How'd you like to ride along with a couple 'public detectives' while we investigate murder? Take maybe five, six nights of your life to get a taste for it. Any more than a taste takes years plus a badge you ain't got. After you get a taste, maybe then we'll see about Janet Armstrong."

"You know my answer is yes and I . . ."

"I'll call you in a few days." He hung up.

The world stayed busy during my prolonged convalescence. As I lazed safe within my apartment, three congressmen were indicted because of ABSCAM and a sniper gunned down a civil rights leader. The Ku Klux Klan was enjoying a resurgence and 60 million Africans were officially starving to death. Air Force early warning computers malfunctioned twice, sounded false alarms of a Soviet nuclear attack, and ordered America's doomsday warriors to retaliate. Our boys double-checked, discovered the error and didn't destroy the world. Their caution was understandable: the computer had goofed like that before. Spring glowed in Washington as I walked toward the Capitol. Birds singing, sun shining, crowd smiling.

"I read about you in the papers!" The black woman stood five feet tall and was almost that big around. She'd come out of the drugstore, seen me, hollered. Her hair was grayer than I remembered.

"Mrs. Smith! How are you?!"

"I read about you in the papers. You all right?" She watched while I raised my chin: most of the scab came off when I shaved, but I was far from a pretty sight. "Lordy, Lordy, and I thought you was in a rough neighborhood when you lived next to us!"

"You been careful?" I asked her.

"I'm always careful." She shook her head. "I been living here all my life and I'm tired of being careful. Seems like it don't get no better and you can't tell me it hasn't gotten worse."

"I wouldn't try to tell you anything, Mrs. Smith. How's your husband?"

"He's doing OK. Nobody's building much. Most folks don't want to pay to do the fixin' up they need done. But so far he still gets enough work to keep him busy—and out of my hair!

"You should see little Christopher!" She smiled as she spoke her grandson's name. "Remember how he used to come up to here?" Her hand dipped to her knee. "Well now he comes up to here!" Her hand reached her hip.

"Pretty soon he'll be there!" I pointed to her chin. "You still work at the hospital?"

"Yes, though I don't know how much longer."

"About time you took it easy."

"Huh! Day I take it easy will be the day I ain't taking nothing no-way, no-how. But the hospital, they talking 'bout not having as many aides."

"Sure isn't because people stopped getting hurt and sick."

"Ain't that the truth? But we talking budget, Mr. John, not blood." She brightened again as she said, "Did I tell you? Charlene is going to have a baby come September!"

"I haven't seen you since way last summer," I said.

"Then I couldn't told you 'cause it couldn't have been since then that she's been goin' to have it!" She laughed nervously at her own good news. I remembered once her sighing about "how certain things been changing." Remembered no mention of a husband for her granddaughter who couldn't be older than 17. In 1980, 58 percent of D.C.'s children were born to women without husbands, to lives apart from the "nuclear" mom-pop-kids family American textbooks declared normal when I was in school. In 1980, society's unwed mothers weren't all poor or black or victims of ignorant circumstance: two of my "professionally" employed white women friends decided that with too few years of youth left they better be a mother now regardless of the marriage they didn't have.

"You tell Charlene congratulations," I said to Mrs. Smith as I backed away. "And all of you take care."

"You too, John!" She called out after me. "And keep your name out of the newspapers!"

I met Senator Woodson in the restaurant's small waiting room just off the Senate Chamber on the Capitol's first floor. My early arrival left me standing around pretending I wasn't bothered by stares from the maitre d' guarding the door of a room full of tables. His face lit up whenever a senator bustled in from the marble halls. Uncle Sam's hired help smiled at me only after Senator Woodson arrived, shook my hand, and said, "I hope I didn't keep you waiting, Mr. Rankin."

"I was early," I said, apologizing for him needing to apologize.

The maitre d' bowed, led us inside the dining room. There are 18 various restaurants and carryouts in the Capitol complex. To use this particular dining room you need to be with a senator or his number one aide—or a reporter able to find space at the table reserved for "members of the working press." Woodson pointed to a corner table for two at the back of the room. The maitre d' immediately decided that was precisely where he wanted to take us. I assumed Woodson wanted to be able to watch who came through the door so he could know when to smile and shake a hand, but he gestured for me to take the back seat and leave him facing the wall.

"We'll order in a few minutes, Jimmy," he told the black waiter who scurried over with menus.

"Very good sir." Jimmy smiled at me, and was gone.

Woodson slipped his glasses on to study what he'd probably read a hundred times before. "We should order first," he explained, "they get busy." I silently chose something, skipped "The Story of Senate Bean Soup" printed in the menu for my edification, and stared around a cozy room I'd visited only twice before.

There sat George McGovern from South Dakota, a senator who'd run for president and lost. Beside him was another never-made-it president, Frank Church, senator from Idaho, who'd beaten cancer, fought his way to the Senate, and had probably the brightest mind in Congress. There was Scoop Jackson, a senate power and presidential contender for so many years Washington city seemed more his home than the state of Washington he (like my host) represented. Jesse Helms—in 1980 a vastly underrated power from North Carolina—looked in, looked around, walked away. In Washington such names, faces and facts are known like American boys once knew baseball cards.

All the men in the room wore expensive suits; all the women were as beautiful as their combined circumstances of natural looks, age and wealth allowed. For women like the slim ankled, silver tipped brunette with flashing blue eyes, the combination was dazzling. The faces of tourists who were lucky enough to be there showed that they now understood how a taste of Washington can sour the rest of the world for someone. It's not the second-class joys of urban life or culture or money. It's the taste of power. Those crazed Air Force computers that almost destroyed the world were given purpose and life by the men who sat around us, by men whose eating place we shared. That taste of power is never forgotten, no matter what else crosses the palate.

I close my eyes, it's that spring noon, 1980, and I'm there again. The smell is warm and rich, thick like fine coffee waiting to be served. The walls of that select room are pumpkin-orange; the window well boxes, baseboards and wood moldings are painted ivory. The carpet is faded green, with burnt-gold eagle seals of America woven into the material. A huge chandelier dangles from the center of the peaked ivory ceiling. Tables crowd the room: round tables, rectangular tables, tables for two, for four, for six—for more if the senator has enough clout. White linen tablecloths and walnut chairs. Phones on mahogany stands. Portraits of presidents. A back-lit, stained-glass caricature of George Washington riding a white horse dominates the main wall behind me. The portrait I face off to my left shows a seated, smiling Harry Truman wearing a white linen suit. He'd been president at my birth. Thick green outer drapes and wispy white inner curtains are tied open on the window by my right arm, but the blinds are tipped so all I see beyond them is sunlight. There is silver and china, black waiters in white waistcoats, and everywhere—*everywhere*—is the taste of power.

"Thank you for taking the time to visit me," Woodson said as Jimmy retreated with our lunch orders. The senator tucked his glasses inside his three piece, navy blue pinstriped suit. "I know you're busy."

"Not that busy."

"I wish I could say the same. Between the campaign, what must be done here, and now that volcano, my minutes are lost. But I want to make time, to apologize to you for the strain of our first meeting."

"There's no need to apologize."

"Perhaps not, but I disliked it. So cautious, combative. Conflict is the element of politics I hate most."

He paused to sip water and I wondered if he wrote his own speeches.

"However, I regret we must return to topics we covered that night. For my sake. For my daughter's. Perhaps for yours. Please feel free to be absolutely candid with me. I promise you your answers will go no further. Did what happened to you have anything to do with what we talked about? With Tara or that murder or . . ."

I interrupted a U.S. senator: "No sir, absolutely not."

"Ahh." He leaned back in his chair. "You don't know how relieved I am to hear that. What worried me most was Tara's safety." He smiled. "I think perhaps that is a major concern of yours too."

103

"Of course. She's a close friend."

"So she told me. We talked after she moved into . . . your office. She speaks quite highly of you. 'A special friend,' I believe she said. Remarkable, given the short time you've known each other."

"She's a remarkable person."

"Yes, she is. I'm ashamed to say I can't claim much credit for that. We're not as close as parents and children should be."

I let that pass.

"I appreciate everything—lodging her, helping her find a job."

"She got that on her own."

"Of course, but you helped."

Our food came and we ate without speaking for several minutes. His tension hadn't eased, not even after I'd reassured him. Then suddenly his face went slack. He frowned— as if he'd resigned himself to the best of bad choices.

"I worry a great deal about Tara. You seem to be her only friend that I know. Do you know much about her?"

"Probably more than most."

"I wouldn't be surprised. Does she . . . Has she talked at all about her family? Her mother? Brother? Me?"

She hadn't, but what I told him was, "Sir, with all due respect . . ."

The U.S. senator interrupted me: "You're right, of course. Don't tell me. Her secrets are so important to her."

"Then shouldn't they stay her secrets?"

"I'm becoming increasingly less sure secrets are good for anyone. I don't know why I'm telling you all this. Maybe I'm passing a mantle I wore too poorly on to you . . ."

"I never want to be a substitute anything."

"I'm not asking that. Please, just listen. Tara says you're a good person. You decide what to do with what you learn.

"Her mother, my wife Ann . . . We were far different than we believed the day we married. She wanted something else from me even as she encouraged me into politics. I don't understand what. She and the children stayed home in our small town when I came here for my House terms. I saw them on trips back, when I could. Many children grow up that way, especially those who have congressmen for fathers—or traveling salesmen. Even after the Senate election, when we could afford to come out here, when we knew I'd be safe for six years, Ann stayed there. She loved that land—hated small-town life, but loved the land, our small farm. That fertile country is called the Palouse, rolling green hills that belong in heaven.

"She committed suicide." He blurted that out almost loud enough for everyone to hear. "That's not what the record reads. No political subterfuge: simple human kindness. Small-town kindness. No one wanted to brand suicide on our family, even though most everyone knows it's there. The record says she had a heart attack one winter morning after she started the car and before she could open the garage door. Quite possibly she staged that ambivalence, her last gesture as kindly made as she could. She didn't leave a note. Just Tara and me.

"By then my son James was dead too. Maybe Vietnam killed them both. Ann lost him, lost something else . . .

"Poor Tara lost them both. James was like I should have been. He and Tara were inseparable. When she was 14, still recovering from Jim's death, Ann sent Tara to her aunt's for a week, fed the animals, and then sat in her car, started the engine, stared around that dark, closed-tight garage while the motor ran. She drove into death."

"I'm sorry."

"What else is there to be?" He waved for the waiter to take away his unfinished food.

"After that, I tried having Tara out here. It didn't work. She made herself so strong, so independent. Kept her own control. I was so busy. We found no comfort in being close, agreed the best thing was for her to go back home. She finished high school living with her aunt. Went to college. Now she's finally living in the same town I do. But not with me.

"I have a favor to ask, John. Keep watch over her—if need be, professionally. I'll pay whatever—No, don't wave me down: I know. But, if necessary . . ." I nodded. "You say there's absolutely no connection between that violence that hit you, that murder and her. Be sure. Do what you must to protect her. Be her friend."

He smiled. "I wouldn't mind having a son again, though that's not what I mean by any of this.

"That's all," he said abruptly. He signed the tab and was guiding me out. I needed directing. His last comment numbed my mind. He shook my hand before he walked through the double doors leading to the Senate Chamber. Men inside that room gossiped about the fate of the world. I suddenly felt that too much had slipped from my grasp, that my loss had nothing and everything to do with the man shaking my hand and waiting for at least a polite farewell.

"Thanks," was all I could say.

16

The Homicide squad room still smelled of stale sweat, sour cigarette smoke and industrial cleaner. The aqua green walls, fluorescent lights turned on against the setting sun, all seemed the same that Thursday as it had been the night Eddie Hampton's murder first brought me there.

Bogart still wasn't smiling in the cops' wall poster of *Casablanca.* I wondered if I'd be able to see him in *The Big Sleep* when it played at the Kennedy Center the next week. Earlier that day, when Tara and I went to a matinee of Woody Allen's *Manhattan,* we'd agreed to see that Bogie-Bacall classic if our schedules permitted. Cheryl would go too, of course.

I wondered if Bogart ever felt as foolish as I did then, sitting at a desk all proper in coat and tie while a Homicide shift changed. Twenty detectives milled around me. Each one shot his eyes through me, then went about his business. I'd been buzzed in, OK'd as the guy waiting for Nick Sherman, seated and ignored. A white detective to my right grunted as he read yesterday's newspaper: I wondered what interested him—the House censuring a congressman for misdeeds or the volcano expert who warned President Carter of impending disaster. Detectives coming on shift strolled down the aisle between the rows of desks, found their place or headed to the back room for coffee. They'd shed their suit coats, shift the guns holstered on their belt to a more comfortable position or shove them in a desk drawer. They'd joke with each other, shoot me that look, then go about their business.

Suddenly I wanted desperately to be part of them, to carry

power strapped to my belt and purpose in a black case that flipped open with a glint of badge and ID. I'd long ago discarded myths about badges turning men into more than they are, just as I'd long ago discovered that few other legal employments besides *cop* bring with them the ability to matter *right now,* live or die, explode the situation or let it grow unchecked and the hell with what the courts or bosses said later. Senators have the power to create and control from afar; cops wield power *right now, right there,* all-the-way power and responsibility each time they leave home with that metal on their hip. And both senators and cops had more worthy purpose to their work than me. Hell, so did a street cleaner. My job isn't to make the world a better place to live. Sometimes—*maybe*—it works out that way. Mostly I'm just a guy earning my buck from other people's problems.

The black detective fussing behind me slammed his desk drawer. He stormed over to a file cabinet, jerked its drawers open then stood there, a simmering ebony giant, while the skinny white detective who'd buzzed me in quietly reasoned with him. I couldn't hear the angry detective's replies, but I heard the other man say, "I know, I know it's shit. But there's nothing you can do about it now." The black detective spat out some words. The other man shrugged. I tried to look like I'd noticed nothing when the black detective stalked toward the desk beside me. He had to squeeze between my chair and the desk behind me to get where he was going. I started to rise, let him through. His hand moved faster.

"Excuse me," he said as he pushed me down, squeezed by.

"Sure. If I'm in . . ."

"You know what time it is?"

The clock on the wall showed its perpetual 9:08. I looked where my watch should be, remembered the muggers, said, "About 8:30."

"Can you prove that?!" He didn't wait for an answer as he stormed back to his desk, slammed a few drawers, then stalked out.

"Yes sir," said the detective reading yesterday's news. He pushed up his metal glasses, lit a cigarette. "Yes sir. Another day in D.C." He looked at me, shook his head—but smiled.

"Hey big Nick!" he called out as Sherman walked past the

command desk, headed our way, a bundle of papers in one hand, briefcase in the other. "What's happenin', Bruder?" The detective affected D.C.'s street accent as if he were black and a hoodlum, not white and a cop.

"B.J. gone, Mama," Nick called back to him, smiling. Detectives throughout the room smiled too. One groaned, one called out, "Not that shit again!" A woman cop in pants and sweater (Where did she carry her gun? I wondered) shook her head, walked toward the front. A black cop muttered, "When you white boys going to learn how to talk?"

The detective sitting by me yelled to Nick: "B.J. gone?!"

"B.J. dead," called out Nick. "D-a-i-d, dead!"

"B.J. dead?! I know'd him when he was comin' up!" called out a third detective.

"That's nothing, I know'd him when he was nuthin!" proclaimed another.

A chorus of voices cut him off before he could continue: *"AND HE AIN'T MUCH NOW!"*

"Ain't we a bunch of nasty sons o' bitches?" asked Nick as he dropped two printed forms in front of me. "Sign your life away on these releases, then we'll hit the street. You meet that ugly character?" The detective who'd been reading old news worked his mouth, dropped his top plate of front false teeth so they stuck out of his lips. He sucked them back in place after he saw my startled face, reached out and shook my hand while Nick continued. "His name is Dan Barlow, but he gets called worse."

"Don't listen to him," said Barlow as he shook my hand. "Pleased to meet you, John."

"Danny's my new partner," said Sherman.

"Don't tell him what happened to Gustafson," said Barlow.

"Wasn't my fault those stairs broke under him!" insisted Sherman.

"Explain that to my widow, would you, John?"

"Glad to," I said.

"You haven't met her."

"Barlow should be riding with us tonight, but he ain't, on account of he has some 'splainin' to do when our lieutenant comes in."

"The guy's got a hair up his ass," said Barlow of the lieutenant.

"What you going to tell him 'bout what happened?" asked Sherman.

"Nothing about anything that put a hair up his ass. No question 'bout that. *No ques-chone!*" he said with a cinema Nazi accent.

"I love it," said Nick. "It would bee-hoove us to be gone before you two tangle." He turned to me. "Got them signed? Soon as I find us a cruiser that runs and a radio that works, we'll start your education. We'll catch up with this wild man later."

Danny stuck his teeth out again.

And found us an hour later by a radio call:

"Cruiser 914 to Dispatch. Could you raise the Homicide cruiser with Detective Sherman, please, and have him meet me on Tac-1?"

We'd slowly, carefully worn the edge down, become Nick and John as he drove through the city pointing out buildings where he'd been on police business, tour highlights such as "this corner sells bam" (phenmetrazine, a heroin booster), "that liquor store is a fence." Now Nick twisted a knob on the radio, lifted the mike. "Cruiser 47 to 914: What you got, Danny?"

"Looks like a natural death, middle-aged male, no signs of violence, but there's lots of blood."

"What's your location?" Barlow radioed back an address at 9th and O streets, Northwest.

As he drove, Sherman mulled the address aloud several times, smiled. "I got it: had a murder upstairs there once.

"Danny just transferred to Homicide. Good man, but he hasn't seen enough death." Nick frowned. "Bet I know what we'll find. There'll be a lot of blood, and kind of like brown coffee grounds everywhere."

"You know what killed him?"

"If I'm right about the address, that's a drunk house. The guy probably drank so much he burned his guts out. Everything suddenly gives way and you bleed to death out your ass. The coffee-ground stuff is discharge. Want to bet?"

"Not against you."

Half a dozen citizens milled around the three-story, wood frame shack tucked between two large brick buildings. Three scout cars, an unmarked cruiser, and an ambulance with spinning red lights drew a far smaller crowd than I expected. A man walked between the peeling white shack and the police cars without looking either direction. Every face I saw except those belonging to a badge was black.

"Glad you got here, Nick," said Danny, walking out the sagging front door. "The blood trail bothers me. It starts here . . ."

With that they walked past two uniformed officers, through the front door, and down a dimly lit hallway. A uniformed black officer nodded to me just as he had to Nick: he didn't know any better. I walked inside as if I too belonged.

No one should have belonged there. The hall ceiling drooped three inches above my head. A cockroach raced upside down across a patch of ceiling light, disappeared in one of a thousand chipped-paint cracks. I hunched down, followed the flashlight beam Danny slowly swung from side to side over the trail of dried rusty splotches on the cracked linoleum floor.

"Yup," said Nick, "bet that's what it is. That room back here by the door is the bathroom. He felt it coming, thought he had to shit, found out otherwise and worked his way back to his room. Let's take a look." He pointed to one of two open doorways at the end of the hall.

"Landlord finally broke down the door when nobody answered," explained Danny. "The people in there," he jerked his thumb to an open room across the hall from the splintered door, "they were all drinking together last night. They couldn't get him to answer their knocks today." His voice dropped. "I'm betting our guy had the bottle with him and they were concerned for its health, you un'erstand."

"You talk to the landlord yet?"

"Got him upstairs in his room."

"Locked him up once." Nick smiled. "Ain't he something?"

"A truly fine citizen. *No ques-chone.* He wants to know how soon he can rent the room. Keep the real owner happy, you un'erstand."

"Look here," Nick called to me. He pointed Danny's flashlight to blotches on the linoleum. "What did I tell you? Coffee grounds." He explained to Danny what I'd already heard. I looked back down the hall, saw a uniform coming our way, saw a gold bar glint on the white shirt, nodded and stood aside.

"Hello, Lieutenant," called Sherman. "I didn't know you had this District now."

I glanced toward Danny, who frowned back—then smiled, shook his head: this wasn't the lieutenant with the hair up his ass.

"Two months, Nick," said the senior official. "Homicide or natural?"

"Without seeing the body, I'm betting natural. As natural as you can call a liver blowup."

"Don't talk about livers," said the lieutenant. He touched his side. "Makes me nervous. You guys need anything?"

"I think we got it all, thank you, sir."

"Take care of yourselves." The brass nodded to me and we exchanged good nights. I added "sir" to mine.

At the front door the building smelled of human excrement, urine, rotting food, damp mildew from walls that pipes burst in once too often. A sweet, ham-and-cabbage smell filled this end of the hall.

The thing on the bed had arms and legs curled up and in, like a fat gopher begging in a fetal position. The thing wore a tank-top T-shirt, Jockey shorts, pants pulled down around its ankles, one sock. The thing had been a black male in his early 50s sometime the day before, a man perhaps of slack face, droopy expression. The closest the thing had to an expression now was a closed-eyed, skintight squint, as if something tasted sour. The thing lay on its back in a sparse room the size of a walk-in closet, atop a bed with one sheet, no pillow and a patched quilt, a bed stained with what wasn't rust and littered with what weren't coffee grounds. The thing was dead.

"Yup, that's what I figured," said Nick. He checked the window lock, the unbroken panes. I swallowed when he walked to the corpse, pushed it over on its side.

"No signs of violence or penetration," he said two minutes later, pulling back down the thing's shirt. "I'd hold off writing

112

it up, check the body at the morgue, but it looks like an alky death to me."

"I figured that's what it was," said Danny, "but I couldn't believe all that blood."

"You'd be surprised," said Nick.

I stepped back to let the two cops talk, almost stumbled into the room across the hall. As I regained my balance, I looked inside.

Every possible inch was filled—a small shelf with a few foodstuffs hung from one wall; boxes of clothes and pots and pans were piled chest high. The bed ran along the wall opposite the door. A bureau filled the space to the window's left, and on it perched a color TV. A movie based on an Agatha Christie novel flickered inside that screen, but the sound was off. Two living persons looked from that movie of elegant murder to me, looked and waited with nothing but acceptance on their faces. The scrawny man sitting in a chair at the foot of the bed wore an outfit similar to the corpse's: this living man could have been any age between 40 and 80. His cigarette was about to burn his fingers. Sunken lips implied no teeth. The woman sagged plump inside her multicolored sheath dress the Salvation Army would reject. She looked 60, should have looked 20 years younger. Her jaw was slack, her mouth open, but I knew she wouldn't speak. I knew that if I were really a policeman and my partners didn't object, I could do anything I wanted to those two living human beings and they wouldn't complain or fight back; maybe they wouldn't care. These neighbors had forfeited their lives. They were sadder than death across the hall.

"You ready to go?" asked Nick.

I led the way out.

A dozen spectators watched us leave and tried not to show their faces. This was the ghetto; we were the man; that was that. The white lieutenant stood by his marked cruiser, laughing with a black boy and girl, both about seven. Maybe he had children their age at home. Maybe his chatting with these kids would keep "that" from being "that" for a few more months in their lives. Probably not.

Neither of us said much as we drove to a District station house. Nick spent 14 minutes washing his hands in a spotless bathroom. "That's the part of the job I hate most," he said. We'd both relaxed by the time our cruiser rolled back on the streets.

Then somehow we were on Church Street, with the numbers drifting by my window adding up to an address I knew.

"This is where it happened," Nick said, turning the cruiser down a narrow cobblestone alley between rows of three-story brick dwellings. The alley emptied into a long, partially paved parking lot. Nick turned the cruiser around; he rode the brake, making the cruiser crawl back to the street as he talked, pointed.

"That third-story apartment was where Janet and her pimp Mr. Magic Murphy lived. The fight started in there. She ran to that back porch, down those wooden stairs, him chasing her. Somehow the window of the first-floor apartment's kitchen got broken. Magic grabbed a long, jagged chunk of that glass."

The cruiser cleared the building's edge; a tan stucco wall slid by my eyes as Nick talked.

"From the bloodstains, he caught her about here, stabbed her a bunch of times, hacked her face. She fell and he took off—jumped in his pimpmobile, tore out of the alley. Drove right past her. A witness living across the courtyard heard screaming. He saw brake lights of a big car with no lights on as it swerved out of the alley. Just as that big car turned, a second car drove past the alley and caught the dark car in its headlights. Our witness was sure that the fleeing car was a black Caddy, that a man was driving it, that he was alone. We never found anybody who'd driven by. Longshot to look, but we did.

"Janet wasn't dead yet, but the witness couldn't see where she lay in the alley from his apartment: bad angle. She crawled along here, crawled to her right, almost like she was trying to crawl back inside the apartment building." He pointed to a spot on the sidewalk beside a telephone pole. "That's where she collapsed.

"And that's where Magic came back 20 minutes later and picked her up. Gutsiest—no, wrong word, he's got no guts. *Cockiest* and smartest move he made. Magic knew he'd be

Suspect Número Uno. He had her blood on him. And he probably wanted to be sure. Hell, maybe he thought he'd hurt her bad enough to scare her but not bad enough to kill her. Magic isn't always the brightest of cocksuckers. She was damn near dead when he got back, so he decides to play the hero, bundles her in his Caddy—which also legally accounts for the blood all over him and it—and rushes her to George Washington hospital."

"Same place I went."

"Yeah, but you left by the front door."

The radio crackled: "Any Homicide cruiser, please respond."

"Shit," said Nick, picking up the microphone. "Cruiser 47."

"Please respond to scout car 33 on a closed case, 717 11th Street, Northwest, apartment 8."

"I copy," he told the dispatcher; to me said, "We just came from up around there."

"What's a closed case?"

"That means they already got the guy who did it." He leered: "Excuse me, who allegedly did it."

The neighborhood was better than the alky's street, but barely. The uniformed officer at the door nodded us inside. In the second-floor hallway we met two more uniformed officers leading a squat, balding black male away from an open door. The man's hands were handcuffed behind his back.

"Is this the suspect?" Nick asked. One of the cops nodded. "Has he been fully advised of his rights?" Again a nod. "Is that true, sir? Have you been advised of your rights?" Nick asked the man.

"They read me a card 'bout all that stuff they talk 'bout on TV," he said. A gruff voice with little beyond its gruffness. This was a short man with a potbelly and a bald head. He looked as dangerous as a fire hydrant.

Nick instructed the two uniformed officers to take the man to the Homicide office, hold him without questioning until Nick arrived.

"Hey Mr. Detective?!" the suspect asked Nick.

"Yes sir?"

115

"My stuff, my medicine: they won't let me take it with me."

"It's on the kitchen table next to where the victim fell when he . . . when she was shot," said one of the uniforms.

"Sir," Nick said to the suspect, "your medicine is part of a crime scene. It can't be moved until we've finished with that area. Is it for a heart condition?"

"No, I got a cold."

"I'll bring it to the station when we talk." The two patrolmen led their charge down the hall.

"And my glasses!" called the man who'd allegedly just seen well enough to kill another human being. "Bring my glasses too! They're on the table. Don't forget my glasses."

"Are you always this busy?" I asked as we walked down the hall.

"Naw, lots of times you citizens get lucky. We work *investigating* or sit in court for days in a row or handle nothing but natural death reports from hospitals."

The body on the floor was still warm, said Nick: a middle-aged woman. The pool of blood was beginning to gel. If left, what didn't soak into the well-scrubbed hardwood floor would crust, flake off. The kitchen table had been pushed aside, covered with groceries and overturned canisters. I saw a pill bottle in the clutter, a pair of eyeglasses. And a shiny, pearl-handled, palm-sized automatic pistol.

"Phew!" said Nick, pointing to a jagged Listerine bottle in a blood-stained paper bag next to the corpse. That antiseptic odor filled the room. "It appears we've had a hygienic domestic disturbance."

We laughed, and that set the tone. The lab men came, took photos, helped track the angle of the five bullets that had been fired, two of which entered the woman (one upper chest wound, probably minor; one head wound, hidden by her thick, kinky hair), three of which punched pencil-thick holes in the wall. Nick summed it up:

"She came home from shopping. Maybe she was touchy, maybe he was grumpy from his cold, maybe they always fought. This time he gets real mad as they sit at the table, jumps up, blasts five times with his pretty little piece, blows her ass away. She crashed to the floor. Sometime during the commotion, the table gets pushed around. When she's lying there oozing he picks up the spent shell casings, dumps them into the garbage can all nice and neat, calls the police, sits down until they come. Nice and neat."

We spent 40 minutes photographing, measuring, sketching, all to be sure everything truly was nice and neat. Then Nick crossed the street to a house where a neighbor sat with the woman's teenage daughter who'd been waiting tables when the call came about how the man her mama lived with had done her wrong.

"B.J. gone," muttered Nick humorlessly as he headed across the street. "I was wrong about handling corpses," he told me as I walked with him part way. "This is the part I hate most." Then he went inside that concerned neighbor's house to officially notify the next of kin that her mother had been murdered.

I sat around the squad room while Nick finished his shift by interviewing the murderer, wrapping up enough reports so he could leave for the day. I saw my second dawn from the Homicide squad room.

"Got a ride home?" he asked as we walked down the front steps. When I nodded to the Porsche, he said, "Looks like I'm the wrong kind of detective."

"Not as far as I'm concerned."

"You did OK tonight, son," said this man who was nowhere near old enough to be my father. "You are going to finish out this tour of night duty with me, aren't you?"

I nodded. "Think I'll know enough by then?"

"Think you'll ever know enough?" He shrugged. "Depends on what happens, on how well you learn." He glanced toward Union Station: half a dozen early risers walked to work.

"Most people get murdered over nothing," said Nick. "Like that woman, killed over nothing. Or whatever is next to it. Motive isn't why most people get killed. It's the means, the ability the murderer has to do it. Just to do it. That's why people get killed. Because somebody can kill them. Murders usually give you a reason. Sometimes it's got substance, most times it's bullshit. A motive doesn't cause a murder, it just sets the stage. The murderer plays his part because he can. For a *de-tective,* there's nothing to solve and nothing he can stop. I get paid to explain what happened, you're getting paid to say why. I just told you why.

"You know what happened to Janet Armstrong? She got murdered. She came to the startling conclusion that going back to Harvard was better than whoring for Mr. Magic Murphy. Her conclusion crimped his ego, to say nothing of what it would have done to his pocketbook. She figured he wouldn't be too happy with her choice, so she faked a phone call from a john, met a weirdo who hangs around with whores, tried to fly. You know how she ended up dead? Magic was sly. He'd sensed she was getting restless. He figured to win her back, *no ques-chone!* Don't know what else he tried, but the week before Janet died he gave her two presents: a plastic potted plant and a beagle puppy.

"The faked call worked. She figured Magic would go off like he usually did. And instead of having that weirdo drive her straight to the airport, she had him bring her back here to get that goddamned pup. But Magic was there. When she walked through that door, there was no fooling him. He wouldn't take such shit off his whore. He could kill her. He could, so he did. So she died."

"Have you found anybody besides her pimp and her family who cares about what happened to her?"

"Have you?" he asked.

"There are three guys who wear masks I'd like to ask."

"Me too."

"But I don't buy the link. Yeah, maybe like you said, somebody at the courthouse cared about you pulling her file. A sharp black dude and a Jewish lawyer type are who you remembered—once you got around to remembering . . ."

"I've been busy," I said.

". . . Maybe somebody else heard her dad and you hooked up. I doubt it. Nobody gives a shit. She's dead, Magic's locked up . . . Nobody in the street remembers her name. I'm betting you bought your trouble elsewhere."

"Maybe," I said, "but I'm going to keep poking around."

"Besides, you got a job."

"Yeah." I shook my head. "I never figured to keep it long. Figured I'd do enough to ease the old man's conscience, earn my pay or do a freebie. Chasing the cosmic why isn't my line."

"You're stuck on it now."

I shrugged. "Gives me a place to start what else I need to do."

"That's how I got hooked."

Sherman studied me, came to a decision. He put his briefcase on the hood of his car, opened it, and handed me a heavy cardboardlike box.

"You're turning out better than I figured," he said, grinned that chip-toothed grin and nodded toward the file in my hands. "That's the Janet Armstrong case jacket. You might want to browse through it before you give it back to me."

My smile told him my gratitude.

He slid behind the wheel of his Chevy, rolled down the window.

"You told me you had more than 200 homicides under your belt," I said. "You don't even know how many hundreds of natural deaths you've covered. But Janet Armstrong got to you. You *want* me in on it, regardless of anything else. I don't know what or why, but you want something from her—and me."

"We'll puzzle on what I want another time." His Chevy coughed, chugged to life. "I'll see you tonight."

The Porsche took me back to the Hill, another "day" ending for me while most everyone else began theirs. I ate another breakfast that should have been dinner, climbed my apartment stairs while other people walked down theirs. I wanted to call Tara, talk with her about all I'd seen and done because—obviously—because she was a friend who would understand. We were that much alike, weren't we? But she'd be in the shower, maybe running. I called Cheryl as promised, let her know no bad guy gunned me down. She promised to cook me dinner—which would be my breakfast—that night before I hit the streets again. She mumbled words of endearment, heard mumbles back. Janet Armstrong's case jacket *thunked* when I dropped it in the bottom drawer of my metal file cabinet. Her horrors could wait until tomorrow. I turned off the desk light I'd left burning through the night.

Then opened the desk drawer. The .357 Magnum revolver Paul gave me waited there, camouflaged under empty manila files. The .25 automatic used to kill that woman had a polished chrome surface. My revolver was blue black, clean and glossy in the sunlight. My pistol, my drawer, my office. Ability spawns its own end, said Nick. I shut the drawer.

17

Steam fled the coffee cup on my desk, vanished before my eyes. I felt as if I could ride that rising vapor. My life seemed clean and clearly drawn.

The odds said I'd only been mugged, but just in case, I was honing down the possibilities.

That morning I'd go to the courthouse. "Excuse me," I'd say to the file clerk: "A couple weeks ago when I was here I haphazardly stuffed some papers in my briefcase. Now I've found them, and they aren't mine. I remember two guys standing beside me . . ." and then I'd describe the black dude in the white suit and the wire-rimmed glasses and chrome-domed Jewish attorney. I'd ask, "Do you know who they might be? I have something that might belong to them." The clerk was probably innocent and just might know something.

He didn't.

That afternoon, before I met Nick Sherman for another homicide lesson, I would call the woman president of a *concerned parents* group whose beloved children deserted the family fold for one of a hundred cults. The woman's daughter gave her soul to the Rev. Sun Myung Moon, a Korean pretender to Jesus Christ, who in 1974 rallied his masses to support Watergate-wounded, about-to-resign President Richard Nixon. Moon expanded his political efforts, sent lobbyists to Congress and organized right wing political fronts. In 1982, Moon's church started a daily newspaper in Washington to counter the *Washington Post*. The parents' group zealously monitored Moonie activities, as well as the antics of every other cult they discovered. Like Janet Armstrong's father, those parents had hearts full of questions about why and what to do. I'd worked with the parents' group on a cults-in-politics story for Ned Johnson. Now I wanted to know if its president had heard of any activity by Jim Jones disciples in Washington.

She hadn't.

Despite my puzzles, I felt back in control.

Beyond my work, I had Cheryl. And even if some of our dazzle had dimmed, and even if she weren't as in step with my life as I'd thought, and even if . . . Well, even if, she was still Cheryl and she cared about me. Very much.

I remembered laughing with Tara as we described the first Thin Man movie for Cheryl—who *said* she loved movies yet seemed not to have seen many. Tara and I insisted Cheryl see that Hammett classic when it played D.C. next month. Cheryl agreed, tried hard to share our enthusiasm, her eyes flicking from Tara to me and back.

Maybe Tara will go with us, I thought. She was such a good friend, such a special friend. Maybe after I visited the courthouse I could swing by Tara's office, grab lunch with her.

Right then I had work to do. Nick Sherman would expect me to have read the homicide file, Janet's father expected me to find answers in its prose. I expected titillation ending in frustration: I still hadn't figured a graceful way out of her business. Indeed, she was proving to be a profitable necessity for me. The lessons Nick taught me in the street, the contacts with other policemen I made through him, all would be invaluable for future use. Plus my mugging left me no choice but to be sure that kindly fool's errand I accepted from her father hadn't cost me blood. But each step I took into her life yielded only more curiosities that I doubted I could ever resolve. Nothing seemed certain about Janet Armstrong. Except that she was dead.

D.C. homicide case jackets are rust colored accordion-style folders that expand to hold regular manila files, detectives' notebooks, lab reports, miscellaneous evidence, whatever the investigating officer chooses to stick inside the case jacket and store in the squad room file cabinets. Eventually all case jackets, crimes solved and unsolved, find their way to a musty warehouse in suburban Maryland.

Somehow I knew Nick Sherman hadn't given me everything in the Janet Armstrong file. He'd hold back anything truly secret, truly sensitive. There were half a dozen manila folders in the accordion binder. The first thing I noticed was the absence of photographs: none of the death scene, none of the victim.

As I flipped through another file folder I found half a dozen pages with single columns of names. I turned back to the cover page, read: COMPILATION OF SIX TRICK NOTEBOOKS KEPT BY VICTIM.

Six pages. Only one name per single spaced typewritten line, but Jesus: *six pages!* Most of them were simply first names with no notation. On some I noticed a comment, like "one time," "chrg. more next time" or "friend of Jenny's." Before I went any further, I had to know. Without noting the names I counted their number: 404. I counted twice, to be sure. Four hundred and four entries, presumably 404 customers, presumably only a total of those she'd bothered to write down. Harvard encourages note taking. I turned back to the first page, began to read the list of men.

The floor fell away.

Page 3, halfway down:

"Martin M."

According to the typist, in Janet's trick book there'd been a mark beside this name.

My hand shook. I walked away from the desk trembling, came back, still found that name on that page in that file.

There was no escape. My mind raced with infinite *could be's*. This could be nothing. Janet's notation could refer to a million Martin M.'s besides Martin Mercer, Administrative Aide to Senator Robert Woodson, right hand to the father of, man whose path had already once crossed mine. But unless I knew for sure, any innocent possibility meant nothing.

Suppose Martin Mercer was the Martin M. in Janet's trick book. He could have been just another john for her. He could have meant nothing to her and she the same to him. Him being there could mean no more than that, a seamy circumstance, a plausible though unflattering aspect of an unpleasant man. What was it Janet told her parents, her aunt? She had "important" customers. Maybe Martin M. was Martin Mercer, and he was just another one of those.

And yet.

And yet.

Cause and effect, circumstance and coincidence, such benign theories when I talked about them with Janet's father, with Tara. Where did they start, how did they line up? Were Janet and Mercer linked, did that connection have anything to do with me? With my being attacked? I flipped through the trick list, found no other known names, not Woodson's, not Eddie Hampton's.

Poor Tara. She had no idea of her jeopardy. If Mercer were smeared, her father showed the stain. She'd had enough pain, she knew enough tragedy. I *had* to protect her, and I dared tell her nothing: she deserved neither wound nor worry.

Then there was me. I hadn't thought my attackers were linked to Janet Armstrong, but I hadn't known Janet Armstrong might be linked to Martin Mercer. Why he would wish to harm me because of that I couldn't say, but such a possibility was now both a question and an answer. I knew the truth of neither, and needed the truth of both. I dared not confront him, for I knew too little: to warn your enemy that he's been discovered is to give him yet another weapon. I dared not ask Nick Sherman for help, for if I loosed him on my problems I couldn't control the effects of his search.

My coffee was cold, bitter, a dark lake. I couldn't see the bottom of the cup.

18

"This isn't really my job," explained the man behind the desk, then he answered his phone.

"Hello? . . . No, you surprised me . . . I'm glad you're home from school early too . . . Daddy's busy right now." He loosened his tie, ran his fingers through his thinning hair. Five pens waited in the pocket of his blue shirt and his suit jacket lay crumpled atop a file cabinet next to a picture of him shaking hands with the pope. "She'll be home soon . . . I know . . . Did teacher say when? . . . I know I promised . . . Remember what you promised? . . . No . . . That's right . . . I got to go now . . . I'll see you later."

He hung up, spoke more to the phone than to me. "When I came home from school my mother was there. Just like in the commercials. Cookies and milk, the whole bit. My wife would work even if we didn't need her to. We're ambitious. You know what our ambition costs? Our child comes home to an empty house. Bad enough in a world with fires and sex fiends, but you know what worries me most? My kid comes home to a TV set.

"I'm sorry," he said to me. "Where was I?"

"You were telling me how this isn't really your job," I said.

"Right." He tipped back his swivel chair. His office was one of two dozen glass boxes surrounding a "word processing center" of secretaries' desks. Individual domains like his had transparent walls, doorways without doors. The black lettered number on their front glass wall gave the fishbowls their identity. *Functional architecture.* "Like I said, Jonestown really isn't my job."

125

"You're listed as the State Department rep in all the studies, and when I called the Department operators . . ."

"They said I was the man, I know, but it's not really my job.

"I'm a senior action planner and response coordinator for the Crisis Coordination Cooperative Response Team— CCCRT in government gobbledygook. I'm a doomsayer. I study the bomb."

"I understand."

"You do, don't you?" He smiled, leaned forward. "Our parents would have asked, 'What bomb?' We're the first generation that doesn't need to ask. Try to explain that to your father if he's still alive.

"Know how I got to be one of the bomb boys? Exeter Academy, Yale, Georgetown Institute for Foreign Policy Studies, foreign service. I kept graduating into new curricula. My first 'job' was a fellowship, then I was posted in Africa where I was the only cultural affairs officer who really wasn't with the CIA. Those guys had more 'discretionary funds' than they could piss away. But they had to spend it, or next budget time they couldn't claim they still needed it. And if they didn't need money, who needed them? You like movies?"

"I love them," I said, wondering what difference that made.

"What American doesn't? That's how *we* were raised. Not that damned isolating-and-dominating idiot box. *Movies!*

"So the spooks have money and we all love movies and it's boring as hell in this jerkwater African stinkpot. I figured, what the hell, organized a film festival, paid for it with covert-action discretionary funds.

"Best damn thing to hit the embassy in years! We flew in 30 movies. Thirty! One of them was *Dr. Strangelove*—you know: Peter Sellers plays three parts and there's a crazy American general who starts nuclear war to save our purity of essence. I loved it, the spooks loved it, other embassies we invited loved it, 'representatives of the indigenous population' loved it—everybody loved it. Except our ambassador. Who thought my choice insulted the infallible decision-making process of the U.S. of A. Christ, he was a sausage king from Cleveland who bought himself an ambassadorship!

How could he allow anything to mock the wisdom of the powers that be?!

"Sausage King is pissed, so he 'promotes' me into limbo with a detailed assignment to NATO's interagency nuclear planning conclave: *'Since nuclear warfare interests you so much, you should have a hand in it.'* His final words to me.

"But the joke was on him because I loved it! Juggling kilokills, wearing color-coded security badges, hobnobbing with generals who used my first name . . . ! God, to think of the decade I sincerely, solemnly wasted in bullshit!

"I'd go to breakfast strategy assessments at State, lunch at the Pentagon, play zap the Red Chinese all afternoon with a million-dollar computer game. Masturbate my mind into reports and memos and position papers and refutations and analyses and talking points and letters for the secretary of state to sign. I got so popular I started zipping in and out of the White House. The fucking *White House!*

"When I started, mankind's hope lay in the strategy called Mutual Assured Destruction—MAD. Nobody would start the war because everybody would lose it. Well, that's 'evolved.' As the bombs got bigger, so did the delusions. Now we have Limited Nuclear Options—LNOs. We're sinking toward a belief that something called Nuclear Utilization Target Selection—NUTS—could work, allow us to use the bombs *just a little, just enough*—but not too much. Ergo if NUTS could work, then it does; if it does work, then it cries out to be tried. We can do it, so we must. Which means that some day we will. *BLAM-O!* Armageddon. We'll get to pay the ultimate price for learning exactly how brilliant we are.

"One day it dawned on me: I was a living absurdity and other people were using me as their measure of judgment! I said, 'Where are all the adults?' I was the *forever young* academic artful dodger, but where were all the wise, competent big people who made reasoned, sensible decisions? You know where? *Nowhere*, that's where! I was the adult, the big person. That scared me shitless."

"What did you do?"

"Became a leper as soon as I opened my mouth about how nuts all this was. Not a goddamned person disagreed with me, *not one*, from generals to White House aides to my fellow 'diplomats.' But their faces would glaze over, maybe they'd say, 'So what?' or pat me on the back, flash me that *oh-so-wise* smile I used to wear. They wondered how I became so naive. One of them mumbled something about 'burnout,' which implies failure. Failure—hell, I finally succeeded in realizing what I was doing!

"My 'negative attitude' didn't win me any contests. I couldn't find squash partners after three months. When Jim Jones orchestrated his White Night in Paradise and State needed someone for the cleanup committee . . ."

"You got nominated."

"Dead on ground zero. Jonestown kept me away from their 'important' stuff, like impending global suicide. Now, what do you want?"

I got as far as mentioning a lawyer representing next of kin before he interrupted me: "You're too late."

"Late for what?"

"Don't you know about the receivership?" I shook my head. "The courts created a Receivership for the Peoples Temple, appointed a California attorney to act as receiver. By now there have been almost 700 claims filed, about $2 billion. There was a deadline for filing—last year, I think. Your clients are probably shit out of luck.

"Hey, cheer up!" said the man banished to bureaucratic limbo as I left minutes later. "Jim Jones may be dead in Guyana, but Dr. Strangelove is alive and well in Washington, D.C.!"

America's diplomatic headquarters rises from a drained swamp called Foggy Bottom. "State" is a concrete maze of interconnected tan blockhouses about halfway between the White House and Arlington. I made my calls from an old fashioned wooden booth in the lobby of the 21st Street entrance. The booth is tucked in a corner outside the chest-high, brass-bar–topped wooden partition borders of the "secured" foyer. Very Important Persons (or so their walk claimed) bustled through the border's metal-detecting gates, marched down the halls to foreign affairs while I dialed. Those VIPs passed beneath a vast marble portal running across the top of the main hallway. A WPA-like mural filled that overhead expanse: human figures blended with war machines in a surreal style. The border partitions, the security desk, the newsstand inside the secured hallway, my phone booth, all were made from the mahogany that dominated this atmosphere, a rich brown fog I could almost taste and smell. Where I was seemed like a blend of an airport, a fine old hotel and a museum.

"You're not going to like this," I told Art Dillon when he answered my call.

"Of course not," he replied.

"All I talk to these days are fatalists."

"We're getting smarter."

"What happened to my crusader in shining armor?"

"He had a bad night." Art surpassed rueful laugh, listened to my report. "Send me the receiver's address with your bill. I'll nail it down."

"I didn't do enough to warrant a bill."

"Come on, Rankin, even crusaders need to eat."

"How about a trade instead of cash?"

"What do you suggest?"

"A grand jury indicted one Herbert Jerome Murphy for murder."

"What the hell you doing handling criminal cases?"

"Murphy is a pimp who killed a girl who worked for him . . ."

"What the hell you doing working for a scumbag pimp?"

"So much for everybody deserving an equal chance under the law. Besides, Murphy isn't the client."

"There are only two sides in a criminal case. You aren't working for the accused and you sure aren't working for the state."

"Maybe I'm being creative, like a lawyer who tries to sue a dead messiah."

"Let's hope you have better luck. What do you want?"

"Whatever you can get me on the grand jury proceedings."

"That's dangerous ground. Got a good lawyer?"

"You're your own answer."

"In that case, I'll do what I can. No trade-offs, though."

"One more thing: Who knows you hired me for this Jonestown affair?"

"Just our clients, my staff. Why?"

"Remember my three friends?"

"What are you telling me, John?"

"I'm just asking."

"And you think . . ."

"People take religion and money seriously, Art."

"And people die because of that every day, but Jones already had his White Night. Sure, there was some wild talk right afterward, but nothing ever came of it. It's a paranoid world, John, but even I'm not that spooked. Besides, with what you've found, we're out of it. No reason for you to care. Or worry."

"I'll keep my eyes open just the same. You had any trouble?"

"Nothing like you mean."

"How bad was your night?"

"Worse. One of those times that happens to every man, right? 'Cept maybe you. I hear you're running a harem on Capitol Hill."

"Who have you been talking to?"

"Cheryl wasn't enough, you had to set up a sideshow with that resume kid. I hear she has legs all the way up to her asshole."

"Tara is a friend of mine, Art."

"Touchy, aren't we?"

"Just trying to keep things in perspective. And accurate."

"Sure. I'll be in touch."

Keeping things in perspective. And accurate. About Tara. That had become an increasingly demanding chore. I kept telling people how we were such good friends. How remarkable she was. How much we had in common. But how we were just good friends. I even needed to explain it (again) to Mad Dog that morning as we walked through downtown's Lafayette Park wondering where yesterday's sun had gone.

"Sure she's special," I said and he didn't bat an eye, "but she's only 22. But so damn smart! Good thing she's not two years older or she'd probably eat me up."

"And then there's Cheryl," he said.

"Yeah, and even if that isn't going so great . . ."

"Since when?"

"Well . . . since the start, probably."

"Didn't seem that way to me."

"Even you make mistakes. It's just lucky for me Tara is still a kid or I might end up hooked like you. How is Katie?"

"Incredible!" I smiled, said nothing. "I just . . . I might want to talk to you about . . . I might . . . She's wonderful!"

"Then how could you have snagged her?"

"I tricked her!" He snickered. "Not really, but sort of. I got in close, like working a source. And after a while, she figured what the hell. One thing led to another." He shuffled nervously.

"And so you won."

"Well . . . I think so."

"You think so? Is that what you wanted to talk about?"

"No, not . . . not now. I may need your help on AB-SCAM."

"I've been trying, Dog. Nobody I know has access to the tapes or videocassettes, transcripts or . . ."

"Don't worry about that," he said. "I probably got them."

I blinked. Blinked again. He grinned like a boy hitting his first home run.

"I'll need a place to store them, listen to them. If they use a search warrant on my place or Ned's, they'll come up empty. I don't want to lose the tapes until I'm through with them. They don't have enough probable cause on you to get a warrant. Besides, I don't have a stereo in my place." His "place" was a rubbish-filled hole, mattress on the floor and a bathroom that shamed a gas station. "I can't use Katie's because of her house partners."

"Sure!" I said. "We can work it out. We have before."

"Those were good days, John."

"Great days."

"It's . . . it's not the same now."

"What's this—*sentiment?!* Katie must be a miracle worker."

"Yeah," he said. "Yeah."

Tara wrought a miracle that day. We met for lunch at one of the restaurants on the Senate side of the Hill not far from her magazine's office. The restaurant charged twice what the

Tune Inn did for a hamburger that was only as good, but this establishment was *swank*. Rendezvous with Tara weren't unusual. We'd phone each other at least daily, eat lunch together when we could. A couple of times she'd called me when her work was slack and we'd met for coffee. Suits with ties and tailored skirts swirled around us. My shirt collar was open and my jeans faded; Tara wore black avant-garde pants and a purple sweater that highlighted her strawberry blond hair. She was gorgeous, something out of a slick magazine's fashion ad. I tried not to stare at her, noticed men at other tables didn't share my discretion, smiled because they wouldn't be eating with her.

"She went back after a puppy!" Tara shook her head. "I remember when you showed me the newspaper clippings thinking that she was from Oregon, I was from the state next door, we both went back East to school. Both the same age. I spent a lot of time in Boston when I dated that guy Peter from Harvard. I might have walked by her, gone to the same party. She could have been me."

"No she couldn't." I was from the West too, had more in common with Tara than Janet did, more with Tara than anyone did.

My assertion won her smile. "Do you know how fascinating this is?! How much I envy you?"

My nod said yes. She frequently asked if I knew what this or that meant to her; I always did. I always said yes. I knew Tara better than anyone. I knew so much in 1980.

"I can't take blood," she said. "I fainted in lab when a friend of mine cut himself. But your cop stories . . ."

"You want me to keep you up on the case?" How could she say no?

"Of course!" She looked like I was crazy to ask.

"You know what Sherman is arranging? He knows the best cops in the Prostitution and Perversion squad. He's setting up ride-alongs with them for me. And I may get to meet one of that pimp's other women."

"You weren't going to do much on this."

I couldn't tell her the whole truth; I couldn't lie.

"I've got no choice. I agreed to help her father. Besides,

maybe I can find some answers to what's going on in my safe little life by walking down Janet Armstrong's street. Maybe I was only mugged, but maybe . . ." I shrugged.

"You'll probably never know," she said.

"You're right. But I have to try. Besides, the more I chase her ghost, the closer she pulls me, the more she and I seem . . ." I smiled. "I guess she's caught me. Guess I've been trapdoored."

"I'm not sure I understand."

"You're standing *oh-so-cool* on top of it all, then the next thing you know somebody or something trips the trapdoor, and you drop down the hole."

"I know that feeling," she said, shuddered. "I hate it."

"It's not always bad," I said. "Nowhere near as bad as I always thought."

She shrugged, smiled. "So, *The Big Sleep* tonight?"

"We promised, didn't we?"

"Yes, but . . . I figured if you didn't ride with Homicide it would be your first night off and Cheryl would want . . ."

"Don't worry about Cheryl. She's coming with us."

"OK. I . . . ah . . . Remember that guy I met who works for Senator Barnes?"

"Yes." I remembered his shadow.

"Would you mind if he came along? I wasn't sure if you'd be able to make it, figured you wouldn't mind if you could . . ."

"No problem," I said evenly. "No problem."

"He's not a bad guy."

"How could he be? But what does The Man From Time think?"

"I'm a free person," she insisted.

"Aren't we all?" We laughed again. "Maybe it's better if he comes along. Makes things easier."

"I had a feeling Cheryl wouldn't be too happy about tonight."

"I doubt we need to worry about Cheryl much longer."

"How do . . . How do you feel about that?"

"It's always sad." I shrugged, put it simply: "Relieved."

She looked down at the chewed quarter moon of a hamburger bun on her plate, looked into the crowd past my right shoulder. "Do you have any idea of what . . . what you'll do next? Any . . . adventures lined up?"

"Not really," I said evenly. Neither of us challenged my answer.

"I knew it!" Tara proclaimed. "I like Cheryl. She's nice and she's smart and kind, she helped when I was looking for a job and . . . And I'm sorry for her. Not only does she get hurt, she loses you."

The noisy crowd faded away. Tara curled her slim hands before her face as if she held a large bowl. "Cheryl was just so wrong for who you are, who I see and know you are!" Her hands swayed with her words and I knew—*I just knew!*—that by some miracle Tara cradled my whole life in her wise and carrying hands. "There's so much else!"

Such was Tara's magic and the scope of her miracle.

We broke the gaze locking our eyes together. I dropped money on the bill. ("Who earns more?" I insisted.) We walked out. As we passed another restaurant I thought I glimpsed a man whose face I couldn't see through the frosted glass turn, hesitate, stand in the doorway as if he were staring at us. At her, I assumed. Who else could he ever stare at but her?

Spring seemed betrayed by the time we reached the corner where we'd part. I zipped my leather jacket closed against the frigid wind. Tara wore a snappy mid-calf-length black trench coat that tied shut with a long black belt which she had misplaced. I knew she'd turn down the belt from my jeans; knew she didn't mind the chill; knew it was bad for her and worried and wanted to help. Her magazine office was in a converted townhouse two blocks down 2nd Street, not far from Union Station and its subway stop. Parked cars lined the street. Congressional aides and lobbyists scurried between the demands of the Senate office buildings one block away and the sustenance of restaurants behind us. The trees stood fully green against the sharp gray sky. The wind pushed dust and last year's leaves down gutters.

"See you later," she said, smiled. Walked away. At the stoplight she turned, waved. The light changed and she once more faced where she was going, ran lightly across the street, her long black coat and golden hair flying in the wind.

"He seemed like a nice enough guy," I told Cheryl as we walked through my office door that night.

"How would you know?" she snapped back. She'd been a ticking time bomb all evening. "He barely got a chance to talk. I didn't get any chance at all. You and *Tara* got plenty. Before the movie, after the movie, in the bar, on the way to drop them off at his car. Maybe you two should have gone to the movie alone."

"That wasn't the plan," I said as I walked toward my desk after unlocking the door to my private rooms.

"Oh. I see." Cheryl stalked inside my apartment. I decided to check my answering machine while she cooled down. Hard rain beat on the streets outside. This was no time for a bloody scene.

But Cheryl didn't agree. I walked back into the apartment and found her rummaging through the bathroom medicine cabinet. Her briefcase gaped open on the toilet seat beside her. The sleeve of a yellow blouse dangled from its leather yawn.

"What are you doing?" I asked with complete understanding of her all too familiar tactic.

"I have some things here. I'm taking them home."

And then I got mad: I wouldn't obediently jump into her game on cue! My question spoiled her script: "Why?"

"I'm not comfortable here."

"It's a little late at night for this nonsense, isn't it?"

"I hope not." She slammed the medicine chest shut, grabbed the briefcase and whirled to face me as if she meant to charge. "I'm not coming back until I feel comfortable!"

"Your choice," I said. "Just remember . . ."

"Fuck you!" she yelled.

She once told me that when I looked like I did then that I went *all over cold*. I held her in the bathroom with that glare, waited until I was sure she'd understand, said, "You don't need to worry about that anymore." Then turned my back on her, walked away, called out over my shoulder, "I'll take you to your car."

"Don't bother!" She bustled by me clutching her briefcase to her heaving breasts. They were so ripe. Scarlet blotches stained her face but she hadn't—wouldn't cry. Yet.

"It's got nothing to do with you," I said. She rolled her eyes as I continued. "It's a rough neighborhood and if you get mugged . . ."

"Fuck the neighborhood and everybody in it!"

"It doesn't matter anymore why you did this," I said. *"How* you did it is enough."

"I don't *believe* you!" She leaned against the door. "Listen to yourself. You were never like this! Even before me!"

"You'd be surprised."

"No, I wouldn't, John . . . You're . . . such a fool! You don't even know what kind of shit you've stepped in!"

"I thought with you I'd stepped out of . . ."

"Spare me. But you should know that I'm going and I'm better off for it than you."

"That's *your* bet." I didn't blink.

She shook her head, clumped down my stairs.

By the time she got to her car parked at the corner of 7th and Pennsylvania I was standing at the window in my office turret where I could watch over her progress. I couldn't let the sharks get her on my street, no matter what she said. She trudged through the rain, wiped her face with her sleeve as she unlocked the driver's door. The briefcase flew into her backseat, she climbed in and was gone.

19

The bulky manila envelope that arrived the next day showed no return address, contained an inch-thick pile of Xeroxed documents with an attached note typed on plain paper: "You may get more of this material you're not supposed to see, but right now all grand jury stuff is tense. Gruesome reading. Your anonymous friend."

Named Art Dillon. He wasted no time. The grand jury reference was a shrewd assessment: that morning's *Post* reported that a grand jury had indicted two congressmen—both chairmen of powerful House committees—as a result of ABSCAM.

Art's packet gave me the government's indictment of Janet Armstrong's pimp for multiple charges of second degree murder, pandering and assault, as well as a thick, stapled report on 14-inch "legal sized" pages labeled "Superior Court of the District of Columbia, *United States* v. *Herbert Jerome Murphy*" and entitled "Government's Proffer of Discovery Given": law school jargon for the condensation of evidence gathered by the prosecution to argue its case before the grand jury. Some of this stuff had been in Nick's case jacket, some of it was fresh.

But just then none of that seemed important. I'd been restless all morning, waking before dawn, tossing fitfully until it was too late to run, too soon to work. Tara went to her office early. Better to call her there than at home, better early than late.

"Cheryl is no longer an operative factor in my life." I'd contemplated, revised and rehearsed those words. As they echoed in my telephone receiver I felt stupid, not funny; contrived, not clever. How could I expect Tara to understand my parody of government garble? My fault for thinking she might.

"Oh! I'm . . . I'm . . . No, I'm not sorry!" She laughed. "I expected it, but not this soon. Are you OK?"

"Yes," I said, and she perceived that there were limits to my truth without understanding them.

"Do you . . . Would you like to talk about it?"

"Yeah." I kept the excitement out of my voice. I didn't want to scare her. "I'd like to talk to you. What are you doing tonight?"

"Ah, The Man From Time is supposed to meet me for dinner."

Pause. "No problem. Maybe tomorrow?"

"Sure. I can cancel tonight if you want . . ."

"No, hey, it's . . . it'll keep. I'll talk to you later."

"Take care," she said, hung up.

I pushed the purloined reports from one corner of my desk to the other, then restacked them and pushed them back to their original place. I couldn't stay still. Pacing didn't help. "Fuck this shit," I said, threw the reports in a case file, changed for running.

All energy oozed out of me after I'd run down Capitol Hill, barely 20 percent of my course and yet I had to stop, walk part of the way back. The preceding night's rain had drenched the city with deep shades of green. The clouds were gone, the sun bright. Summer was due any day, I could feel it, see it all around.

Rich was washing The Eclectic's front windows. He wiped the red rubber squeegee blade on a dirty white towel. "You look terrific," he said, sarcasm covering his words like the wash water covered the windowpane.

"Had a rough day, Rich. Rough night."

"Doing what?"

I told him about Cheryl. He shook his head. "I doubt that was too rough." I didn't reply, couldn't hold our gaze. "Now," he said, "what are you really up to?"

Talk about work, I thought. That's certain. "I got a packet of nightmares in the mail."

138

"You aren't afraid enough of your own nightmares, you need to send away for more?"

"More people are afraid of their dreams than their nightmares."

He squinted at me: he was supposed to be the cryptic one. "Are you more afraid of your dreams than your nightmares?"

"Sometimes they come together. Sometimes I can't tell the difference between the two."

"Try getting more sleep. But not now. Now you've got somebody upstairs waiting for you. Stop that! I know, I remember the last time. This is somebody special. Somebody you know."

I didn't dare ask; could only hope.

Rich leaned forward, twisted toward me, his face contorted like a grotesque movie monster. He growled his words in a harsh stage voice: *"The Mad Dog!"*

"Shit!"

"Well, pardon me!" he said, straightening up in an exaggerated huff. "I thought you two were partners and best of friends."

"We are," I said, "it's just . . . I wasn't expecting him."

"You never expect a mad dog."

"Yeah," I said. "How long has he been up there?"

Rich shrugged. "How long have you been gone?"

The Dog paced back and forth in the same path I'd quit.

"Look, Saul," I said as I walked through the door, "I know I promised to help, but today I don't . . ."

"It's about that thing we talked about."

"The ABSCAM tapes and I'm just not . . ."

"Not ABSCAM, that other thing."

"What other thing?"

Neither of us moved.

"You mean Katie?"

He nodded. "I . . . Her internship is almost up and she's talking about going back to a guy in New Mexico. She doesn't really like him that much, I know it. She doesn't say so, but they're just playing it out from habit. I know I can win . . . So . . ." He forced himself to look me straight on, to stand rock still: "What would you think if I told you I might ask her to marry me?"

Four months earlier I'd have said for Saul "Mad Dog" Lazarian to even discuss marriage was unthinkable. So much can change in so few months: a mountain in Washington State blew up.

"Do you love her?" was all I asked.

"Yes! A whole lot!" He shuffled his feet. "And she loves me. I'm afraid . . . I'm afraid of losing her. That's what you do, then, isn't it? Isn't that the rules of the game? You love, you don't want to lose it, so you get married."

"Why not?"

"No argument? I never expected you to . . . As many times as you've gone down the court . . ."

"This isn't sports, Dog." I paused. "I know how you feel." First admission, I thought. Smiled.

He wrinkled his brow: "Cheryl?"

"She left last night."

"Have you been to Tara yet?"

"What makes you think . . ."

"We're not blind, John. None of us are fools."

"Maybe none of you." I shook my head. "I'm probably going to see her tomorrow night."

"Why wait?"

"Bad timing now."

"I like her."

"Don't start hearing my wedding bells! Everybody is a long way from that. I like her too, and . . . And I don't know where it will lead or what will happen or . . . you know."

"Yeah," he said. "I know."

He raved about Katie for another 10, 15 minutes.

"When are you going to ask her?" I said.

"I did last night." *That* stunned me. "I figured you were going to get mad, so I'd slide it to you easy. Guess I was wrong."

"What did she say?"

"She wanted some time to think about it, couple days."

"Sounds fair."

"Of course it's fair! And I . . . I know I'm going to win. I just know it. I just know it!"

"I hope so, Dog. More than you can imagine."

I stood in my tower after he left. I tried to think of Saul and Katie, but they didn't come to mind.

The phone rang.

"I got stood up!" Tara laughed. So did I: who could be so foolish? "The Man From Time canceled, so you can see me tonight if you want. How about dinner?"

In a public place. Even in private, needing to go through the motions of an ordinary event . . ."Can I drop by afterward?" "Sure. How about seven—no, eight o'clock?"

"Fine."

"You OK, John?"

"I'm fine," I said. "I'm just fine."

20

There are memories difficult to believe, detached moments crucial yet curious in the sum of our time. We lived them with stormy intensity, remember them with quiet awe: Did we *really* play such a scene? Was there *really* such a time?

Fire ached in me as I walked toward Tara's that evening. All life seemed suspended, all purpose fixed.

And she opened the door as a golden vision, wispy white mohair sweater, slim blue jeans.

"Hi," she said as she hung my leather jacket on a doorknob. "It's messy in here."

"It always is." The clutter of her life brought charm to an otherwise dingy apartment of board and brick bookcases, plywood-slab and folding-chair desk. A worn stuffed chair lent her by the landlord was the only other furniture besides her new bed pushed into the corner. A counter separated the living/sleeping room from the stove, refrigerator and sink kitchen with its two overhead cabinets. A single electric ceiling fixture colored more than lit the subdivided room. Clothes overflowed from the one closet by the bathroom. Pull-down shades obscured the window bars protecting her ground-floor dwelling. The first apartment: we've all lived there. She'd taped a poster from a New England jazz festival to one wall, a dark and moody Rembrandt print to another.

"I hope I didn't cause you any trouble with the mix-up tonight," she said.

"No trouble at all."

"Are you really OK? You don't look . . ."

"I'm fine. Really."

"You keep saying that, but getting rid of Cheryl . . ."

"That was nothing." She moved back, folded herself cross-legged on her faded blue bedspread. I paced, looking not at her, seeing her no matter where my eyes pointed. "That's harsh and I don't mean it badly about her, but it's true.

"This is . . . This is hard and strange. Could you . . . Would you just listen to me for a while? Please?"

She nodded, set her face: God, I was scaring her!

"It's nothing bad! Don't worry, please don't ever worry." I was worse than a teenager who'd showered and shaved and tried not to sweat through the clean blue shirt and fresh jeans he wore to look his "natural" best; who'd brushed his teeth three times and still tasted his own foulness. Words stumbled from my mouth like lemmings charging to the sea cliffs.

"This might sound dumb to you," I said, brushing away everyone else in my life, "but you're my best friend."

"I know what you mean," she said. "My friend from college I lived in Europe with? I feel guilty because she's not as close to me as you. Nobody has ever been."

"I don't want to lose that. Ever."

"Me either." Her chin trembled.

"I love you," I said.

Tara started to cry.

"I couldn't help it," I protested. "I tried not to, told myself not to, told myself I didn't, but I couldn't help it! I love you, Tara, I love you like I never believed I'd get to love anybody. I loved you the moment I saw you and it keeps growing. I know it's bad for you and . . . I didn't want to tell you but I couldn't help it!"

Her face was slick. I crouched beside her slumped form as she sat on the bed. "Don't cry!" I pleaded. "Please, please don't cry!"

She waved her hands to ward off my worry, rubbed her eyes. "It's OK," she stuttered, soft and low. "It's OK, they just do that."

Slowly, ever so slowly, I moved my hand toward her cheek, stopped so close I felt the warmth of her wet flesh tingle my fingertips. Then I touched her, slid my hand through that soft hair as she leaned into my neck and cried. We stretched flat on our sides. She lay tucked safe against my chest, silent streams flowing down her cheeks.

"I've made a mess of this, haven't I?" I said and she shook her head. "You don't need me in your life like this."

"I tried so hard, Tara!" I floated above the bed, above my words. My life stood at its utter extremes. I was suspended; vulnerable to everything, oblivious to nothing, a total slave to circumstance. And yet I felt curiously freer than I'd ever been. I had nothing left to lose. My only reward would be what she gave me. What did I have to fear?

"Tara, I tried to dodge you by pinning you down. So much for brains, so much for whatever. But you fly off any scale. I know your faults, but . . . You're beyond all that."

"You too." Her eyes roamed my face. "You know that, don't you? I can't . . . I can't put you in a neat little box."

But then she pressed her head back to my chest, cried.

"I don't want to be an adventure like The Man From Time or Peter from Harvard or Senator Barnes's Brightest Young Man or . . ."

"You could never be like them! I don't want you to!"

"I love you, Tara. All the way down always love. And I think you love me too. When we walk into a room everybody feels it! I know it's spooky. Maybe I'm asking too much." She shook her head against me. "But this is so much! I don't want . . . I mean, maybe you need some time to think about it. I'm not giving you deadlines or schedules or ultimatums or . . ."

"I know," she said, "I know." And she nodded. And cried.

So it went. I lay beside her on the bed, talked and tried to make her smile. Kissed her once or twice. Told her as few hundred times as I could that I loved her. Held her at the door as we said good night.

Between when I said good night and when I saw her again I coasted through life, filling my hours with mindless routines.

When she let me inside her apartment the next night I had to take her in my arms, hold her, tell her again. And again. I kissed, tenderly, slowly, my passion surging yet held in check by my heart and my head. She held me loosely—but she held me; her tongue flicked lightly, teasingly at mine. And I told her again.

"I know it embarrasses you when I say that . . ."

She smiled. "I like hearing it."

All I could do was stand there grinning like a fool.

"Shall we go?" she said.

The night was too nice for the car—her car, though I'd started to forget which possessive pronoun properly belonged to the Porsche. We walked to the French café on the far side of the Hill.

"Thanks for the four record albums. And that note. How did you get them inside my apartment?"

Even her landlord with his passkey knew we were special, but I didn't tell her that. Never spoil a surprise. "I have my ways." She didn't ask again. "Besides, I had to do it: Springsteen calls his group the E Street Band. You live on E Street. I could have *not* given you the records, but . . ."

". . . it would have been wrong." We laughed as she finished the Watergate routine.

"What's on line for tomorrow night?" I asked.

"Oh. Some friends from the office are going to that seafood place written up in the *Post.*"

Four steps, five. "Sounds . . . nice."

"You, ah, you can come if you want."

I knew enough to say, "I don't know if I can."

She shrugged her shoulders, we walked on.

Dinner was wonderful. The night was warm, we sat at an outside patio table. The maitre d' and cook were old friends of mine, they fussed over us. She looked beautiful and I didn't look bad. We chatted, eventually reached laughter. I glanced around: we were A Stared At Couple. Everybody knew.

But behind my smile, dread gnawed at my soul.

"I'll put water on for coffee," she said as we walked inside her apartment after dinner. "We can listen to the Springsteen albums."

She turned toward the kitchen, hesitated, then turned the other direction toward the stereo. My hand touched her sweater sleeve and she froze.

"Tara." She turned, put a smile on her face. "The answer is no, isn't it?"

The smile tightened, her chin trembled. I saw her eyes fill. "You don't know!" She cried through her words. "You know,

145

don't you? You know how important you are to me? How much I care about you and . . . I just don't know! I want to oh God how I want to! But I can't . . . I just can't! I'm not ready and I can't and I . . ."

She couldn't go on. I pulled her close. She clung to me, sobbed violently. "It's OK," I said. "It's OK.

"Doesn't make any difference. I love you, Tara. We're best friends too. We can't stop that." Her head dug into my chest as she nodded. "You are my life." She tried, but I wouldn't let her speak, held her closer until she stopped trying. There was still that last chance, that last grand hope. I wouldn't throw it away. I couldn't throw it away! "I know you can't now. But you're saying no to now. You're not saying *never*."

"How can I say never to you?"

"Right man, right woman, wrong time."

She nodded, sobbed even harder than before.

"I love you, Tara. I don't know what or how we'll do . . . but we will." She nodded and we clung to my logic: such wonderful, insightful and *wise* logic.

There was much, much more. I held her and held on for maybe two hours, talking and telling. Explaining. Understanding. Justifying. I promised much; she asked nothing, said little. I held her at the door, told her I loved her one last time, drifted away.

Four blocks, I told myself. Don't stumble like that. Your legs aren't broken. Your arms aren't gone. You can still see. Four blocks and one flight of stairs. A dying man could crawl four blocks. A dead man.

This is your home, this is where you live. This is your office. Not anymore. Not ever again. This is your couch. This is where she slept. That bathroom is where she showered. She laughed in here. She really did.

You're supposed to get drunk. You don't like to drink. Won't do that cocaine in the gun drawer, the gun drawer. Don't need to be awake. Don't want to intensify. Don't need don't need don't need need only her. Don't have her. But she didn't say never, couldn't say never, wouldn't say never, won't be never.

Who left that bottle of gin who cares? Maggie or was it Cheryl who liked gin and tonics and left tonic too and who cares? Wouldn't they laugh now? Wouldn't they all? Wouldn't they like it now. Who cares.

Don't spill gin on the answering machine. Wait: four-block walk, long time gone, maybe please please maybe . . .

—My name is Cliff Palefsky, I'm a *Washington Post* reporter. You've been leaving messages for me. I've been covering campaigns. I'm back in town for a few days. Who are you and what do you want, anyway?

—Mr. Rankin? I called before but this machine wasn't on. This is Fred Thomas, Senator Woodson's attorney. We met at his house. I'm so glad we resolved that problem. I'm calling about my law firm. I happened to mention to Martin Mercer, the senator's A.A., that we are swamped with detail work—depositions, research, interviewing, file searches, that sort of thing. He suggested I give you a call. I'm sure we can work out mutually beneficial professional arrangements. Please call me when you can.

—It's Dog! She said yes! Katie said yes! I won! We're getting married, you gotta be there! Call us at Katie's!

—How you doing, brother? This is your buddy Paul. Just checking to be sure you're OK. I'll be in touch.

—This is Nick Sherman. You're all set with Prostitution and Perversion. Call 555-0959, ask for Detective Ben Clay, work it out with him. He's a good man. Be talking to you.

—Hey, Rankin: it's Malletta. Talk to you soon.

The tape whirred, messages over. I turned off that machine, wandered to my stereo. Noise. Life. Something. Slapped in a tape.

And watched my guts burst all over the floor. *Crashed and burned* was my last coherent thought. Crashed and burned. The ice in the glass I held rattled and suddenly I was hyperventilating, panting in-and-out sobs. I didn't know I was crying as well until I felt tears soaking through my shirt. Each time I thought I'd stopped or thought about stopping I'd break apart a little more, start all over again. I knocked down three, four gins waiting to stop and didn't. All I could do was sob, call her name over and over again. I did four, six, maybe eight megalines of cocaine; didn't care and didn't feel them, couldn't feel anything but falling. I repeatedly played one song on a bootleg tape of Springsteen doing a benefit for a Philadelphia nightclub, Bruce groaning a soulful piano and violin rendition of "I Want You," Bob Dylan's rage against fate. Jimmy Carter quoted Bob Dylan as he rose to the Presidency. I listened to Dylan sung by my man as I crashed and burned.

Saturday was fog. Sunday evening I discovered I was still in the world. The world didn't care. According to the newspapers I found outside my door, forms of life created by man in his laboratories were now patentable. Maybe she'd care even if the world didn't. That was enough. That and believing with invincible certainty that this wasn't *never*. I was born to win her. I'd live out that fate if it killed me. My redemption would come when she'd realize our truth. That's the way it had to be, that's the way it was. Whatever I had to do, I had to do, and I could do whatever it was. No limits. You want it all, you give it all, isn't that what the wise men say? That was fine by me. Hell, that proved everything, didn't it? If I was willing to put it all on the line, then I deserved to get it all back. And I would. Right? I was John Rankin. Tough guy, smart guy. I could do that. I could do that. Now that I knew what love was, now that I had it, all I needed to do was live it out, fight to keep it and make it work.

I built that rational world, then found enough strength in it to follow its rules. That prompted me into action, to clean up, leave and look for food.

She turned the corner headed toward the Safeway I stood in front of just as I heard Joey Malletta call out, "Hey Rankin!" She saw me, maybe heard him too. She hesitated, but there was nowhere else to go. She and Joey reached me at the same time.

"You remember Tara, don't you Joey?"

"How's you doin'?" He smiled through his Chicago accent. He'd seen us together before. "Glad I ran into youse guys."

"Is this store closed? I need some things," Tara said, looked away.

"Me too," said Joey, "but we're shit out of luck. John, I called to be sure you came to our party. We have a police permit, live band, eats, kegs of beer. Couple hundred people. We'll have the whole alley and courtyard behind my place. You two can't miss it."

"When is it?" I asked.

"Fourth of July, of course! Independence Day! When else?"

I spoke to Tara with cautious precision: "What do you think, *friend?*"

"I'd like to," she answered in a whisper.

We declined Joey's invitation to get a beer, watched him amble off.

"I think we can handle it, don't you?" I said, hoping she didn't notice my dissipation.

She smiled. "Yes, I think so."

21

We met Sunshine during my third night on the Stroll—
"sneaker night," as ordained by Ben Clay, the white detective
driving our unmarked cruiser. His black partner Willy Franklin and I complied. Walking the sidewalks wearing our
"felony flyers" with windbreakers and cords we looked like
aging fraternity brothers from a liberal college—until you
noticed their granite eyes.

"Who we got here?" asked Ben as our cruiser turned off
Logan Circle and chugged toward 14th. Two women leaning
against the wrought iron fence surrounding an unrestored
mansion looked at us expectantly. The slender black woman
in hot pants saw the radio antennae, muttered to her companion, a squat white girl with bouffant hair bleached the color of
pale straw. The black woman stepped away from her companion who shuffled but didn't leave the fence.

"I do believe that's a new face," said Willy.

"Which one?" I asked from the backseat.

"The white girl," answered Ben.

"Who's the black woman?" I asked.

"A friend-girl," answered Willy. "One of Cisco's, isn't
she?"

"Last I heard," said Ben as he pulled the car to the curb.
"Hello ladies!" He turned on the blinkers and we walked to
the sidewalk slow and easy.

The black girl had a model's face, classic features, red
lipstick and thick brown hair cascading to her shoulders. She
was five feet tall, but black patent high heels and slim
chocolate legs shown off by her hot pants made her seem

taller. The blond suffered from an obvious excess of everything but intelligence: her hair was too white; her cheeks too puffy; her lips too thick; her hot pink lipstick too poorly and too heavily applied; her pants and sweater outfit too tight and too electric blue; her manner too cool for her timid and too wet eyes. She couldn't decide whether to stay by the fence or move closer to the black woman; couldn't decide whether to speak.

"Step into my office, ladies," said Willy. Neither woman moved, so he called out, slightly louder, "Excuse me?!"

"You talkin' to me?" The black girl's voice was a trill, like a songbird. She smiled—even, white teeth.

"Darlin', who else is there to talk to out here?" asked Ben.

"I bet you could find somebody else to pick on," she said.

"Oh," countered Willy, "is that what we're doing?"

"I suppose so." She shrugged. "I don't got no beefs against me."

"Now," added Ben.

She shrugged again.

"Who's your little friend?" asked Willy, angling his head toward the blond who still hadn't moved.

"I don't know. Some girl. We was just talkin' now."

"Who are you?" Willy asked this black beauty.

"You know me!" She shook her head at such foolishness. "I be Star."

"Well, Star, why don't you come over here and talk to me?" said Willy. He led her up the sidewalk, leaving the dyed blond alone with us. Ben pulled a white index card from a stack snapped round his notebook by a rubber band, clicked his pen. "What's your name, darlin'?"

"Who, me?"

"Yes, you. I know my name. I know his."

"What you *axxed* me?"

"*I asked, a-s-k-e-d,* I asked you your name. You have one, don't you?"

"Sure."

Ben closed his eyes, shook his head. "What is it?"

"Sunshine."

"Not your street name, girl, not the name your man said to give the johns and the police . . ."

"I ain't got no man."

"Un-huh. But you got a real name you're going to give me, don't you?"

"Sure." Ben's eyes narrowed, and she stuttered, "Ah, Mary."

"Ah, Mary: Funny name. Got any ID?"

Ah, Mary fished in the cheap purse dangling from her shoulder, pulled a plastic laminated card out of a wad of tissues.

"Says here your name is Janey Grant, not Ah, Mary. Or Sunshine."

"Well, that's my real name."

"And this is your real address? 531 I Street, Northwest?"

"Sure."

"There is no such address."

Sunshine glanced down the sidewalk to Star, but the other girl couldn't rescue her. Willy smiled our way.

"How old are you, Sunshine?"

"Eighteen. Says so on the card, don't it?"

"You had the card made up—No, *excuse me:* your man had the card made up in a store downtown for $5."

"I told you, I don't have a man."

"He such a coward he won't let you talk to the po-lice about him?"

Again she glanced toward Star. Again she found no rescue.

"Who's that woman?"

"Who, her? Just a friend."

"And you're 18. And you live someplace that doesn't exist. And your ID is phony."

"I just moved here. I don't remember the address. Maybe I made a mistake on the card."

"Maybe you did. Where you from?"

All her lies were played out, her meager script exhausted. She didn't have enough imagination to create any more. "Pennsylvania. Martin City."

"You got family there? Mother? Father?"

She nodded. Ben scribbled Martin City in the appropriate blank on the small white card he'd later file with thousands of others. "Suppose I called them, told them you were here and what you were doing? What would they say about Janey Grant then?"

"Well, they don't actually know me by that name."

"Last time you get to play, girl: What is your true, God-given birth name?"

"Debby Grummer."

"Bullshit."

"I wouldn't bullshit you! My name is Debby Grummer and I'm from Martin City and I'm 18 and I probably fucked up writing down the address for the card!"

"You wanted anywhere?"

"No." She paused. "I spent some time in a juvenile home, but I'm out now."

"Free as a bird, right?"

"That's right."

Ben used the car radio. Sunshine and I avoided looking at each other while we waited.

"Well, you're right about that, darlin'. No wants or warrants for Janey Grant or Debby Grummer."

"See? I told you!"

"I had to ask you enough times. Why you make it so hard for yourself?"

"I didn't know who you was."

"You know who we are now?"

"You're Clay, right? The Salt cop. And the black guy is crazy Willy. Pepper. I don't know 'bout you, officer," she said, looking at me.

"Hey Willy! She says she heard about two cops named Salt and Pepper!" Willy smiled. Ben quickly turned back to Sunshine. "If you don't have a man, who'd you hear about us from?"

Sunshine didn't know what to say.

"What are you doing out here?"

"Nothing."

Ben softened his voice. "This is your first night on the Track, isn't it? You haven't even broken luck. You know you don't have to do this, don't you? You know doing this is dumb."

"Doing what?" She was stubborn, or feared something more than our questions.

"You know. You know, Sunshine. If you stay stupid and stay out here, then you tell Cisco to get you some real ID 'cause we'll check back. If you want, we'll give you a ride somewhere right now." He paused, but she refused to acknowledge his offer. "We don't want to hassle you. You give us no problems, we give you none. Maybe we can even help you, if you let us."

"Yeah, sure."

"What are you doing out here, Sunshine?"

"I'm here."

"Yeah," said Ben. He nodded Willy to the car. "Yeah," he said as we walked away, "you're here."

"What we have here," explained Willy as we drove to 14th Street, hung a left toward downtown, "is a classic turnout situation. The girl Star? She's the bottom lady for a pimp named Cisco. That means she's his number one woman. Until Sunshine, she was his only woman. Nasty bitch. Straight razor sweetheart. Cuts and runs on her customers if she gets a chance. Charged with assault with a deadly weapon last year, but the complainant never showed: too nervous about the publicity. Star's job, in addition to making her own quota, is to pull other women when she can, help Cisco turn them out, which is probably fine by her except when she gets jealous of them. The more work they do, the less she needs to do."

"I figure Sunshine for 17, don't you?" said Ben.

"Then you can pick her up as a juvenile, right?" I said as Willy nodded yes to Ben's question before answering mine.

"How? She doesn't need to carry ID. What she has says she's 18. What right do we have to pull her in? She's got the Constitution too. Probable cause is shaky. She ain't breaking any law we can prove until she solicits. Let's say she is a juvenile, 17—that's not that young. We picked a 13-year-old girl off the streets last week, a 15-year-old the night before you came on. Runaways, castaways. Say we get Sunshine to the office. We can figure up some charge. We can tell her it's LNC . . ."

"Leaving North Carolina," chimed in Ben.

"Sometimes we'll tack WP on to that charge."

"Without Permission," said Ben.

154

"A heinous crime. About the most we can do is crimp her, piss her pimp off at her and make her pay for his anger. Maybe—and I do mean maybe—we can send her home for some reason. But I doubt it. Unless we charge her cold with solicitation—a misdemeanor—she'll walk, because no prosecutor downtown will take the time to paper anything else. They call it bullshit, victimless crime."

"What about her pimp?"

"What about him? Cisco is like most of the others, like your friend Magic Murphy, though maybe not quite as successful. Magic would have two, maybe three ladies, but he was still just a pimp."

"Could he have been more?"

"He could have been less," said Ben. "Could have been a simp."

"Popcorn pimp," added Willy. "Kind of guy can't hook a girl without a fishing rod. Walkin' pimp, drives maybe some raggedy piece of shit for a car, maybe shares his mother or his sister or wife with some other simp equally as lame. Turn out your next of kin to supplement her welfare checks."

"Your man Magic was a step above that," said Ben, "if you cut layers in a shit pile. Magic was a regular pimp. Two main kinds of regular pimps out here: your gorilla pimp, who beats up on his girls all the time, and your sweet pimp . . ."

"Daddy, you're so good to me!" mimicked Willy.

"And that's it?" I asked.

"What more do you need? A pimp usually works one solid bottom lady at a time, maybe has two or three other girls. Gets one and loses one. Pulls in between $100 and $100,000 a year, tax free. Did you know most pimps don't fuck their women? They will at first, fast and furious, pull them in with how great they are. They make the girls believe that so deep they forget how true it really is even when he's quit making them burn. That's usually deliberate on the pimp's part. After time on the Track, sex loses its mystery for anybody. If he is a steady romp for her and she's doing it with 60 other guys a week, the comparison gets dangerous. Maybe the girl will say, 'Hey, this joker ain't so hot.' If a pimp does fuck his whores, it's usually oral or anal, anything to degrade them.

But most of them don't, most of them don't like women, especially their own, because they're just whores. Most pimps are switch-hitting bisexuals too. All of them are scum."

Ben leered out the window at three women walking down the street. They waved at him, giggled.

"Now on top of your pimps are your macks, your sweet macks," said Willy. "A mack doesn't need to show his shit in the street to take care of business. A mack's girls hold his money for him. He might have six, seven ho'es working the Stroll. And if he gets real fancy, really starts cruising the circuit, he turns into a player working maybe a couple strings in a couple towns at once, with the girls working under bottom ladies and wiring him the money."

"Big businessmen," said Willy.

"But your buddy Magic was a long way from that," said Ben.

"You know what amazes me?" asked Willy. "Pimps are utterly useless to the business. The girls don't need them for a thing. They work their ass off out here, rain and snow, sixty, seventy hours a week . . ."

"Usually never on Sundays," said Ben. "Sometimes."

"They work harder than for a straight job and get nothing. He takes all the money. All. Does shit."

"All that figurin', man. Worryin'."

"And beating up on them when he gets bored."

"That's the way life is. Just ask a ho'e. They know everything."

"Why do they do it?" I asked.

"You mean be a ho'e?" said Willy. "You find out, you tell us. The only thing that makes less sense than being a ho'e is being a ho'e with a pimp, which almost all of them are."

"Why do they have them then? What makes them go with a pimp?"

"Any line of bullshit that'll work," said Willy. "Going to be rich and run a club, whatever. Mostly they do it for the big L."

"*L-o-v-e*, love," spelled Ben. He mumbled and whistled the Beatles song "All You Need Is Love."

"How could anybody love a gorilla pimp who turns them out to be abused by creeps, then takes all their money?"

"You tell me how and why anybody loves anybody," said Ben.

I said nothing.

"It's not just love like man-woman anyway," said Willy. "The pimp become everything, keeps it that way—father, family, priest, friend, only contact with somebody who ain't a customer, only 'man' in her life. The name of the game is *control*. That's why you don't see many junkie whores. The junk gets in the way of the pimp's control and it cuts into his take of the girl's trap. All a whore gets is expenses. If he runs up her expenses by letting her become a junkie, he cuts down on his own take and the junk cuts his control. Then she belongs to the pusher. There's some crossovers, some exceptions, but not many. Not here, anyway."

"What about organized crime?"

"Not in these streets. O.C. swings weight in the porno shops, lots of other shit, but not out here. Too hard to centralize. Some towns, the streets pay off up the line. But here the pimps are the top. There's one or two players, guys like Bobby V., who owns a new 'Vette, a new Mercedes, a new Caddy, a house in Maryland, more gold than a jewelry store, and lists his occupation as mechanic. He's got a couple walkin' dudes who work for him, one as a driver, one as an enforcer—and the enforcer runs a ho'e of his own. But that's about it as far as organized goes. Players don't last beyond themselves, like a Mafia don passing on his family. Bobby V., he's a rare breed."

"Outlived his own existence," said Willy.

"It's like high-class call girls," said Ben. Maybe D.C.'s got them, maybe it doesn't. We got massage parlors and outcall services, all of which are a bitch to even think about policing. Anything we can't see nobody complains about and few people tell us about."

"Nobody even really sees much of this street stuff," said Willy. He saw me start to protest, start to rant about the highly visible, almost mile long, sometimes three block wide jungle of ho'es and pimps. He cut me short.

"I know what you're thinking, but that's true. I have a friend who had to show a *Washington Post* reporter who'd worked here for three years where the Stroll was and explain as much of how it worked as he could—and the Post building is two blocks away from one of the main Stroll corners. That reporter was stunned. More people don't see what goes on in front of them than we like to believe. Either they don't want to see it or they look at it and are too blind to know what's there or they don't care enough to focus or they believe they know the truth and *that ain't it*. Some of the people who live here, big shots and poor folks alike, some of our best and brightest, know less about this town than millions of people who vacation here each year."

"Too many people are just tourists in their own time," I said.

"You got it," said Ben. "You got it."

Whatever I got from those streets Ben and Willy took me down cut deep. This was my third night and I was played out. Maybe because I'd seen how ignorant I'd been about what I thought I'd understood, like Willy said. Maybe I'd just plain seen too much on those seamy streets that make up Washington's Stroll.

I'd seen the same alleys hundreds of times as we cruised through them, and I learned that, besides "garbage, basketball, vertical bathroom activities and rats," Washington alleys were used for commercial oral sex, with male customers paying by the score all along 14th Street during almost any hour of darkness for that prostitutional service. We'd rolled our cruiser up to one Chrysler with Virginia tags parked in a loading dock just off a major downtown D.C. street. Our headlights outlined one man sitting in the front seat, one man sitting in the back. Ben blared our car horn, the trio of whores standing on the corner screamed, and up beside each man popped a ratted-haired woman. Thirty seconds later those two whores, both about 25, both black, both not ugly, ran from their frightened customers' car, stuck their heads in our cruiser windows, and giggling through voices fit for a church choir said, " 'Bout time you showed up, we been suckin' on those guys long enough!"

Then I'd learned that whores often chewed condoms like gum, the better to use their lips and tongues to manipulate those devices over their anxious and unknowing customers:

"preventive health maintenance," Willy called it as he laughed over my shock.

One of those spring nights turned unexpectedly cold. I'd watched a whore walking past our cruiser engine-running at the mouth of an alley turn, bend over to warm her tight-skirted bottom against our radiator grill, then shake it at us and smile as she returned to her appointed rounds.

I'd seen a white whore so fat her sex was hard to distinguish standing on the corner, blood gushing from her slashed hand, urging us to get the cutter who'd wanted something other than sex. She wanted us to get him, she couldn't describe him, she wouldn't get in the car and help us find him by cruising the streets, she wouldn't go to the hospital. "All I need is some fuckin' freebase!" she said. Freebase—an incredibly expensive, brain-tissue-destroying drug refined from cocaine and smoked. That spring of 1980 a comedian who'd had his own movie almost died from burns he allegedly acquired preparing freebase. We drove off, left her cursing on the corner. "How can you care about that?" asked Ben. I had no answer.

The first night out I followed the rust-colored splotches of a sidewalk blood trail from another cutting, whore versus whore in a dispute over the attentions of a pimp. No one was ever charged because no one ever agreed to press charges.

I'd learned some of the language and customs of the Stroll. If the whore who'd been stabbed pressed charges against her fellow businesswoman, she *signed papers*. If the prosecutor downtown agreed to prosecute any such crime, he *papered it*. Sunshine was being *turned out* by Star, her pimp's *bottom lady* and her *friend-girl* or maybe *wife-in-law*. With her first *trick* of the evening, Sunshine or any other whore *broke luck* and acquired money to make her *trap*. When a pimp picked up his whore's trap, he *broke her*.

Customers were *johns*, and a girl's quota was usually $250 no matter how many johns she needed to service or rob to make it.

When the whores on a corner spotted our cruiser rolling their way they'd yell, *"L-Train!"* Sometimes, when Ben or Willy wanted the whores to get out of the street and back on the sidewalks, they'd switch the radio mike to loud speaker and boom out, "L-Train!" If the girls were in a playful mood, they'd take up the chant, yelling, *"L-Train! L-Train! L-Train!"* while all the squares and johns and straights wondered what the hell that urban chorus was about.

I heard how a pimp would *bump* a girl if he could, finagle her away from her rightful owner. I learned that if a whore got caught by a rival pimp showing disrespect or talking to him, he could and often would *put a charge on her,* maybe take her off and rape her for her folly, charge her pimp $100, $125 for her infraction too. The whore would have to tell her pimp she erred, make the penalty money, take his punishment beating, and suffer the shame of knowing she'd embarrassed her man. "A heinous crime," said Willy. Maybe she'd *sting*—rob—to make her money, probably she'd work overtime. "Tell your old man you cost him a buck and a quarter," she'd hear from the creep who, because he was a pimp and she was a whore, became her judge, jury and executioner. Tell her old man she would, for what would happen to her if she didn't was even worse than if she did, probably as bad as if he caught her *playing out of pocket*—talking with pimps who didn't put a charge on her, sleeping with anyone and holding out money from her trap, or doing the ultimately absurd act of not charging for a sexual relationship. Then the pimp would whomp up on her but too good—unless he was a *simp,* a fool, a bluffer who'd sold her a *wolf ticket: wolfing* meant bravado one couldn't back up, like the pimp arrested by the undercover policewoman he mistook for a whore and tried to bump into his *stable.* He failed to impress her with his charm: "Deep down in your heart I know what you are like, because all women are the same, need the same things." He tried wolfing her, showed her his holstered .32 revolver. Ended up meeting all of us in Prostitution and Perversion's tiny basement office, his hands cuffed behind his back while his mouth wolfed off even more.

"He's a Tennessee pimp," said Willy. "They're the dumbest and the nastiest." Like the Atlanta pimps, the Nashville boys pull farm girls who've never seen much of the big time. The Michigan pimps wolf gangster tough when they come to D.C., usually end up caught between the local do-right boys and the cops, usually book out after three days' street time. The northern pimps and the ones from the Deep South (Mississippi, Alabama) are the most respectful of the police, but the whores from New York and Philadelphia are the most arrogant.

"A pimp may have a color preference for his ho'es," explained Willy. "Some won't work whites, some won't work blacks. But the only color that really means anything to them is green."

Willy and Ben showed me a street where green and white were the only two colors that mattered, 14th and U, the major heroin dealing block in Washington. On the second night, shortly before 10:00, we drove down yet another alley, lights out, emerged in the middle of the block next to a shack called Success Café. At least 100 persons—men, women, children, black, some white, some Hispanic, all dressed mostly in rags—shuffled in groups of three and four up and down the sidewalks and pavement. Gray rats ran out of the alley ahead of the cruiser; they mingled freely and unafraid in the crowd of junkies.

"When I count three, open your door," said Ben: "One, two, three!"

All three of our cruiser doors opened, their creaking metal echoing down the street, the car's inside dome light flashing for our exit. Rats and junkies alike scurried away from the alley and the cruiser as if it were about to explode, slinking far enough away to run further if need be, but not so far as to leave this street of dreams.

"Beautiful, isn't it?" asked Willy as we closed our doors, drove down the opposite alley towards the Stroll.

I'd seen whores walking the Stroll seemingly like any other whores until Willy pointed out the size of their hands and feet, told me they were "gators" which came from "nators" which came from "female impersonators," which is what they were. I'd heard about the marine from Wyoming who flipped out after Willy and Ben arrived in the parking lot too late to interrupt his purchased oral sex act with a stunning blond whore in the backseat of his waiting New York marine buddy's customized Trans Am. The cops had not been too late to ID the marines and the blond, who answered Ben's

"What's your name?" by booming out "Ralph!" in a deep bass voice. This blond creature then fled, high heels clattering in the night, as the Wyoming marine screamed, "Oh my God!" grabbed his crotch and collapsed to the pavement.

Willy explained to me that I hadn't really seen six pregnant prostitutes working the Stroll, stomachs bulged way beyond their breasts. "Only four," he said. "Rose there won't turn tricks, she's a thief. Her little bowling ball buddy is her accomplice. Pickpockets, mainly, though Rose has a mean switchblade. Maybe ten holdups and snatch thefts a night around the Stroll. Maybe one a night gets reported. Maybe one a week makes it through the system. So you've only really seen four pregnant whores." *Basketball city,* he added. *Must be something in the water,* said Ben. "All of them swear it's not a trick baby," said Willy, "that it's their old man's. And a lot of johns will go with a pregnant whore because they figure she's just naturally got to be *clean.*"

I'd seen a lot of johns: old men, young men, ugly men, handsome men, all colors of men. They came to the Stroll on foot, in cabs, in pickups, in raggedy-ass cars that put popcorn pimps to shame, in Mercedeses and Porsches and Chevys and Toyotas and vans—including one regular who always shopped for a pleasant, dyed-orange hair, coffee-with-cream skinned whore Willy and Ben called Moon for the time they'd driven up to that van and seen her enormous bare bottom going up and down against the van window: "You may not be able to reach the stars," Willy told me, "but you can always have the moon." Mixed in with johns I'd seen psychos, crazed men and even a couple of crazed women drawn to the moving river of the Stroll like screws to a magnet. I'd seen three men who were whore groupies: they seldom tricked, but they spent their time on the Stroll, chatting with the whores, maybe buying them coffee, letting them warm themselves in their cars when the weather turned cold on a working girl. One of the groupies cosigned a Cadillac's loan note for a woebegone whore who was slightly smaller than a Japanese economy car. One of them had driven Janet Armstrong to her Church Street apartment the night she'd been murdered.

And I'd seen pimps: Oh yes, *gentlemen of leisure* earned by the flesh and blood of the hundred-some whores working

Washington's Stroll. The pimps were incredibly unimpressive. A few were pleasant looking, one was handsome, more than one ugly. They were all black: "This is a black town," said Ben; Willy flashed his ebony-on-white smile, said, "At least out here in the street." I saw pimps in their Cadillacs, their Lincoln Continentals. "The car is the thing," said Willy. "That's status, that shows what your stable can do for you. And everybody wants to keep up. Jewelry, suits, though more of them are going for the casual look. Laid back and all that California mellow shit. They watch the soap operas. They follow fashion."

"Look there!" said Ben, pointing to a long, white Lincoln double-parked in front of a pimp bar. The form behind the steering wheel turned and caught our gaze. Snappy white hat, long curling black locks, wispy mustache and beard. A lean, pretty-boy weasel face that flashed a pointy-toothed smile.

"Grin sucker," said Ben as he smiled back. "Come August 23rd, your ass is ours."

"What's August 23rd?"

"His 18th birthday."

"Who the hell is he?"

"Jesus Riaz. JR on the street. A pimp." For Ben, that summed it up.

"At 17?"

"Ambitious fuck, ain't he?" said Ben.

"And connected," added Willy. "His mother serves on some regional commission for Hispanics. JR got busted for burglary across the river in Virginia. She pulled some strings so he walked without even a diversion charge. Maybe you can judge your degree of 'ethnic assimilation' by the clout you have to bend the rules. A Virginia cop happened to tell the story to Ben the day after we noticed one 'J. Riaz' put up bail money for a ho'e who used to be a secretary. We figured, hey: burglary is one thing, slavery is another. Tell his mommy. She's a solid, freedom-loving citizen, *a sister*. She'll slap her wayward boy's wrists till he flies straight. Maybe send him through a shrink. Ben and I go talk to her. She looks at me, midnight complexion and all, calls me a motherfuckin' racist liar. Her JR wouldn't do no such pimping shit, so I must be a racist liar. Guess nobody told her 'bout the sergeant I flat-assed when he called me nigger. Anyway, after her righteous indignation, we got properly pissed off. We went down to a certain newspaper. Dumped the whole story in the lap of a certain editor."

"What happened?" I asked.

"Did you read about it in the paper?" asked Ben.

"Neither did we," said Willy.

"So we figure, long about his birthday, JR is going to fuck up again. And then he ain't tied to no mama's apron no more."

"What happens to pimps and whores when they get old?" I asked.

"They fade away," said Ben. "One day you notice she or he ain't around anymore."

"Maybe the whore gets killed, another whore or john or a stickup man or a pimp like Magic done—oops, like he is *alleged* to have done. I've never known a reformed whore."

"Once a whore, you're never without a career," said Willy.

"The street is hard—hard on pimps too," said his partner.

"They have to think," added Willy without total sarcasm. "Live by their wits."

"They need to keep up a constant show, always be watching for the younger guy who wants to bump him. A pimp can't work a straight job unless he's playing it for a con. If he goes to jail, which lots of them eventually do, he comes out busted. Jail time is hard for a pimp. Those guys behind the wall all have sisters or girlfriends or wives or mothers. They know all about pimps. A pimp loses touch with the street when he goes to jail. The street always changes even though it's always the same. Like a river. Besides, suppose he gets locked up for something like Magic: hurting girls. Hard to keep a whore after you've been *convicted:* once you cross that line you can't slap them up near as much and still make them buy it. And you lose face with jail time: 'You were chump enough to get busted?!' "

"Busted pimps die or become con men," said Willy. "Or both."

"They all trip themselves up," said Ben. "It's that one girl they abuse too much, too often, who signs papers on them. It's that one time they sell a little smack on the side. One time we're lucky and they're not. But we only need to be lucky one time. Bad guys need to be lucky all the time."

We drove toward 14th Street, took a right on K, cruised past the McDonald's hamburger joint and the U.S. Passport Office, turned north at the end of the block—Vermont Avenue, Janet Armstrong's corner.

"How is territory carved up on the Stroll? Who decides who works what section?"

"The whores," answered Ben. "Maybe the pimps get into it, maybe it gets rough. Especially with the guys from Tennessee. Your better looking whores tend to work this area closer to downtown. They look for what any business looks for: market accessibility. This is an easy block to cruise around. They all hate weekend nights: traffic backs up for blocks, bumper to bumper two lanes deep. But 90 percent of those cars are gawkers, not buyers. I don't know how territory works, don't think they do either, but some sort of natural selection gives whores a customary corner or beat they walk on the Stroll. Just happens."

We circled the block, headed down 14th Street again. The cute Oriental girl who always wore a white suit giggled and waved.

"You dating?" Ben yelled at her. "How much you spending?"

All the whores who heard laughed.

"God this gets old," he said.

Ahead waited a block of strip joints where women jiggled naked onstage then after their performances came down into the crowd to con half-drunk fools into buying splits of champagne for five times their value. One of the marquees flashed "THIS IS IT!" in 20-foot electric gold neon letters.

"Ever think how many people make money off the whores?" asked Willy. "About the only person who doesn't is the whore. The pimp takes all but her overhead and spends it on things like cars and home video games and jewelry and suits from the finest stores. Then there's the 24-hour convenience stores where the whores buy their coffee and burgers to fuel them up so they can go back on the Track. There's the trick pad, deserted warehouse with sheets separating mattresses, or fleabag hotels that charge by the hour, double if they change the bedding. Maybe some elder of the church really owns the trick pad in his investment portfolio. We got the drugstores doing a booming business in condoms to keep the clap away, then penicillin when the condoms fail. Doctors who do the abortions and fix the clap and stitch the wounds. Taxi drivers who shuttle whores and johns around. Hell, Ben and I got jobs. Nobody wants the whores but everybody profits from them. Except the whores."

"I'm willing to quit if they are," said Ben.

"Hey there!" yelled Willy, his long black finger following a late model Chrysler with Wisconsin license plates as it headed up 14th Street. The knuckles of the man gripping the steering wheel were paler than his white flesh, paler than the blond hair of the woman who sat beside him or the faces of the two children pressed against the rolled-up windows. "You're going the wrong way, tour-ees-ta!" Willy laughed. "I bet those doors are locked tighter than frog's pussy. Nobody happy in that car. Hey mister!" he called out again, though the Caucasian car was now two blocks away, grimly headed from bad to bleak. "Watch out! There's nee-ga-roes loose out here!"

We all laughed. Willy laughed differently.

"I've been in that car," I admitted.

"Me too," said Willy. He laughed again, stroked his black chin. "Me too."

"Either of you ever talk to Janet Armstrong?" I asked.

"Sure," said Ben, "We chatted with her like Sunshine. When she got busted for soliciting, they dropped her by the office so we could take a snapshot of her for our whore book."

"We use her in the spread now," said Willy. "You know, the half dozen photos of ho'es we show citizens who want to press charges against some lady of the evening who done them wrong. Now that she's dead, we know somebody's wrong if they ID her."

"Janet was just like the others," said Ben. "Maybe a little more interesting to talk to. I might have been surprised that someone like her was out here, but I've seen too much before."

"Be fair now," said Willy. "We don't often get Harvard

women working the Stroll for money. Now Harvard men *spending* money . . ."

"Harvard just started taking girls, didn't it?" asked Ben.

"Don't ask me," said Willy. "I never went to college. I'm just an ignorant po-lice."

"We got all types out here," said Ben. "One nurse who found she could make more on the streets than in the operating room. She does it without a pimp—we think. One of the few who does. We got some part-timers, though they usually get themselves into trouble and this kind of life doesn't stay a weekend job very long. Once you step in, you're in. You can buy a class background out here for the same price as a ghetto girl. Democracy. Grant you, poor and bad-educated girls are more likely to be hooked by a pimp or decide, what the hell, fuckin' for money honestly is easier than faking it all the time just to shack up for security under a marriage license."

"Besides," said Willy, "they need love, they can always get themselves a pimp."

I said nothing.

"Ain't life grand?" said Ben.

"You said Magic wasn't any different from other pimps." They nodded. "Janet told her father Magic was writing a book. Did you ever hear . . ."

Ben laughed. "I didn't even know Magic could *read!* A book? Hey partner: how about that?"

"I can see it now," said Willy. "Magic on Johnny Carson, pimping himself on TV to all those folks in Kansas who can't go to sleep."

"Sure he was writing a book," said Ben. "Just like me and you. Only maybe Magic scribbled bullshit on a few pages. A book for a ho'e: he ain't no jive-ass, no-count pimp, he's writing a book!"

"And she gets to be part of it! Hell of a deal," said Willy.

"We got pimps who've done all sorts of things to be . . . more legit, I guess. We've seen formal codes of conduct a pimp printed up all nice and neat for his ho'es. Spelled a few dozen words wrong, but what the hell: written laws equal civilization! We have a price list from a pimp to his ho'e revising rates due to the 'inflationary wage-price spiral.'

Big-time business. They all going to be honorable to the world someday, and the gates of heaven will swing wide because they've suffered so much at the hands of the squares."

"Especially the police," said Willy.

"Yeah, we're a bad-ass lot."

"Mean motherfuckers."

"One player did it. He pimped some publisher in New York. Iceberg Slim. He got himself a real, honest-to-goodness book glorifying a gentleman of leisure—with proper rationalizations and justifications, of course."

"Just like he had himself a string of broken women tagged with lines like, *'I'm sorry we need to do this—it's just for a little while—I love only you—we'll retire rich, baby!'* "

"I guess as long as you get applause for what you are, you aren't bad," said Ben.

"No," said Willy, "what Magic does is pimp. 'Writing' spells 'whoring' for him."

"Is there anybody out here who'd want to help Magic?"

The two cops glanced at each other. I wondered what Nick had told them.

"Help him what?" asked Ben.

"Whatever. I'm fishing for who out here would care enough about what happened to . . . to do anything."

"Nobody," said Ben. "Magic has no friends. No pimp does. Just because they hang together, running their jive and being cool, that means nothing. They're all sharks. They swim together, feed together, but let one of them get bloody and the rest will turn on him."

"There's no percentage for anybody out here to waste any blood, sweat and tears over Magic," said Willy.

"How about Janet?" I asked.

"Nobody besides her family gives a shit," said Ben. "Except you. And Nick Sherman."

"What about her johns?" I asked.

"What about them?" replied Willy.

"Do you know any of them? If any of them were special?"

"They were johns. How special could they be?" said Ben. I said nothing.

"We don't know any," said Willy. "Hell, I bet Janet didn't

know who most of them were, even if they used their real names. She wouldn't care. They were all just another dollar for Magic."

"And I ain't happy about saying it," said Ben, "but Janet was just another whore. Me not being happy about it doesn't make a damn bit of difference. That's what she was, that's what is."

But what was didn't seem enough to me as I drove the Porsche home at 3 A.M. Or maybe it seemed too much. Maybe there wasn't a distinction there worth making.

I followed P Street from the police station to 12th, then took Massachusetts Avenue to the Hill. Just after I crossed 14th I saw Sunshine. She was standing where we'd stopped her hours before, pacing through a few-steps loop on the sidewalk. Star was nowhere to be seen. They'd been on and off that corner all night. Working. That's what was. Sunshine had broken luck. On the Stroll. At 17. Sunshine smiled lamely at the Porsche and the male figure in it as I drove by, didn't recognize me. I saw her working the Stroll off and on for the next two years, and each time I did her eyes were more brittle. In the spring of 1982, Cisco—Star and Sunshine's pimp—died when the stolen Toyota in which he and his two friends fled suburban Maryland police flipped off the interstate and exploded in fire: the trio had terrorized the D.C. area as a roving rape ring for six months and dozens of victims before someone could finger them. Star eventually went with another pimp, stayed on the Stroll. No one ever saw Sunshine again.

22

"How you been?" Martin Mercer's brown eyes darted from me to a flashing light on his desk phone before I could reply. He lifted the receiver, spoke into it: "Yeah? . . . What's his name again? . . . He the L.A. or the A.A.? . . . OK, give me a few seconds, then put him through." Mercer leaned against his cluttered desk top, waved me down to a chair beside it, spoke to me: "This won't take long. Coffee?" I shook my head and he said, "What have you been doing?"

"Keeping busy," I said.

"I hope not with that shit from when we met."

"I have other concerns."

"Glad to . . . Hey, Larry! How you doing? Christ it's been a long time! . . . Yeah, we're busier than hell. Between the volcano and the campaign it's like I'm on fire."

This man who was Senator Woodson's official right hand looked over to the four-foot aquarium running across the bottom of the window box. A dead fish floated there. A dozen others swarm idly beneath it. The tank's air circulator bubbled gently.

"No," he said, "I don't think we're going to have much trouble . . . Not in the primary, and the opposition isn't on his team's presidential bandwagon . . . Let's *hope* he's a token sacrifice! . . . Your turn is coming in two years."

He reached over to the aquarium and picked the dead fish off the water's surface. He turned, still listening to the phone, black angel corpse dangling from his thumb and forefinger grasp. His brown eyes roamed around the C-shaped cubicle office, fixed on a wastepaper basket next to my feet. His arm

170

extended like a crane, held the body over the can for a moment, then opened his grasp: *plap!*

"Your boss put S.807 in the hopper . . . We've been getting mail on it, mostly canned stuff and coupon printouts. Normally we don't pay much attention to the canned stuff but . . . Right, it's that year . . . Pretty much all in favor . . . Just a few perpetual rabble-rousers, the two-dozen-letters-a-year kind . . . We're safe with no time for it to go beyond committee, right? . . . Will he stick it in next year? . . . Un-huh . . . Pretty much the same form? . . . We'll worry about that later . . . Larry, I've read the damn thing, but could you tell me in English what the sucker does and is for and how come and all that good shit?"

Tara's father the senator had a suite of offices in the Russell building on the third floor totally in keeping with his seniority and party's clout—factors which decide almost all the mechanical functions of being a senator, from which office suite he gets to the number and location of his assigned parking places in the street outside the office buildings and the number of public employees he can call his own. Senator Woodson's receptionist hummed as she worked, a wall at her back and a door to either side. A.A. Martin Mercer summoned me through the door to her right five minutes after I arrived. There I met the senator's personal secretary, the stylish, early-40s "Sue" who'd gone from stranger to opponent to ally on the phone, all without a direct word in her carefully controlled voice. She smiled at me from behind her desk parked flush against another door: the room beyond that door would be the inner sanctum, his private office. The senator might have a secret hideaway office in the Capitol itself, but this was where his work was officially done.

This intermediary room between the inner sanctum and the reception area was cut into professional and probably personal turf by two partitions, one giving a woman all of 20 a small open closet to type in where neither she nor Sue could see each other. Beyond them, with its entrance next to the wall so he could lean back in his swivel chair and see anyone going through the senator's private door, was Mercer's lair. I sat behind his plastic wall while he talked on the phone. Mercer's lackey typed a rapid-fire electric chatter. Sue made diplomatic phone calls answering this invitation or that request. The walls were aqua green, a pleasant and probably accidental coordination with the huge aquarium filling the well of Mercer's ten-foot window. I could see the park separating Union Station from the Senate office buildings through those venetian blinds, but the photographs covering Mercer's walls interested me more.

Some camera caught Mercer in a group of expensively suited and visibly serious men banded around former Secretary of State and architect of the Vietnam War Henry Kissinger.

To the left of the Kissinger picture hung photographs of Mercer with the last three presidents: laughing in a huddle at a black-tie reception where it seemed Lyndon Baines Johnson had just made a joke; sitting in a room at the White House while Richard Nixon stood behind a lectern sternly delivering a monologue; walking in a cluster of casually dressed golfers as a smiling Gerald Ford strode across the links of an unidentified country club. And there, at eye level on the wall by the door, was Mercer with the current president, Jimmy Carter—the two of them in shirt sleeves, ties loosened as they pored over papers held in their hands like the other dozen men seated in their circle in yet another White House scene.

There were other pictures: Mercer meeting with the pope at the Vatican, probably on a congressional junket. Mercer at a skeet range, shotgun over one shoulder and smoked black sunglasses covering his brown eyes, ostensibly the companion of the ultraconservative senator standing beside him. Mercer on a platform with the ruling elite of the National Association for the Advancement of Colored People. Mercer snapped one on one with faces I didn't recognize. A dozen pictures of Mercer and senators whose faces would be unfamiliar to the average American: visitors to Mercer's office who mattered *of course* knew the names and ranks of all the creatures hanging on his wall.

The photographs were in color as well as black and white, framed with the standard basic black wood provided by the tax-supported Capitol frame shop. Most of the pictures were signed—perhaps forged by an aide or a machine, but nevertheless signed, usually with some effusive phrase of gratitude for Mercer's existence. The second time I looked over Mercer's glory gallery I noticed that the pictures which were cropped to center him with the person who made the picture important were curiously conspicuous for the absence of Senator Robert Woodson, the man to whom Mercer owed his job, that vehicle of power and prestige that put him in those photographs in the first place.

Are there any pictures of you and Janet Armstrong? I wanted to ask. But not yet. Not until I knew enough to trust his answer. *Someday,* I promised myself. *Someday.*

"Un-huh, I get it," Mercer said into the phone. He used his free hand to shake flakes of food from a box onto the water of his aquarium. A dozen brightly colored fish swam wildly to the surface. "Who came up with this? . . . Who's with them on it? . . . Who will this piss off? . . . You sure only them? . . . Hell, don't worry, then: they're dopes. They don't have enough clout between them to get any good press . . . Who you got for cosponsors? . . . That many, huh? Well, then, you better add us on it too. And send over all your 'Dear Colleague' letters, your endorsement correspondence, *Record* statements, the whole nine yards so we can crank out our letters to let our allies know we're with them 100 percent. Press releases too, that'll help my people writing ours . . . Yeah, no sweat. Let me know what happens. We'll probably go with you on it next year . . . Of course we'll be here . . . And tell your boss that the next time I see him on the Floor I want the $100 he still owes me from the Super Bowl . . . What can I say? He didn't back the winner."

"Sorry," he said after he hung up, "business. You ever seen how a Senate office works?"

"Been a while," I said.

"Come on, I'll show you the *real* Congress."

Each time we met a staff member Mercer went through a fast though warm introduction, as if I were a friend they'd see again. The men and women would raise their eyes from their work, maybe shake my hand or pass a few polite comments to me on Mercer's prompting, then we'd move on. Other than Sue and Mercer, no one on Senator Woodson's staff seemed to be older than 25. The office looked like an on-the-job training program or a summer camp for graduate students with Mercer and Sue as the adult counselors who called the shots.

"This office is our legislative shop," said Mercer after we passed through the reception room door. Half a dozen aides huddled in individual cubicle work areas partitioned off by snazzy red and blue pegboard. Each staffer had a video screen-typewriter combination, a set of file drawers, a desk with a phone and a work area. Staffers pinned postcards, small art prints or photographs of friends, maybe a political cartoon to their walls to personalize the slot where they spent their days. Their slots were open boxes—privacy feigned by design. "Like a precision engine, everything planned for maximum efficiency. There's some spillover between here and the casework section, but these people handle all the constituent inquiries about Congress and the fucked up world.

"The VDT computers revolutionized our work. No more need to traipse back and forth from the file room. We're linked to a computer bank that could handle all the letters and bills Congress has ever seen, connects to everything from the Library of Congress to the *New York Times* morgue. All our standard response letters go in the computer, as well as a summation of all letters we receive, cross-referenced by name, town and topics. Every time somebody visits the office, even if it's only to sign the guest book, they get processed in too, along with a summation of what they wanted.

"Here's how it works." Without bothering to excuse himself Mercer pulled a letter off a woman's desk, took over her work area. She excused herself quietly, vanished in the canyon of partitions. "This guy is writing to say he's a right-to-lifer, abortion stinks and America should reinstitute the death penalty for about a dozen crimes—sucker must have been robbed. Let's pop him up."

Mercer hit some keys. The video screen lit up. He typed a series of code words on the typewriter, saw them flash on the screen. Finally he entered the man's name. Almost immediately a row of green-light electronic words appeared behind the screen's glass, then another row, and another, until seven lines showed on the screen.

"This guy's written before. If he'd met the boss, that would show too." The lines summarized each of the man's previous letters, plus the responses he'd gotten from Woodson. The responses were described by topic, and usually as 'Std. Letter 1 (or 2 or 3).'

"OK," said Mercer, inserting a sheet of Senate letterhead stationery in the typewriter. He flipped another switch. "Now we mix and match him."

Mercer's fingers flew over the keyboard and the machine obeyed, duplicating and displaying his words as electronic lights on the screen:

> DEAR MIKE:
> IT'S GOOD TO HEAR FROM YOU AGAIN.

"Most letters all you need to do is type in the name. The computer already has a programmed friendly greeting. If the person has written more than twice, we automatically use his first name. If he signs his letters Mike instead of Michael, that's covered too. If he's a winner, somebody the boss really knows or somebody who's written favorably more than three times or given us money, we scrawl the guy's name in pen over his scratched-out typed name. All 'Dear Mike' type letters get signed 'Robert.' The others get his full name. Both are on the signature machine. I tried to get him to use 'Bob,' but the guy's too stiff. Probably costs him about 100 votes. He personally sees and signs about 50 letters a day. The rest are all the machines'.

"We've got two standard response letters covering most hot topics. The sympathetic tone is different for each side. And the letters are long: shows careful, reasoned consideration. What we'll do with Mike is program the 'pertinent paragraphs' from a form abortion letter." Mercer tapped a short command into the machine. "Next we'll do the same from our capital punishment letter." The words "Capt. Pun., Pro" appeared beneath "Abortion, Anti." on the screen.

"If the guy were worth it, we'd have other stuff on his computer printout—if he had contributed, palled around with Woodson, jokes they shared over baseball, notes about Mike's brilliant son Todd at Harvard. In five seconds we can summon up every previous contact with us, all without leaving this desk. Every letter we get has a turn-around response time of three working days. If it's one of the 20 percent that can't be answered by a form letter or we need more information, then an interim *'Thanks for your letter I'm working on it and will get back to you as soon as possible'* gets sent. When the full response goes out . . ."

"You plug it into the system."

"Right. We also cross-reference the computer so any time the senator makes a speech, a copy of his remarks with a 'because I know you're interested' letter gets shipped out to everyone who would like whatever he said. If you write us and you're not already on the computer's list, at the bottom of our response is a standard paragraph thanking you for your interest in America's government and asking if you'd mind receiving the senator's weekly newsletter. Not many people take the time to write back and say they don't want it. If they do, we woo them."

"And if they don't," I said, "they keep getting whatever you want them to read about Senator Woodson. But how many people like that actually read those newsletters and send-outs?"

"Doesn't matter if they read them or not. It's the presence that counts: there's Senator Woodson, in their mailbox again, hard at work, always with a little form questionnaire asking you to check what you want him to do. We structure the question choices, of course. Gives us a poll 'bout which way the wind is blowing. That's what we got the government free-mailing frank for."

"Keeping in touch with the constituents."

"You got it. Try to be the opponent dumb enough to attack that system. The incumbent's the hardest battle out there."

"We'll see this year."

"Yeah, well, if the incumbent sets himself up to be a target of a hardball political group or doesn't keep fertilizing his base of support, then he'll be in a whole lot of trouble."

"Doesn't look like Woodson made that mistake."

"No, we didn't," said Mercer. "Now watch." He typed a command onto the screen. After a safety/cancel pause, the typewriter machine-gunned characters onto the blank page. "Two hundred words a minute, letter perfect. All you need to do is be sure the machine gets fed paper. Types the envelopes too. Records its own efforts. Makes us the most efficient office on the Hill."

"Impressive."

"Each of these legislative aides has areas of responsibility —environment, budget, defense, foreign affairs, welfare, social security, whatever. Oddball letters get parceled out. For each of Woodson's committees we've got someone who works with the committee staff. One legislative assistant supervises the whole operation and reports to me."

"You run the show," I said.

"He's the senator." Mercer didn't smile.

"Back here," he said, leading me to the rear office, "is where we keep current files and where our caseworkers sit. They have the same setup as the legislative aides, but they deal with the thousands of *want* letters: I *want* my kid to go to West Point. I *want* my Social Security check delivered on time. I *want* the Bureau of Land Management to stop telling me I can't graze my cattle on public lands. I *want* my garbage picked up on Thursdays instead of Tuesdays. *Gimme, gimme, gimme.* We help everybody, or at least sympathize. For lots of people we're the last chance they have to keep from going down the tubes. A lot of them have been shafted by some stupid bureaucrat safe in his cubbyhole. We're the only place people can go to stop him from turning the screws."

We headed toward the front office.

"Back there they also handle requests like flags and photos and . . ."

"Research for high school term papers," I said.

"You got it. There's a lot of overlap between the legislative and casework shops. If it's something big, like a small businessman having trouble with the SBA or a sugar beet plant that's closing down and taking the only industry from a town, it gets special treatment." He pointed to the wall behind the receptionist. "Back there is the press secretary, who makes sure the media gets our message, handles reporters, writes the press releases and newsletter. He shares that office with a guy we call Oddjob. Oddjob handles everything that falls through the cracks. The sugar beet stuff, that kind of thing. Coordinates with our people in the three state offices

177

back home, with the other offices when it's not in somebody's particular area. Spends his whole damn life on the phone or in meetings."

We passed by Sue's automatic smile. Mercer paused when we reached the senator's inner office door. "This is what it's all for."

The grand room Senator Robert Woodson used as an office seemed colder and lit with a richer, more hued light than the other rooms of his kingdom. The same sun shown through this ten-foot window, but in here it traveled unchecked through the entire room. No partitions blocked its glow from the white splendor of the marble fireplace on the far wall, the huge flat oak desk in front of the window. A leather couch and two leather easy chairs looped around a coffee table made from a redwood stump from Woodson's home state. Beyond the couch on the wall opposite the window was a door leading directly to the outer hallway: senators need a way to dodge anyone waiting in their outer office. This room smelled of leather and new books—in addition to the couch and chairs, leather-bound law books lined the walls in antique bookcases.

The wall with the fireplace mantle was a shrine. No doubt the oil portrait above the fireplace of the short-haired, smiling blond woman had been inspired by a photograph then inflated with awe and flattery by the painter. What I'd heard about her from Tara implied she hadn't been the kind of person to have her portrait painted. Two framed black-and-white snapshots stood sentry to her icon on the otherwise bare white marble mantel. The photo on the left showed a young soldier in combat fatigues and flak jacket, M-16 hanging almost forgotten from his shoulder as he smiled to a friend's camera on the jungle helicopter pad. The second sentry snapshot showed the woman from the portrait holding the hand of a special little girl, a tall not-quite-teenage boy gawky by her side, a much-younger-than-today Robert Woodson nervously obeying her gesture to grab the hand of campaigning presidential candidate Senator John F. Kennedy at an airfield somewhere in America. Tara told me later that Woodson once kept several solo pictures of her around this room, including one on his otherwise somber and pristine desk, but that he complied with her request to remove them from his political facade without understanding her unease. The snapshot of the happy family stayed on the mantle.

"Come on in," said Mercer, closing the door behind us. He walked across the thick maroon carpet, settled himself in the senator's high-back leather swivel chair. Flags of America and Washington state stood on appropriate sides of that throne. He indicated two captain's chairs in front of the desk. "Sit down. I'm glad you called. What did you want to see me about?"

"Why did you set me up for Fred Thomas to hire?"

"Oh, that," he said. He tipped the senatorial chair back, propped one shoe on the desk's mirror surface. "He mentioned that he called you some time ago, but that you hadn't returned his call."

"I've been busy. What made you suggest me to him?"

Mercer shrugged. "We were tough on you when you were just trying to do your job. The boss still feels bad about it. Then I saw you with Tara one noon. Week or so ago, during that cold snap. I knew about your rough luck from the paper. And once when Tara was in here to see her father, we talked about you, your business, how good you'd been to her. When Fred mentioned his firm needed help, I figured why not help *everybody* out by putting the two of you together? No harm in that. The boss likes you. Seems like so does Tara. Seen her recently?"

The night before had been my first night off the Stroll. Tara and I drove to Georgetown, ate in a Vietnamese café, talked until 11. She said she was glad I'd finished that risky bit of business. I drove us home in her Porsche, playing "the game" as we went.

The idea is to never completely stop. We made it fine out of Georgetown, over the parkway to Independence Avenue. Construction just beyond an over-the-road walkway connecting two Department of Agriculture buildings threw my driving rhythm off. I turned left to Constitution Avenue to avoid the red light near the Air and Space Museum, made the Porsche crawl to the top of the Hill where the Capitol glistened like an ivory cathedral in the night. Then I had to floorboard it, hit 45 mph and roar by the Senate office buildings to keep from getting trapped at 1st Street. All of which did me no good, because a block later the light beside the Supreme Court turned red and stayed that way so long I had to stop the rolling silver car or blow through the intersection. Violation isn't part of the game.

Tara laughed, said better luck next time.

We smiled good night to each other at her apartment building. I waited until I saw her get safely inside, then drove away in the Porsche. Tonight we'd catch a Bogart double feature at the Biograph: *The Maltese Falcon* and *The Treasure of the Sierra Madre*. Tomorrow was Saturday night. She was busy. That's where that sentence ended. I'd see her sometime Sunday, unless something came up.

"Yeah," I told Mercer. "I've seen her."

"Hell of a girl, isn't she? I'm glad that bullshit worked out so we can all be friends. You came out of it pretty good, didn't you?"

"What do you mean?"

"Well . . . Without mentioning Tara." His smile was man-to-man sly. "There's Fred Thomas. You going to take him up on his offer?"

"I'm going to listen to it first."

"Smart. And you tracked down why he made the offer. Double smart. You got brains as well as luck."

"Yeah," I said.

23

Independence Day turned our city into a vast sea with marble beaches and a hazy green horizon. Temperature and humidity hovered near 90 degrees. The air was thick with summer—wet grass and sweet flowers. Pollution was mercifully marginal. Time rolled gently around itself, lapped against the shores of morning and midnight on that Fourth of July, 1980.

By midday half a million people drifted on the Mall between the Lincoln Memorial and the Capitol. Many were there for free "classical" entertainment—the Park Service's night fireworks show after the National Symphony's dusk concert; most of them came for the sunshine rock 'n' roll concert by the Beach Boys, balladeers of gentle White Anglo Saxon Protestant fantasies. The Beach Boys recorded the first album I ever bought. In 1983 a right-wing secretary of the interior refused to let them repeat their July 4, 1980, concert because he considered the band dangerously un-American. In 1984 that right-wing apostle had left office, and his presidential mentor interceded with the federal bureaucracy so the band's drowned drummer could be buried at sea. On the Mall that bright day in 1980, standing with many who survived high school before me, were thousands of teenage bodies who swayed and laughed and sang to "Surfer Girl," a Beach Boys song popular before they were born. Tanned flesh showed from halter tops, shorts, T-shirts. There were picnic coolers and Frisbees. The day's sentiment was as warm and wonderful as its sunshine.

By noon I'd drifted to the Mall to meet Tara and Katie:

Mate of Mad Dog, as Joey Malletta called her. I dared put no such possessive on Tara even though we spent most of our waking hours together. It was only time, I told myself. Bittersweet time. The more of it I spent with her, the sooner she'd realize the truth. Redeem us, redeem me. Finding Tara and Katie among half a million faces on the Mall was logically impossible, but logic made no difference then, so I found them. Few things made any difference that day. Vital questions from earlier in the week concerned me not at all: this was Independence Day.

Friday's confidence had been harshly won during the week. Martin Mercer was too much to believe. Perhaps he had no idea I was trying to link him to a dead prostitute, from that bond somehow to the foul on me. Perhaps he and his senator boss were being so solicitous to me because of gratitude. But perhaps not.

After I left Mercer I walked down the hall, ended up at an office I knew well. David Henderson's secretary said he was "at a meeting." I sat behind his desk, pulled a copy of the *Congressional Record* from a pile stacked on the floor, and opened that staple-bound magazine at random for stirring words from the self-proclaimed "world's greatest deliberative body." Congress records its daily ramblings in tiny print on cheap, pale pulp paper. I started at the top of the second of three columns, right below a box score that showed David's boss, my ex-boss Senator Applegate, and Tara's father, Senator Woodson, lined up on the losing side of a roll call vote.

So Mr. MELCHER'S amendment (UP No. 502) was rejected.

Mr. LEAHY. Mr. President, I move to reconsider the vote by which the amendment was rejected.

Mr. DANFORTH. Mr. President, I move to lay that motion on the table.

The motion to lay on the table was agreed to.

UP AMENDMENT NO. 503

Mr. BAUCUS. Mr. President, I send an unprinted amendment to the desk and ask for its immediate consideration.

The PRESIDING OFFICER. Will the Senator suspend?

Will the Chamber please be in order? Will Senators please clear the well?

The amendment will be stated.

Mr. LEAHY. A parliamentary inquiry, Mr. President.

The PRESIDING OFFICER. The Senator will state it.

Mr. LEAHY. Is an amendment appropriate without unanimous consent to my amendment; all time not having been yielded back?

The PRESIDING OFFICER. It is not in order except by unanimous consent.

Mr. LEAHY. Mr. President, I suggest the absence of a quorum.

Mr. BAUCUS. Mr. President, will the Senator withhold his request?

Mr. LEAHY. Yes.

Mr. BAUCUS. Mr. President, this amendment is not addressed to the amendment of the Senator from Vermont. I suggest that it be deferred until the amendment of the Senator is dispensed with.

Mr. LEAHY. Mr. President, I am not necessarily going to object. I just want to know what the amendment is.

Mr. BAUCUS. This amendment, for the Senator's information, addresses a section of the bill which extends section 505 of the 4–R Act for another year.

Mr. LONG. Mr. President, the Senator has discussed this amendment with me. I have not had the opportunity to discuss it with other Senators, but basically, this amendment would make it discretionary with the Department of Transportation———

The PRESIDING OFFICER. The Chair inquires of the Senator from Montana, to what is the amendment being offered?

Mr. BAUCUS. The amendment being offered is an amendment to the 4–R Act portion of the bill. It is not an amendment to Senator LEAHY's amendment.

Mr. LONG. Then the time in opposition would be under the control of the manager.

The PRESIDING OFFICER. Is the amendment to the bill or to the committee substitute?

Mr. BAUCUS. Whatever is appropriate.

Mr. LONG. Mr. President, I would just as soon consider the amendment to the bill. It is in order.

Mr. BAUCUS. Mr. President, the amendment is to add a new section. It is my understanding that it is, therefore, an amendment to the bill.

The PRESIDING OFFICER. The Chair informs the Senator from Montana that his amendment could be offered to the bill, the committee substitute, or the Leahy substitute, but it cannot be done except by unanimous consent at this point, because there is still time outstanding on the Leahy substitute.

Mr. LONG. Mr. President, how much time is outstanding?

The PRESIDING OFFICER. Twenty-nine minutes.

Mr. LONG. I ask unanimous consent that the amendment may be offered at this time.

The PRESIDING OFFICER. Is there objection?

Mr. LEAHY. Reserving the right to object, Mr. President,

how much time will the Senator from Montana consume?

Mr. BAUCUS. No more than 2 minutes.

Mr. LEAHY. Mr. President, I have no objection.

The PRESIDING OFFICER. Without objection, it is so ordered.

The Senator from Montana is recognized.

"This is the real you, Rankin," said David as he came in: "Blue jeans, open shirt, sneakers, sitting at somebody else's desk, rifling their stuff." He glanced at the *Congressional Record*. "But I'm disappointed: not only is that public record, it's damn near a year old. That's the junk pile."

"Figures that it's back here," I said, tossing the *Record* to the stack on the floor.

"Don't you wish they didn't edit it so we could read the *unhs* and *duhs* and other stupid shit they really say?"

"Been busy?" I asked, still not getting up. I didn't want him settling in.

"Two months cutting a deal with the goddamned Business Roundtable types. Gut stuff, trade you this for that. We're all set to hit the Floor, then today they bring in this new guy who wants to show everybody how clever he is. Just after we get it settled that my boss won't object when their guy stands up on the Floor and how they'll guide it through together, this new Mr. Slick has the fuckin' balls to say, 'Well, I assume this means your guy won't do such-and-such'—which is totally unnecessary horseshit but shows everybody at the table he knows one way to queer a deal and is a tough guy."

"What did you do?"

"Got royally pissed off! I leaned forward, said, 'Not only will my guy not do *that*, he won't do this or this or this!' I tick off about six other ways we could screw the deal. 'Where I come from,' I says, 'your word stands for something. When you say you won't, you won't; when you say you will, you will; and we resent anybody implying that we're rats!' The smart guys on his team shut Mr. Slick up and we go on about our business. Now what do you want?"

"What about the deal?"

"Oh, we'll go through with the deal. But I'm pissed off. They already had a run-in with my boss about me. He told them I was twice as reasonable as he was and anything I said went, only I'd need to convince him that they weren't getting too much. I won't take their cheap shit. One way you keep from getting slapped around is to slap back harder. About five phone calls from now everybody everywhere is going to know how Mr. Slick almost blew the whole ball game."

"They won't fire him because of you. You're not big enough or a good enough friend. Fact, they probably . . ."

"They hate my guts, but you need to remind them that doesn't mean they can't treat me right. Or that I can't deliver.

"What do you want from me, Rankin? More shit on Jonestown?"

"How about a couple minutes in your private office?"

He shrugged. We went into the hall. I leaned my back against the wall so I could see who might be able to hear.

"Look," I said, "I want to ask you a question, one of those questions that never got asked and that you don't question. I need your help and I'll owe you big."

"What's this hardball drama, Rankin? Never been your style."

"You ever hear anything about Senator Woodson?"

"Checking out the future father-in-law, Rankin? I saw you two uptown the other night. I never figured you'd chase after her kind."

"What do you mean?"

"Man, I've seen her before, a hundred times: She's one of this year's gorgeous girls. Little high strung and kind of anorexic for my taste, but she makes the cut. The names change, the style is always the same. Sexy. Chic. Always in the know. Always got to be where it's happening, always playing it cool and collected at the edge of the crowd. They don't get dirty. They're a tough act, but that's it. They disappear when they get old, or they turn to stone. Nice diversions, but that's their limit. How'd she hook a smart guy like you?"

"You're wrong about her. She's not one of those kind. She's . . . special."

He shrugged. "Maybe. It was dark. But she's still a kid. You trying the Svengali routine?"

This wasn't what I'd come to him for but I couldn't let it drop. "What do you mean?"

"The get-'em-while-they're-young-and-innocent, shape them how you like, make you the savior of their precious soul . . . and their sweet young body. That lets you play the messiah bit, only it's a whole lot more fun than walking on water."

"She's no innocent," I insisted. "Not like you mean. She's . . . I don't want to shape her into anything. And I'm sure no saint."

"Then what are you? I hear she's got you dangling."

Didn't occur to me to wonder how he'd heard that. I'd been repeatedly failing to resist the compulsion to talk about Tara with everyone I met.

"I love her, David," I told him.

"Jesus, don't give me that shit," he said. "You're no country hick anymore. You're supposed to be beyond folly."

"Why?"

He shook his head. "What's this crap about her father?"

"Could he be . . . could he be crooked?"

"Of course he could! What kind of stupid . . . If you mean have I heard or do I think he is . . . hell, no offense to your dream girl, but her old man is a balloon: pretty, full of hot air, and so lightweight he'd float away if his crew didn't tie him down. Who'd buy him off? Who'd want to, when you can get a real ball cutter?"

"What about his A.A., Martin . . ."

"Martin Mercer. Yeah, I know Martin. We aren't buddies, being as how we have different types of bosses and different attitudes. Don't fuck around with him, John. You know that *I am the toughest son of a bitch in the Valley of Death* poster? That's his life story. 'Course, with a balloon for a boss, somebody has to play heavy or Woodson's political turf will

186

blow away with the volcano. Mercer still can't make his boss more than a lightweight."

"Is Mercer crooked?"

"Who knows, who cares, what difference could it make? I know, I know: it pisses me off and I'd like to see the crooks up here hung and come the revolution we'll wash them all away so we can stick in new crooks."

"Do you know anything about his personal life?"

"You becoming a gossip columnist or what?"

"I just wondered if you knew about him and . . ."

"I know enough to never let him get behind me. Other than that, he's just another public servant. I don't know if he likes little boys or little girls or German shepherds, cheats on his taxes, blows dope, pops pills or drinks too much, and I don't care. He does his job. I may not like it, but he does it good.

"Maybe . . ." his voice softened. "Maybe I don't need as much certainty as you do. It's been a bad day. As far as Mercer being crooked, it's hard to believe in the first place, probably silly in the second, and me not knowing doesn't mean a whole lot in the third. He's too smart to steal. Same goes for Woodson—not the smart part, but he only cares about being a senator. But hell, what do I know about crooked and corruption and all that shit: that's supposed to be your game, Rankin."

He was right.

I went searching for corruption in other men while an unlicensed gun and a felonious portion of a prohibited drug waited in my desk drawer. I broke those laws not from such worthy motives as political conscience or journalistically licensed necessity but because of a hazy concept of personal power and for pure, selfish pleasure. While I was a criminal, I did not judge myself as evil: arrogant, somewhat hypocritical, probably foolish, but not evil.

But in 1980s America there *was* right and wrong, good and evil, with righteousness more often than not being found well within the law. Not always, but far more often than not. There's a basic principle of good and bad beyond the wispy and sometimes hypocritical sentiments of society and its jungle of laws: find the victim, determine who is hurt, how badly, and why, then judge the wrong. We may all be victims of this hard world and our own folly, but evil comes from those who force us to bleed even more.

The most dangerous criminals for a democracy like America in 1980 are those who steal from the democracy itself, those crimes that mangle an easily fouled, humanly flawed system with calculated or even chance cunning beyond the casual abuse its citizens inflict on it every day. The thief steals your wallet and the killer rips your life; the crooked "public servant" steals your country and the political assassin savages your soul.

Political corruption is as complicated to judge as it is dangerous to allow. So much of politics is showmanship, so much of showmanship is structured sham, so many shams are lies of corruption rotten to their core. So many politicians win applause for doing what is ultimately or even immediately wrong. Blending all that into a clean, provable judgment in a world of exploding complexities is an act of cautious faith. I knew better than to concentrate on lofty ideals while I tried to dispel ghosts that might lurk behind Tara's father and his henchman. As they said in Watergate, I needed a smoking gun, or at least a clean whiff of gunsmoke. And I knew where to look.

Once upon a time the eight-story boxlike building at 119 D Street, Northeast, was called the Immigration building and presumably sheltered functionaries who administered part of this nation of immigrants. But Congress has grown since once upon a time. In 1980 Immigration had become the pigpen of Senate buildings: peeling yellow walls, freight elevators, mazelike floors of dingy offices. Immigration housed unglamorous committees like the special committee on hunger and subcommittees given to junior senators as learning toys. Some senators bottled their typing pools in the Immigration building. And on Immigration's eighth floor, safely away from the public tours, is the Office of Public Records.

For years, senators and representatives filed personal

wealth reports. For years, the House of Representatives allowed routine inspection of its members' records by the press and public. For years, the Senate, in its upper-house wisdom and dignity, kept its records secret. After Watergate, the Senate grudgingly voted to open its records. That same era generated disclosure regulations for senior congressional staffers and lobbyists.

Every year Senator Woodson was supposed to file a nine-page income disclosure form covering everything from interest earned to stocks and bonds to real estate transfers to outside income for the preceding year. His 1979 forms had just been filed—right on time.

Forms are as revealing as the person who fills them out. I found no indications that Woodson had lied, though I always wonder when I see a senator reporting that his assets and outside investment income (for equally laudable, anti-conflict of interest reasons) have been bundled into a blind trust. Woodson's filing showed a modest income of $1,000 per month from his blind trust—which didn't mean lawyer Thomas who was listed as manager of the trust hadn't turned the senator's assets into bigger bucks, it just meant that the money was managed so Woodson got only 12 grand a year of it as income.

Woodson made another $11,500 in the "honoraria" category—speeches, all but two of which he gave in this town (a Harvard forum in Boston and a bankers' convention in Los Angeles). He usually got $1,000 plus expenses per speech, though Harvard bought him for $100 plus expenses. The private local lecture circuit was fast, easy and quiet money for a senator. He could show up for a businessman's dinner group like the National Forum, have a few drinks with a bunch of the boys as they bent his ear about this and that—not lobbying, you understand—eat a free dinner, stand behind a lectern and mouth platitudes for half an hour or so to a semisober audience, then pocket his $1,000 and hop in the group's limo for a ride home. Besides the National Forum, Woodson had delighted the National Bankers League, a business group called the Capital Discussion Panel, the National Labor Council, the Construction Alliance and Association, and Pulver/Maronic, Inc., all for $1,000. I wondered who Pulver/Maronic, Inc., was and what they did, but $1,000 meant little: if somebody could buy Woodson for that, then nobody would.

According to his microfilmed forms, Woodson owed a "minor" mortgage on his Virginia estate. Period. Which meant he must have paid off any money he owed on the ranch he listed as his "personal state residence." That deed was part of the blind trust's assets.

I photocopied each page of Woodson's report as it rolled through the microfilm machine, then did the same for Martin Mercer.

Mercer showed up as clean as his boss in the income reports. He made money off his savings account, owed money on a swank co-op apartment he owned on Connecticut Avenue and on his Maserati, reported no other outside income, unusual debts or liabilities.

Nothing, I thought as I counted my slick-papered copies and paid the clerk. She handed me my change and I handed her the signed form I had to fill out in order to look at any Senate records: the persons whose files I examined would get a copy of my request form. I thought about filling out a false name, address and occupation, as do many of the people who use this system: why tell some politician that you've zeroed them? The hell with discretion, I decided. Let it bother Mercer; if Tara's father were upset and called me, I'd play it straight. Under the form's "Reason for Request to Examine Records," I wrote, "curiosity."

The subway took me to the Federal Elections Commission downtown at 14th and K—block and a half from Janet Armstrong's old corner. More money went through the FEC in 1980 than is spent on the Stroll in 100 years.

Every politician running for senator, representative or president files periodic election reports with the FEC listing contributors and expenses. Most candidates form a political action committee, an election committee to receive funds, run their campaign, employ their political staff and volunteers in the great cause. It is to these committees that money is legally given, within broad guidelines for amounts allowable and reporting required. Some of the money used to elect federal officials comes directly from average, ordinary citizens who donate their dollar or two, but most of it comes from other political action committees—PACS—alliances usually based out of business or labor groups or "employees of Acme, Inc." or associations like the plastic surgeons or hard-line political groups from both the right and left. PACS changed American politics: in 1980 their institutional, systematized clout eclipsed the specter of a human power broker, of one man opening his private purse to pull a politician's strings.

In the 1980 election 2,155 PACS gave $60,189,696 to candidates for elected federal office. Sixty million dollars. More than a million dollars for each state in the Union. Add to that $60 million another $14,220,000 spent as "independent expenditures" through a loophole in the election law that allowed them to drop unlimited money as long as they had no organizational ties to the candidate they were supporting or—as was most often the case that year—the candidate they were smearing with massive TV-oriented campaigns. There were other PACS floating around that year who for one reason or another didn't spend any money in that election. Maybe they figured they didn't need to, what with the $74 million already on the line from other PACS, plus the additional individual contributions and the federal matching dollars given to major presidential candidates. In 1980 it seemed like there was a PAC for everyone: there were 1,204 corporate PACS, 297 labor group PACS, 574 "trade, membership and health" PACS, 378 "nonconnected" PACS and 98 more PACS juggled into two other general categories. The PACS spent 42 percent of their money in congressional races like Woodson's.

Everybody—that is, all the PACS—seemed to love Woodson, but then that isn't unusual. PACS will give money to candidates they dislike if he has *any* chance of winning or staying around the political game, just so they won't be caught completely unconnected. The more they like you, the more you get. If one PAC has given you its legal limit, it might secretly arrange a swap with another PAC: your gang gives their gang's buddy bucks in return for them giving you the same. This was July, only mid-campaign, but Woodson was doing fine. I didn't pay much attention to the total given by the FEC for the "Woodson for Washington" committee—catchy slogan. He'd probably used it for years as the basis for his political life. Besides getting some money from most of the major PACS of labor and industry, Woodson cleaned up from the banking PACS (he served on that committee), local construction companies (he was on the D.C. Appropriations Subcommittee), several do-gooder groups and local attorneys who throw $1,000 contributions around congressional campaigns as casually as the average American throws chips around the $2 Las Vegas blackjack table. The lawyers were usually those mirror-image lobbyists who "represented the legal interests" of their clients on Capitol Hill.

But I saw nothing extraordinary in the Woodson for Washington thousands. No pattern of a dozen contributors giving the same amount, the same day, from the same address with a blurred answer in the "occupation" blank on the FEC form. No cadre of "housewives" giving $1,000 contributions so their husband wouldn't need to list his name, title, occupation and principal place of business for the public to see. No unduly surprising contributions from PACS or persons. Nothing at all, but still I Xeroxed everything—more out of habit than reason.

No *reason* for my paranoia about why Woodson and Mercer wanted to be my friends, no links to Janet Armstrong or any other mystery in my life. They're modern American politicians, I told myself, they want to be everybody's friend. They were worried you were pissed off. Nonentity that I was, I had connections: to my ex-boss and their current Senate colleague Applegate; more importantly, to my other ex-boss, the 1,000-newspaper syndicated muckraker Ned Johnson. They knew that much, and in Washington, the assumption is you are more connected than anyone knows. Besides, there was Tara: Woodson probably loved his daughter, and his daughter . . .

And his daughter. I smiled at her as she, Katie and I walked through the crowd that Fourth of July, headed to Joey Malletta's block party where we'd meet Mad Dog. *And his daughter*. She'd also seen no reason why I shouldn't take her father's lawyer up on his offer, so I had, getting half a dozen legal legwork chores that a first-year law student would have done for $7.50 an hour instead of my $30. I hushed my paranoia, took the work and glad of it: mine is not a lucrative profession. I still hadn't figured out what to do with Eddie Hampton's $1,000. But never mind. This was summer, the Fourth of July. I had no room for worry. I had Tara.

We heard the band long before emerging from the kitchen door connecting Joey's house to a T-shaped alley courtyard that ran half the length of his block. Dog had been waiting for us—well, waiting for Katie and we who happened to be with her. I didn't watch as they giggled and embraced. Didn't watch them or Tara. Joey sauntered up to us, beer in hand, as we stepped into the courtyard.

"Mad Dog and company!" he nodded exaggerated graciousness. "The day is complete. Even The Hammer of Justice is here."

Tara looked at me, but I shook my head, smiled and waved to a six-foot-two, dark and intensely Jewish man in blue jeans and sports shirt who shuffled nervously beside a garage. He nodded back as I spoke.

"Not me," I said, "him, Ken Goldstein."

"Why The Hammer of Justice?" Tara asked as we walked further into the alley's sunshine. Tables covered with food dishes, hot dog and hamburger buns, waited to our left behind three houses. The five-member band set up at the far end of the alley started another song. The hard-edged woman singing lead wore a tie-around blouse and shorts. She slapped a tambourine against her uncovered thigh. Burned-hamburger and roasting-chicken smoke drifted our way from barbecues sizzling to our right. A volleyball net hung across the wide mouth of the courtyard's alley entrance. Two girls and a boy, all about six, giggled and chased each other beneath its web.

"Joey named him that last year. The Hammer is an attorney for the Federal Communications Commission. One day he was going through some routine documents and he noticed that AT&T earned $100 million more than it was supposed to that year—in effect, overcharged its customers. The company wasn't lying or hiding anything. They reported it, just like they were supposed to, for the FCC to adjudicate.

"Which meant nothing would have been done. But then struck Ken, The Hammer of Justice. He bullied and beat the $100 million question all the way from the bowels of the bureaucracy to the official attention of the politically appointed commissioners who pass judgment on whatever they can't avoid while they're in office."

"And?"

"And nothing. Well, not officially nothing, but in reality nothing. At least so far. The commission issued an official ICC notice asking for public comment as to what should happen. AT&T, consumer groups, all sorts of people responded. The Hammer bets the current commission will keep the comment time open as long as they can, stalling a decision until most of them leave office. The guys who come behind them may do the same."

"What about the $100 million?"

"Well, eventually, if AT&T has to somehow pay it back, they'll also probably pay an interest penalty. But I'm betting it will be simple interest, say 7 percent. They should be able to earn twice that from the $100 million while they hold it. Maybe more."

"That's . . ."

"That's why we call him The Hammer of Justice," I told her. "Without him, nobody would have done anything."

"What are you guys doing this weekend?" Mad Dog asked me. I glanced at Tara. She answered: "Movies."

"Henry Fonda in *Grapes of Wrath* at the Kennedy Center tomorrow night," I said. "*Taxi Driver* rerunning at the Circle on Monday."

"I never saw *Taxi Driver*," said Katie.

"Robert DeNiro plays a psycho New York cab driver who wants to shoot a presidential candidate, flubs that but ends up rescuing Jodie Foster who plays a teenage whore. It's like life: the connections are vague, the whys are twisted, but it works and is real as hell."

"You've been spending a suspicious amount of time on prostitutes lately," Dog laughed.

I shrugged. "It's the work I do."

"Tara!" called Katie. She giggled. With her white blond

hair and easy laugh 27-year-old Katie played at being a little girl without offending your intelligence. "Look at this!"

Tara joined Katie at a table, laughed over something I couldn't see. As I watched her walk away I felt Dog's eyes on me.

"Don't worry," he said. "You'll win. You have to."

"I know," I said.

Someone called his name. He hesitated, then grabbed an offered hand: wedding congratulations, no doubt. I drifted to the middle of the courtyard, sliding through almost 100 people. I shared acquaintanceship with many of them, friendship with a few, a generational kinship with most of them. In 1980 we were largely between the quarter-century mark and forty's hump, the baby boom generation, defined by the 10,000 days of the Vietnam War and spawned by its biggest predecessor. The bomb counted too, although we were only the first children to live beneath it. The oldest of us were the first to reach for John Kennedy's "torch [that] has been passed." The youngest qualified with special dues of conscience or circumstance, like Tara, who'd helped her mother's political crusades (and her father's career) and lost a brother to 'Nam. Besides *us* there were maybe two dozen "middle aged" adults of 50 or more milling in the crowd, one gray haired grandmother of 70-some smiling from a lawn chair by the plates of burned chicken, a dozen fresh-faced "kids" who shared Tara's age—but not, I'd decided, her generational bond. It was *us* who celebrated Independence Day in that alley in 1980, the core ones some small minded media power once absurdly lumped together as "the Woodstock generation" after a historical rock extravaganza.

Suddenly it seemed natural that Mad Dog was getting married. America created adolescence when it took children out of the sweatshops and kept them in school; made "youth" a universal class with college days common and not just a plaything of the lucky and rich. The baby boom poured bodies into this new social slot. We grew up as a new class. In 1980 we had all unavoidably graduated. I thought of the bomb man in his numbered fishbowl. We weren't kids anymore. Some of us survived and prospered as holdouts against what our parents considered adulthood: family, 20-year career plans. For some, like Saul and me, part of that was trappings, part of it was true. Looking around, I realized we were all someplace new.

Everywhere were couples with wedding bands, some sporting their second set. A few of the "singles" showed a white-flesh band on a finger not long before encircled by gold. There were children, dozens of them, not just babies but *children*—laughing and screaming and playing amidst *adults* while the band labored its way through a new-wave rock song.

There stood a longtime source of mine, one of Bobby Kennedy's '60s rebels, talking to his teenage son. It was that long ago. So many of my friends were bald, converting to athletics like jogging or squash or weight training or "aerobic dancing" to avoid ugliness and old age. So many of them seriously discussed mortgage rates and real estate. So many of them talked about "mid-career changes" like "going back to law school." Especially the women, who were flocking to law schools as if such factories could somehow manufacture whatever they'd found lacking in the world before they "went back."

There were picnic tables of cooked food, pot luck dishes where once we'd been lucky to produce beer and fresh potato chips. Once so many of us had laughed at the stuffy Georgetown parties where the ancient and established primly socialized over hors d'oeuvres and white wine. "They" wore suits and dresses as they ate dinner the caterers served. Now most of us had been to such Georgetown parties or embassy receptions; some of us hosted them.

All around me I still saw blue jeans, our class uniform. But they were fresh, weekend worn; some of them now bore a chic designer's name over what in years past had been only a pocket. I saw Gucci loafers and sneakers that like mine cost a small fortune. Many of the women wore makeup, earrings, gold chain jewelry. Hairdos. There were sun dresses and sandals, and the scent of expensive perfume drifted over the food. This was fashion, not the casual conforming styles of *youth*. People here had titles and positions of trust and authority once held by those who gave us our first angers and opportunities. On the faces of a few of the "young people" spending their first postcollege "professional" summer in D.C. was that same cocky, nervous-awe smile I remembered on our faces from what now seemed a frighteningly long time ago.

The band ground to a merciful pause. The female lead shook her tambourine in sarcasm, looked at the stringy-haired guitar player, smiled. I wondered if they were stoned. I'd seen an occasional cluster of two to five people discreetly disappear into a house, emerge ten minutes later smiling and smart and coughing. The woman singer tipped the microphone toward her.

"Ah, thanks for the wild round of applause, folks. Some of you may not know it . . ."

"And most of you may not care," boomed the guitar player.

". . . but Ringo Starr today announced that he's gonna marry or has married or some such goddamned thing this actress named Barbara Bach . . ."

The guitar player leered as the woman continued.

". . . so we thought we'd sing a song to honor them that was written by his two ex-Beatle buddies, John Lennon and Paul McCartney."

She started to beat out time but the band wasn't ready; started again. The guitar player twanged his opening chords, took over lead singing as they hacked their way through "Drive My Car."

I wondered if Tara were listening.

Nobody but me seemed to notice when the song ended. The guitar player caught my eye, shrugged as he exchanged that instrument for an accordion. He lightly ran his fingers over the squeezebox's keyboard, pumped it a few times with low warm-up notes while his female partner addressed the uncaring crowd.

"OK, well, so much for sentiment. We, ah . . . this is the Fourth of July, as you all know, at least, I guess you all know. Can't tell, really, what you guys know and what you don't but hey, never mind that. We tried to think of a patriotic song we knew that we could sing for you . . ."

"We failed!" interrupted the now-accordion player.

". . . seeing as how it is Independence Day," continued the woman. "The only thing we came up with that was halfway appropriate was a song called 'Sandy: Fourth of July, Asbury Park' by . . ."

"Dog!" I turned and yelled and he was moving toward me, listening now to the band as she continued. Dog was by my side, standing deep in the moment before she finished saying "Bruce Springsteen." Her partner coaxed plaintive melody out of the accordion while she joined the band in a slow-beat ballad about a man at his crossroads.

"Happy Independence Day, Dog," I whispered under the music. "You won." He shuffled, smiled.

I glanced behind us in time to catch Tara motioning for Katie to look at us. They both smiled, two blondes in sunlight, and I thought my heart stopped. The band sang far off key. We didn't care. Later in darkness I'd drop Tara off outside her apartment after the party's pilgrimage to see Uncle Sam's fireworks burst over the Capitol dome. A little drunk, we talked about tomorrow, fell into silence. A moment, two, then she touched my hand and was gone and I knew my heart still beat. Her Porsche took me home. Midnight found me staring out the tower window of my empty apartment, Springsteen on my stereo wailing that same damn crossroads song.

24

Summer is seldom sweet in this city. Outside the dark Holiday Inn bar where I waited the temperature hovered at 103 degrees. The afternoon air dared you to breathe its blend of carbon monoxide and jungle rot. Wise and lucky bodies shuffled from air-conditioned building to air-conditioned building; wise and lucky souls sought a languid pace. I wondered what it was like in Detroit, where the Republican party faithful were saving the world at their presidential nominating convention. The Democratic extravaganza was scheduled for later that season. That Wednesday another member of Congress had been indicted for ABSCAM, and a California cultist was in trouble for hiding a rattlesnake in his rival's mailbox.

Nick Sherman suggested meeting at this bar: "a neutral zone" where we'd all feel more comfortable.

Betsy Kranz didn't look glamorous enough to have been a whore. She belonged behind the counter of a franchised donut shop on any seedy strip in America. At 25, a sagging gut stretched her white blouse and a broad-beam bottom threatened to burst her blue slacks. Her hamlike thighs rubbed together when she walked; the slacks made a *zuzzing* sound. Before Nick had a chance to introduce us she plopped down at the corner table where I waited, brushed the stringy brown hair away from her pale face, lit a cigarette and put two packs in front of her. Small brown eyes waited behind her cheap glasses. They were just eyes, empty of everything but life. A few pimples dotted her plump cheeks. Nick told me she'd been brought back to D.C. from California by subpoena for the grand jury to talk about her younger days when she, like dead Janet Armstrong, had worked for a pimp named Herbert "Magic" Murphy. Nick convinced her to talk to me too. He said she was going straight; didn't smile when he told me.

"Look, Betsy," he said as the waitress brought us beer, "we've been through this before, but I'm going to take you through it again for John—OK?"

She shrugged.

"When and where did you meet Magic?" asked the cop.

She'd told this story so often her voice had lost most of its emotion. Like a well-trained dog, she needed little prompting.

"After I dropped out of high school, I, you know, like, I hitchhiked from Santa Monica to here. Back then I was into traveling between California and D.C. I was fat, had short hair. I had no friends, except my girlfriend here."

"How old were you?" asked Nick.

"Twenty-one. I went to a bar called Baghdad. We drove by it on the way here, and now it's got a different name. I forget what."

"Doesn't matter," I said.

"I was standing at the bar, and there was this one guy standing behind the other . . ." She gestured vaguely with her cigarette to reference points that made sense only to her. "That guy asked my name, so I told him. Over his shoulder I saw Magic smile and I asked him why, which started us talking. He told me he was a pimp. I'd never met a pimp before. He was so cool. That was when I wanted to be a great dancer, and he could really—I mean really—dance. We went to the Presidential Hotel, room 442, and we made love for hours. It really impressed me that he'd make love to an overweight girl." She smiled, apologized: "I used to look better. Anyway, the next morning I moved out of my girlfriend's house and moved in with Magic and Chris."

"Chris was Magic's longtime . . ." I groped for a word.

"She was his bottom lady," said Betsy. Like a bureaucrat, she automatically expected me to know that peculiar language of her small and specialized world.

200

"Magic said he was helping support Chris's sick mother in New York or Philadelphia, I forget which. He said Chris couldn't marry him because she was still married to her first husband, and besides, she meant nothing to him. If things went right, he said we wouldn't need to worry about her. When I met Chris, she fed me that stuff too. That morning the three of us sat around her apartment and talked about my never having been out on the street before."

And other trivia, I thought.

"Chris turned me out. For the first two weeks she stayed with me all the time, made sure I didn't get hurt, that none of the girls beat me up. Magic would drop us off at the Track, pick us up later. Her quota was $100, mine was $200. He promised me that in a year we would have a ton of money saved up to open a business. I could go back to school, take up my dancing, not have to worry. A disco, a bar, a massage parlor, whatever. Something so we could fix up our money so the tax people wouldn't give us shit."

She lit another cigarette, followed Nick's nod to continue.

"We'd get to the Track about seven. Magic would stick around for a while, then go look for other girls or gamble. When we made our quota and it was still early, he kept us out there anyway. He bought us things when we did good. When we had a bad night he sent us out early the next day.

"At first he let me take anything, just as long as they paid. I was making crazy mistakes, getting hurt, so he told me to take only $40 and $50 tricks. I never had the guts to keep any money back, because he'd told me I'd die if I did."

"Talk about that time Chris went to Baltimore," said Nick.

"Oh yeah. Magic sent her there to try to pull some new girls. She stayed with this guy, and Magic got real mad since she was giving up free stuff. He called her back. I was at the apartment, getting ready to go to work, when they got back from Union train station. He walks by me when they come inside, gives me this funny look and gestures. I followed them back into the apartment and saw him beating her up. He said not to interfere or I'd get the same. He made me watch when he put on those black gloves. He kept backhanding her, calling her names. When she fell on the floor, he kicked her.

Tore her clothes off and told her how unfaithful she'd been. He had this crazy look. Drooled. Like a mad gorilla. He threw her on the bed and . . ."

She looked for a proper word, found what she had.

". . . and had sex with her in the anal area. That hurt her a lot, because she already had a bad back from other beatings.

"I told Magic I didn't want to be treated that way. That if he ever beat me, I'd leave. A week later I got my first beating."

She leaned forward through the fog of her cigarettes to explain herself.

"It really wasn't a beating. He wanted me to go to work, I was tired. I got out of bed mad. As I went into the kitchen I slammed my brush down on the table. He jumped up from the couch, slapped me a couple times. I was so scared I wet my pants. I screamed for the police. He got madder, said, 'Oh, you trying to turn me in!' Slapped me a couple more times, laughed and called me names, made fun of me because I peed on the floor. Then he made love to me. That anal sex way. That was the first time I'd ever been treated so rough. After he made love to me he said I was such a whore that was the only way I could come. I felt rotten. When he and Chris were in a good mood they used to tease me about this time.

"I got my first real beating a couple weeks later. I had the clap and told him I wanted to leave. He hit me while I was sitting at the kitchen table. He hit me so hard it knocked me from the chair to the floor. He slammed his foot down on my back and when I turned to look at him he was putting the gloves on. He'd kick me, then pull me up by my clothes and hair, backhand me. He hurt his little finger and that made him madder. I was cooking a pie in the oven. He dumped it on my back and rubbed the hot pie into my skin. I think this was the beating where I got this scar on my cheek when my tooth cut through, but I'm not sure. He beat me until he got tired. After he calmed down he made me sleep with him because he was afraid I'd run away."

"Did he beat people often?" asked Nick.

"I saw him beat Chris another time, using his gloves and this belt with one of those Western buckles. I don't know what she did wrong. She left him for a while, but came back. She did that a lot.

"I ran away too, but when I got to Indiana I was run down to empty. I was too ashamed to call my parents. I called Magic for help. He drove out in his Cadillac, brought me home."

"Then?" I asked. I needn't have bothered, she paused only to light another cigarette. She'd relive her tale of woe with little prompting.

"Then I went back to the street for him. Then I got the herpes. The doctor told me I needed two months' rest with no sex. Since Magic and Chris depended on me and I was the only one making big money, I had to work. That meant I had to do that anal sex stuff and give blow jobs. Magic still got upset, beat me. I couldn't get rid of the herpes and needed rest. I left him because he beat me again, this time in front of the White House. Two nights later a trick gave me bus fare and drove me to Baltimore so Magic couldn't catch me. I got to Arizona.

"I stayed there about a week with some cousins. But I couldn't stand on my own two feet.

"Hell," she said, leaning closer to me again, "I was still in love with Magic. I called him, he sent me a plane ticket.

"When I got back I worked the Track. I had a temperature of 104. Turned out I had the clap again. Hurt so bad I screamed every time the doctors touched me. They said I was gonna have a nervous breakdown. Magic thought I was so cute, crying and all, that when he took me home from the hospital he fucked me. Then he let me have about two days off. Chris run off again, and he needed money, so he put me back on the Track. That was when I saw he didn't love me."

How could you have been so wrong so long? I wondered, but didn't ask. Instead, I said, "Did you ever meet Janet Armstrong?"

She nodded, showed some pique: Betsy knew her story didn't matter, but at least she got to tell it and tell it *first*.

"I'd run away again for six months," said Betsy, "but had nowhere to go. So I came back. It was near my birthday. Magic was giving *her* a birthday party at the Athena disco. He invited me and another girl and some guy named Harry. We all went to Janet's apartment on Church Street. Magic took me into the bathroom, called me his whore, told me I was a piece of shit and belonged to him. He acted crazy. He let Janet take Harry into her bedroom and make love to him. He was trying to prove it didn't matter to him that she was giving it to a good-looking man for free. He told me that if I came back to him I could make love to anyone I wanted. I got out of there. Later I took a job dancing in a topless club not far from the Stroll.

"This January I ran into one of the oldest girls on the street—Misty. She asked me how Magic was. I told her how should I know, I don't go with him no more. Then she said, 'Well, have you heard what happened? Do you remember Crystal?' I said, 'You mean the pretty girl that left college to go with Magic?' She said yes, and that Crystal had been found cut up dead in front of Magic's place. I said, 'So Magic has finally killed somebody.' I told Misty that if a trick had killed her, a trick would have tried to hide her. Besides, she was good to her tricks. And Magic sure as shit would have killed her if she tried to leave, which she probably had. Magic went crazy sometimes. I knew all about that. She said Chris had stuck with Magic until the police grabbed him, then she took off too.

"Me, I went back home a couple days later. I would have stayed there too, if . . . if I hadn't wanted to come back and help with the police and grand jury and all."

And if you hadn't been subpoenaed, flown out here by the government, I thought. "Did you ever talk with Janet?" I asked.

"Not really," said Betsy, ending any hope I had of asking about a john named Martin. "I just saw her that one time. She was too busy for me. It was her birthday party."

Betsy ground out her cigarette in the crowded ashtray.

"Did Magic ever promise you anything special?" I asked.

"Oh yeah. He kept telling me he would marry me, but he never did. He wanted to get me pregnant, because that way he'd have a better hold on me. Whenever I ran away he said he couldn't live without me. Promised that soon I wouldn't need to turn tricks, that he'd get other women to work for us, which was why he was always after them—he said. I told him that if he got married he was not supposed to have other women. Magic told me that I couldn't expect him to give up his way of life, because he was a pimp and a man."

"Did Magic ever send you after other women?" Sherman asked.

"He wanted us to pull other girls. Chris went to Baltimore that one time, but she quit that, told him that was his job."

Nick leaned toward her. "Explain how Magic beat women up."

"You mean a real beating up," said Betsy, "or just a little knock-around?"

"Was there a difference?" I asked.

"Sure. If he just blew off, you know, over some little thing you done wrong, or if he didn't have time or if it might be in public like that time in front of the White House, he'd just slap you a couple. He was careful never to hit too hard because of that time he hurt his finger.

"If it was real important, over something major and he had you boxed in, he put on his gloves and beat you up good and proper. I saw him do that with Chris, and he did it with me a few times."

"Tell us about the gloves," said Nick.

"They were beautiful, all smooth and shiny and black, very thin leather. Dress gloves. Special. He wore a regular pair for winter. He wore those to protect his hands. He always bragged about being a great guitar player, though I only heard him play once when he stored some hot stuff for a guy. It didn't sound like much to me, but Magic said the amplifier was bad. He said he was more than good enough for my dancing. He kept them gloves folded in his back pants pocket. He didn't want to dirty or bruise his hands if he had to do something. He only wore them for special occasions. He'd say, 'Please don't you go making me have to work the gloves.' He never wanted to hurt us with his flesh on ours because he loved us too much. That's why he needed the gloves. Because of us. But he loved to put them on. Once I saw him kind of stroking them, like a woman. Or a dog."

"What happened after he put the gloves on?" asked Nick.

"He beat the hell out of you."

"How . . . How did that go?" Nick asked, and I didn't know why.

"He would jerk you up, start hitting you, backhanding you. If you fell he put the boots to you. The beating went from room to room. He would rip your clothes naked. My glasses always fell off."

"Do you remember any big scenes when Magic lost control?"

"Well, there was that time in Georgetown."

"John doesn't know about that," said Nick.

"OK," she said. "We—him and me and Chris—were in that Athena disco and he got mad at this woman over something like sitting in his chair or a drink or something, so he took out his thing . . ."

"His thing?" I asked.

"You know, his thing."

I shook my head.

"His penis!" she said, exasperated at my foolishness. "He took it out and shook it at her and everybody yelled a lot."

"Other than that," said Nick, "did Magic ever do anything weird?"

She frowned, shook her head. "No, not that I can think of."

"Did he ever make you take drugs?" asked the cop.

"He made me take acid three times. He gave me a drink every time I went out to work. He would get some dope to smoke when I got home. A couple times there was coke around, but he usually kept that for himself."

"Betsy," I said, "can you think of anyone who wouldn't want the truth about Janet to come out?"

"What truth?" she said, looked from me to Nick, back again. "Everybody knows all about her."

"Do you know anything else, do you . . ." I groped for the right words. "Is there anything else you can tell us?"

She shrugged matter-of-factly: "No, should there be?"

We were drunk.

Well, I was drunk and Nick Sherman was drinking. All night long he'd matched me, bourbon for beer. We'd walked Betsy to her room, climbed in Nick's ancient Chevy and plowed our way through the evening heat. Now we were in a two-story blue box building at the base of Capitol Hill. The blue metal letters "FOP" hung above the locked door: Fraternal Order of Police, the cop clubhouse. Inside was a standard bar, a small dance floor with a few tables, booths. Framed replicas of 50 or more police badges covered the walls. The clientele was male, white. Hard. Half a dozen men sat at the bar, one table besides ours was full. Everyone checked us out when Nick used his key to open the door. He rated several nods and smiles. I rated suspicion, but I was his guest. He told me he'd get the drinks; I asked for a beer and he came back bearing a pitcher. The barmaid with huge breasts walked over a large bourbon for him. She brought him fresh ones all night long without him so much as nodding his head. "She knows me," Nick explained. Now he was upstairs in the bathroom and I sat staring into a plastic mug of golden brew.

The woman Betsy met called Chris—Magic's bottom lady —had talked to the law too. As I waited for Nick, I remembered her statements from files I wasn't supposed to have.

Chris claimed to have been with Magic longer than anybody. She had contempt for the other women who drifted in and out of their lives, and denied any wrongdoing such as drug use by Magic even as she bragged about being his whore.

Of Betsy Kranz, Chris said, "Magic told me he went to a club, saw her dancing in hot pants, invited her for a drink and slept with her and she was with him. Just as simple as that, that's how it's done. She fell in love with him."

Chris was older and black, factors she regarded in economic terms: "You know the white girls are always going to make the most money, that's just the way it is."

She remembered when Magic brought Janet back from Oregon:

"He was gone and then they both came back. Magic is a sex maniac and he wants his sex every night. You know when you are out there in the street and screwing all the time to make money, you don't want to have to come home and screw some more. You just want to get in a hot tub and relax. But Magic

207

wanted to screw all the time. Some women leave home 'cause they don't get enough. I left home because I needed a rest. I was getting pains. That's how he got all his women, 'cause he could last a long time. Janet already knew about me from Magic talking in his sleep. When they came back it was me who suggested keeping separate places. A man wants to have all his women together so he can feel like a king, but that makes trouble. I guess Janet felt I was living apart just to spite her. But she never did like me, because until he came back here she had him to herself."

In the story Chris spun, her wonderful Magic found Janet a jealous woman, one who grumbled when Magic spent time with others—that is, spent time with Chris. Janet's best quality as far as Chris was concerned was her ability to make big money fast. She usually netted her quota by 3 A.M. Early and easy hours.

Chris told of Magic's remorse when she met him at the hospital just before dawn after he "rescued" Janet from a lonely death in darkness:

"That was the first time I ever seen him cry. We sat there in the waiting room, all them people and nurses and police around. Magic would not have told me if he was in love with her, just like he would not have told her he loved me. I know he cared for her, 'cause she was for him and she loved him."

Magic's affection for the other woman, Chris explained, stemmed from her own absences. She spoke nonchalantly of being beaten. The closest she came to criticizing her man was to say, "He always had a violent side and wanted his way. He told me that he loved me because he couldn't break me. I was the only black woman he ever had. He always been around white women, went to white school, dated white girls. They just fall all over him. That's what made me so special, that I was black and was with him. That's what he said."

And, of course, Magic didn't lie, Magic didn't kill Janet.

The grand jury file included a statement from another prostitute, another woman Magic acquired in a disco. One thread ran through her story that troubled me more than anything else I'd learned. The morning after Magic seduced the girl, *Janet* had been the one to pick her up, drive her to the Church Street apartment. *Janet* took her to dinner. *Janet* explained the intricacies of prostitution to her. *Janet* chaperoned her on the Stroll the first night while the girl only watched. *Janet* tricked with her and two johns in a hotel the next night. The third night this new girl was arrested. *Janet* was the one who met her in court the next day. On the fourth night the girl was raped. On the fifth night she left, despite Magic's pleas of affection and promises of introductions to influential people who could enhance her modeling career.

Janet "helped" her. What could I tell my client who waited in Eugene, Oregon, that mellow town with a sparkling river running through it and everything green all around? Your daughter served a man who drooled like a rabid gorilla and wore beautiful gloves while he beat and debased his slaves? What happened to the little girl who always put her piano books away, waited for her cousin the teacher to bring milk and cookies?

"You look lost," said Nick as he sat down. He didn't seem even a little drunk.

"I'm chasing spirits," I told him. "Ghosts. That's all I seem to do, and I can't figure out how to catch them."

"You mean with Janet?"

"Yeah," I answered, "sure. Janet Armstrong. I guess that's the ghost's name."

"You aren't running after Eddie Hampton, are you?"

"No—should I be?"

He shrugged. "You tell me, cowboy."

"He's just somebody else who died," I said. "Happens all the time."

"And he still don't mean nothing to you?"

Maybe then I should have told him the whole truth, all the whats and whys and what ifs, how I'd handled that letter from a dead man and where I'd found myself. About Martin M. and who he might be. But protecting my vision of Tara was all important. That night my heart told me to be careful with the truth so it wouldn't get bruised or misunderstood.

"You found me stuck in his vest pocket, and that makes me unhappy as hell. But I've got enough ghosts around me. I'm through with him. What about you?"

"The investigation is proceeding."

"What the hell does that mean?"

"It means if we knew what to do, we'd do it. It means we know he's dead and a whole lot of trivia about that, but that's it. Eddie Hampton is somebody else who got murdered. Like you said, happens all the time. So do muggings."

"Yeah. *The investigation is proceeding.* And my only ideas are turning out to be dead ends."

"You sure?"

I shrugged. "Sure as I can be."

"You still going to work the Armstrong stuff?"

"You mean now that I've concluded it's not the answer to my questions about who hit me and why? Hell, I guess I'm not important enough for anybody but muggers to notice. Janet . . . She won't give me my answers, but she's got me hooked on her questions. How could anybody be so damn smart and end up such a dumb victim?"

"You talking about her or you?"

I laughed. "Sometimes I'm not sure. Sometimes I think I understand her right down to her core. The more I chase her, the closer we seem. Makes my flesh crawl, but I can't stop. Not yet. Not until . . . Not until I know who's who."

We each took a long drink.

"How could I get anybody to believe all this?" I asked.

"Best you can do is tell them," he said. "I gave up trying to make people believe a long time ago. They do or they don't, or maybe they figure it out better than you. Once you tell them, ain't nothing left for you to do.

"You figure out the big 'why' to tell her father yet?"

"Seems like all I'm doing these days is asking why, and I'm not getting any answers."

"You're moaning like you think you got troubles," said the cop.

Didn't matter about his tone right then; didn't make any difference that I needed to beware the dangerous ears of the law. The wonder is that I hadn't launched into stories of Tara and me before. As long as I didn't let him link her to that inconsequential ghost named Eddie Hampton, or mention any Martin M.'s, there'd be no problem. I rambled on for maybe 15 minutes about being the right man at the wrong time, about how she was stuck, about how right we were for each other. All that blood and guts that looks so silly in print.

"If I had a dime for every time I heard a story like yours in this bar, I could buy the whole jukebox," he said as the barmaid walked a bourbon toward us. His eyes followed the tremorous bounce of her breasts. He sighed after she left the drink, walked away. "You sound like a country and western song."

"Country and western isn't my style," I told him. I tried to sneer, but too much beer made me drool instead.

He laughed. "Everybody's got a song on the country charts. Sometimes I think the only things you can count on besides your own dumbness are . . ."

I waited expectantly while he double-checked his reasoning.

"Baseball and country and western music," he finally said. "They're more certain than the old standards: the rich never pay taxes and true believers cheat death."

"A gangster fixed the World Series in 1919."

"Before my time," he said. He squinted, and that chipped-tooth grin turned serious. "You really got it bad, don't you?"

"You're a great detective."

"How come?"

"You mean 'why'?" I grinned at my own cleverness. "I can give you a million words: fate, free will, circumstance, kismet, I've looked them all up and I'm living them all out. Every time I come up with an answer, I come up with a question and none of it changes a thing. Nothing to do, 'cept to keep on pushing because it's bound to work out right."

"You mean work out like you want it to. You're like a junkie, giving yourself the needle."

"I didn't give myself this needle."

"Don't be so sure."

"Look," I said, "you just don't understand. It's complex, complicated, it's . . ."

"I learned something a long time ago," he interrupted: "The more complex and complicated it is between a man and a woman, the more likely they are to be messing with their complications instead of their real lives."

"If this were any more real, I'd be dead."

"And that would prove how sincere and true and real all this stuff is, right? That would prove only that you were dead.

"I can't understand you, Rankin. You're not a walking fool, but you're acting like one. You've put your life in the clouds. You talk about this Tara woman like she's an angel. You better deal with her like she's flesh, not fantasy."

I stared at him as if he were a Martian.

"Can't you figure anything out from what we've been doing?" he said. "We're talking about love, and what is, is; what ain't, ain't."

And I got pissed off. "You sure know a whole lot about love for somebody who spends his days dealing with hate!"

"I've been both places," he said.

"Really?" I said, oh-so-smart. "Let's hear your country and western song. You live by yourself. What do you know about love?!"

"I was married for 11 years."

"If you know so much," I told him, "how come you blew that one?"

"She died."

Trap-doored. Again. My stomach and all my smarts fell away as I dropped down the hole.

"She was a nurse," he said, his black eyes on me, "and a damn good one. If things for women would have been like they are now and she'd have had money, she'd have gone to doctor school instead of nursing. She worked the emergency room over at George Washington hospital. We used to joke that everybody ended up meeting our family, one way or the other.

"She got cancer. Maybe she'd always had it living in her. Maybe that's why we couldn't have kids. Hell, my big worry was that I was firing blanks. Big, manly tough guy like me didn't like that idea. Pretty dumb, huh?"

"Nick, I . . . I'm sorry, I didn't know." My sentiments pushed me as close to sober as possible. "I feel like an asshole. Stupid and ignorant."

He flashed that chipped-tooth grin. "I'll give you the ignorant and some of the stupid. You're still working on the asshole part."

I told him I didn't feel like drinking or talking much anymore and he told me he'd give me a ride home. His Chevy was parked at the end of the block, down past the tall bronze statue of a heron perched on one leg erected on Constitution Avenue by the Temperance Society and unnoticed by Washington's masses. I stopped him as we walked past it.

"I still don't understand something," I told him. "You want something from me, from this. Just like her father."

"Maybe so," he said. He looked over my shoulder to where the Capitol dome shimmered all ivory and distant in the night. "Maybe so."

"What?"

He looked back at me. The chipped-tooth grin was rueful. "Maybe I can't say. Maybe because I know that what I want I either got or I don't. Like those answers you think you need. What is, is; what ain't, ain't. We just gotta learn how to live with that."

"Yeah," I said, knowing exactly what he meant and not knowing at all.

25

"I think you've been looking for me."

That man standing in my office door was younger than me, taller too, lean and curly black-haired handsome with laugh lines at the corners of sparkling blue eyes. He wore a sports coat even though the bank's sign across the street kept flashing 96 degrees. I'd abandoned all office decorum for running shorts and a cotton pullover; a print skirt and sleeveless blouse draped Tara. Beads of sweat glistened on our brows: my air conditioner was broken.

"What makes you think so?" I casually moved away from the bookcase, positioned myself between Tara and the stranger. He didn't seem threatening—at least not violent, but you can never tell.

"Are you John Rankin?"

"All day long."

"I'm Cliff Palefsky from the *Washington Post*. You've been leaving messages for me for weeks, something about Janet Armstrong."

"Oh, right," I said. We shook hands. I followed his gaze. "This is Tara Woodson."

"Nice to meet you." He beamed as they shook hands. "Are you a private investigator too?"

"I work for *American Media* magazine," she said.

"A fellow journalist," he said, and they both smiled.

"Hey," I interrupted, "instead of us staying here in this sauna, why don't I buy you a beer?"

"Ah, sure." He turned back to Tara. "I have to confess: I've never read your magazine."

"Everybody reads the *Post*," she said. "I have to confess: I don't know your by-line."

They both laughed.

"Mostly metro stories so far," he said, "but that's how Woodward and Bernstein started." He turned to me. "That's why I got the Armstrong story. When we heard . . ."

"Why don't we wait on business till we have a beer?"

"You only do local stories?" asked Tara.

"No, I got lucky. A guy got sick and I made the team that covered the Reagan-Bush sweep in Detroit. That's why I haven't been around until now."

"Ready?" I said, headed toward the door. I asked Tara, "You got your keys so you can lock up?"

She nodded.

"Nice to meet you," Palefsky said, stalling our progress again. "I'll have to pick up your magazine."

She shrugged. "I'll send a couple over to the *Post*."

"Thanks," he said. "I'd like that."

"Hot out, isn't it?" he said as we walked up the avenue.

"Yes."

"More than 100 people have died from the heat in Kansas City so far this year."

"I read the *Post*," I said.

We walked a block without speaking.

"I hope you don't mind me asking," he said as we entered the Tune Inn, "is she doing a story on you or . . ."

"She'd forgotten some books." I carefully told the truth as we slid into a booth. "She needed to get them before tonight."

"You two married?"

I smiled, slow and easy. "We're very good friends."

"Lucky man."

"Yes," I said. "I think so."

"I hope you don't mind my asking," he repeated.

"I don't mind you asking at all." I smiled again.

When I explained what I was doing *he* didn't mind me asking about his story. He even agreed not to do a follow-up piece on "the father's quest." He was careful and crafty, never telling me as fact anything more than he'd reported: journalism ethics and healthy caution.

215

"Did you ever hear anything special about her as a whore?"

He ignored the hook. "Beyond the whole weirdness? No."

"How about her death? Hear anything special about that?"

"There's more rumors than reality about someone like her. Especially after she hit the big time on page 1."

"Anything specific?"

"You can make up just about anything you want to believe."

"But you heard nothing solid enough to chase it down."

He smiled. "No, nothing *special* like you mean. Besides, I wish I'd never done that story. Too seamy, brought some things into my life I'd just as soon avoided."

"I know what you mean," I said.

"Made me queasy, like I was afraid some of it would rub off. I hate asking strangers to tell you dead people's secrets. Spent hours talking to kids who knew her up at Harvard. I'd buy them espresso while they'd not talk for hours and use a lot of words to do it. Like they were guardians of some ultimate truth hidden in a Pandora's box they wouldn't open. I doubt any of them will help you."

He was wrong, but I didn't tell him so. Eventually we started swapping reporter stories. When he left, I never expected to hear of him again.

Palefsky had been wrong because I'd already taped telephone interviews with two of Janet's friends and they'd opened up as easily as that fabled Pandora's box. Of course, I wasn't hunting headlines.

Excerpts from *Ellen*, who in 1980 was working in a San Diego bank's executive training program.

We were incredibly normal kids. Eugene was a Disneyland. The university influence. Beautiful environment. No real poor people—none we saw. No minorities except for a few Indians.

It's amazing how many details you lose in time! My classic picture memory of Janet is her singing with incredible intensity. Her laughing at class elections, seeing them as a farce, as "this is not serious because the only decisions a class president makes is what colors will the prom streamers be."

Her social life? Maybe things have changed from when you were in high school. No real dating. A group of us went out together. Occasional pairs, a closed door, but within a group. I don't remember Janet ever having a "relationship" in high school.

Sure we talked about men. I know what you're after here. The things that come to mind are hostility toward men or an over-concern with needing men. I don't think of those things when I remember Janet [Laughter.] I always felt she was just normal. We all were.

Something happened that summer after graduation. Janet was hanging out with Mary. They worked at Alice's Restaurant. After graduation I became more conservative, they headed toward the wild side. I stayed in Eugene, went to the local university. The only times we saw each other were like Christmas vacations. Then I saw a sense of confusion. She'd always been so confident.

Even after she dropped out and came back to Eugene I rarely saw her, although I was just at the U. I don't even know what she was doing. Cleaned apartments? Took a couple classes? I didn't know that.

I met Magic Murphy one night that summer at a bar. Janet introduced us. Um, danced with him a couple times and he was . . . Well, a real sexual kind of dancer. I felt like I was being mugged to music. He was very smooth, lots of complimentary lines. I remember being confused about them, wondering, "What's the routine here?" He started calling me at home. I don't know how he got my number. He was a character I didn't want to know.

Yeah, I know people say maybe she had "mental problems." We did some crazy things, but they were normal crazy. When I look back at some of the things I did in high school, I had to be nuts to do them.

For so many years everything went so well for Janet. There's this nice path being laid out for her to success, whatever the hell success is. Things happened well and easily for her.

Why did she do it? That's the $10,000 question. Maybe just searching for something. Maybe Janet was at a point where there was a whole lot of not much in her life.

Excerpts from *Mary*, who in 1980 had a master's in drama and was living in New York, trying to get a break as an actress. She landed rare modeling jobs ("My hands are in the Sears catalog"), was hoping for a panty hose commercial the night we talked, and took acting classes between shifts as a waitress in a trendy SoHo café:

I was pretty rowdy and Janet liked that. Although she didn't overtly challenge the establishment, she always complained bitterly. We used to piss and moan about the slaughtering of baby seals, whales, the environment and the war, that kind of stuff.

She loved music. I remember how she wanted to sing some great opera piece for her senior recital. She loved jazz, Billie Holliday, who I guess was once . . . Never mind. Janet cared about the music inside herself, she wasn't just a crowd pleaser. She was an aesthete.

People outside our group might have considered us aloof, but that's not fair: people hung around people who were alike. We didn't hang with people who lived in mobile homes. She sometimes talked back to teachers, told them they were ridiculous, laughed at their stupidity. She had a temper. Nothing ever really out of control.

We lost our virginity on the same night within ten feet of each other [Laughter], *which bonded us pretty close during that summer of debauchery after graduating from high school. We were working at Alice's Restaurant as dishwashers. Seems like I can't get out of restaurants, doesn't it? We went to this hot springs resort outside of town with the cook. I was with a friend of hers.* [Laughter.]

She wasn't about to let any boy, any high school guy

get moony-eyed over her, nor was she apt to do that toward anyone else. She was very independent. Control was her game. She never got talked into anything she didn't want to do.

On the one hand she was the moony-eyed or dependent type, but on the other she had a great love for loving. Was very affectionate and "touchy." A romantic: colorful. She loved art, her music, bright people. Beautiful men and beautiful women and . . . beauty.

No, she was bright, not just clever. Impulsive, and that got her into stupid things. Throwing caution to the wind for a bit of fun. We did quite a few drugs then too. [Laughter.] Quaaludes and Jack Daniels in Memorial Park. Pretty silly stuff.

Janet was naked under her graduation gown. Not a stitch. Those little braid things on the hats? Tassels? She tied it on like a bra outside her gown, almost marched into the auditorium that way. One of the teachers caught her and demanded that she set it straight. The whole time he didn't realize she was naked underneath.

She was looking forward to Harvard. We cried and cried when we said good-bye, made a pact that we'd never lose touch. She was going to take it all by the balls—but she was scared, too.

That first year away at different schools we kept pretty tight. Our summer of debauchery left Janet pregnant and she had an abortion within a month of hitting Harvard. I came down with mono and nearly flunked out. We'd call each other, say, "Oh, I miss you! I want to go home!" That kind of thing.

In Boston she fell in love with some jazz musician who was good to her. So much is fuzzy now. Like I can't remember when she fell in love with a guy in Eugene and when she fell in love with my brother who was also out there.

I wasn't in town when Magic came through. Stunned me when my brother called, said, "Janet has run off with this pimp. Lois and I are trying to get her back." He felt terrible because they were looking for Magic's car to

*sugar his gas tank or something, but they'd already split.
I heard from her about a month later: "Don't worry, I'm
OK, doing all right."*

*She loved this Magic. She talked about how he was
"incredibly perceptive." That he knew how to read
people, was bright, and music was big in his life. My
brother and Lois told me he could immediately tell a
woman her good points, yet also get to her with what was
wrong: "You've got beautiful eyes but you should lose a
little weight, you'd be just smashing." He was into
astrology. I have this mental picture of him in a beat-up
Caddy with "Taurus" letters plastered across the back
window.*

*Writing had always been a big deal with her. Leave a
record, she'd say. Put all that truth down so you never
lose it. Her letters read like essays. But I quit getting
them after she hit D.C. From then on it was strictly
phone calls. We'd talk about movies. She said she went
to lots of movies. She'd talk about her jazz club she
wanted to start, about combining our efforts. She could
manage the jazz bar and I could put on a cabaret. They
wanted to buy this yacht together, she and Magic. Sit out
on the ocean and take it easy, write their books. They
had plans to go to Hawaii. Vacation. [Bitter laughter.]
She never got a vacation. She was going to work that life
five years, then get out. Everything was all played out
perfectly in her head.*

*Once she told me, "Mary, I'm an actress, just like
you." And, "I hate these guys." She liked to take money
from johns, because they were shits. I got the impression
that it was all men who were shits.*

*She always had a thing for black men. I think it was
the jazz she associated them with, the muscle in the
music. Somehow, in spite of herself, she ended up
buying a whole bag of stereotypes.*

*She never really talked about Magic, except how good
he was and how he protected her, was always in the next
room behind one of those reverse mirrors. He enjoyed
watching her with johns.*

The last phone call I got, couple weeks before she

died, was different. She always urged me to visit her. I wouldn't because I was broke and refused to take her money. This time she says, "Mary, I saw a great movie, this Julia thing, and those two women's relationship reminds me of us in high school. How close we've been. I know we'll be together to help each other if we ever need it." And I said, "Yeah, I loved the movie too." We talked a bit, then she said, "So why don't you come out and see me?" "Come on, Janet," I told her, "you know: same old story." She blew up: "If you weren't so fucking proud you'd just take my money and come see me!" So I said, "OK, it's been two years, I'll come during spring break." "Great," she says, "tell me when and I'll send you tickets." Before I could do that, I got the call that she was dead. I think she wanted me to help her get out of there, and that movie stuff about that writer Lillian Hellman and her friend was kind of a . . . I don't know, it's hard to say.

She was so bright—and yet thought she could walk through shit and come out clean. I think you're perceiving that correctly, John. It's hard to articulate what it was, but . . . The impulsive nature or something. There was this definite flaky bone in her body. She must have been in love with this Magic guy. So weird.

I don't know why it happened. Maybe . . . A lot of battles she won in high school were because of who she was, not like she done it herself. You know what I'm saying? Then she didn't make it at Harvard, lost a couple guys, ended up cleaning houses. So this guy rolls into town, this Magic Murphy. He's a smooth-talking black man. He's been to cities and he's talking fur coats and good food and . . . Why not? Why not pick up? Have a little adventure? You can get out of it clean. That's what I think it was. Janet didn't really believe in consequences.

"You know what's fascinating about those two transcripts?" Tara asked me that night as we sat on bar stools at the Tune Inn. I hadn't wanted any more beer, but my air conditioner still wasn't fixed. Tara's apartment was small, too intimate for us. We'd seen all the good movies in town. Which left a bar, which meant the Tune Inn. It was crowded with after-work softball teams loudly rehashing their glories while the jukebox blared country and western music. Tara found the dead woman's story intriguing—which was another good reason for me to chase it: Janet Armstrong was something safe we could share. I used anything I could think of to hook us together—well, almost anything. *If Tara only knew Janet's most intriguing secret,* I thought. By then I believed Janet's secret, her mysterious Martin M., forged no link between the lives of these two women who'd come to dominate my time. But with Tara's well-being I took no chances. She filled my life. When she wasn't working, we'd grab a bite somewhere, go to a movie, maybe go somewhere with Mad Dog and Katie. There were a few nights or weekends when Tara was busy. But fewer than before, fewer still with each passing week.

"What's fascinating," she said, answering her own question, "is how two people can walk through the same time and place and see whole different worlds—and maybe neither of them is right."

I'd known she'd seize on that. Her eyes saw shades of meaning: *how perceptive!* I told myself.

"What are you going to do next?" she asked.

"You mean with Janet Armstrong?"

She nodded.

"When you step through a trap door, you fall until you hit bottom." I shrugged. "I made a commitment."

"And you're worth your word." And God did she smile!

"Things at the magazine changing any?" I shifted to more comfortable ground for her.

And God did she frown! "Same old shit. I can't get promoted or given anything good because the associate editor is crazy and the managing editor says it will make her crazier if I do too much too fast—even though he agrees I'm capable of more and deserve it."

"At least you got to go along on the interview of that French movie producer. You never know when a contact like that will help."

"Like that reporter Cliff Palefsky," she said. I lowered my

bottle to the bar. "I'm going to send him the last three issues, the ones with my name on the masthead. He's a contact worth having."

"I guess so," I said evenly.

"You don't . . . You don't think it could hurt, do you?"

I swallowed some beer. Cold. Tangy. "How could it?"

"That's what I think too. Play all your cards for all their worth—right?"

I stared into the bar mirror as I answered. "Right."

"Did I tell you I talked to my aunt? I got worried when Mount St. Helens erupted again yesterday. She says it's nowhere near as bad this time, but there's ash over everything."

"It'll give your father something to do," I said, then immediately regretted my words.

"Yes," she muttered. "Sure."

A Marty Robbins gunfighter ballad twanged Spanish guitars from the jukebox.

Tara raised her eyes from her beer, looked through the mirror behind the bar. "God I remember that song! I was just a kid, six, seven. They used to play it all the time back home on the radio. Probably still do. Probably don't have any Springsteen. My brother Jim would always ham it up to make me giggle. 'Keep the kid laughing,' he'd tell Mom, 'and she won't complain.' We had this old Ford pickup, black and rusted through, always smelled like a gas station, especially in the rain. I don't know how he and Mom kept it running. One of his jobs was to check the fence line. He took me with him everywhere. We'd pile in that pickup, roar off to inspect our borders. That song would come on the radio and he'd act it out, shouting along with the words while we bounced over hilly green fields. I'd be giggling and . . ."

I saw the first tear run down her cheek, then the mirror showed me a second roll down the other side and blue eyes so wet they looked like stones underwater. Scarlet blotches marred her cheeks. She wore baby powder and baby oil in the summers, always smelled of their fragrant warmth. Sometimes, though not that night, she'd wear a little musk. I touched her arm, let my hand press against her trembling back. My fingers spread wide, gently covering as many as possible of those ribs I felt through her thin red cotton top. She shook her head.

"It's just the heat," she said, sobbed softly, then hardened her voice. "The air is filthy. The goddamned heat. And those transcripts, they . . .

"Goddamn the heat," she said. "Just goddamn the heat."

26

"You understand I agreed to this with great reluctance?" said the public defender for the fourth time. When I nodded, he settled back in the chair. Nick Sherman leaned against one of the cubicle's transparent walls, black eyes glistening as he watched the two of us sitting at the small table.

"I really didn't plan on being here this morning," said the lawyer.

"Neither did I," I told him. "I'm going to a wedding and jail isn't on the way."

The lawyer nodded, cleared his throat.

Washington is a city of many jails: simple lock-ups at police stations, bullpens at the courthouses, contracted detention facilities like halfway houses for those on their way back to the world, six major prison facilities across the river in suburban Virginia for those who won't be roaming the world for some time, and, in 1980, two major facilities east of Capitol Hill actually called jails—the Old and the New. Jail in D.C. is where you wait for the courts to decide how long you'll be behind prison walls. Sometimes that takes a year or more. By the end of 1980, all the prisoners had been cleared out of the Old Jail moved through the system or at least across the square to New Jail, where Sherman, the reluctant lawyer and I waited in one of the half dozen Plexiglas-walled interview rooms on the third floor. The interview areas on each of the three levels are like warehouse floors filled with old fashioned phone booths. Each cubicle has a small table and two chairs so lawyers can talk with their clients in relative privacy. Relative privacy is more than you can hope for in jail. The Plexiglas walls kill all noise. I saw a woman lawyer arguing with her client three cubicles to my right, a pantomime of soundless gestures.

On that July Monday morning the former shah of Iran had died in Egypt and I'd been packing, frustrated but resigned to the fact that the others hadn't agreed with Tara and me about leaving at dawn rather than midday. Then Nick Sherman walked up my stairs.

"Looks like I got here just in time," he said, eyeing the gaping suitcase on my desk. He smiled. "Skipping town?"

"My ex-partner Mad Dog is getting married in Maine."

"You picked a good time to escape the heat."

"Their choice, not mine."

"You know Tyrone P. Harris?"

I shook my head. "Should I?"

"Tyrone P. Harris, 19 years old, busted one week ago for armed robbery and assault with a deadly weapon. He shot the liquor store owner. Tyrone also stole a car. Tyrone also got caught. Since witnesses tie him to three other holdups and his fingerprints were left all over a burglar scene, and since he's already on probation for a narcotics violation, Tyrone wants to assist the police how-some-ever he can. Make a good impression on the judge. Cut a plea with the U.S. attorney to settle for this, forget about that in exchange for some information."

"And?"

"And one of the things he coughs up is how he and two of his buddies were hired to rough up some white chump private eye on Capitol Hill a couple months back. I convinced him and his attorney it was a good idea for you to meet Tyrone this morning. What do you think?"

"I got time to make a phone call?"

Sherman grinned: "We always let you make a phone call."

In the outer room's far corner a dull gray steel slab door marked "Cell Block" slid open. A stocky black youth with a thin mustache entered the maze of transparent walls. His eyes took in all they could see. He hesitated a moment, then came our way as his legal services attorney opened the Plexiglas door.

"Let's go over this one more time," said the attorney. "Mr. Harris has agreed to talk with Mr. Rankin alone and in strict confidence, off the record. My client does this in a full spirit of cooperation with the authorities and in order to further . . ."

"We all know why Tyrone is talking," said Sherman. He smiled at the prisoner, who couldn't help smiling back. Sherman jerked his head toward the hallway, and he and the attorney left us alone. They stood outside the Plexiglas door, not talking to each other, not watching the two of us inside that glass cage.

I sat down, waited. Tyrone took the chair on the other side of the table. He tried to tilt the chair back, but it was bolted to the floor.

"You got a cigarette?" he said.

"I don't smoke."

He grunted, stared toward though not at me.

"You know who I am?" I finally said.

"Yeah, I know."

"You beat me up."

He shrugged. "I was there."

I waited for him to go on, but he only stared.

"Listen," I told him, "the deal not to prosecute you for that number you pulled on me was for you to talk about it. To the cops. And to me. So far you ain't said shit."

"You weren't so tough in the street that night."

"You didn't give me a chance."

"That ain't the name of the game, Jack." He reached inside his denim shirt pocket, pulled out a cigarette. He found a matchbook in the other pocket, lit the cigarette. He blew smoke my way.

"Suppose we start with why you came after me."

"Doin' a job, man. Just doing a job. Got paid 50 bucks plus whatever we could rip you for."

"Paid by who?"

"Some nigger."

I winced at that word that rolls so casually out of the Tyrones of this world. "What guy?"

"This nigger used to hang 'round the parking lot up 15th. The cops know where. Not far from dis corner where dis other dude sells bam. This nigger he be just hanging there. I be hanging there too." He grinned. "When I ain't hanging 'round here."

"Why did that guy want me beat up?"

"He was just doin' a job too."

"Who for?"

"He didn't say. I didn't ask. But that sucker got maybe $50 more than the chump change he paid me and Freddy to help him."

"Who paid him? A black guy or a white guy?"

"A green dude named Ulysses Simpson Grant." Tyrone was proud of his knowledge of the president pictured on a $50 bill. "The big green dudes do it every time."

By now I'd recognized Tyrone's voice. "But you were the one who did my car."

"Made a hell of a bang, didn't it? Must have been one wild sight. I was too busy makin' tracks to get a good view myself."

"Who was the boxer?"

"That be Freddy. Crazy mutherfucker. Thinks he's a regular Sugar Ray Leonard. Since that homeboy won the Olympics and the championship, seems like all the dudes think they's Sugar Ray. They ain't shit." Tyrone smiled as he dropped the cigarette butt to the floor, ground it out with his heel. "Though he done you pretty good."

"I'm not Sugar Ray either."

"No shit."

"How did you know who I was?"

"That dude . . ."

"What's his name?"

"He said Jackson. I didn't buy his shit, but so what?"

"Go on."

"This dude, he got your name, your car, your address, the whole number. We hung around waiting for you three, four times that weekend. I be standing there telling them how pissed off I be 'cause you ain't been 'round when looky here: there you be, driving by the dime store looking for a place to park. We be lucky you didn't have far to go. Had to jog to follow you."

"Then what?"

"Then we did our job."

"Which was?"

"Come on, man! Don't be jiving me! You was there. We did you good, like we was supposed to. We was supposed to deliver a message."

"What was the message?"

"If you ain't smart enough to figure it out, don't ask me, man. I just helped deliver it."

"How did Jackson know to ask you to do the job?"

"Everybody knows me! Everybody knows Tyrone's a righteous dude!"

"Did you ever hear of a man called Magic Murphy? A woman named Janet Armstrong, maybe called Crystal?"

"Naw."

"Do you have any reason to think this job has anything to do with pimps or prostitutes?"

He leered at me. "You changing your action, Jackson? Which you going to be, bro: the Mac or the meat?"

"You keep fucking with me, I'll be the one who screws you inside this place so tight you'll forget what sunshine is."

"You wish, white boy. You wish."

I spent another 15 minutes questioning Tyrone, learned nothing more about a man who might have been named Jackson. The third man, Freddy, already had warrants out on him for my assault, two robberies and two burglaries he'd been fingered for by his longtime friend the righteous Tyrone.

I looked through the Plexiglas, caught Sherman's eye, stood.

"Hey man!" called Tyrone. I stopped with my hand on the doorknob. "Something I don't un'erstand. You be a private detective, right?" I nodded. "Then, shit: what's this *major crime* jive? I ain't no chump, Jack. This is supposed to *be!* I see you private eyes on TV all the time. You always be being beat up, knocked around. No big thing. So what's the matter with you?"

"This isn't TV," I told him.

He rolled his eyes around the Plexiglas walls. Where he was going there were steel bars. "No shit," he said.

Sherman drove me home.

"When I talk to Tyrone this afternoon," said the Homicide

cop, "will he tell me that you two came up with anything I don't know?"

"If he does, he'll be lying."

"What else is new." Not even a question. "We seem to have eliminated the idea that you only got mugged."

"I still can't believe that."

"Believing doesn't make any difference to the truth."

"What happens now?" I asked.

"Well, unless you got any bright ideas . . ." I shook my head. Sherman continued. "We got warrants out for Freddy. Tyrone is looking through mug shots for Jackson, the guy who hired them and the guy who gave you that message. The manager of the parking lot where this Jackson supposedly hung out may or may not remember anybody by that name. He doesn't recollect Tyrone or Freddy either. It's a downtown lot, not far from the Stroll and junkie paradise. Lots of guys drift there. If Tyrone picks Jackson out of the books, we'll show the picture to the manager. Right now we're going easy on him: he isn't the most cooperative citizen. Maybe Freddy will help us when we pull him in. The business between you and them isn't my ballpark, so I can't push too hard.

"But you and I don't really give a damn about Tyrone or Freddy or Jackson, do we?" He grinned. "I keep wondering who doesn't like you enough to hire three thugs to deliver a message."

"Me too."

"We can't put Eddie Hampton in it. Everybody says they never heard of him or saw him."

"Is that true?"

"You tell me."

I laughed.

"Ain't being a real detective fun?"

"Yeah," I said, "more fun than TV."

"Could this be tied in with Janet Armstrong?"

"I doubt it." Nick stopped at the red light. "I should have pulled Magic out of the cellblock for you while we were there. He makes Tyrone look like a saint."

We drove through an emerald tunnel of trees on a residential street. Children and dogs played in the summer heat.

"I figured something out last night," I said as we turned onto Pennsylvania Avenue and headed toward the Hill.

"What?"

"Why Janet Armstrong's murder got to you."

He stopped for the red light on 8th Street. The Eclectic waited two blocks ahead.

"I know about you now," I told him as he stared down the road. "About how your family busted up when you were a kid. About growing up dirt poor in a piss-ant New Mexico town. About working your way through a two-bit community college which was all you could get into because you were too wild and smart to have flashy grades from shitty high schools. About your wife. You busted your balls getting to be a big time homicide detective in a big time city. Somewhere you could use all your brains and guts and toughness, somewhere where you can lock up assholes who crap on those great American fantasies we both believe in and never seem to get."

Sherman pulled the cruiser into a parking space across the street from The Eclectic. Those black eyes stared straight ahead.

"So what happens? One night you roll up to GW hospital for a routine homicide and find Janet Armstrong. A girl who had it all, from birth to Harvard. Great family, great record, great future. She even came from out West like us. What does she do? She pisses on it."

His knuckles turned white on the steering wheel.

"Then she goes and lets this scumbag Magic kill her. If he walks, she's helped a creep rip one more victory out of what's supposed to be, rip one more out of us. So on top of that hunger that you've got to close every homicide, you're mad at her."

I was out of breath and out of words. Nick waited for me to go on, still not looking my way.

"You think too much for a cowboy like me," he finally said.

"Bullshit," I replied softly.

"Yeah." Strength reentered his words. "Bullshit. You driving that pretty silver car to your buddy's wedding?" I nodded. "Your lady friend going too?"

"We're both in the wedding," I answered. Tara had been a

last-minute substitution bridesmaid for a friend of Katie's: "Lots of things happen at weddings!" Katie had said, giggling as she told me how I'd march down the aisle beside Tara. Lots of things, I told myself.

"Sounds elaborate," said Nick. "None of you are 18 anymore."

"Last great traveling road show," I said. "Might as well do it up right. We got T-shirts printed up, the whole bit: *a savage journey into the heart of the American dream.*"

"Sounds like a party I shouldn't miss." He grinned. "Maybe I should alert all state patrols over the teletype."

"Tell them we're dangerous but decent." I felt like those black eyes saw the cocaine vial I'd hidden in my suitcase.

"Just you worry about being careful," said my friend the cop. "From what Tyrone says, you've got enemies somewhere."

But on that journey it seemed like I had only friends everywhere. Katie's family lived in a house secluded out of Millbridge, Maine. Small Town, America, where everyone is born. The family's backyard ended in an inlet of the sea. Friday we nursed hangovers from on-the-road revelry there. Family members and friends bustled in and out of the big white house, frantic with preparations. Long tables with elaborate decorations unfolded on the grass. At the far end of that lawn we sprawled out on granite boulders and smoothly worn slabs of solid lava, the gently rocking, frigid Atlantic Ocean a few feet below us. New England's warm sun bright above our baking flesh. Three seals fished a hundred feet away from our shore, their brown heads bobbing through the blue gray glint of slow ocean swells. Half a mile beyond the seals a grayish white blanket of fog hung low over the water, but it never moved closer to shore, never spoiled the brightness of that day. The air was tangy with ocean salt, clean and fresh. The foul sauna city of Washington, D.C., seemed a galaxy away as we waited for that night's wedding in a grove of trees two hundred feet from Katie's front door.

"I used to play there when I was a little girl," Katie told me as we walked toward the house from the rocks. She'd asked me if I'd get a beer with her, but what she really wanted was a break from the others—no secret, no offense. It was this flaxen-haired woman's wedding day. She wore a one-piece black bathing suit and thongs. I slipped into my sneakers, threw a towel around my neck. My skin and swimming trunks were wet from spray off one of the rocks. Katie smoked a cigarette. She'd quit two years before. "I used to daydream about how some day it would be time for my wedding and I'd have it in the grove and how beautiful it would be."

"Looks like you're going to get it," I joked as we walked past the kitchen door leading to the refrigerator full of beer.

"Yeah," she said. The lawn along the side of the house was freshly mowed by her brother. "Looks like it."

The gravel on the driveway crunched beneath my sneakers as she led me toward the trees. She dropped her cigarette, didn't bother to crush it out. Behind us in the gravel we left a plume of smoke.

"Feel how different the air is in here?" she said as we walked into the trees.

"It's cooler," I said. It made no difference what we said. She just had to talk.

"Yeah, that must be what it is.

"How are you and Tara doing?" she asked suddenly.

I shrugged. "You know. Better, I think. I'm glad you asked her to be a bridesmaid. This way she has a reason for coming besides me."

Katie stared at me, then looked away as we separated to walk around a young sapling.

"Sally and Tara had a talk," she said. Sally was a college friend of Katie's who'd flown to Maine for the wedding. "About you."

"Should I ask?"

Katie laughed. "It doesn't make any difference if you should or shouldn't, Rankin. If I let you sweat long enough, you will.

"They were in the house this morning, fitting their dresses. I heard Sally say something like 'Rankin is cute,' and then she asked Tara how long the two of you had been together, if you were getting married or something. Sally didn't buy whatever Tara mumbled back, asked something like 'What's this routine?' "

My face glowed like the ember of her discarded cigarette.

"Then Tara said something about the two of you being undefined. When Sally pressed her on undefined, she hemmed and hawed, *drifted* away."

"Undefined?"

"Undefined."

I shrugged. "She is technically correct."

"Undefined isn't the word, Rankin. You two are completely defined by whatever Tara wants, whenever she wants it."

"Whatever she *can* want," I insisted. "She can only go so far for now."

"How 'bout that." Katie stepped to the middle of the clearing, turned slowly around, her face tilted up, her eyes skimming over the treetops. "Isn't it amazing what people can do?"

"Yes," I told her. "Like me. I never thought I could get where I am today."

"Me either," she said. She smiled. "I'm getting married, Rankin. To the Dog."

"You two are lucky as hell."

"Aren't we though. Aren't we all." She looked around again. "I had a nightmare about this place once.

"Come on," she smiled. "We better grab a beer and get back to the rocks or there'll be talk about the bride and the groomsman."

"Don't worry," I told her. "I'm safe."

"So I hear," she said.

An excess of enchantment is the only way to describe that night. Clear, cool, crisp air laced with the scent of pine and the sea filled the grove where a crowd of 300 gathered. A string quartet played Vivaldi and Mozart in the shadows. Ten of us—five men, five women—formed a V pointing to an outdoor ecumenical vestry fashioned for the occasion, Jewish *chupa* covering a crossless Unitarian altar. The men wore powder blue tuxedos and black pants; the women brightly colored, cotton gauze dresses made in Mexico. The bride and groom wore white. Tara's dress was lavender. She wore her golden hair tied back by a lavender ribbon in a high, thick, ponytail fall, carried a sprig of lavender roses and purple lilacs.

234

Before the ceremony I helped Saul dress, giggling with him in the basement of a neighbor who lived at the far end of the twisted country road leading to Katie's house. Tara was billeted next door. I had to loan Saul a pair of socks. Joey Malletta stopped by to pick us up. "I'm going to win the bet," Saul told him. "It's going to happen. Want to give me new odds?" Joey laughed, but nervously: such humor was too irreverent for him. He touched Saul's arm, spoke softly when he spoke at all. Katie cried during the ceremony. Saul giggled. Nervous.

What was probably the entire population of the county milled around Katie's family yard. A three-piece combo played palatable wedding reception music. Couples danced in the soft glow of lights from the house and lanterns hung in the trees. Tara stood apart from me, the center of three male friends of Katie and Saul's whom I barely knew. I watched her, wondered if she'd want some of the cocaine I carried in the pocket of my rented tux. I was a little stoned, a little drunk, in absolute awe of life's beauty when Saul stood before me—married.

"I won, Rankin!"

"Yes you did."

He followed my gaze. "Don't worry. It's just a matter of time."

I smiled, nodded. "I wish you two didn't need to be back in D.C. on Monday."

"Are you kidding?! Of course we do! My first story from the ABSCAM tapes runs Tuesday!"

"Can't have you miss that. Not for something like this."

He shrugged his shoulders. "As an experienced married man, let me tell you: a wedding is no big thing."

We laughed. Across the yard Joey Malletta and Saul's sister, a buxom, sultry woman two years younger than me, joined Tara's group.

"Ah . . ." Saul looked to both sides, steered me to shadows past the edge of the crowd. "There's something . . . I tried to talk to you before we left town last week, but I could never find you."

"I've been pretty busy."

"Yeah, well . . . I don't know what it means, but . . .

235

There's something I think you should know. Because of Tara."

He won my full, sober attention.

"One of my sources told me . . . During ABSCAM, one of the names mentioned to the FBI as somebody corrupt to target was Tara's father.

"Nothing was ever done about it," Saul quickly continued. "Probably because it was all nonsense."

"Is this in your story?!"

"No, I could only get one source. He only had it as rumor."

"Then it might not be true?!"

"Sure."

"Besides, what the hell does that mean?! Nothing! Somebody in the Bureau had a hard-on for him or Woodson was the only senator's name he could remember or a crazy once dropped a dime on him and the bureaucracy went wild or . . . or anything!"

"Probably."

"I went over him myself! And Mercer, his A. A. I found shit. Nothing!"

"Knowing Tara, I didn't think so," said Saul quickly. "But I figured I better tell you. You never know what'll come out someday." He paused, saw I'd shifted my gaze back to her and how she was laughing, how she stood at the center of our friends, of those men. "Don't worry," Saul said. "About what I told you. Or anything."

"What's to worry about?" I said. "It's your wedding."

A beehived, blue haired woman with a wrinkled neck, powdered white face, red lipstick and booming voice grabbed Saul's arm. As he turned to be polite, I marked where Tara stood, drifted into the house. Two minutes later I walked to her side. My closed fist slid into her hand. She stiffened for a moment, then realized what I was doing and cupped her fingers beneath mine.

"Use the key for a spoon," I said. "The bathroom line is gone."

When she came back I was talking with Sally and Saul's sister, who stood laughing at some joke I'd made, her hand on my arm, her huge brown eyes fixed on my face. Tara moved alongside me. Saul's sister had to lift her hand, step

236

back to give her room. I felt something drop in my pocket, but I don't think Sally or the sister noticed a thing. The band paused for applause, didn't get any, then started a slow, rhythmic Broadway show tune. They knew no Springsteen. Tara shifted her shoulders in time to the music, hummed along with the song as she smiled at me.

"Want to dance?" I asked her.

"Sure." She walked three steps onto the floor, then turned into my arms. I held her loosely, easily. We slid through the crowd, turning, swaying, drifting as one with the music, as if we were fused together, her motion matching rhythm and pace with mine, dictating mine even as it did so. The scent of lilacs lingered on her, lilacs and a trace of musk. We'd turn and whirl. I felt the warmth of her flesh through our clothing where her arm lay across mine, the pressure of her fingertips between my shoulder blades. Her other hand curled soft and gentle in my grasp. The glow of her slight sunburn rose through the wispy lavender dress where the palm and fingers of my right hand rested lightly on her back. The band missed a beat but we never faltered, pivoting, spinning back through the crowd. We glided safely through their chaos, untouched except by each other. A strand of her hair came undone, brushed my cheek. I could look straight into her face, to her blue eyes bright this magic night, to her full lips turned up with joy so close to mine. She moistened them with her pink tongue.

"Isn't this absolutely perfect?" she said. "Isn't this the most wondrous night ever?"

"The most absolutely wondrous," I answered. She nodded, smiled. We danced.

And it was true, the absolute most wondrous night, a night of extreme enchantment. A night of living in my best dream. And my worst nightmare. This was heaven: I held her in my arms amidst all life's beauty. This was hell: I held her in my arms only as close as she let me. The circle of my grasp around her marked the divine borders of the universe; as we danced, I was everywhere at once and nowhere at all.

27

Excerpts from interview with *Desmond Jones,* who'd grown up with Janet Armstrong in Eugene, Oregon. They'd been the only two students in their high school class to go to Harvard; only five students from their high school had *ever* gone to Harvard. By 1980, *Desmond* had graduated, landed a job with the Department of Interior in Taos, New Mexico, working as a "programs and systems analyst"—"but what I'm really doing is writing fiction," he said. "Nobody is buying, but I'm still writing. Like everybody else."

I remember when Janet and I were in eighth-grade orchestra. We wore white armbands to a concert along with a few other chic, intellectual kids to protest the Vietnam War. Must have been 1970 or 1971. That sounds more sophisticated than it actually was because we didn't understand what we were doing. It was the times and the town. We had our liberal parents' approval, so it was more an act of conformity than rebellion, even though we were in the minority among our peers. We led a very bucolic adolescence, though we didn't think so. During adolescence most people are unhappy, usually because they contrive to make themselves so. We were no different.

We knew each other pretty well, though people have private lives no one ever plumbs. We were interested in music, knew we were the hottest shits in the state. That doesn't portray me in a terribly flattering light, but that's what we thought, and that's what everyone around us implied. I was the hottest piano player and she was the best singer and we were going to go to Harvard, blow their doors off back East. Maybe we needed that extreme confidence to force ourselves to be as good as we were. Didn't matter that it didn't fit in with reality, the myth gave us the strength to storm the world.

I was her accompanist, which meant we faced each other for two years in a row, practice sessions every night. I was in a couple high school cliques, though not completely part of any one. One clique included my high school girlfriend. They were all "Christians." I wasn't. Janet wasn't either. That was when the Jesus-freak cults swept through American high schools. Now it's sweeping through Washington, isn't it? Only you don't call them freaks up there. "Born again" bullshit. Besides the freaks, there was a group of Janet, Lois, Mary, other people you may know about.

In terms of Eugene high school, Janet was sophisticated as well as being smart. She always knew what was going on, or thought she did, which may be the same thing. Which probably wasn't the same thing as far as the rest of the world was concerned. She was bright, she was talented. She was very physically attractive. I never dated her, but I knew she was extremely aware of her sexuality and contemptuous of people who weren't as sexually sophisticated as her. She perceived high school dating and pairing off as immature. She was certain that her opinions were right. That's an extremely easy attitude to have when you're living in a small town without a wide spectrum of real-life examples to prove you wrong.

Janet was popular with her friends, but some of the young Christian types and kids whose fathers worked in the mills . . . I don't know if "fear" is a big enough word, or if it's precise, but they were kind of afraid of her. She could make you feel so silly.

No, she didn't have clearly defined goals. None of us did. Maybe there were people in my high school class who knew they wanted to be lawyers, but there weren't many of them. For people like us who went somewhere like Harvard, that was the goal. Just getting out of

Eugene. Being in this big-name school that none of us knew anything about. That might be one reason Janet had trouble when she got there: Harvard's not a goal, it's just a beginning. When you get there, it's scary to find out you haven't really won anything.

If you can ascribe mistakes, one she made was going into premed as a sophomore. She took biology, mathematics, chemistry, and something else all in one term. She underestimated the cutthroat nature of Harvard premed. She never wanted to be a doctor. But "doctor" was a title, a solid, grabbable goal. Beginning, end and reward. Most people at Harvard didn't have any clear direction when we got there. Our map ended at Harvard Square. Everybody flirted with one major after another. Janet started her first year in intensive Russian.

During high school, premed or Russian never entered her conversations. She wanted to study English when she got to Harvard, talked about being a writer. I decided to be a writer after I read books at Harvard I could have written better. During our senior year of high school I remember Janet being very moved by Tess of the D'Urbervilles, *by Thomas Hardy: a young woman driven to despair and destruction. A fucking classic, right? Tell me all about it.*

I rarely saw Janet at Harvard. That was an unspoken but quite conscious decision on both our parts. When you're 3,000 miles from home you don't want to need crutches and you don't want to appear that you have a crutch.

One of the few times I ran into her she said she'd just come from one of those intense coffeehouse discussions with some Long Island suburbanite coed types. Janet had been arguing that Jimi Hendrix's music was more legitimate—Jesus!! What the hell does that mean?!— anyway, that Hendrix's music was more legitimate than Bob Dylan's because Dylan came from a nice, white, bourgeois background whereas Jimi Hendrix came out of the ghetto. Did you ever have those kind of conversations? Crap. But that was like Janet. She didn't like the kind of music most people in Eugene listened to. No rock 'n' roll or country and western for her. She listened to jazz. Maybe to be unique, also because she had taste. Nobody listened to black music in our high school. She did. Everybody from Billie Holliday to . . . Jimi Hendrix.

Janet decided not to do music at Harvard. That's not so uncommon. Part of it was that there were other worlds to conquer. You must be smart to be a musician, and people like Janet who were good musicians had a lot else going for them. I knew lots of people who were intensive in music all through high school, then after graduation they stuck the cello in the closet and never looked at it again. Same thing with sports, acting.

We had no friends in common at Harvard. Of course, after that story hit the Washington Post, all of a sudden "everybody" knew her.

The week before Thanksgiving our sophomore year she visited me in my room, said, "I'm going back to Oregon," and I remember being jealous, because I wasn't having an easy time. If you make that kind of radical shift from small-town Oregon to Harvard, it takes a while to get acclimated. Janet never gave herself enough time.

Yeah, there might have been something forceful, something in the background that could have caused . . . It was always easy to be unique in Eugene. But once you leave there for the real world, Boston, Taos, probably even Washington, that isn't quite so easy. I think she wanted to be unique. Everybody does. She wanted to be doing something different than everybody else, something more interesting, more exciting. Which is why it was silly for her to become a premed, but then I don't think what you keep calling cause and effect was an important philosophical construct in her life.

Also, when we got to Boston, there was this disorienting discovery. There were a lot of smart, aggressive people there, and one thing you discover is that it doesn't necessarily matter how smart you are, it's how aggressively you handle what you got. In Eugene, you didn't need to be aggressive. She didn't have any competition *in Eugene. We didn't need to study and we got all A's. Musically, nobody could touch her.*

I think Janet was ultimately very cynical, and I don't know when that process starts. Does it go all the way back to the war when she's 12 years old? Or is it from high school and having everything handed to her on a plate? Or is it seeing all those Jesus freaks hiding behind the crosses they wore around their necks so they didn't need to confront sinning or being a good Samaritan? Or is it from seeing this cutthroat and pretty shallow but extremely prestigious society at Harvard? Is it never finding a knight in shining armor and knowing the huge odds against such a thing even existing? Maybe a Freudian would trace it back to her potty training.

I remember the last time I saw her, that summer after my sophomore year when she'd dropped out and went back to Eugene. She was about to leave for Washington. I didn't know why she was going. Janet seemed to be doing very well, had a nice apartment. We were driving around and talking about what we were going to do with our lives. I remember her saying, though I don't remember the context, "Desmond, any job is prostitution." By that time she really thought that no matter what you did you were basically selling yourself, your soul, or your mind or your body. I don't think that's a terribly irrational conclusion to come to. But a lot of people may think that, and they don't become literal prostitutes in the streets of Washington. Maybe cynicism is too weak a word for what Janet felt. I guess it's despair.

But I don't know if she ever thought she was doing wrong. From all accounts, she . . . she kind of enjoyed it. It's easy to think it's a very glamorous existence. I don't know if you can think that about it when you're doing it. I didn't speak to her then, I wish I had. I feel guilty about that, plenty of times. We could talk about my guilt, but I don't think it's very interesting.

The only contact I had with her was through Lois, who I saw every couple months because her school was close and she was dating my roommate. I knew Janet had been thinking about leaving the streets, coming back to Cambridge, that Lois was helping set that up. In fact, Lois was in my room when we got the call that Janet was dead.

Can't help you there, I really don't have one strong impression, one clear visual snapshot of Janet. It's easy not to retain anything like that because you assume everyone is going to keep living. It's only after something happens that you go back and resurrect memories, so in some sense they're false, invoked. Janet was the first death for me. That's what I can't forget. You want ideal images of her? No? "Real" ones? Yeah, I know: what's real. Maybe her standing by the piano, singing an aria while I play. You give me one: her whoring on a street corner while I'm studying at Harvard.

Remember how we talked about Janet wanting to be unique? The saddest thing of all is she blew that. The only thing unique about her becoming a prostitute and getting murdered is that she went to Harvard first and made the front page of the Washington Post. *Yesterday's papers. If she hadn't been from exotic Eugene or gone to Harvard, I bet she wouldn't have made the front page. Maybe not even the back page.*

What about Janet for me as a writer? That's funny. You can picture yourself as a character in a book. But you never really believe that's how you'll end up. I wouldn't write this story.

That tape waited in the Porsche parked in front of the small house Katie and Saul rented that summer. Katie and I sat inside on the living room floor, surrounded by cardboard boxes and crumpled newspapers, sorting through their wedding gifts while watching the Democratic party's presidential nominating convention on TV. Mad Dog was somewhere in the city still digging dirt out of the ABSCAM investigation. That night's evening news told how the jury in Philadelphia congressman Ozzie Myers's ABSCAM corruption trial heard the videotaped phrase he made a Washington classic to rival Watergate's "but it would be wrong" cliché. As Myers bragged to undercover FBI agents, he proclaimed, "I'm gonna tell you something simple and short. Money talks in this business and bullshit walks. And it works the same way down in Washington."

This August night Tara was also out. That's all I knew for sure. On TV, incumbent president Jimmy Carter took the podium to accept renomination and a lukewarm reception from the party faithful who'd been fed a myopic theme revolving around the greatness of their party's history, an evening dedicated to the memory of Franklin Delano Roosevelt and Hubert Humphrey (who always just missed grabbing his presidential dream). This President Jimmy Carter, who'd quoted Bob Dylan and talked about the future four years earlier to win his first term, now stood before the world to praise the past; in so doing, he bungled, called one of the convention saints "Hubert Horatio Hornblower . . . Humphrey!" That night it was easy to see that this time Carter had already lost.

"Nothing happened between you and Tara at the wedding?!" Katie asked.

"Nothing you didn't see."

"I wasn't everywhere all the time," she teased, hoping.

"You might as well have been. We played it straight."

"That's terrible!"

I shrugged. "For now, that's the best there is."

"Really?" she said, unwrapping an out-of-town newspaper from around their third silver-plated butter dish. We'd been using the second one they got to chop and spread cocaine lines. "If that's the best, I hope none of us ever sees the worst."

"I've got no room to complain. I bought the game, we both play it by the rules. Honest and clean."

"Not quite."

The butter dish with its two-thimble mound of my cocaine, the rolled dollar bill tube and single-edged razor blade lay between us. I leaned forward on my elbows, drew four inch-long lines out on the silver mirror surface, snorted two, pushed the plate in her direction. "I don't know what you mean," I said.

Katie hesitated, did her two lines.

"John . . . You two really aren't doing the same thing."

"Of course not, I *know* and she doesn't."

"But that's not all of it. You keep using metaphors and cosmic explanations. People in love like you say strange things. Nothing you say is *wrong*. But that doesn't mean you're *right*. You can die in that gap.

"Those 'straight and honest' rules, sure, you both play them. You love her, she says she doesn't know. If she says anything. Ever notice that? Like when I was with her the other night. If she does talk, it's all the time questions: give me answers. Give her questions back and you don't get a thing. Her brother and mother, right? War casualty and suicide. The Great Tragedies. But I lost a brother too in that car crash. I answered all Tara's questions about that heartache, but when I asked about her brother, she says, 'I don't want to talk about it.'"

"That's because there's still so much she doesn't understand, still so much pain . . ."

"Yeah, well, pain is a shield and ignorance an armor. They're both great excuses."

My words were bitter, defensive. "Armor against what? Shield against what? If you've already got pain, what's left to protect?"

"Everything." Katie shrugged. "Protect against the chance of other pain. Or pleasure you can't control. If you're smart enough, tough enough, thorough enough, you can grow to love that pain. You get trapped inside it. Where it's safe. Maybe not pleasant, but safe. At least you know it will always hurt. In this world, any certainty is hard to throw away."

"So you think that's Tara's problem?"

"I don't know, John." She shook her head. "I know all that trouble pulls you together. You love to solve problems, make things right. That's your compulsion. You know she needs more in life and you could be the center of that. She knows you're a better deal than the ghosts on her shoulders, and you . . . you charge her batteries. Right now, she's got the best of both worlds. But she's enjoying an illusion. She can't have either if she holds onto both. You talk about playing it straight, playing by the rules. You both do, but . . . she uses the rules to her advantage. You play your advantage within the rules."

"Same difference."

"Then why are you two so fucked up?"

"We could go 'round on this all night, couldn't we?" She laughed. *"Again?!"*

"I figured this kind of talk ended when I left high school."

"Guess again, Rankin." She reached for another taped box: the fourth toaster-oven. "Nobody in America ever leaves high school."

"You know what scares me most?" I asked. "All my life I *believed*. Built my life around one great inflexible dream. Ultimate love, one special woman. That's what you wait for. That's what you fight for. You know it when it happens because it obliterates everything else. The rest, for all its problems—and I know there are problems. You know that better than me . . ."

Katie's expression didn't change.

". . . the rest is how you shape heaven.

"Well, I found that woman. But something went wrong. Right man, right woman, wrong time. I'm just hanging there. Nowhere. If I was wrong about it all, then what have I been basing my life on?"

My turn to laugh. "I can't console myself with the myth that I'm unique, that nobody has ever bled like this before."

"I know what you mean," Katie said. She looked around the walls where her paintings now hung. "I know what you mean."

Her voice grew more excited. I assumed it was a coke rush.

"You don't cast yourself an image, not do anything that isn't cool for it. Get so good at it you fool yourself even though it's got you trapped, fool yourself and everybody else too."

"I don't need to worry about that," I said, though I wasn't sure what she meant.

"Good," she said. "I'm glad you don't."

On television, Jimmy Carter finished his speech. We turned to watch the applause.

28

August surpassed July as the hottest month on record, according to the *Washington Post*. Muggy, filthy air wrapped itself around the city like an ever-thickening wool blanket. Even thunderstorms couldn't wash away the stench or sweat of summer. On that September 4th morning, the air quality was "in the unhealthy range." The *Post* credited the right wing, evangelical organization called the Moral Majority for the defeat—in his own party's primary—of an Alabama Baptist minister turned congressman who had served in the House of Representatives for 16 years. The proselytizing politicians of the Moral Majority found the incumbent minister insufficiently pure for public service in the capital of the greatest democracy on earth. The *Post* also said that Abbie Hoffman, a cheerleader of the rebellious 1960s, planned to turn himself in to the cops after six and one-half years of well-publicized outlaw life. Hoffman was a fugitive from cocaine, not political, charges. I imagined the burning red glow of the plastic bag still heavy with white crystal powder hidden in the top right hand drawer of my desk, a shimmering scarlet ember clearly visible through the wood paneling, but I didn't have enough energy to worry about such trivia.

August surpassed July. September was following suit. I felt trapped in a race that wouldn't end, running where milestones signified nothing but their own passage, the ultimate illusion of progress. Each day I'd wake from a fitful sleep, stand before my mirror and say, "Well, at least you can't get any smaller than you've shrunk now." Then the next day I'd get up, look in the mirror, and discover I was half the size I'd been the day before. The world kept disappearing. Existence seemed like a vast, three-dimensional jigsaw puzzle. Chunks fell from the mosaic, replaced by yawning, burning, black gaps. Each lost fragment pressed down on my back.

"Did you see my story?"

Mad Dog stood in my open doorway. I hadn't heard him climb the stairs, open the door. Lucky he wasn't anybody who wanted to break my skull. Lucky, I told myself.

"The lead story on toxic chemical waste dumping?" I said. He nodded. "I didn't know it was yours. Nice job."

"No big deal." He grinned at me, but his smile left when it wasn't matched by mine. "I came to get the last ABSCAM tapes."

"You know where they are," I said, nodding toward my apartment.

"If the FBI had hit this place with a search warrant, I wonder whether they'd have looked under your dirty laundry. That would have been real bravery." He grinned at me again, waiting for a response.

"Probably," I said. He went back into my bedroom on his errand.

I had more control when he returned. "How are you and Katie doing?"

"Oh, you know. We . . . There are those things. I guess you're right. I'm not the easiest person to live with, neither is she. We'll always have . . . What did you call them? Rocky times."

"At least you have times."

"Yeah," he said. "We got that. Want to get some coffee?"

"I can make some. I don't want any but . . ."

"I just thought . . . Let's go for a walk or something."

"It's hot out there."

"You can stand it." I hesitated. He said, "Come on, you can't stay in here all the time. We haven't hung out in a while.

"What are you working on?" he asked as we bounced down the stairs. I had to move quickly to match his pace.

"Nothing. Lots. Bullshit, some of it for the law firm Tara's father steered me to, some for Art Dillon, a couple clients on the side. The Janet Armstrong mess. I keep busy. Make a living."

"Good," he said as we reached the bottom of the steps. I surged past him, jerked open the door, looked back over my shoulder as I lurched out into the heat while I replied, "Sure it is."

My shoulder slammed into something that bounced back. The impact registered as aftershock as I watched the creature I'd knocked away from the wall stagger four steps to the gutter.

Radio Woman. She regained her balance, a bent, twisted gnome of a person, almost sexless, almost unhuman—and by her species, almost unavoidable in the streets of Washington that year. Radio Woman was Capitol Hill's Queen Bag Lady. She'd once walked her miles followed by her son, a tall, vacant-eyed man who held a transistor radio pressed tightly against his ear. When his mother carried the radio, crackling static blared from it: she kept the dial between earth stations. In 1977 one of the social service agencies channeled Radio Woman's son into a therapy program. Suddenly she walked our streets alone in her hidden world. A tannish gray dust settled over her. She wore sacklike dresses and in summer shoes seldom hit her dirt-caked feet. Black greasy stains worked their way up her tanned, thick-veined legs. Her dusky brown hair was chopped short around her head. Freckles dotted wrinkled leather skin. Someone seemed to have pushed her face against a brick wall, held it there until all her features flattened out. One snaggle tooth stuck up from her lower jaw through cracked, dry lips. Her brow was perpetually furrowed, her eyes like asphalt. She walked hunched over, usually carried two brown paper bags stuffed with her treasures, sometimes loading them onto a squeaky, pull-along stewardess's luggage cart. In 1980 she seldom carried the radio that won her name. Maybe there was nothing left worth listening to.

"I . . . God I'm sorry!" I called to her as she shrugged her shoulders to readjust the weight of the sacks dangling from looped handles at the ends of her arms. "I didn't see you! Are you OK?"

Her glare dismissed me as if I were a fly. She regained her balance, her bearings, shuffled to the intersection at 7th and Pennsylvania, headed toward the Eastern Market.

"Jesus," I said as Saul joined me on the sidewalk.

"You want to go upstairs and shower?" He wasn't joking.

"I didn't see her!" I said. "All of a sudden, *Boom!* There she was."

We watched her cross the street, seemingly unaffected by her brush with my reality. She looked to see if cars might kill her, but ignored the traffic light.

"You OK?" asked Saul.

"Back when we were bachelors, we'd have tried to get a date with her."

He didn't laugh. "You are a bachelor, John."

"Yeah," I said, "I am, aren't I?"

We drifted toward Seward Square.

"John, I . . ." He touched my arm. "A lot of your friends are worried about you."

I wondered who, but knew he wouldn't tell me. "That means so . . . I'm OK. Really," I insisted to his skeptical frown.

"You sure?"

"Really. At least, as much as you see."

"That's what's got us worried."

"Worrying doesn't do any good. I don't even worry anymore."

"What are you going to do?"

"I'm doing all I can."

"You're . . . You're not drinking or doing lots of coke, are you?"

"Don't worry," I assured him, smiled. "I'm already hooked. You can't live with more than one obsession. Staying alive with what I got is hard enough."

"You're not thinking of anything else?"

A car honked its horn at the Metrobus which hadn't started rolling the instant the light turned green. I wanted to hug Saul, him and everyone *who*. But I didn't have the strength then. The thought went through me that I must be worse off than I figured. My friends projected me past a fate like Radio Woman.

"If I don't stick around," I told him, "I'll never know how it ends. You know me. Insatiable curiosity."

"All of us would do anything to . . ."

"I know. I'm sorry I'm such a pain in the ass."

"You'd talk about anything, wouldn't you? You wouldn't do anything without talking about it, would you?"

I laughed. "Aren't you all tired of me talking about it?"

"Promise me—*promise me* that you won't do anything . . . major without talking to me first."

"Saul . . ."

"Promise me!"

"Still that much faith in my word?—OK, I promise . . . I promise I won't do anything like you mean—and I promise I'll talk with you about . . . anything.

"Hell," I added, "that's easy enough. You've heard it before. A thousand times before."

"Is she worth all this, John?

"I mean," he quickly said, "she's gorgeous and bright and you're both from the West, love movies and politics and it's amazing you met, but she's . . . she's just who she is, not the world."

"You just don't know her like I do. She's more than you think. Different than she seems, than anybody but me knows. Better."

"You've never been to bed with her," he said.

"I want more than that," I insisted.

"Sure, but it's a good place to start."

"We're already something special!"

"Yeah, but is it worth it?"

I stared at my friend as he pleaded for me to show him my salvation. "It's all I got," was all I could say.

All I had, I had that night. Tara and I sat across from each other at a downtown jazz club's sidewalk table. Traffic whizzed by us on Pennsylvania Avenue's sticky blacktop. Cicadas sang their shrill electric whine in the trees of George Washington Memorial Parkway one block away. The odor of dank foliage from the parkway mingled with cigarette smoke drifting from the open door of the jazz club. We sat at one of the half dozen outdoor tables; our waitress and two of her friends occupied another. The other customers were all inside where it was cooler even though the owner kept apologizing for his air conditioner's sporadic performance. Tara wanted to sit outside, so that's where we sat, the scratchy jukebox sounds of Duke Ellington's "Take the A Train" flowing out to us with the smoke.

There'd been little to do that night, no movies she hadn't seen worth seeing at all. The night before she'd stayed home: the *Post* warned of rumblings in Mount St. Helens, and she wanted to stay close to the phone in case her aunt called. I wondered whether "the Senator" was back home campaigning, whether he might be in danger, but neither of us mentioned him or her mother and brother unless absolutely necessary. The night before that I hadn't seen Tara either. She said she went to a dress-up birthday party for one of her gay male friends, a waiter at the café where she'd briefly worked when she first hit town. She had many gay male friends. One of them told me he'd let me use the birthday party mansion for my wedding. I didn't thank him; it wasn't even his house. Tara told me the birthday party "was quite a scene." She volunteered nothing else. I asked for no more.

"It's September," I said. "You think the heat would break."

She shrugged; listless, nervous.

Try to talk her out of whatever ails her, I thought: "What do you think you'll do if things at the magazine don't get better?"

"I don't know," she said.

"Me either," I joked. "I may know you better than anybody, but I don't know everything."

"WHAT DO YOU WANT!!?" Her right hand groped toward me, her face contorted tight across her bones. "Do you want to play 20 questions or . . ." She shook her head, covered her face with her hands. Her lower lip trembled, slickness suddenly glistened on her cheek. The waitress approaching our table to ask if we wanted another beer stopped, turned, went back to her friends. They all pretended not to see two lives unraveling ten feet from their now strained banter.

Tara let me pull her hands from her face. Her fingers held mine—trembled, didn't lock tight, but they held mine. "What's wrong?"

"It's . . . Nothing, I . . . I just don't know!" she moaned.

But I knew. I knew so much in those days. A man carrying

a briefcase through the night walked past our table. He looked at me gutting my soul in public. Suddenly such indiscretion didn't matter.

"It's us, isn't it? You want to and . . ."

"Do you think that if I *knew* we'd be sitting here?!"

She started to cry again. My voice shook, fire stung my eyes. "I know what you're going through," I said. "I know you're trying. It takes time. This probably isn't the right thing to say, I know it hurts you when I say it, but I love you. You're so special, so . . ."

"No I'm not." A pronouncement chiseled in ice.

"Tara, I . . ."

"Don't you see that?! I'm not. You find all these things in me that aren't there. All of you do. I'm just *here,* and that's all there is."

"That's a lot."

"That's hollow. All I am is hollow. Not like you. You've got something inside you that makes you alive and different. You don't care if you're a Don Quixote. So you make it work. Like a wolf in the city. You don't belong here and there's no better place for you to be. Don't you see? You got this sense inside you, this vision or dream that makes you strong so you can . . . Don't you see?!"

"Everybody's got . . ."

She shook her head.

"You don't think you've got something?"

She nodded, sobbed.

"Nothing inside you? That's why you're running scared?"

"That's all I am," she said. "Just running scared. That's being nothing at all."

"If you only knew how wrong you are, how . . ."

"Sure," she said. "Sure."

"Look: you wouldn't cry, you wouldn't care, not if you were hollow. It wouldn't make any difference to you if you didn't have a dream locked up in there."

"I just cry because I cry. That's all." Her lips trembled to a frown. "Besides, what difference does any *dream* make? What good did dreaming do Janet Armstrong? All this precious *life* ends up in Nazi death camps or down in Jonestown sucking its own poison. It all ends and the best go hardest and first, so why fight for more? We're like a movie. We don't make any difference. We don't last. We're not even on film."

"You make a difference to me. Forever." I could barely whisper, barely stop my tears. I felt her almost there—and I felt her slipping away.

"Yeah." She sniffled, forced her tears to stop. "I've been so wonderful for you, haven't I?"

"Yes, you have."

She started to cry again. I leaned across the table. Right there, in a jazz bar where any fool could watch, we wrapped our arms around each other.

"I love you so much, Tara! You've made all the difference in the world for me. You are my dream!"

"Oh God please don't say that! Please don't say that!"

"I have to. It's true."

"I can't," she moaned. "I don't know and I can't."

"You will," I said, my head pressed in the crook of her neck, hers in mine, our cheeks slick against each other, the warmth of our bodies spicing each dry breath. "You will. I promise. You know I always keep my word. I promise you will."

"Sure," she said. "Sure." But she didn't stop crying.

I dropped $5 too much on our table. No one at the waitress's table looked at us as we stumbled, shuffled our way to the sidewalk. From inside the bar I heard Billie Holliday singing "All of Me." The Porsche waited around the corner by the park. We had to pass alongside a mammoth brick building under construction. I led Tara into the shadows, held her in my arms while she sobbed, tilted her head until I saw that beautiful face again streaked with tears, forced those blue eyes to look into mine.

"I know it hurts." Her lips trembled. "But it's all either of us has got. We're the best in the world for each other, even with all this." She tried to look away, but my hands locked her tight. "It's . . . We must know this after all we've just said: nothing has changed." I smiled, tried to say it lightly so as not to hurt her. "Except maybe I love you more." I felt her shudder, but wouldn't let her look away. "I know: you don't know. But that means . . . You're not saying *never* to me. You're still not saying that, are you?"

"No." A barely audible whisper. She shook her head, leaned into me.

We held each other. And she cried.

The phone started ringing as soon as I opened the door at the bottom of my stairs. It had taken longer than usual for me to find a parking place after dropping off Tara. She would expect me to be home by now, if she wanted to call me, to tell me . . . anything, I thought as I rounded the second-floor landing at top speed, tore up the last flight three stairs at a time. I stumbled but didn't fall and the phone kept ringing. I bent the key in the lock, almost broke the door down before it flew open and propelled me inside. I grabbed the receiver: "Hello?"

"You were wrong, cowboy," said the answering male voice.

"Most likely," I replied, catching my breath, not sure who he was. I heard background voices, tinkling glass, the *cachunka* dinging of a pinball machine.

"Where you been?"

"With a friend," I said: Detective Nick Sherman, though his voice didn't sound right.

"Your pretty lady friend?"

"Yes."

"You're a lucky guy, Rankin."

"Are you drunk?"

"I'm working on it. How about you?"

"No. What am I wrong about?"

"You remember our friend Magic Murphy? Indicted on 17 major counts? Couple assault charges from a couple different complaining witnesses, a couple of his girls he beat up? A weapons charge? Couple pandering raps? Even a referral to the tax people? Plus the big one, the second-degree murder count for Janet?"

"I remember," I said.

"He's gonna skate."

The room caught fire.

"The grand jury thought he should get a trial," said Nick. "So did the first prosecutor assigned to the case. Then she got promoted. The second prosecutor wanted to try the case too. Then he got a job downtown defending people. The third prosecutor lost the case for a while. The fourth one figured, hey: hard case to try, hard case to win, ugly publicity all the way around. Since he wants to be a U.S. attorney or judge or some other political job some day, he's shy around ugly, risky cases. So it somehow bounces to a fifth prosecutor. He ain't bad, but he's four steps removed from what happened and at the bottom of the totem pole. Not long out of school. He's handling maybe 70 cases, lots of pressure to generate 'closed' statistics with 'conviction' stickers on them. Meanwhile Magic, that fine, maligned, police-abused citizen, he's been sitting in jail for 'most a year with the same attorney, some legal eagle who ain't no fool and who wants to do his ethically sworn best by Magic."

"What happened, Nick?"

"Final score? Plea bargain. Down from 17 counts. Down to 2. No more murder count. One simple assault, one pandering. The most Magic can get is five years. Which means he'll serve about a year, maybe less. He'll get credit for his jail time. He goes for sentencing in November. Do a few months, hit the streets again. You were wrong."

"Wrong about what?"

"About why Janet got to me. You were wrong."

"Doesn't seem like that makes much difference."

He mumbled something to someone passing by him in the bar. When I heard him come back on the line, I tried for more. "Was there any reason the prosecutor gave . . ."

"Oh yeah!" he interrupted. "There were reasons. Bullshit and bureaucracy. Plus our new boy prosecutor is shaky about Magic's guilt."

"Nick, if there's any question . . ."

"That's what the jury decides. Ain't no question here. But maybe the jury might think so, because our prosecutor isn't quite bright enough to *believe*, to realize what a piece of evidence means, let alone get it introduced in court.

"Go back to that night. Janet was going to fly. She fakes a john call, leaves Magic at the place. He tells her he's going out. He tells us he did. Probably he meant to, maybe he did. For a while. She comes back for the puppy. Next thing nobody disputes is she's dying in the alley. Magic drives up, takes her to GW hospital. Big hero, right? You know why I know he killed her too?"

"No."

"Those pretty, black leather gloves. The ones he wore to protect his hands when he taught his whores the way of the world. He was wearing them when he brought Janet to the hospital. They were soaked with blood and freshly scratched. He says they got that way pulling chunks of glass out of her. I know they got that way when he stabbed her with a jagged glass knife broken from the windowpane as they brawled down the back stairs. Our prosecutor says the gloves will never fly in court. Says it was cold that night and Magic might have worn them for that reason, not because he put them on to do Janet when he tumbled into her game. Doesn't make any difference that the other women all say Magic never wore those gloves for anything else, that he had other gloves for the cold. Who'd believe them? They're just whores. He's just a pimp. Not a strong enough murder case to excite a jury over a little thing like a pimp cutting up his whore.

"And that's where you're wrong, buddy. That's where Janet got to me.

"She deserves better than this treatment. This ain't the way it's supposed to be. I don't care if she was a shit or a psycho or whatever, she wasn't supposed to end up a dead whore out there in the street. Nobody is, but especially not . . . not somebody who walked through all that love. She deserved better. Where did it all go wrong? That's your job, right? But it hits me too. So OK, so all *that* went wrong. Now she's in my game. What does she get? The shit end of the stick. We can't even lock up the guy who cut her down for any more than bullshit. Doesn't make any difference who she was or what she did, she deserves better than that. If *we're* somebody, then no matter who *she* is, she deserves better than that."

"So do we, Nick."

"Ain't that the truth? Maybe things have never been right, but were they ever this confused? Half the time I don't know where I'm standing. Everywhere I am seems like one big lying commercial that sells you junk you gotta buy. Right and wrong don't add up like they used to. I need someplace that won't keep changing on me, someplace I can stand that won't be bought and sold from under my feet. Baseball and country and western music: I can't play neither.

"Back when we started all this I figured . . . I don't know. Maybe that you really would come up with a 'why' that answered everything and made it all right. Maybe that me pulling somebody else into this shit, making them see it and making them care, maybe that would help wipe it all away. Make me feel cleaner. Make me feel like I done something worth doing. Now I don't even know what I done."

"You did right, and you did good."

"That sure made a whole lot of difference, didn't it?"

"You never know," was my only answer.

"It's all so fucked up."

"I wish I could help."

"Me too."

"You called the guy who was wrong, remember?"

"Yeah," he said. "Yeah.

"Look," he said after a moment's silence. "I thought you should know. I already talked to the Armstrongs in Eugene. You don't need to do that. Told them you'd do a good job. Whatever it is."

"Thanks."

"For what?"

"I'm glad you called."

"Yeah," he said, "so am I."

29

Life lost another season in October. Leaves turned crimson and gold as they died. It was beautiful to see.

Autumn reigned on that Sunday, October 19. I lay in bed, full of the certainty that I was doomed to but two choices. One was to fade with the leaves, dry up and blow away. The other was to believe in spring, a dubious assumption of no comfort. The phone beside me rang. My arms were as sluggish as tree branches when I moved to answer it.

"Good morning!" Tara's voice was chipper, excited. "Have you seen the *Post?*"

"No," I said.

"There's a major story about how oil companies have swindled $2 billion from consumers, but the *big* story is on Bruce's new album! It's by somebody named Peter Knobler. Do you know him?"

"No," I said.

"Listen to this: 'Bruce Springsteen is more than simply a rock 'n' roll performer, he is a man who has been taken to heart. Where Elvis's power came from sex and isolation, and Dylan's visionary magic derived from his struggles with desolation, Springsteen has moved people with the course of his life.' I'd say the *Post* likes him, wouldn't you?"

"Yes," I said.

"Did your friend get us tickets for the concerts?"

"Both nights. Two sets."

"Why not go both nights?"

"Why not," I said.

"Ah . . . Have you had any coffee yet?"

"No," I said.

She laughed. "Well, call me when you get going. Maybe we'll catch a movie tonight. I'll be here all day."

"I'll probably come by," I said.

We hung up.

Once I got out of bed, it was over. The rest was just the doing. I lay there, the weight of the dying world pressing down on my chest. Nowhere else to go. My right leg slowly dragged across the sheet, over the edge, bent my foot to the hardwood floor. Like ripping an oak from the earth.

These books I'd borrowed from her. Into the box. That record album of Billie Holliday she brought over so I could understand more about Janet Armstrong. Into the box. The blue sweatshirt and gray sweatpants from when she'd been running and gotten trapped by the rain, dashed laughing to my apartment for shelter, a towel, and a ride home. Into the box. Here was one of her casserole dishes from when we'd cooked dinner for Saul and Katie, gotten drunk and stoned, stayed up all night playing Risk. Into the box. Here and there were things she gave me—a Springsteen button, a novel she loved, a small art print to thank me for letting her camp in my house when she first came to town. Part of me wanted to put them in the box too, banish all presents of the past. But that would be cruel, that would be wrong. I put two tickets for one night of Bruce's D.C. concert schedule in an envelope, poured a couple grams of cocaine into a vial, put that in the envelope too. Power and poetry, a few crystal moments of illusion, my last gifts to her. I taped the envelope to the outside of the box. I did some of the coke before I put it back in the drawer, did some then did some more. It didn't matter. I stared at the plastic bag as it lay next to the gun, that heavy, black gun. The last thing I did was slip the Porsche key off my ring.

Tara was sitting on the stoop of the E Street townhouse where she lived in an English basement apartment, a steaming cup of coffee beside her, the newspaper spread over the concrete. Maybe she was reading more about the story of the ten-year-old heroin addict that the *Post* blew the town apart with three weeks before. The story won the Pulitzer Prize as America's best journalism of 1980; it later turned out to be a lie from a reporter who'd also lied about her credentials. Tara waved as I drove up. She wore sneakers, jeans. The shirt sleeves of her snap-button, blue denim shirt were rolled up as she soaked in the last warm sunshine of the year.

The car engine turned off. My forehead pressed against the leather-padded steering wheel. I heard the creak of the small gate in the wrought iron fence, the scuffle of her shoes on the sidewalk. I got out, stumbled to where she stood with questions and concerns shaping her face. She looked at me, then past me to the car. To the packed, bulging box on the passenger's seat. I held out my hand, hers came toward mine automatically, and just as automatically her fingers closed around the Porsche key I laid in her palm. Her lips trembled.

"Don't say anything," I told her. Words fought their way past my sobs. "Not now. Not after all this time. There's nothing you can say anyway, is there? Nothing you can do. I love you and you love me and none of that makes any difference anymore because there's nothing we can do about it. You won't say yes, you won't say never. Because you don't know. You say you can't. So you won't. I can't stop loving you and I can't go on. I can't solve your mysteries so we can take the best we have. That's never going to happen. Never is when there are no choices left. It doesn't matter if you speak the word. Never is now."

Her shoulders shook, her face was wet. I put my arms around her, held her limp, shaking form next to mine. She smelled of the sea, she smelled of the sun. My tears fell everywhere. "I love you," I whispered.

Then I turned to leave. Last chance was for her to reach out, pull me back. Nothing touched me. I walked away.

30

Lois didn't deserve my mood when we met. She was on her way to Atlanta to work for IBM in a job whose vague title implied bossing people. She'd reluctantly scheduled her trip so I could interview her. My conscience kept me from trying to cancel our appointment. Besides, she'd been unreachable while traveling. Lois grew up with Janet Armstrong, came back East (though not to Harvard) for college, visited Janet in D.C. when that old friend worked the streets for Magic, helped set up the escape plan that failed, had been in Desmond Jones's room when her mother called to say Janet was dead.

I didn't feel dead enough as I rode the subway to the airport. Bitterness dripped from the jagged hole I'd blown through my core two days before. There didn't seem much left to life. Certainly not a lot of sympathy or concern for a dead whore and her mysteries or a woman who like Janet—and Tara—was beautiful, bright, a "young professional" their same sweet age and on her way up. *Over how many broken bodies,* I wondered when I saw Lois's thick black hair, high-cheekboned, classic features and lithe frame. Her clothes were designer chic. Half a dozen businessmen idling around her in the airport lounge over martinis and scotches were wondering how to get her into a bathroom on the plane or maybe even in a dark corner of the terminal. She thought I was one of them, seedier than most, perhaps, but still predictable in intent when I walked up to her. We surprised the hotshot hustlers at the bar, retreated to a deserted corner of the carryout. Day and night get lost in airports. There were no windows in this hallway. The yellow electric lights and piped-in Muzak made everything nauseatingly timeless.

Lois read my mood, matched it. "What if I don't know anything?" she argued as we sat down.

"I don't expect cosmic answers from you," I said.

"You're not going to get any."

More pessimism was not what I needed. I led her through the usual routine: when she met Janet, where, what was Eugene like then, what was important to Janet. Got the usual family-and-music answers.

"The music part I need to understand on faith," I confessed. "I like jazz a little, but the rest . . ."

"What do you know about opera?" she asked.

"Juan loves Maria, so he kills her then sings about it in Italian for four hours."

"That's not funny."

"No," I admitted, "it isn't. You said her father is wonderful and Janet cared about him most. He had all his hopes pinned on her."

"That's right." Guarded, wary of a trap. She had much to protect, from the wisdom and virtue she'd exercised in being Janet's lifelong friend to memories that would define both of them. Lois's jaw was steady, her words evenly paced. She'd hacked her way through the social and academic jungle of exclusive New England colleges; had that blasé toughness such success brings. Everything is reduced to a clean, intellectual wit, and on that level, no one gets the best of one of those clever survivors. Her fortress was made of glass—totally secure until someone pitched the right rock.

"There's a world of difference between Janet's father and what she did," I said.

"If there was, she rationalized it. She talked about her independence as a gift from her father. Janet played that rule all the way. She concluded that what they wanted her to do was to be happy and preserve her independence. Even if it meant hurting them."

"Or herself."

Lois shrugged. "Independence has its price."

What would you know about that? I wondered. "She sold it to Magic pretty cheaply."

"Maybe she didn't think so."

Tread softly or you'll lose her, I thought. Shift: "When you were teenagers, what did you do for fun?"

"What do any kids do for fun? We'd sneak into this hot springs with a cement house where the water comes into the pool."

"No cruising Main Street in cars?" I asked.

But I doubted energy conservation prompted the negative shake of Lois's head. "We didn't hang out at the shopping mall either."

"How about drugs?"

She glared defiance: "Janet didn't smoke grass until her junior year in high school. Cocaine was too expensive. Maybe once or twice. Quaaludes a couple of times. All of us did acid after graduation. Tequila was our drug."

We barely used beer, I thought, said, "Was she a good friend?"

"She could be cutting, bitchy about people. She wouldn't hesitate to tell someone what she thought of them. But she was a good friend to those of us she cared about."

"Did she ever do anything unusually wild or rebellious back then?"

"Well . . . senior summer was different for everyone. By then we'd all had our first affair." *And it took me until the middle of college,* I thought. "I think for Janet it was that spring. She started going out with Mary's older brother Karl. She used to sneak out at night. The morning she was to leave for Harvard she still hadn't come back in. Her parents woke up, the window was open, Janet was gone. Maybe she slept in. Maybe she just didn't care. Maybe she wanted to get caught, to prove a point. Whatever, it shook her parents. They called our house at six in the morning. I tracked her down, got her home and to the plane on time."

"How would you describe her then?"

"Good humor—biting, but good. Bright. Tenacious, very proud. Impulsive. Practicality was the first thing to go. Thoughtful, but rash. Brave. Obviously she put herself in danger. She didn't believe in God like her parents, but she wasn't a true atheist, because she had this religious sense of life. Nothing to make a cult of, but still strong.

"She saw herself as very attractive to men. She was, especially in the confident way she carried herself. She was good at rebuffing people, which makes anybody more attractive."

I couldn't think of a clever comment. "Did she understand cause and effect, consequence?"

Lois frowned. "I think so. Whether her understanding was accurate is another question. She was reckless. The immediate was her focal point."

"If you had a snapshot memory of her from high school days, what would it show?"

The loudspeaker announced the departure of a United Airlines flight for Portland, Oregon. Less than two hours driving time south of Portland waited Eugene, where Janet and Lois grew up. Everything was green there. Clean. A river runs gently through the town.

"Before we left for college," Lois said, "we exchanged gifts. I don't know what *the* book that everyone is reading this year is, but that year it was Tom Robbins's *Even Cowgirls Get the Blues*. Janet had this motto she blended from it and something some guy once told her. She gave me that book inscribed with that motto: *'If you don't like it, get on your horse and ride.'* That's how we went to college." Lois shrugged. "She wore coveralls."

"She changed her image at Harvard."

"Who didn't change their image when they left home?"

"Why did she end up at Harvard?"

"Harvard gave her more money than Yale. She also wanted to go to Boston. She'd been back East—family trips, school programs. Europe too. Harvard was another adventure. *The thing to do.*"

"But she didn't do it. She quit."

"She was disappointed." Lois leaned forward to reinforce her justification. "She didn't think other students took their opportunity seriously. She said she felt sorry for the teachers because they didn't have students who cared.

"Part of her leaving Harvard was that disappointment, part of it was personal. She started going out with Byron the summer after her freshman year. She fell convincingly and deeply in love with certain people . . ."

"Why do you say *convincingly?*" I interrupted.

"Because she really believed it at the time. If she were here today, she'd say, 'I don't know how you define love, but at that time it seemed like the thing.' Maybe Janet was more in love with the abstract, with being in love than with any one person. But she always believed love was real with whoever he was *then*. The man kept changing, she kept claiming the love was genuine—no, better or bigger or more real. She would throw herself into it, change her life for him. She left Byron working in Eugene after our freshman summer, came back to Harvard briefly, then dropped out and came back home to him. I think he cared for her, but she'd just altered her life's plan for him. He didn't want to share that big a commitment with anybody. He didn't.

"There'd been men at Harvard too. Janet had an affair with a black man on campus that they kept secret because he was part of a . . . he and a black woman were a prominent public couple, so he and Janet kept their relationship a secret."

"How nice for him."

Lois shrugged. "I never understood it either."

"Oh, I *understand* it," I told her. "Usually the guy is married and can't leave his wife *because*. It's as common as hell.

"How did she feel about sex?"

"She loved it!" Lois laughed, probably remembering some innocent conversation. "She went to bed with a lot of men. She cared deeply about some. If she didn't care about someone, that wouldn't prevent her from going to bed with them—any more than it prevents every man I've ever met from acting the same way."

"This was before she got into prostitution?"

Lois nodded. "Don't get me wrong. She wouldn't hop into the sack with anything. There had to be something more than sheer physical attraction. That was maybe less true summer of our senior year in high school, but we were young then, less discriminating. How picky were you when you first had your chances at passion?" I didn't answer, so she continued.

"In prostitution, she said she could split herself off from . . . from the bodies who were doing *that*. Maybe she could do that before. Lie there and think about baseball or movies

266

or what happened in class. She'd been to bed with people she could have cared less about later, but in the throes of passion or a hot summer night . . ."

"How was she after dropping out of Harvard?"

"Extremely depressed. She couldn't explain why she was home: *What was wrong with Harvard? Why did you quit?* How the hell *do* you explain when you choose the unexpected? So you try not to care, shove those people out: They don't understand. She developed an elitist attitude about that. Which increased her sense of isolation. She probably would have left Harvard without Byron. She may have gone someplace besides back to Eugene, though. When he didn't work out . . . she'd just sit and cry. Crying over Byron in part, but everything else too. He was the easiest thing to focus on. She was depressed because she didn't know who she was—and because she didn't know who she was, she was depressed." Lois laughed bitterly. "Trapped in her own circle."

"Did Byron change her outlook on love?"

"No. She fell just as deeply into the next person. Which was basically Magic. Ultimately Magic."

"Ultimately?"

She smiled without amusement. "That's how it worked out, *the big one,* but that's not what I meant.

"After Byron, she had a few flings. Then fastened on a black deejay at the Eugene nightclub where I worked that summer as a cocktail waitress. We used to joke that he was the only real black in Eugene. He played up that cool stereotype, claimed to be an ex-heroin addict, a jazz player. Thought he'd been around. Thought he was bigger stuff in the small pond than he was even in the small pond. He was nothing in a larger pond. He was exotic for Eugene. Being black in Eugene means that's all you are. Then it's just a question of which stereotype you get branded with.

"Janet usually came by the bar when I was working. She dressed up when she went out. She shined in downtown Eugene. That didn't take much. A simple gauze skirt and a halter top. Plus the way she carried herself. When I came to work, Magic was there. *He* stood out because he was the second black in Eugene and he had on knickers." She laughed: "A gold velour knickered jump suit. With boots. And many rings on his fingers. One was a coiled serpent with diamond eyes. Real flashy. Hanging on the railing with a drink. When I went by him delivering a drink he made some comment, something that required a retort. That started a battle of wits. He's the master of bar patter. Janet saw him that night. He talked to me, meanwhile dancing with several other women. After I got off work he asked if he could take me out for a drink. I said no. He asked if we could meet the next night. I tried to fob him off with *we'll be around downtown,* which is a way of saying *no.* You know: *If you see me, fine; if you don't, fine. I'm not that interested.*

"But the next night he followed Janet and me from one bar to another, sat down at our table. I was next to him. Janet sat next to me. They hadn't met. She watched the band like she was miffed or bored, but she was real aware of our conversation. Playing it cool right back at him. He was hard to put off. Gave out a lot of drivel about astrological signs, and the kind of person you are, and *'I can see this and I can tell this about you,'* and the fact that there was something *different* about me. Really special and unique. And could we go out, could we do this. Could we just go and talk. I think you're interesting. Let's just go and talk. Meanwhile Janet was kicking me under the table, whispering, 'This is crap!' When she and I went out for coffee later that night she said, 'What he is saying is straight out of the book of pimps. I've heard it before, that kind of patter, that kind of come-on.'"

"So she knew—or thought she did—right from the start."

Lois nodded. "I couldn't believe that was what it was. But it upset me. The next night at work I told the bouncer I didn't want Magic bothering me. When he came to the door the bouncer told him to stay away from me. Magic blew up, put up a terrifically indignant scene, was finally let in. He came up to me livid, said, 'Why did you insult me like that? If there was something wrong, why didn't you just refuse me?'"

"He took the slack you cut him, spun it back to trap you."

"He's clever. He hung around that night, maybe the next. He ran into Janet, probably with the black deejay who Magic had been conning with this *soul brother* rap. Janet brought us back into contact again, only now he was centered on her. A couple nights went by.

"The next time I saw Janet she said they'd gone to the ocean. I hadn't known they'd been seeing each other that much. A couple days later, she said she was leaving with him. Out of the blue—although I knew when she called what she was going to say—no reason for me to. But that's what she said. That's what she did.

"They knew I was extremely upset. She said, 'We'd like you to talk with us about it.' We met in a bar to 'iron things out.'"

"Had he identified himself as a pimp yet?"

"We all knew by that time."

"Did he say she was going to work for him?"

"Let me get to that. She told me that at the ocean she realized she loved him. It was not love at first sight, but after she came to know him. She felt that he was different than everybody thought. That we didn't understand or know him like she did. That he was someone else, somebody special.

"I found out then that the black deejay threatened Magic because he was seeing Janet. He showed up at Magic's motel room with a pistol. The deejay was in over his head. He didn't know that, but Magic knew it. Magic conned him out of his anger."

"So much for the big fish."

"Yeah. When I met them, he took me for a walk, got into an extremely personal discussion about things I wasn't able to handle then. Stuff Janet must have mentioned. He got me to admit far more than I had to other people at that point. Upset me. But also drew me closer to him. To thinking he wasn't such a bad person, so understanding: *My, look at how perceptive he is!* He used all sorts of hooks and questions and teases, bullshit empathy and calculated crap. Any 'understanding' was solely for manipulation's sake.

"Trying to iron things out was all to his benefit so Janet wouldn't have second thoughts. The night before she was supposed to leave, she and I went to see Karl, Mary's brother, so she could say good-bye. He told her she was out of her mind. That she would end up a cheap whore, no two ways about it. She was almost persuaded not to go, then she went back to Magic. According to her, they talked all night. When I went to sleep I thought, *maybe she won't, I don't think she will*. She called the next morning and said she was.

"I helped them pack up. What else could I do? Even now, looking back and knowing what I know, I think: *What could I have done? What could anybody have done in a situation like that?* You're required to make so many judgments and decisions, and usually don't have a whole lot of wisdom and power to do it all. She wrote her vacationing parents a note saying she was going to work in Washington, D.C., at a restaurant. She said she'd call them Thursday or whatever.

"She told me she was going with Magic because she loved him, that he was bright, street smart but more than street smart. He had . . . perspicacity or some sort of insight that she admired. And that they had a terrific time in bed. Sexually, she said he was wonderful. There was this . . . power between them, like a secret strength they shared. That showed that everything was right, that this was the right thing to do. And that they loved each other."

"What was her plan?"

"When she left, she . . . *he* said she'd never have to do *that*. Be a prostitute. He wanted her to be his number one lady. They'd go back East, make money. She could manage. Maybe find a singing job for fun. Open a small jazz club with the money they earned. They could have a nice life. Money was never going to be a problem. She could pursue the things she always wanted to do. Jazz, books."

"Had she ever talked with you before about prostitution?"

"Sure. We'd discussed it *hypothetically* or in fooling around. All women talk about it that way. You're right: it was posed whether I wanted to go with them. We toyed around with what all that meant in the whole scenario he described. Her best friend and her lover off to win the world. I had no intention of doing that. You think about what might happen that's exciting, but finally you realize that your adventure would hurt too many people. That's what I told her. But she thought she'd found a line to walk that justified everything."

"She probably also felt like the star of high drama."

"Absolutely. The atmosphere was adventure. You go off in a Cadillac with clothes and this and that and money. You won't even stay in this country long. You'll go to Europe, the Riviera, have a chalet in Scandinavia and a villa in Spain. High drama."

"High horseshit."

"And you've never fallen in your own horseshit?"

Lois caught me by surprise. I froze for a second, cracked a wry smile. The tension between us eased.

"What happened then?" I asked.

"She was supposed to call her parents when they got home that Thursday." Lois shook her head. Her manner softened as she remembered. "She didn't. Three days later she still hadn't called. It had been a hellacious *déjà vu* of the time she'd snuck out the open window, with her folks calling me 15, 20 times a day. Karl and I finally decided to tell them because something might have happened. Maybe they could go to the police, put out an APB or whatever.

"God that was terrible! Saying, 'Janet is not working in restaurants.' Telling them who she went to see America with. When I finished, the phone rang: Janet. Her parents never said to her, 'We know what you're doing.' She gave them the excuse about going back East to work. They let her know they were scared to death."

"Did she say she was alone?"

"She said she'd gone with friends. She never admitted to them at this point what she was doing. But she called me at home that night, and I told her I'd told her parents.

"The next time I heard from her she called to give me the name of her Chicago hotel. My mom took the message. I called back right away. Magic answered. In an offhand manner he asked if I'd told her folks what he did. I said yes. He said, 'No, but did you tell them what I did? I mean, *really?*' He got nastier: '*Did you tell them what I did?!*' I told him Janet hadn't called like she promised and I was worried. I said, 'I told them everything I could think of about you.' He said, 'I never want to speak to you again, bitch!' Slammed down the phone.

"Janet called me a couple days later, so he probably cooled down. By then, everybody knew that everybody knew. At that point, she said she was working."

"When you say working, you mean being a prostitute?"

"Yes, not just *managing*." Lois's face twisted as if that word tasted foul. "She said there was a convention and they were going to be staying there. They were looking for more people to work. Later on, she said that was one of the toughest parts of her life, working in Chicago. Getting used to the business. They stayed there for a couple months. I went to Rome on a program through my college. We were out of contact until the following January when I returned to Eugene. She called me from Washington.

"The next time I saw her was spring break of my junior year. I went down to Florida with a girlfriend. On the way back we stopped in Washington overnight. Magic was very nice to me. Went out of his way to give us drugs, cocaine, anything we wanted. Still tried to convince me to come and work. But by this time it was only an exercise in words because we both knew where the other stood.

"We went to some disco in Georgetown. My girlfriend had something else to do, so it was just Magic, Janet and me. Drove up in a white Cadillac that had a little makeup mirror you turn on and off, a skyroof. Three of us sitting in the front seat. We were very dressed up. Janet wore a lot of makeup. I borrowed some of her ritzy clothes: I was a college kid on vacation, what did I have? The car was parked by a valet, we were ushered in and given very good seats. Everybody knew who he was. I don't know that he was anyone special there, but they gave him royal treatment. He was a good customer, a showman when he went somewhere. He knew all the cocktail waitresses' names. And we were his ladies. That was very clear."

"Did he give you instructions on how to act?"

"No, but you fall into it. Just because of what's going on around you. It's unusual to see a black man walking through the night with two white women who are slickly dressed up." She shrugged. "You know that's how people look at you, so what can you do? You fall into acting, you perpetuate the look.

"Janet and I and my friend stayed at the Church Street place that night. Magic stayed somewhere else with his other woman—Chris, I think her name was. We left the next morning.

"I didn't see Janet again until May, though we talked on the phone frequently. After I got out of school, I flew down here, stayed a few days, again just nightclubbing it, talking. The last time I saw her was in August, for about a week here in D.C. But I talked to her right up until she died."

"How did Magic treat her?"

"In front of me, always very well. I never saw or heard them argue. He knew he had to, or there would be trouble for him, because it would get back to her parents."

"Did you talk to her alone? What did she say about herself?"

"I asked her if she were doing a lot of drugs. She said she was staying pretty clean. He had it and could get it, but she didn't do much. Cocaine. But nothing . . . nothing more than what we'd done in high school. Less. She wasn't doing pills, and I believe that, because she was trying to keep her health up. She was disciplined about getting enough sleep, eating right. Because she had responsibility, because she was working. At first five days a week, but then constantly. Seven days. Christmas Eve, Christmas Day even. Trying to pay huge bills. They had material things. One of those giant TV screens. A Betamax. Full sets of living room furniture in two apartments, exotic waterbeds. Two color TV sets in the one-room apartment. Upkeep on the Cadillac, on her Volkswagen that they'd driven out from Eugene. Plus they spent a lot. She said he gambled.

"I asked if he ever hit her. She said only once, when he blew up. He slapped her. And he felt terrible afterward. It wasn't only once. I know that now. She'd been beaten. Had huge black eyes, everything else. But at first she wouldn't tell me that."

Lois paused, looked off toward the crowd shuffling down a corridor to catch a plane. She didn't look at me when she started talking again.

"Once we went up on the roof of that Church Street place. He wasn't around. She said that one night she was so depressed she drove her Volkswagen to the Potomac, took a bottle of pills with booze because she just . . . she wanted to leave there, but she didn't care about living anymore. She fell asleep and a cop came by, woke her up. She didn't take enough. How badly she wanted to die, I don't know. But that scared her. I don't know how many times she tried to do that. She promised she would call me if she ever felt . . . in that frame of mind again. Or that she would fly up to New England or I would fly down.

"She constantly talked about leaving—should I or shouldn't I? More so as it came closer to the time she died. But she'd said that before, then she'd say maybe it would work out."

"Did she still talk about loving him?"

"Yes, but there were more things she had to put up with. That he spent any time at all with Chris, the other woman. Janet was largely supporting her too. Chris wasn't very good at the business. Janet couldn't understand the obligation Magic felt to her. Janet wasn't jealous of other women, because they tried to recruit women and there were some she liked. Chris was a jealous, spiteful bitch. I met her, but she never said a word to me. She stared out the car window."

"Did you ever get the impression Janet was trying to maintain any separate identity? Any freedom?"

"She talked about hiding money. She knew if she ever left she would have to split without saying anything. She knew he'd react violently if she ever tried.

"She told me how once in the spring before she died she took a client up to his hotel room and he was . . . really disgusting, fat, self-infatuated. Smelled. She knew he was carrying a lot of money in an envelope in his suit coat. They were in bed, he'd fallen asleep, and she decided to sting him. She described the whole thing like a terrifying short story. It took 45 minutes for her to ease out of the bed carefully so he wouldn't wake up, listening to his breathing and snoring the whole time. Ease over to the closet, open the louvered shutter doors. Every time she moved he'd breathe or turn over or something. But she got the envelope. Got dressed, got out of there. In the elevator she discovered she got $3,000. She kept some of it, gave some to another prostitute who hadn't made her quota, turned the rest of it over to Magic. I don't know what happened to the money."

"How did she feel about the men who were her customers?"

"That they came to her put them beneath respect because that meant they were lonely or deceitful in some way."

"There's an old Groucho Marx joke about not wanting to belong to any club that would have you as a member."

"Are you always so full of ugly jokes?" But by now her pique was more for life than me.

"I don't know," I said.

"There were some johns she liked," said Lois. "Some interesting people, high-level officials. People who offered to fly her to Panama, put her up, not expect favors but just take care of her."

"That sounds like a twist on Magic's line."

"Who knows? She said there were people interested in her because of her past. She told customers she went to Harvard —if she ever talked to them much. There were some that cared enough about her to want her out of that life. Some that loved her, some that brought her gifts all the time—clothes, jewelry."

"Did she ever mention anything about a john from Capitol Hill?"

"She said they came from all over."

"Does the name Martin or Martin M. ring any bells?"

"No."

I hadn't expected it to; I didn't much care.

"What was her life like?"

"Work. She made as little as $200 a night or as much as $500. Four hundred dollars was a good night and there were some great nights. She used two apartments, one in Georgetown, one on Church Street. She hung out in the Regency, sometimes on the Track. But she also had a book with a lot of clients. At least 60."

More than that, I thought as I remembered the six-page trick list: 404.

"She often got calls from those regulars. She also didn't mind going down to the Track. She had friends down there. Some of the police officers liked her. She said she didn't fit into any of the categories on the Track, that she had a good corner. It was simply a job, something she did."

"Did she enjoy her music when she wasn't working?"

"There wasn't time, especially toward the end. Losing her

music and her reading made her irritable, worried. Volatile. There was so much fatigue. It got harder and harder to go on. She worked and she slept. It was as if there was a tunnel and she wasn't sure if there was a light at the end of it. Maybe there was and maybe there wasn't.

"After Eugene, did she ever try to recruit you?"

"No, she knew that I wouldn't. There may have been a couple times when she asked, 'Are you sure you don't want to come down and be with us?' But nothing serious. And she told him not to bother me about it."

"Was she ever afraid of Magic or johns or the streets?"

"Well, she knew Magic was violent. But remember: she didn't always tell me the truth. She threw out a couple instances where a john pulled a gun on her. Once she figured the gun wasn't loaded, grabbed the guy's arm and it went off, put a bullet hole in the wall. Her reaction was that she'd pulled a dumb move. She figured if she knew enough, then she wouldn't get into trouble. She figured she knew enough."

Didn't make much difference, but I wanted to know.

"How about you?" I asked. "Didn't you ever question your wisdom in coming here, hanging out with her in a life of danger and crime? One wrong second, and you could have been raped or killed or who knew what."

"Let me tell you about wisdom. And responsibility. Janet was my friend. Had been forever. I loved her. Slowly, step by step, she walked out where . . . where it was bad and dangerous. And I knew that. But let's not get too hypocritical here. I'd done bad and dangerous things with her even before Magic entered our lives. What we felt between us was honest and true. How could I turn that off, deny my responsibilities to a friend, maybe just when she needed me most? How much slack should you cut a friend, especially when they cut you all they got? All those great theories and written rules of right and wrong, they're easy to cling to when you're a million miles away and standing still. But when it's up close, when it's your friend and you're walking down the street with her . . .

"Sure, there was more. There's a rebel in me, a yen for excitement. Adventure. That street world . . . it's the exciting undercurrent the high and the mighty never admit the whole time they're riding on it and more. It's *real*. There's a seduction there, especially when you got a friend like Janet, who lets you walk in her shadow and see as much as you can about how it is to be on that line and across a hundred more, all without actually taking those steps yourself. She gave me as close to a free ride out there as you can get. Sure, it wasn't free: tell my boss I hung out with whores and pimps, I'd be fired, even though I bet he's secretly had a whore. Sure it was wrong: I was part of crime, even if I didn't do any. I didn't call the cops. I wouldn't and I couldn't. Forget about Janet, I knew my ass was the price of that phone call. Sure, I knew my ass could have gotten blown away. But I was younger then, life is easier to risk. That's why generals like young soldiers. The young die eagerly; their imagination is less refined.

"The danger dues weren't the big cost. It was looking in the mirror, wondering where your loyalties lay and knowing you might not know for sure until it was too late, until after you'd made the wrong choice. There may have been a more right thing to do, but if there was, I didn't see it. If I saw it, I ignored or didn't recognize it, maybe fooled myself. Maybe I just plain fucked up. I pay for that, even if nobody else sees the cost. That's life. It's all risk and reward and chance. Sometimes that's a shitstorm. Can you understand that?"

"Yes," I said, remembering. "I understand."

"I had a friend," she said. "I didn't like where she was, but I stuck by her and did the best I could."

"Friendship's a two-way street. Did she know the effect she was having on you, her other friends and family?"

"That bothered her. But she had that logic. Because she was all up front with no lies, because they wanted her to be independent, that smoothed things out enough for her to keep going."

"What choice did her parents have? They either wrote her off as dead and cut off her best link to salvation, or they tried to keep her as their daughter."

"I don't think Janet interpreted the equation that way."

"That didn't change it. Except that made it easier for her. Given that, given that she was breaking all sorts of rules, breaking even her sales promise by robbing johns . . . What happened to her 'religious' view of life, of honesty and morality?"

"She felt a knowledge of a more . . . real reality, that *I am of the streets and this is how things are* stuff. And: *Who are you to talk of morality when there are these two different worlds?* She believed she knew the worst of both worlds. She felt qualified to judge in both. For her, it was all basically shit.

"I think she wanted to live honestly—but not the way you define honesty. Like stealing that $3,000. She would see that as quibbling in the larger picture. Which she believed she was at peace with. I think she wanted to live truly to herself. And grab as much of life as she could at any given moment. That's what she wanted out of those streets. To know them, take life from them."

"Did it make any difference to her that she was in Washington, D.C.?"

"The capital of our country? No, but working as a prostitute here didn't do anything to curb her cynicism. For her, Washington, D.C., was just another tough town."

"Lois," I said, "you've been living with this from the start. Can you figure out the why in what she did?"

"I'm not sure I even know *what* she did. I don't find her life surprising, no decisive cracks, no 90-degree turns. Everything seemed to grow out of what preceded it. Given the people she met, the way she thought, it seems like a logical development —as crazy as that sounds."

"Does that answer why and how she died?"

"She reached the point where it was time . . ."

". . . to get on your horse and ride," I said, finishing the motto Janet once wrote in her friend's book.

"Yeah. *Get on your horse and ride*. I guess she was in the wrong spot when she made her move."

"Remember how I asked for a mental snapshot of her from high school?" Lois nodded. "Could you give me one that summed her up? One picture when you think *Janet*."

She blinked, paused, sighed. "Not one, but three. Any scene from high school when the three of us—Janet, Mary and me—are sitting out in the woods, drinking Tequila, her in her coveralls. Whipping through the forests in her Volkswagen. One at Harvard, Janet in her tapestry skirt, boots—*in* that environment but still not a part *of* it. And then sitting on the roof in Washington, talking about the time she drove to the Potomac and . . ."

Her voice cracked. She looked away. Time passed, she glanced at her watch as if to prove its journey.

"Look," she said, "I . . . There's nothing more I've got. Nothing more I can tell you. I can't . . . I've got a plane to catch."

She stood, gathered her briefcase and carryon bags, quickly walked off into the crowd.

31

Lois's memory rode with me on the subway downtown to keep my appointment with Art Dillon. She'd come to Washington out of obligation, and out of obligation I'd peeled back her scars. She found she still bled. I found a few new stories about Janet Armstrong, but not the ultimate answer I'd been hired to find or the secret I'd hoped to unearth. I knew a little more than I'd read in the newspapers. Maybe it's always like that. Maybe the only ultimate answer you'll ever get begs the question itself: Janet Armstrong did what she did because she did it. History. Things happen. As my train pulled to a stop at Dupont Circle I didn't much care if I ever knew any more about Janet Armstrong. I could chase small questions about her all over the world, drag more people back through a time they wanted to leave behind them. I doubted any of it would bring me an ultimate answer worth believing. I hit bottom. My only concern right then was how to live up to my promise to her father. No matter what I did, he wouldn't feel it was enough.

As usual, Art Dillon started talking as soon as he opened the door to the law library where I waited. "Did you see the Phillies win the Series last night?"

"I saw part of the game at Saul's," I said. When I took the car back I'd borrowed from them—but I didn't mention that.

Art took off his glasses, looked my body up and down. "Have you been sick?"

"I've been running a lot."

"Too much. Nobody should be that skinny. You keeping busy?"

"I left town for a couple days. Went to the sea."

"Probably did you good. The case I called you about seemed bigger this morning. Car accident. Counterclaims, witness problems. I thought there were more issues, but now . . . Tell you what: you should earn some money for coming down here. Could you run a couple license plates for me?"

He could have done that with one call. But he felt an obligation. I was too drained to convince him he was wrong.

"Sure," I said.

The outer walls of the public building by police headquarters are gray, its corridors are painted institutional green, it smells stale and tired. I went to the proper room and to the proper window, filled out the proper forms with the two D.C. car license plate numbers Art had given me, paid my $2 per form. Outside dry leaves were skittering over the sidewalk with October's dirty wind. Inside tired people fed the paper monster that records America for America's sake.

Call it sentimentality, call it nostalgia, call it foolishness. I picked up another form off the stack by the window, filled out the license plate number of Tara's Porsche. I knew the small answer I'd get back; I didn't know why I wanted it. Maybe to reaffirm what I already knew—that it wasn't my machine.

The clerk brought back the two forms for Art's question first. I put them in an envelope along with the proper receipt for my reimbursement. The pittance I'd charged him above expenses would cover my subway fares and the request on the Porsche.

D.C. license plate registration forms are returned completed on four sheets, one atop the other: white, yellow, pink and orange. They all said the same thing. The 1978 silver Porsche, coupe body style, license plate number 813-407, serial number 394857029387, was owned by Panchax, Inc., with an address in care of an office on K Street. I knew the address, I'd worked there: Fred Thomas, her father's lawyer. But I'd never heard of Panchax, Inc.

Whose car had I been driving?

32

I sought the truth by hunting down the lies. There'd been so many, they'd been so smooth. She'd called me a wolf in the city and they'd fed me garbage. I'd played their game simple and straight. No more mistakes like that.

Washington's civic bureaucracies are scattered at the base of Capitol Hill. My hunt started there, and I ran each step of it as steadily as I'd run my route the day this all began: May 19, 1980, so many months before, so many lies before. Eddie Hampton started it all; I couldn't foresee where I'd find his corpse, but I knew I would. Just like Janet Armstrong, who wrote a name in her trick book. Somewhere down the line I knew she'd step out of the shadows, into the spotlight, in place once and for all. A wolf in the city. They didn't know how right they were.

The flag signifying that the Senate was in session still flew over the Capitol that afternoon when I finished two hours of sifting through public files in three different municipal offices. Panchax, Inc., was a duly registered D.C. "investment management" corporation, with its 1,000 shares of stock privately owned by three men: Martin Mercer, who was also corporation president; Robert Woodson, who was vice-president; and Fred Thomas, the corporation secretary-treasurer who listed his law office as the corporate headquarters. All nice and legal.

Of course, neither Senator Robert Woodson nor Administrative Assistant Martin Mercer listed their holdings and titles in Panchax, Inc., on the disclosure forms I'd examined not so long ago. Perhaps Woodson had an excuse: the stock could have been held in his anonymous blind trust which *was* reported. But he should have listed his vice-president title. Mercer had no such legal loophole. Woodson and Mercer were not alone in their *inadequate* compliance with federal disclosure law. A March 4, 1981, General Accounting Office audit of Congress's compliance with its self-policing system found that approximately one-third of all such financial reports in the Senate contained omissions or errors. The Justice Department, however, had no interest in prosecuting these violations of law and had been given no money by Congress to do so.

The city bureaucracies yielded two business permits for Panchax, Inc.: one for parking lots, one for vending and electronic video game machines. No agency had a public master list of the corporation's holdings. The corporate registration dated back six years. Her father's second term in the Senate started then; his third election was little more than a week away.

Maybe not, I thought.

Twenty minutes later I sat in a prestigious, cluttered office waiting for a roll call vote to finish. Law books filled this office as they had Senator Woodson's, but these well-worn volumes were not for decoration. A sense of intimacy drifted through the bric-a-brac and political mementos, the photographs on the walls. Woodson's office was a carefully crafted showpiece; someone lived and breathed and worked in this room.

He lumbered through the door with the lilting gait I knew so well. While an infantry captain in World War II, three German soldiers surprised him and his sergeant one foggy morning in the hills of Italy. The meeting was accidental; intense. Two German soldiers died, one got away. The sergeant was unharmed. The same bullet slammed through both of this man's knees, damaging the second one more than the first. Now, at age 64, arthritis and rheumatism locked those rebuilt joints in constant pain, forcing him to always seem a little drunk when he walked. Most people didn't know about the wounds, didn't know that he took massive doses of a prescribed painkiller just so he could move. Most people knew him as a lush: look at the way he walks—would a sober man stumble like that? The fact that he also drank too much didn't help dispel his alcoholic image, nor was the truth helped by his refusal to dignify such slurs by denying them, by explaining his war wounds. *The hell with that,* he'd say. He kept lumbering, kept drinking, kept too silent. Somehow he also kept getting reelected.

"Hello John!" He rolled toward me, big as a bear, silver haired like a grizzly. But he was 64, wounded, and it showed.

"Hello Senator Applegate. How are you?"

He lowered himself into a stuffed leather chair, motioned for me to sit down. He sighed his reply. "I'm tired. God-damned tired of this goddamned place. When are we going home?"

"I don't know, sir."

We both knew yet never admitted the answer as far as he was concerned. He had two more years left in his term, and only conscience kept him from resigning that moment, flying back to mountains and valleys he loved but left to serve elsewhere. Practicality kept him from announcing any earlier than necessary that he wouldn't run for reelection: the moment he publicly committed to that choice, he lost 90 percent of the power he'd spent a quarter century accruing. At that point, his foes only had to stall, which is the easiest action in the U.S. Senate. Stall until they didn't have Senator Applegate to kick them around anymore. The smart bet in the city said he wouldn't run again. But stranger things had happened in the Senate, so no one pushed the gamble too far. The longer Applegate kept his secret, the longer he functioned with any worthwhile power.

"You're the only person who ever worked for me who then did something totally unexpected," he said. "Being a reporter was one thing, but a private detective . . ." He shook his head, grinned.

"Senator, I . . . Something big has come up. I normally wouldn't ask you, but . . ."

His grin faded and the quick nod told me to skip the sales pitch. His life was measured in seconds.

"Senator, have you ever noticed anything . . . peculiar or wrong with the way Senator Woodson conducts his business?"

"Haah." He rubbed his eyes, they slowly bored through me

with their glare. "You know, John, the United States Senate is not supposed to be a marketplace for idle gossip."

"There's nothing idle in my question."

"I'm sure you believe that. But I wonder if you know what such a question means.

"We are all prisoners of our own power here. Whenever the mob outside these marble walls clamors for one of us—for whatever reason—we all tremble. We protect our own, John, because that protects us. No one wants to fight up here. The genteel rivalry of the parties reflects self-preservation, the Senate rules enforce it.

"The meek may or may not inherit the earth, but they certainly manage most of it. In politics, timidity is rewarded, true courage is punished. Perhaps that's not totally unwise. Bold men drag us into nightmares more often than not. The meek act as brakes, give reason its chance to prevail. Right and wrong get sorted out in that process.

"I've given my life to this system. Maybe knowing what I know now, I wouldn't do it quite the same. But I've made the commitment. I'll keep it as long as I'm here."

"I'm not asking you to compromise your principles, sir."

"We both know what you're asking. I have my obligations, as do you. I also have a great deal of faith in you, so I'll tell you this: "I have never seen Senator Woodson do anything I construed as corrupt. But then, I know little of who is corrupt. I choose not to know. You need to ask someone else, a wheeler-dealer, not a man like me." He raised his hand against my interruption. "I'll say this: Woodson is not much of a United States senator. Not that I am, but given what should be . . .

"I've never served on a committee with him. We both belong to the Western Caucus, and I've watched him operate on the Floor. And, of course, in the party. It's my impression that he got into politics at his wife's urging. My wife and I knew her slightly. She wanted him to *do* great things, he wanted to *be* great things. I think she eventually saw there was no bridging that difference. I think that contributed to her disappointment and ultimate death. She committed suicide."

"I know," I said.

"Peggy told me you've been dating their daughter, so I assumed you did."

He sighed, stared off into space. Then startled me:

"Woodson is an idiot. A well-intentioned idiot, mind you, but an idiot nevertheless. He has no depth—not in intelligence, not in character or personality, so . . . perhaps not in morality or integrity either. All he seems to acquire in life is polish. He is, unfortunately, not unique in the Senate. Worse, his type—the smooth, glib, handsome face—is becoming less the exception and more the rule. Television. No debates or reprinted speeches or reasoned arguments of hard years of experience recorded and rewarded. Machine politics is passé. People stay locked in their houses now, not connected to their neighborhood or ward or . . . They are wooed behind their closed doors by careful control of mind-numbing media. Sixty-second movie miracles, that's who wins elections now. I'll be so goddamned glad to leave them I . . .

"I don't know what evil you're after, John, but I doubt Woodson is it. He's not worth pursuing. For all I've said, he's not a bad man. He's just not much of a man at all."

"He's a United States senator," I said.

"Yes," said the man who was one too, "he is, isn't he?"

So many somber suit-and-ties and fashionable dresses swirled by my phone booth in a hallway of the United States Senate; so much frantic importance attached to this sentence of the proposed amendment to the pending and doomed resolution about the shadow of yesterday's problem. I watched every form, saw no one watching me back.

Don't slip, I commanded myself as I waited on hold. Stop your hands from trembling. Don't let *them* perceive your churning bowels. Don't let *them* make you lose control again. You're a wolf in the city. Don't break on their streets now.

The on-hold buzz ended. That spry male voice sounded more alert in mid-afternoon than most people are in the morning.

"Thank you for taking my call, Mr. Shaughnessy," I said. "You probably don't remember me, but . . ."

"My secretary said John Rankin."

"That's right, sir."

"Of course I remember you. You work for Ned Johnson."
Ned had me call this man on stories—only twice, with the last
time being three years before. Yet Jack "the Mack" Shaughnessy remembered who I was; it wasn't that he remembered,
I thought, it was that he never forgot. "How is Ned?" One
legend inquired about another. "I haven't talked to him in
months."

"He's fine. I must tell you: I don't work for him anymore."

"I hadn't heard." There was no reason he should have. "I
hope everything is going well for you."

"Well enough. I need a favor. I hate to ask it, but it's more
important . . ."

"Than I can imagine?" He laughed. "What is it, John?"

"I need to talk to you about corruption in Washington."

He laughed again. "John, I'm 73 years old. I doubt I'll live
the second 73 years we'd need to cover that subject."

"Not the whole subject, sir. Just a specific group of men."

"Ahh." He thought for a moment. "And no doubt it would
be best if we met. And no doubt you're on some sort of crisis
schedule. Is there any particular reason you called me?"

"Ned says you know more about Washington than any
other man alive."

"While I appreciate his kindness, I doubt his accuracy—but
that's a flattering hook to throw an old man. Let's see . . ."
He probably consulted a desk calendar in his expensive K
Street lawyer's suite. "Could you be on Capitol Hill tomorrow for lunch?"

"Anytime, anywhere."

"Do you know what Club 116 is and where it's located?"

"Yes sir, though I've never been there."

"Then our meeting definitely won't be wasted."

I used the public-records room on the House side of the
Hill. I could have gotten the same stuff on the Senate side,
but why risk being seen on that turf by anyone who might
mention it to Woodson or Mercer? Their staff all knew my
face. No more small errors. Not for a wolf in the city. It took
an hour to go through the payroll books for the last 12 years,
but I found a chance.

Her name was Carol Kenwood. She'd started work for

Senator Woodson in March, 1976, with the impressive title of Legislative Assistant. She'd stayed until September of that year. Not long, even by Hill standards. I borrowed the clerk's *Congressional Staff Directory* for 1980, got lucky again: KENWOOD, Carol, still on the Hill, with a biography that showed she'd been there since the mid-1960s and listed all her former employers. For three years she'd been number one staffer for a congressman from Tennessee.

Cross-checking payroll books gave me a list of other staffers with whom Kenwood had worked. One of them was an acquaintance whose philosophy appalled me; another was a man who I'd tried unsuccessfully to turn into a source during my tenure at Ned's. We liked each other enough to transcend my fruitless efforts. That flimsy bond had to do. He'd been a junior staffer to her some five years before. Now they both worked better jobs for different bosses.

He wasn't happy when I called him from my office late that afternoon. Something about his wife's car being towed. I played on every worthy bone in his body to let her dangle somewhere in the civic bureaucracy while I asked about Carol Kenwood. He didn't buy the lame reasons I gave him for my questions, nor did he answer them as candidly as he could. According to him, she was smart, tough, straight as an arrow. I thanked him, wished him luck, and offered to do what I could if he needed an investigator for his wife's traffic ticket trouble. My offer left him more confused than my questions.

By the time I got off the phone with him it was 4:55. The operator connected me to the receptionist in Carol Kenwood's office.

"Can you tell me if Carol is in?" I said, hoping the question would stump the receptionist enough for my scam.

"Ah . . . I think so. Do you want me to buzz her?"

"If you . . ." I turned the receiver away from my mouth and yelled to my empty office: "Hey Paul! Don't go yet!

"Look," I quickly said back into the phone: the receptionist still hadn't switched me off her line. "I'm sorry, I've got to catch Paul before he leaves. Will Carol be in tomorrow?"

"As far as I know."

"Great." That meant she was in town tonight, probably at

the address shown in the phone book. "Talk to you then." I hung up before the receptionist could say or do any more.

Carol Kenwood lived in one of the many anonymous multistory adult dormitories that rise into the darkness alongside the interstate across the river in Virginia. The building had 12 floors of identical apartments with window balconies, a parking lot, a name like Treemont or Oakflower or Hilltop. The lobby was spacious, decorated with musty yellow carpet and wallpaper. An Arab-looking desk clerk watched me as I stood outside the glass front doors using the security phone to call Carol Kenwood's apartment. The autumn night was cool, the odds less than even that she'd buy my pitch.

"I realize you don't know me," I explained, "and I know it's late, but it's extremely important that I talk to you. We have a mutual friend." I mentioned the name of the man I'd called about her. "Call him. He'll vouch for me, although he doesn't know why I'm here. Please see me, Ms. Kenwood. I took a cab all the way out from D.C. I don't have much time to spare and it's vital."

"To whom?" she said. "A private detective shows up at my door knowing my name and something about me at 9:00 at night . . ."

"I came by earlier and you were out."

"Persistent too." She thought a moment and I worried that I'd lost her. I was already scheming to salvage a meeting the next morning when she said, "Hang up the phone and wait."

People wandered in and out of the building while I waited. I could have drifted in with a crowd, blown right by the desk clerk, taken the elevator up to her door, but I was sure that would have inspired Carol Kenwood to dial 911 and introduce me to the Arlington police. The desk clerk answered his phone, peered out at my form shuffling in the darkness, spoke into the receiver. He gestured to me. When I pointed to the phone on the wall, he nodded. I dialed Kenwood's number.

"He wasn't there," she said, mentioning my friend's name. "His son said something about parking troubles."

"He's lost in traffic court."

"His son doesn't know you. But he knows you're here now. I promised to call his dad back later tonight."

And you made sure the desk clerk checked me out, I thought. "Will you see me? Please?"

She hesitated, but I knew her mind was made up: "Why not?"

"Usually I don't let strange men into my apartment," she said as I followed her nod to sit on the couch. She kept a safe three steps between us as she led me into the apartment. She sat in the easy chair facing me and in a straight flight line to the door. Her apartment was tidy, her bookshelves full but neatly lined, her plants lush and healthy. I settled down on the couch behind the glass coffee table with its selection of newsmagazines, crossed my legs and tried to look harmless. The dead green eye of her TV set stared at me from the corner of the room. A gray cat slept beneath its stand.

"Well," she added, "the men may be strange, but at least I know them."

I bet she did. She was over 40, nowhere close to beautiful, but possessed by a smoldering spirit that made her sexy when she should have been plain. She was a big woman, five-foot-ten and husky beneath her tentlike, flowered dress. She wore her brown hair cut short and puffed out; probably dyed, but so what? Her face was round like the moon, her eyelids thick and droopy, her mouth heavy but not attractive. She had slight jowls and a thick neck, but she moved like a dancer, sultry and sweet. What she had lasted longer than most women's beauty, and probably satisfied those lucky men she invited into her apartment more than attention from a vapid sylph.

"I greatly appreciate you talking to me, Ms. Kenwood."

"Let's get to it." She lit a cigarette, inhaled deeply. "Forget the soft soap. Why are you here?"

"You used to work for Senator Robert Woodson."

"So?"

"You quit abruptly. You don't have to talk to me . . ."

"Tell me something I don't know."

"I'm not sure I can," I said. "But maybe we can figure something out together."

"Like what?"

"Like is he crooked."

"Oh." She stared at me. "You say you're a private detective?"

I nodded.

"Hired by whom? What do you do and where do you come from?"

"I used to be a reporter for Ned Johnson." She pursed her lips: I didn't know what it meant. But at least I'd hit a nerve.

"Who do you work for now?"

"I really don't have a client for this."

"Freelance head-hunting?"

"I have my reasons." She waited. "Good ones." She waited. "They threw a net over me. I got hurt, so did at least one somebody else. The whole world got lied to. And it hasn't stopped."

"How do I know you're not full of shit? Cute, but still full of shit?"

"You don't. But I promise you've got nothing to lose."

"Spare me your promises. I'm sorry if anybody got hurt. The whole world has been lied to before. How can I help any of that?"

"By talking to me."

"About what?"

"About Woodson, his henchman Mercer, their office, why you quit and what stinks about it all."

"I should tell you all this out of the goodness of my heart."

"I don't care why you tell me."

She stared back, then stubbed out her cigarette in the sidetable ashtray and walked toward the kitchen. A phone waited on the counter and again I thought I'd lost her. She opened a cupboard above the counter, brought down a tall glass.

"Do you drink?" she asked as she opened the refrigerator.

"Not much." Bad tactic, but it was too late.

"I do." She came back with a glass of ice in one hand, an open bottle of amber liquor in the other. "I drink scotch. I drink a lot. And I like it. You're probably into that other shit. Don't tell me, I don't want to know. If you want some soda or juice, there's the refrigerator."

"Thanks," I said as she filled her glass with scotch.

She settled down in the easy chair, lit another cigarette. "How much do you think you know?"

"I know something stinks. I know Woodson and Mercer, their lawyer Fred Thomas. I've read all the public records and reports. I've been in their office."

"You've been around."

"Not always by choice."

She laughed and I knew I was home free—for whatever good it would do me.

"Let me tell you how I got there, what it was like, then you can ask your questions.

"I was working for a retiring representative. I was tired of the constant battle for reelection that is the House way of life. Thought I'd try the Senate, six years of security. I heard Mercer wanted someone to help him run Woodson's shop, applied, got the job.

"Supposedly I was the legislative assistant, number two in the office, but that rank was meaningless. I don't know what Mercer expected when he hired me. Maybe he figured me for a bossable broad who'd make sure the coffee fund never went broke. I knew Woodson wasn't much before I signed on, but I never realized what an . . . He's not lazy or stupid, he just isn't concerned with legislation. Which is not the way a senator is supposed to be. I think he's only playing a part he does well. That's not a bad ambition or occupation, if it doesn't get in anybody's way.

"It got in my way. I was the legislative assistant in an office where legislation meant nothing. Oh, Woodson voted and we cosponsored and were always *very concerned*—but it was show biz.

"Mercer is nobody's henchman. He runs that office—and that senator. The kids on his staff call him Iron Man Mercer, or sometimes M-2 or M-Squared. They're all basically kids, except for him and Sue—do you know her? The *personal* secretary?"

She slurred *personal* and I nodded.

"Don't get me wrong. I like Sue. We're both Hill freaks. She earns her public dollar. If there's more to who she is, well . . . it works out to everyone's advantage. Especially

Martin Mercer's, who hired her. It would be like him to put her next to Woodson, then give them both a push. That would leave him one less worry. Give him more time for his goddamned fish.

"Mercer's the center up there. He keeps the staff busy with trivia that keeps Woodson getting reelected. Woodson always sponsors National Pet Week. Mercer keeps Woodson happy in the easy limelight where nobody shoots at him. That's why Mercer likes only kids or burnouts or never-was cases to work for the senator. The kids don't understand the charade and the burnouts don't care.

"Every time something of substance came up, Mercer expected me to do no more than funnel it to him and then funnel it to the kids for them to put whatever he wanted on paper. Nobody was allowed to bother the senator and nobody cared what the legislative assistant thought."

"Any special areas that happened in?"

She grinned. Lit another cigarette, poured herself another slug of scotch. "You know something, don't you?"

"Only enough to ask logical questions."

"Yeah, well, logic is why I got out of there. Nothing concrete. But I'm no dummy, no burnout, and certainly no kid.

"Woodson is on the D.C. Appropriations Subcommittee. He took over chairmanship of that and another subcommittee just before I got hired, which was why I was supposedly needed. But I never got to do shit with the D.C. committee. That should have been the lowest priority. What the hell does a senator from Washington state care about godfathering the city of Washington? Nothing in that but headaches.

"Or supposedly nothing. Everything about that committee went straight to Mercer. Top man handling the lowest priority. He went to all the hearings, sometimes with a kid to carry the papers. Sat right behind Woodson, did the whispering-in-his-ear act whenever the committee staff hadn't adequately prepared the script for Woodson to follow. That made no sense. Nor did it make any sense that whenever anybody called with questions about D.C. they talked only to Mercer.

When I asked him about it, he tossed me two answers, both weak. The first was that handling D.C. gave him something to do. Then he added that they got a lot of political contributions from local biggies and better he should handle them with tender loving care.

"He realized I wasn't buying the game. The kids began to end-run around me, ignore even my bullshit figurehead role. They didn't come up with that move themselves. I read the writing on the wall. Mercer wanted to ease me out. He was too clever to fire me—God knows where I would land and how nasty I'd be and what I'd shoot my mouth off about." She smiled. "Or who I'd let into my apartment late at night.

"And that's it," she said suddenly. "There were too many questions and not enough good answers for me to stick around. I didn't dislike Woodson, what little I saw of him. He's pathetic to somebody who cares about Congress. Mercer is a creep, pure and simple. He'd sell your heart for a penny a pound."

"You have no idea how they're crooked, though?" I asked.

"Or *if* they are, *why*," she replied. "Money wouldn't mean much to Woodson. Mercer always drives a fancy car and has those exotic fish, but he's never been married, has no kids and no high-rolling habits as far as I know. He drinks, but he's no alky. Maybe he's some kind of junkie."

"You nodded earlier when I mentioned Fred Thomas, the senator's lawyer." She nodded again. "Was he around much?"

"I've heard his name but I never saw him."

Most Senate staffers don't even know if their boss has a lawyer. "Have you ever heard of Panchax, Inc.?"

"So you've got a specific. No, should I have?"

"Ever hear of a Janet Armstrong?"

She shook her head.

"How about a man named Eddie Hampton? Nervous guy, wasted appearance, big boozer."

"I don't know every big boozer in town."

"I wasn't implying . . ."

"Come on! What happened to your sense of humor?" We flashed smiles toward each other. "Eddie Hampton doesn't ring a bell. That description fits a dozen bums I've known, a hundred more I've seen. Sorry. Do you have anything else?"

"Not yet," I said.

Club 116 used to be housed in a rambling white stucco building in a parking lot next to the Senate offices, a handy location because Club 116 is the private haunt of Washington's heavyweight lobbyists. Once only a few hundred paces separated the public buildings from Club 116's private door. Bobby Baker, who started as a congressional page, evolved into an attorney and Secretary to the Senate Majority, and ended up serving 15 months in federal prisons for larceny, fraud and tax evasion as a result of a 1960s influence-peddling case, was the guiding light behind Club 116's predecessor, the Quorum Club, which, like Club 116, was located but a silver dollar's throw from the Senate office buildings. Bobby Baker's misfortunes spelled the end for the Quorum Club. But a good idea never dies, and the Quorum Club was quickly reorganized as Club 116, with a private bar and restaurant. Club 116 has always served the best crab cakes in the city.

When construction began on the new Phillip Hart Senate Office Building, Club 116 had to move. Luckily, the men who control the club were able to find and renovate a large townhouse only two blocks away at the corner of 3rd and D streets, Northeast, keeping Club 116 convenient to the Capitol. The move basically changed nothing. The outer walls are maroon brick instead of white stucco, there is no name on the curtain-covered glass door, the windows are fogged so no one can see in, and the club still serves the best crab cakes in the city.

The bartender smiled as he handed me my club soda. I pointed to a table in the corner, he said *sure,* and I sat there, waiting for Jack the Mack and hoping no one would sit close to us. It was 11:17, early in the day, yet Club 116 had five other customers—all men, all over 50, all with a drink resting in front of them. They didn't look like they were sipping club soda.

The inside of Club 116 is exactly the opposite of what one expects of a private club run by wheeler-dealers so they can have a quiet place to lunch and drink and forge their pacts.

The second floor has small private meeting rooms, but the main action takes place on the first floor. A small bar is off to the left of the front door, and the dining room with its white-clothed tables occupies the rest of the space. The dining room has the capacity for about 70 customers. The furnishings are extraordinarily bland, with fake gaslights on the wall and a worn dark red carpet on the floor. Cloth napkins, yes, but functional *first* chairs and silverware. The decor resembles a dining room in any one of a thousand franchise motels scattered along America's highways. Jack the Mack explained to me that this massive understatement is deliberate: during any normal working day of Congress, 70 percent of the world's multinational corporations and major money concerns have a high-paid lobbyist who visits the club, with an especially heavy representation by the military budget bunch. Some top congressional aides—committee counsels and the like—have memberships too. Guests can be anybody. Occasionally a member from the House or Senate drops by, but they are too obvious in the club and too far removed from the quorum bells that run their lives.

"If this building were to accurately, physically reflect the power the club represents," explained a man who epitomized those words, "there'd be such a hue and cry that its worth would be cut in half. The governing committee even hates to give the place new paint jobs for fear some passing citizen will point too nosy and noisy a finger."

But Club 116 still serves the best crab cakes in the city.

Jack "the Mack" Shaughnessy. He took his nickname from the common man's raincoat he wore when he first came to Washington. When he joined the staff of President Franklin Delano Roosevelt, a highly revered newspaper columnist dismissed Jack the Mack as "a probably nice enough young fellow who somehow managed to work and worry his way through law school and has now landed himself a position not unlike a minor court functionary in a Shakespearean comedy." By the time FDR died in office, the world knew Jack the Mack as a major strategist and street fighter in his boss's New Deal. Jack the Mack left public office the day after FDR's successor, Harry Truman, won the presidency on his own. They parted friends: Jack the Mack later said if they hadn't parted then they'd have ended up enemies. As it was, he retained an unofficial tie to the Truman White House, someone who knew the score and could cut a deal out of it, whether in Congress or the courts or the White House itself.

Truman left town. Jack the Mack stayed, his reputation and his clout growing each year. Eisenhower liked Jack the Mack and of course everybody liked Ike. JFK relished banter with this legendary Irish politician and LBJ was canny enough to use Jack the Mack as best he could. Richard Nixon invited him to a state dinner once, but wouldn't talk to him—and wouldn't say why. Jack the Mack went and didn't care; he worked around that man, as did everyone else. Gerald Ford invited Jack the Mack back to the White House for dinner and they talked about great Notre Dame football teams. Jimmy Carter put him on an advisory commission and wondered in the formal announcement if America would ever be so unfortunate as to have a man like Jack the Mack pass from public service, which was a polite way for a Georgia preacher to say *die*. Much of Washington wondered if Jack the Mack could die. If anyone could cut a deal to avoid that, he could. And if anyone would know who had tried to cut such a deal, he would.

"But the world is not much longer for the likes of me," he said as we waited for our crab cakes to appear. His thick white hair was combed in a pompadour, his blue eyes twinkled and I wondered if he'd had a face-lift. His form was trim, his walk steady. He used an Irish brogue that I read somewhere he'd acquired around 1943 to tease Winston Churchill about the plight of the boyos when they came home from fighting tyranny in occupied Europe. The brogue suited Jack the Mack so well he never dropped it from his repertoire.

"This will be the last presidency for my generation," he told me. "No matter who wins. Carter is not quite one of us, but he's close enough. Young Ronald Reagan—whose movies I never liked—he's the last true candidate from my class."

"Then you're not losing power either way it goes," I said.

"Well . . . We're like a great comet crossing the sky, those of us from the days of FDR, the Great Depression, World War II. We stamped our distinctive rule on six decades. Now we're almost gone. But like a comet, we'll flare bright again before we suddenly fade."

"Then who gets this city?"

"Not you, I'm thinking. Your generation will never rule as ours did, not for all your numbers. You've been bonded by blood, yes, but by wars like Vietnam and inflation that will never be officially won—and perhaps never lost either. Victory and defeat were clear for us. Your crises lack clarity. Such confusion saps a generation's strength. So many of you have already peaked, and you've only just begun.

"But I pity more the generation behind you. They suffer from data without wisdom. History is too fast and furious to guide their souls. They'll fight only for survival; that's a struggle so small it never yields true sustenence. There is nothing their TV shows them that is worthy of faith. They believe only sensations, not sincerity or eternity. Living with them may be your biggest problem."

"It's too much for me today," I told Jack the Mack as the waiter set the white plate with its two deep-fried, brown crusted patties before me: the best crab cakes in the city.

"It's probably too big for any of you," he said as he picked up a fork. "Such times as these wear the best men down rather than push them to the fore.

"Of course," he said, "I make no judgment of you."

"You might as well," I told him. "I've not exactly done myself proud."

"One never knows until one stops," he said. "Now, what can I do for you, besides insist that this lunch be billed to someone who likes neither of us and pays my fee for that privilege?"

"I need to know about Washington."

"Don't we all?" he replied, then smiled:

"Washington is a figment of America's imagination. For good or bad, that's all it is, the product of America's dreams and nightmares. True, it is the center of our society's gravitational pull, but equally true, it thus is a collection of what flows to it from the hinterlands. It is like every American small town, only concentrated in intensity and with a grander scale of effect. The forces in small-town America can fail to fix potholes, the forces in Washington can fail to stop

Armageddon. Unfortunately, the same mix of saints and devils end up dealing with both levels of problems. We live within that reality. What do you want from it?"

"I need to know if someone here is corrupt, and if so, how."

"Of course someone is and the hows are infinite. Tell me more, or we have little left to discuss."

He was the ultimate wheeler-dealer, one who might have a stake in whatever I was trying to destroy, but I had to trust him. "I think Senator Robert Woodson, his A. A. Martin Mercer, probably his lawyer Fred Thomas, are crooked. I need to prove it."

He carefully patted his mouth clean with the white cloth napkin, said, "I question whether you *need* to *prove* anything."

I wondered about his precise answer.

"Is suspicion all you have?"

"No, I've got one error I can hit them with, plus an idea where the bodies are buried. He seems clean on the Floor, but the way he runs the D.C. Appropriations Subcommittee is too curious."

Jack the Mack frowned. "I think I understand.

"D.C. is a colony run by foreign congressmen who get little reward from doing that job. The local leaders are puppets attached to Congress's purse strings. The most they can do is make trouble. The only other power in this city is the businessmen who follow the laws of the marketplace and organize semipublic governing groups like the Board of Commerce, which in turn are dominated by a hard core of shrewd horsetraders. That didn't mean much until government here grew so big, so ripe, so ready for plucking.

"Congress determines who makes money how in this city. How many police and firemen D.C. has. Whether a multimillion-dollar civic center gets built and with what kind of federal government funds. Whether the city adopts a backstop internal computerized audit system to track the carloads of money it misplaces each year.

"Perhaps I've heard rumors. I know nothing that would compel me to call the U.S. attorney and say, 'Here is crime.' I have also never dealt with those . . . *public servants* you named," he said, enunciating the words. "Or with certain developers and contractors who have . . . ingenious profit schemes and want my assistance.

"So what can I tell you, laddie? If I were the clever, honest man you think me and not simply a canny old Irish lawyer, the least I could do is confirm your suspicions, maybe drop one or two hints on where to pursue your hunt. I will only wish you good luck and Godspeed and hope that you do well by doing good.

"I also hope," he said as he led me to the door, "that these ramblings haven't been a waste of time."

"Not at all," I said. "Not at all."

I looked across the Senate cafeteria's small table to David, said, "If your boss were still on the D.C. committee, how would the two of you steal money?"

He blinked, blinked again, moved his steaming coffee cup out of the way so he could lean closer to me. "What are you doing, John?"

"Finishing something somebody else shouldn't have started."

"Going after her father won't help anything," he said. So David knew. By now, probably most of my friends knew.

"This has nothing to do with that," I said.

"You sure?"

"Yes," I lied.

"Then why are you trying to dig a grave for Woodson?"

"He dug it himself. I'm trying to keep my name off the tombstone."

David looked around the room crowded with other Senate aides enjoying their lunch. "If I help you now, will that get you free?"

"Sure." Neither of us had much faith in my easy answer.

"You make your friends be too smart, John." He sighed. "What do you want to know?"

"How to steal using the D.C. Appropriations Subcommittee, especially in areas like the planned civic center and contracted services for the D.C. government."

"Those are the kinds of things you joke about when you're drunk and a little disgusted."

"Or sober and a lot crooked."

"There is that," he said. "Although I don't believe it's being done . . . What you do is wire the appropriations process.

"You get bribed for several things. To OK a project—like the civic center—where a lot of people are going to make a lot of money, especially if Uncle Sam picks up most of the tab then lets them reap the bennies. Just guaranteeing approval is often enough. If you can determine whose property is going to get bought to build it, there's another big chunk of money.

"There's a chance to rig the contracts. Low-bid competition, right? Eliminates collusion, right? Wrong.

"Let's say Congress decides the federal GSA is supposed to subcontract $10 million of a D.C. project like the civic center. That's a $10-million price tag, but the contracts that get let on the basis of low bids to that figure are just the beginning. *Contract modification* is the name of the game.

"See, the Appropriations Subcommittee usually allows contracts to have a cost modification clause for things like utility increase that can't be planned for. The clause allows a contractor to revise his approved bid. Add more money to the cost. In effect, increase Congress's appropriation. If the increase is OK'd, the money gets layered in somewhere in the next year's budget as a necessary and unavoidable expenditure, maybe not even under the project's name.

"Approval for a modification is a nice, legal, formal system where the contractor sends his request to the D.C. Subcommittee. The subcommittee, in Congress's name, OK's it. The GSA projects officer gets notified, and the bucks get passed out.

"That approval is a sham. Usually the subcommittee is a bunch of guys too busy doing stuff they care about to pay any attention to something as routine as a modification request for a contract that didn't matter to them in the first place. Let's say the modification request is to increase a $10-million project by 4 percent. Four percent doesn't sound like much, is way below the inflation rate, sounds better than $400,000. Spread out four 4 percent requests over a year's time and nobody notices you've picked a million and a half out of Uncle Sam's pocket. You know how the subcommittee usually handles such requests? They make all contract modification requests subject to the review and approval of the chairman, which . . ."

"Bingo!"

". . . which is usually automatic in the best of times when everybody is moderately straight and God-fearing."

"Suppose everybody isn't straight and God-fearing?"

"Then it's rape and pillage time. It only takes a few somebodies. The fewer, the better. The contractor, in collusion with subcommittee insiders, rigs his bid so low no legitimate contractor can come close to him. He legally wins the contract, which could have been created corruptly to begin with. The bad guys get the low-bid contract, then over the course of a couple years they modify it up as high as they dare. Let's say they double the cost of the bid they submitted and won. Nobody ever really knows. Nobody ever really complains. The chairman approves it. If he's part of the wire from the start, the whole thing is as smooth as shit. The pad gets passed along as a necessary and normal operating cost. In a couple hundred million dollar budget, who notices maybe $10 million of slowly locked in pad?"

"All you need is a crooked chairman, couple crooked jobs."

"Why limit it to a couple?" Articulating *what could be* had reversed David's skepticism of *what was*.

"How can you catch them?"

"You need to show excessive approval or reckless approval of shady contract modification requests. That's hard enough. Then you need to prove the modification approvals were bought. You need to find the bucks that got paid. You then have to make the link proving *why* they were paid. That's a world to lock up."

"How do you start?"

David grinned. "That's the easy part."

David's "easy part" took what remained of Thursday and all Friday morning.

Every Government Services Agency contract has a GSA contracts officer. That official receives copies of all requests for contract modifications—and their approval. There were dozens of GSA projects that came out of the D.C. committee, but I went after only the government-spawned, privately powered civic center, where more than a dozen major contractors labored under GSA's umbrella. Jack the Mack's hint had been too strong to ignore. The GSA contracting officer looked at me nervously when I showed up at his office and requested a copy of his file, but he gave me no trouble. The Requests for Modification file was three inches thick, and took an hour to Xerox.

The next morning I made the same request to a deputy comptroller of the D.C. government. Jack the Mack implied something about a computer contract. The deputy comptroller questioned my right to see the file. I didn't have time to go through the formal legal channels to prove my rights, a fight which would ring alarm bells all over town, so I mentioned that I'd been referred to him by David Henderson, Senate aide. That was true, but the deputy comptroller had no way of knowing the referral was where my clout ended. He knew David's name. They'd done business like this when David's senator served on the D.C. committee. David and his boss were not ones to jerk around. The deputy comptroller stared at me for a full minute, waiting for me to say more or another option to open a safe door for him. Neither happened. He grunted, walked to a locked file cabinet, and ten minutes later I took a two-foot stack of folders to the Xerox machine.

Those two days of Xeroxing swelled my paper file on the lives and times of Robert Woodson, Martin Mercer and Fred Thomas. I paid for the Xeroxing out of the $1,000 Eddie Hampton sent me.

That was the easy, clean part.

Pam was what used to be called *a nice girl*. She came from some small Virginia town with quiet streets, church bells on Sunday mornings, neighborhoods where people didn't lock their doors. She was 20, with limp brown hair chopped off just above her shoulders. The only distinctive feature of her face was its blandness. She wore glasses and should have worn braces as a child. She weighed 40 pounds too much. The best Pam could look was plain. She was cheerful, polite, sweet. On the weekends she didn't go "home," she stayed in her apartment, went to church. Knitted. The city confused

her, but she tried not to let that show. She didn't drink or
smoke, didn't understand the jokes her coworkers made
about drugs. She was easy to excite, quick to laugh, quicker
still to sympathize. For Pam, everyone was basically a good
person. The office scuttlebutt decreed that she probably had
never even been kissed *really* good. Everybody liked her.
Pam was the receptionist for Fred Thomas's law firm.

And I was going to rip her off as best I could.

By 4:20 that Friday afternoon most of the employees of that
law firm had left their office across K Street from the fast food
café where I dawdled over coffee. Firm president Fred
Thomas walked out of the building at 4:10. When I saw his
minions scurrying away in his wake, I knew he wouldn't
return, and that the office would empty as quickly as possible.
The early exodus was easy to predict, especially for somone
like me who knew their operation.

At 4:25 I stood in the fifth-floor hallway outside the law
office's huge door, an empty briefcase dangling in my left
hand. Last chance, I told myself. Say no, walk away, stay
straight. I turned the door handle, and crossed the threshold
into a different world.

The reception area was as big as my entire office. With its
couches, tables and chairs, it had as much furniture as my
apartment. Pam sat inside a tasteful cage, a sophisticated
phone on the desk in front of her. A keyboard hooked into a
video screen, the "word processing system" that became *de
rigueur* for all major offices in 1980, stood a mere pivot away
from her chair. She wore a shapeless brown dress, conservative and correct for a stuffy law firm. The private secretaries
with their long legs and tailor-made skirts provided the sexual
display in that office. They'd all left early, often with their
bosses, for drinks and excitement after work. Pam would
mind the shop, close it up at 5:00. They could trust Pam. Safe,
steady, dependable, honest Pam.

"How are you?" I strolled through the doors, a worried but
happy-to-see-her expression on my face. My words dripped
sincerity. Magic Murphy couldn't have done better.

"John!" Her face lit up, her hands nervously scurried to her
lap, brushed away nonexistent wrinkles, wandered back to
the top of her desk. She was the unassuming angel; the quiet,

thoughtful do-gooder for whom no chore or kindness was too much. I was gambling on her charity and coy remarks by some of her coworkers; on the blush and stammer I'd drawn from her more than once; on the way she always tried to help me, or even just be there, close by; on the way she sometimes stared at me when she thought I wasn't looking. Few men paid her any attention. I'd always been friendly, polite during my piecemeal chores for her bosses. Now I sought obscene payment for simple human courtesies. I'd even dressed as best I could to coax her submission: the blue shirt Maggie once told me made my eyes magic. The last time I'd deliberately worn it was the first night I told Tara I loved her.

Make better use of it now, I told myself. "What's new, Pam?"

"I . . . Oh, I'm just . . . you know. Nothing. How about you?"

Concern clouded my face. "I've been better." I frowned, looked around. "Is Mr. Thomas in?"

"No, he's gone for the day."

"Damn!" I said. "How about his secretary or paralegal?"

"Them too. Is there . . . Is something wrong?"

"Hmph." I shook my head. "Wouldn't you know it?!"

"What is it?"

"Remember that last case I worked on?" She nodded her head though I knew she was only being polite. "I found out that someone I interviewed was wrong. Not much, but enough to screw up the reports I filed. The lawyers will trace the error, and . . . Well, I suppose it's my fault for getting lied to."

"Don't blame yourself! There was nothing you could do."

"Maybe . . . I'm sorry. I don't mean to burden you."

"You're not," she said. Softly. "Is that what you wanted to see Mr. Thomas about?"

"I figured he'd be mad, but before he cut me off for making one mistake, maybe he'd let me go back into the files and correct it, plug the revision through the system. Save the firm some money and hassle."

"Oh I'm sure he would!"

"If he doesn't sue me first."

"Sue" scared her. She knew the trouble lawyers make.

She'd seen anguish parade past her desk. *Why can't people get along, work things out?* she asked me once. *Why tear each other apart?*

"He'd never do that," she said.

"I hope you're right. It would . . . Damn!"

She grabbed the hook. "Is there anything you can do?"

"Sure," I said. "Or at least, I could have. The lawyers review the case Monday. If I could have gotten into the computer, corrected my reports, there would have been no damage. No trouble. Everybody would have been happy."

"That's all you need to do? Correct your reports?"

"More like update, since I didn't make the complete error."

"Of course not," she said.

"But not having done wrong doesn't do me any good now," I said. "If Mr. Thomas were here, or his assistant, maybe even one of the other lawyers—*are* there any of them here?"

"Nobody but me and a couple of the law student clerks studying in the library," she said. "You know Friday: everybody leaves as early as they can. It's not as bad as in the summer . . ."

"But it's still bad enough." I stared off as if envisioning my execution. The idea hit her seconds later.

"John?" she said.

"Hmmm?"

"If you got into the computer, could you fix everything?"

"With a little time. But my temporary employee sign-in code has to be cleared by an executive code. There are no executives here. If there were, the executive might sign me in on his code so there'd be no record of me making the error and correcting it. As long as everything comes out right, nobody but Thomas would care."

Her tongue peeked from between her lips, a gesture of absolute concentration so unconscious that when she saw me looking at her, realized she'd done it, she turned crimson. "I . . . I've got an idea."

"What?" I said, ready to guide her inspiration.

"Suppose you had an executive access code, and the computer was still on? Could you fix things then?"

"Sure. Probably takes no more than an hour." I was

306

guessing. "But I'd also need the central index access code. I'm not sure of everywhere my report data was filed."

"We can do it!" she whispered.

"What?!" My words held hope and thanks, with just a touch of intimate surprise.

"We can do it! We can fix it so there's no problem, so you'll be OK, so everything will be fine and nobody needs to know!"

"That would be perfect!" I said truthfully. "But how?"

"A secretary for one of the senior partners is not . . . Well, I like her and she's a nice person, but she's . . . She's very pretty and sometimes pretty people forget more than they should."

"Pretty people aren't all they're cracked up to be," I said.

Pam blushed. "I . . . ah . . . She's a nice person, though. But she has trouble remembering her access codes. Instead of memorizing them like everyone is supposed to, she wrote them on the underside of her desk pad." My brow wrinkled. Pam giggled, said, "I caught her peeking there once and she told me! I could get them, you could go in an office, use a machine, fix everything!"

"I couldn't ask you to do that."

"You didn't," she mumbled. "You don't have to."

"It can be our secret," I agreed. Her lip trembled. The digital clock on her desk showed 5:07. The computer should have been shut down at 5:00. That menial chore fell to her because she could be trusted to carry out orders. She nervously scurried out from behind the desk, locked the outer door, then bustled back into the inner recesses of the office suite. When she passed me I felt her form tense. She returned a minute later with a slip of paper.

"There's both her access code and her boss's. Plus the code for the central index. And I double-checked: besides those two law students, we're . . . there's just the two of us here."

"Terrific!"

"Ah . . . Where do you want to work?"

"How about the central processing room? That way I don't mess up anybody's office and it might be quicker." And I'd have access to photocopying, but I didn't mention that.

"OK. Should . . . Should I come with you?"

"Got a better idea: if you stay here, you can watch both the front door and the law library door. If the students wander out or if anybody comes in, you can buzz me before they get down the hall."

The need for such security frightened her: "No use bothering anybody by what we're doing," I said. She questioned that rationale, but she was so far committed now she swallowed her fear. "Then afterward," I said, "we should be able to find a place for dinner."

Her hands fussed alongside her stretched-tight tent dress. That was just innocent enough. Not a date offered as a bribe. Not a date at all, *really*. Yet it might be a road to a happier ending—a road with just a small and *of course* legitimate toll.

"OK," she whispered.

We created computers to help us process what we know; by 1980 computers began to shape our knowledge. Grade school children conceived of long division as the consequence of pushing a few buttons on a pocket calculator. I was from the generation that found the now obsolete slide rule sophisticated.

My indoctrination to the law firm's computerized information system was minimal, no doubt at Thomas's specific decree. To turn on one of the typewriter VDT computer terminals required a simple series of commands typed through the keyboard. To get the interlocked maze of high technology machines to perform took a great deal more. The machines were controlled by code words that dictated access to the system. Secretaries had one level of access, paralegals another. Lawyers' access depended on their status in the firm. Everyone had a personal code word which he typed into the computer to "sign on"—let the machine know who it was dealing with and how much authority that mere human had. I'd been given an almost worthless code word to feed the system the reports I'd been hired to make. Now I had a senior partner's access code, the code word to get to the central index system, which would give me access codes for other groups of files, and the fundamental skills to abuse the entire system. Plus whatever time my angel Pam awarded me.

You should be proud of yourself, I thought, as I closed and

locked the door to the roomful of esoteric machines. You used fraudulent means to gain entry to a private premises. You are about to break into a computer. Since you are taking information, you are not only violating privacy laws, you're stealing. Fraud, grand theft, trespass, who knew all the legal names until the judge banged his gavel? Worse, I seduced a young woman's good intentions, ripped off her dreams, made her a criminal too. You should be real proud of yourself, Rankin.

A green video screen asked what I wanted in glowing electric-lettered computer language.

"General index," I typed, then "entered" the code words for client files, followed by "Display all files Robert Woodson; all files Robert Woodson blind trust."

And waited, knowing that the computer logged all requests, hoping that nobody would check on who'd done what with the system until it was too late. Hoping that whatever happened, Pam would somehow emerge with her honor if not her innocence intact.

A flashing row of letters lit up the green video screen:

''INSUFFICIENT ACCESS.''

My unwitting senior partner didn't have enough clout.

"Identify sufficient access," I typed.

''ACCESS LIMITED TO FREDERICK THOMAS, FIRM PRESIDENT.''

And the one item the central index didn't list was anyone's private code name. That avenue was closed.

"Display all files, Panchax, Inc."

''INSUFFICIENT ACCESS.''

Get something. I typed: "Confirm status of Panchax, Inc."

''PANCHAX, INC., CONFIRMED CLIENT THOMAS AND WASHBOURNE.''

I hit the data-freeze button, then typed a series of commands from instructions I found taped to the desk. Within seconds that simple statement was being typed by another machine onto a sheet of the firm's letterhead stationery. I tried a new tack.

"General audit review confirmation," I typed. "Accounts receivable and payable, last four fiscal quarters."

The computer stored all bookkeeping functions separately

from "substantive" functions. With luck, the machine would understand my commands bastardized from the general index and give me something.

"Confirm and report all disbursements from the payments to accounts under/for Panchax, Inc."

The computer took ten seconds—in its time, almost an eternity.

''ACCESS ALLOWED, DATA READY.''

Here we go. I froze the data command, typed in a function command. If I'd learned my computer lessons properly, if I hit the right keys, if I kept fooling the machine . . . if, if, if. I typed the proceed-and-duplicate command, pushed the commence key.

Images flashed on the screen for no more than a second while across the room a Xerox machine *cathunked* them into "hard" copies. I didn't know how long the process would take. No noise came through the closed door when I pressed my ear against it. Only the hum and whirr of the duplicating machine, the computer's hiss, and the pounding of my heart echoed inside this room. The warning phone light from Pam wasn't blinking.

The machine labored for ten minutes. How long before Pam gets too impatient or scared?

Machine noises suddenly stopped. I couldn't risk much more of this. The janitors would be here soon, more eyes to challenge me. The law students might notice the computer was still on.

"Display all client and correspondence, all general reference files relating to HAMPTON, EDDIE."

''NO FILES EXIST THAT TOPIC.''

Why? He must have been deep in it. But then, they could have been that clever, there could have been no reason for him to . . . To be in the computer, which only answered as it was programmed.

"Have any other commands/queries concerning topic HAMPTON, EDDIE ever been entered?"

''AFFIRMATIVE.''

"Display all such commands."

''ALL FILES/COMMANDS HAMPTON, EDDIE PURGED.''

"By who?"

''INSUFFICIENT ACCESS.''

But I knew. Firm president Fred Thomas. Who'd been sloppy with his cover-up. I didn't know if it would hold, but I typed, "Log all commands/queries HAMPTON, EDDIE this date forth, deny new purge commands that topic by any access level." The machine took my command, though that didn't guarantee its obedience. But at least if some government official with a warrant demanded what the computer knew about Eddie Hampton, there was a chance some truth would pop up. I told the machine to duplicate our Eddie Hampton exchange.

The phone flashed as that copy rolled out of the machine.

"John!" Pam hissed at me through the receiver. "Mr. Walters came back for his wife's birthday present and his office is down the hall right past your door and . . ."

"Turn off the computer!" I slammed down the phone, grabbed the stack of papers out of the Xerox tray . . .

A knock on the door. The knob rattled. My eyes riveted on its silver sphere, on the depressed push-button lock dotting its center. I pressed against the wall beside the door just as I heard a new rattle, a scraping: the lock button popped out. The knob turned. The door swung in toward my body, closer, closer, closer . . .

Stopped. Someone stood on the other side of that slab of wood. He couldn't see me and I couldn't see him. Yet. "Mr. Walters," a partner in the firm I'd never met. What did he want in this room where others always did his menial work? Did he hear the quiet hum of the machines as they cooled down? Did he smell the electronic tingle, the motor heat in the air?

And how far was I willing to go?

He grunted. Then reached on the wall to his right, flicked the light switch and dropped darkness all around me. He pulled the door shut behind him. Relocked it. I exhaled deeply for the first time since Pam's call.

She called again 15 minutes later, almost hysterical with relief and fright. Mr. Walters commended her diligence, chastised her for being lax about leaving the lights on: he'd seen the glow through the crack in the door of the central processing room. Good night, he'd said. Have a pleasant

311

weekend, he'd said. Please please please stop now, she'd begged me, and I'd said yes, I'm through.

And taken her to dinner, calmed her down, even cheered her up. Made her blush, giggle. Try a glass of wine. Cemented her silent allegiance to my absolute and total con of her innocence. I smiled at her sweetly, knowingly; she smiled back genuine and sincere, her vision so full of tomorrows she couldn't see the blood in my eyes.

33

His apartment door jerked inward with anger, but fear undercut confidence when Martin Mercer saw me standing in his hall. Ghostly TV echoes of Reagan and Carter quarreling over nuclear destruction drifted around us; a faint bubbling gurgled behind their words.

"What the hell do you want?!" snarled Mercer. The drink in his hand looked like scotch.

"Everything!" I looked like I needed that: rain-matted hair, waterlogged leather jacket and blue jeans, drowned sneakers, a crazed leer on my face.

"See me at the office!" He swung the heavy door toward me. My shoulder crashed against that oak slab, knocked it open and him back. He staggered into the apartment, stumbled against a 50-gallon aquarium on a wall stand. Its air circulation pump shook, but that bubble machine didn't stop. I slammed the door shut behind me. He spilled some of the drink in his backward flight, but not much, and the flicker of attention he paid it was unthinking.

"You just broke the law, Rankin!" he hissed at me. "Forcible entry, assault . . ."

"Tell me about the law! Tell me about what's legal and what's not, about what's right and what's wrong!"

He glanced at his watch, said, "I'm expecting somebody!"

"Gives me a witness."

"How do you know I'm alone now?"

"Because you threw out that bullshit about expecting someone. Because nobody has come running to see what's wrong. Because I've been watching for you, waiting for you.

You drove up alone, gave your red Maserati to the doorman outside, came in alone."

That he'd been *stalked* sank into Mercer; he didn't want to believe it, but sometimes belief counts for nothing. For three hours that Tuesday night, October 28, 1980, for six hours the night before, I'd stood in an alley, waited amidst the garbage for Martin Mercer to come home to his swank Connecticut Avenue residence across from my post. Waited, watched, been soaked by the rain.

"What's the matter with you, Rankin?! Are you crazy?!"

"Yeah," I said, unzipping my rain-stained leather jacket. The sharkfin front sight of the .357 Magnum revolver gouged my flesh as I pulled it from my pants. It was heavy in my hand, awkward but solid, and good. The .357 Magnum can bring down a grizzly bear and looks that way. The bore's black circle stared at Mercer and I said, "I'm so crazy I'm in control."

"That's a gun," he whispered, as if to confirm its existence.

"No shit."

"What . . . What are you going to do with it?"

"Whatever I want."

His brown eyes flicked from the gun to my leering, unshaven face, liked what they saw there even less. I'd spent the weekend poring over Xeroxed files I'd gotten one way or another, eating when I remembered to, sleeping fitfully when I could. Exhaustion rolled over me on Sunday, so I'd hit the cocaine in my desk drawer—not enough for a hard stone, not enough to drag my already fractured form over coke's razor edge reality, but enough to wake me up so I could work over what I had until I knew all my questions and believed all my answers. I didn't answer my phone, avoided ordinary people, stood in the cheeseburger parade at McDonald's behind Radio Woman and felt like I belonged. Monday night Mercer hadn't shown up across from my stakeout. I'd been cocked: waiting and ready, war drums beating my heart. No cosmic battle for redemption materialized. I was waiting alone in a rainy alley. Too much of that year had been spent *waiting* for salvation. By the time Mercer saw me Tuesday night, hell burned in my eyes and no one could have missed its glow.

"What do you want?!" he asked again.

To my left was a sunken living room: couches, chairs, coffee table. Huge color TV with politicians preening as they pretended to debate each other in their quest for victory. Paintings on the wall, subdued lighting. Straight ahead was a hallway, no doubt leading to the kitchen, maybe a dining room, bedrooms. To my right was another doorway, this one on a level raised two steps from the foyer. A light shone from that room where the atmosphere was vibrant brown with wood paneling.

"Go in there," I said, and made him lead the way.

"In there" was another wheel-and-deal world for Mercer. More personality pictures on the wall, some of them duplicates of those in his office. A shelf of books, a second aquarium along one side wall and a third above and behind the couch by the door. Air machines bubbled in them, brightly colored fish swam amidst plants and underwater castles in fluorescent glow. An ancient dime store fishbowl with two electric orange "goldfish" darting around each other sat on one outside corner of the flat, antique desk. A portable black-and-white TV sat on the other. The TV was on, tuned to the presidential debates. I found the knob to turn the volume down, but couldn't figure how to shut it off. Two politicians mimed their TV scene while I pointed the gun toward the couch.

Mercer sat down, automatically putting his drink on the table. That he hadn't been shot yet comforted him. He looked at his watch again, strangely found more comfort there. I moved behind his desk, glanced over the bundles of paper centered among the phone, reading lamp and ashtray full of mashed-out cigarette butts: routine constituent mail with bland answers ground out by "the kids" on their VDT machines, memos awaiting Mercer's OK checkmark. I walked in front of the desk, raised the gun and coldly zeroed it on Mercer. Panic flashed across his face: that's what I wanted. He'd grown too confident here in his private office.

"No! Wait!"

"For what?" I rested my elbow on my hip, kept the .357 vaguely pointed his way.

His breathing slowed, he eased back against the couch. "For a minute there I thought you were going to shoot me!"

"I might."

"Why?!"

"Why not?" I said.

"If you don't know the answer to that . . ."

"There are answers I don't have."

He thought for a moment, licked his lips. Looked at his watch again, smiled. I didn't trust his nod or his words: "Look, any . . . anything you want to know . . ."

"You *will* tell me!"

"Sure," he said. Then relaxed even more, settled deeper in the couch. "Sure." He nodded toward the glass on the table in front of him. "Mind if I finish my drink?"

That mattered only to him, so I kicked the glass over. Scotch splashed on his pants. The glass rolled to the edge of the table, *cathunked* to the floor but didn't break on the carpet. "You're finished," I said as I leaned back against the desk.

"What do you want from me?!" he snapped, but his bravado masqueraded fear he couldn't shake.

"Why did you start Panchax, Inc.?"

"Look, president is just a technical, paper title. It's Woodson's trust money that set up . . ."

"Woodson is too stupid to have thought all this up. That leaves Fred Thomas, hotshot attorney. He doesn't have the guts or the clout, not by himself. That leaves you. Why did you do it?"

He leaned back on the couch, smiled: "Why not?"

I cocked the .357's hammer. He went white as I snarled, "This is the way it is: one chance per question. Understand?"

He swallowed, nodded. I eased the hammer back down, enunciated: "Now, why did you do it?"

"Lots of money," he whispered, found his voice again. "Lots of money to be made. Much more than you can imagine."

"I've got a great imagination. The parking lots, the video game machines: you used them to launder dirty cash, didn't you?"

"How did you know that?"

"Even pimps know about laundering. They use massage

parlors. Or talk about how they will. Tell me about Eddie Hampton."

"Who . . ." Mercer hesitated.

"He's all through the documents I've got," I said, spoiling his pretense. "One of your buddies even modified his computer contract so Eddie Hampton could get an up-front piece of the pie as an accounting consultant. Woodson approved the modification. But Eddie was more than that, wasn't he? He got a whole lot more than that, including what you paid him out of Panchax funds for 'bookkeeping services.'"

"Eddie was the bagman," Mercer said. "He . . . He picked up cash from whoever—the contractors, consultants, lawyers who wanted a fix in for an immigration case . . . Eddie was always the one who picked up the cash. No direct link between us and them in transferring money. And that way he could blend the cash into the business receipts, dummy those books so we'd have clean bucks for the IRS."

"Didn't you worry about Eddie taking more than his share?"

"He was honest. You could trust Eddie to do what he said."

"So I heard. Is that why you killed him?"

"I never killed anyone!"

The revolver locked dead center on him. "We'll work our way back to that. Why did Eddie come to see me?"

Mercer licked his lips. He couldn't shift his eyes away from the black hole before him. "Dumb, stupid, fucked-up move. Eddie . . . Eddie was coming unwound, a boozer getting down toward the bottom of his bottle. He saw red snakes squirming out of walls. Then came the GSA investigations we rode out by the seat of our pants. Then ABSCAM. The two of them maybe starting to cross over. And Tara was coming back to town. She'd shacked up with the chief headhunter of the House oversight subcommittee for the GSA stuff. If the headhunter started looking at the right stuff, added up a couple things there, then got into ABSCAM ideas . . . if she let the wrong thing slip across the pillow not even knowing what it was, if he got too curious and too close . . . Who knew what could happen? I told Eddie there was no problem, nobody would let there be, everything would hold together. But Eddie was shaking apart. I wanted to keep him calm. Told him something like he should keep his eyes and ears open. Make sure we were covered. I was only trying to calm him down! He must have thought hiring you to poke around . . . Who the hell knows what kind of bright ideas Eddie found in the bottle."

"He lied to me."

"That's how business is done in this town."

"So is murder."

He licked his lips again, tore his eyes away from the gun to look at me. "It wasn't like that."

"What was it *like?*"

"An accident." He saw I doubted his nervous offering. "One of those tragic things that happens but . . ."

"But not so tragic," I finished for him, and he seized the chance he thought I gave him.

"That's right! Hell, Eddie's liver was due to go any day, or his mind. I met him that night by . . ."

"By the parking lot you guys own."

"That's right. He was drunk, rambling. He told me he couldn't keep going, he was going to crack. I led him down the alley so nobody else could see."

"I mean," Mercer quickly added, "so nobody would hear what we were talking about."

My eyes blinked. He took that for encouragement, continued.

"He wanted it all to stop and he didn't care how. He said he was sorry, but it had to stop. That's when he mentioned going to see you. Said maybe you could find out how bad things were. I cut him off right there, told him he was crazy. He got all shaky, kept getting louder, kept saying he was sorry. Stupid fuck! Once he got an idea in his head, you could trust him to follow it out. I tried to reason with him. He went crazy, started hitting me. He swung a piece of pipe. I grabbed it away and hit him. He fell down. Dead."

We paused while his story settled around us.

"You hit him once and knocked him down?" I finally asked.

"Down and out." Mercer nodded. "Self-defense."

"So who stood over him and beat his head while he lay in the alley?"

Mercer waited 30, 40 seconds. His halting, hesitant manner turned cold, the sneer broke through his fear and repentant gaze. "What difference does that make? He's dead."

"Then you took his keys and wallet, his money. For lots of reasons. Make it look like a mugging. Delay identification on him. Give you a chance to clean out his home office." That was all guesswork, but Mercer nodded. "You even had Fred Thomas purge his computer. How did he feel about murder, about being an accessory?"

"Fred's a realist. He knows what's necessary."

"And then I showed up. Had Eddie told you he'd already sent me money before you killed him?" Mercer shook his head. "But there I was. So you hired some guys to kill me."

"If I wanted you dead, I do business with the right kind of people for that job."

"I bet you do," I said. "I just bet you do. But you probably didn't want any more heavy duty people in on your problem than necessary, so you shopped for lightweight local talent. How much did you pay the parking lot manager to be a go-between with the spotter and his guys? A couple hundred?"

"I never met anybody like that."

"Maybe not. Maybe you just had his name from Eddie Hampton. Eddie's word that the guy was shady enough to not ask questions about the money Eddie dumped in his till. Maybe you figured if he were that shady, for a bundle of his own he'd fill a contract. Maybe all it took was a phone call and some cash in the mail."

"Nobody tried to kill you."

"Too many bodies too soon—right?"

"Maybe you should think about that, about how times change."

"Maybe *you* can't see who's got the gun."

"What are you complaining about?" he said. "So you lost a car: you got insurance. So you got hurt: you get paid for pain.

"Hell," he said, "you made out better than anybody! You've been getting a classy piece of tail because of all this—don't tell me you haven't milked your protection of Big Daddy Woodson for all you can with Tara! The girl's crazy about you. Play your cards right, marry her, you've cut yourself in on her dad's share of the loot."

My hands started to tremble.

"Oh spare me the pious act! You're nothing but a two-bit snoop. An ex-hack. A hired gun. Thirty fuckin' bucks an hour. Hookers make more than that. I don't buy your big hero scene. All this *outrage* bullshit. You're no knight in shining armor, not after busting in here, not after what you must have done to know what you know. Not with the skeletons you've probably got in your closet.

"What's your play now? Waltz me down to the halls of justice? This isn't the movies, asshole. One: you busted in on me with a gun, so you're the fool up against the law. Two: anything I've said, it's your word against mine. See this watch? Two thousand dollars, some of what I got for a fix on a small contract for GSA's share of the civic center. You know why it doesn't matter that I tell you that? Because it's only your word that you heard it. There's a device built into this watch that lights up when anybody has a mike or recorder turned on within hearing range. Nobody tapes me like they did in ABSCAM. You ain't wearing a wire. Even if you were, all that 'evidence' was obtained by illegal coercion.

"That leaves you three choices. You can be smart—buy in for a piece of the action, plus what you can shake out of Tara . . ."

"She doesn't know about Panchax!" My words pleaded as much as insisted, my fear of contradiction rang loud and clear.

Mercer laughed. "She didn't need to. I sure as hell wouldn't tell her. She probably doesn't want to know anyway. Details like where Daddy gets his money or why Mommy took a dive mess up her tidy world. You pegged Woodson right. He's a fuckin' fool. I tell him when and where to shit, and he doesn't even realize what he's doing. Hell, the only reason we cut him in on the take is to keep him rich and in the Senate—*and* to keep our books clean, use him as a shield if we get caught. We even shake the money tree to keep his campaign afloat. All we need him for is to be there, and that's all he wants anyway. *I* run things. When you brought your Sir Righteous story out to us, I figured if scaring you off didn't work, the way your eyes lit up when you talked about Tara would keep you in line. Looks like I was wrong. But that sure gives you nothing to bitch about."

I fought to hold myself together and the gun on Mercer.

"Like I said, you've got three choices. Number one, you can be smart and buy in. Number two, you can walk away able to do nothing except hope I don't have you whacked some day. Or Number three, you can use that fuckin' toy cannon you've been waving around like some 14th Street cowboy." He smiled: "Which would sure queer any complaints you got about Eddie Hampton."

"I've got you," I whispered. "I've got the gun . . ."

"For how long?"

". . . there's paper, the records you didn't report Panchax on, tax reports you dummied . . ."

He shrugged. "That's bullshit. Nobody cares about it."

"And Eddie Hampton! I got you on that!"

"You got his corpse. Period. Try to tie me to it."

"You knew him, you had a motive."

"You can prove I knew him, maybe you can speculate on motive. Try to prove anything more. In this city. With me pulling my boss's strings.

"You see what you got?" My mind told me his confidence was a pose, the hard bluff backed by years of experience, but it rattled me anyway. "You got shit."

"What about Fred Thomas?" My voice wavered. "You said it: he's a realist. I've got enough to knock him out of his precious law office. How well will he stand up to that? All I need to do is break one crack in your game and everything comes apart!"

"Don't bet on it," he said. "But believe this: you'll lose that girl. You take out her father—*her innocent father*—and what is she going to think of you? If she's ever mattered, you can kiss everything about her good-bye, because he'll go first and worse. And what about her? She'll get smeared."

"She's not in this!"

"Sure she is," he drawled. "Everybody is in this."

My head shook from side to side, more to affirm to myself

that I was there than to deny anything to him. I waved the gun vaguely around the room: "Is this why you did all of it? An apartment, a sports car . . . fish?"

"What difference does that make? Say I did it for fun. So what? It's your ass that's on the line. Buy in or get out."

Crevices split my whole being, my life turned into a jigsaw puzzle mountain ready to erupt.

"What about Janet Armstrong?!" I screamed.

"Who the hell is Janet Armstrong?" His brow wrinkled and my world trembled.

"You know!" I insisted. He *had* to know! "You know. She was a whore who had you in her trick book!"

"What the fuck are you talking about?!"

Truth rang through his words, rattled my bones.

"So maybe a whore had me in her trick book," he snapped, unsure why he'd found a gap in my armor, but determined to pierce it anyway. "So what? What difference does it make? I've seen a lot of whores, I fuck a lot of people. If you're right and she's a real whore, then you got it backward: she's in *my* trick book. Maybe I fucked her, maybe I didn't. Whores aren't worth remembering, even if I used her to pay off some other sucker. Hell, a whore is cheaper than dipping into the 25 grand I carry in a briefcase in the trunk of my car, just in case."

"But . . ."

"But what? I don't know what your beef is on any whore. She's your action, not mine."

"You know," I stammered, logic slipping from my grasp. I had to pull together, even if I couldn't make total sense of it. I had to *control*. "I won't get fucked like her!"

Mercer was riding on top now. He knew it, I knew it, we both knew the other one knew. We both knew that sometimes belief counts for everything, and if I didn't believe the power in my hands . . .

"I don't know who the fuck Janet Armstrong is, but I know you, Rankin! You're a dog lost in a crowd. You got Tara and her old man and Eddie Hampton and me and the whole goddamned world all around you. You don't know whether to bark or bite or run off or play dead or stick around and maybe get a bone and a pat on the head. You're just . . ."

BLAM! The first shot came from nowhere. I don't remember pulling the trigger. The slug tore past Mercer's head, destroyed the aquarium behind him. A .357 Magnum explodes when it's shot: an orange ball of fire flashed around the weapon I held in my hand, the thunderclap deadened my ears. The recoil threw my gun arm straight up in the air. Mercer dove to the floor, desperately seeking shelter between the coffee table and the couch as water and drowning fish swirled around us.

The gun came down still trapped in my fist. I grabbed it two-handed, spun toward the wall on my right: *BLAM!* The second 50-gallon aquarium exploded and fish and plants and sand cascaded out of a jagged foot-wide hole in the glass. I whirled toward the desk behind me: *BLAM!* The telephone shattered, flew across the room. *BLAM!* The dime store fishbowl disintegrated. The roaring air was thick with smoke and gunpowder. *BLAM!* The small TV set with journalist sages analyzing politics died violently, blasted off the desk so hard it unplugged itself from the wall, tubes exploding as it hit the pond on the floor. I whirled back toward Mercer, who was scrambling toward safety. Thirty feet beyond him down the corridor, opposite the apartment's thick oak door, stood another 50-gallon aquarium. Feet planted shoulder width aim over the shark fin sight: *BLAM!* The ball of flame erupted toward the hall. The last glass aquarium shattered and Mercer hugged the floor . . .

I heard the *click* as I flipped open the cylinder, the splashing sound of ejected shell casings hitting the flood on his study carpet. My hand fumbled in the flap pocket of my jacket for bullets the size of my little finger as his frenzied pale face turned to look up at me, see the gun being reloaded.

Mercer charged but he didn't have a prayer as I sidestepped, whipped the three-pound-plus .357 across his head. On the way down he grabbed the desk, but I kneed him in the chest and he flipped over, slumped against its forward wall. He tried one more time to push himself toward me. I backhanded him across the face with the black steel revolver. He sank into the pond on the carpet, dying fish skittering around him, his body sagging against the desk. Blood ran out his left ear because of the first blow; from his right cheekbone and nose because of the second. His breathing was harsh, labored and painful. His eyes glazed with fear, couldn't look away, could only watch me flip the .357's cylinder back open, slide six cartridges snug into black wombs. I snapped the cylinder home, squatted down so he could focus on my face. I was panting, crying, shouting:

"Nobody decides who I am!"

I backed toward the study door, my feet sloshing three steps through the death of worlds he'd kept caged in glass.

Then I dropped into the two-handed combat stance, brought the .357 up a yard from his face where he could smell and taste the hot steel and burned cordite. The black bore lined up dead between his eyes, stone cold certain as I thumbed back the hammer, steadied my feet. His eyes snapped shut, his jaw dropped and he started to hyperventilate, moan as I cried:

"That's my job!"

And I blew a hole in the desk wall a foot above his head, turned and walked away from his hysterical sobs, the splashing sounds he made in the water on his floor.

34

"This isn't going to work out quite like you want," Nick Sherman told me.

"What has?" I replied.

No doubt Sherman was more used to disappointment than he was to late Tuesday night phone calls from combat-shaky men. Together we ruined Wednesday morning first for an assistant U.S. attorney, then for a full U.S. attorney. They shuffled me through the system all day Wednesday. Sometime around noon Sherman drifted off to do his duty elsewhere. Now it was Friday, we were in my office.

"Where have you been?" I asked him.

"Been busy. Saw your friend Mercer. He didn't show up for work Wednesday, so I dropped by his apartment."

Nick showed me his chipped-tooth grin. "He looked like somebody dragged him through Hell—singed eyebrows; face has a splotchy burn; black eye; puffy ear and nose. His apartment got hit by a hurricane. I wonder what happened?"

"Maybe somebody went there looking for a place to stand," I said. And stared back. There'd been enough that I hadn't told.

"I can't complain about that," said Nick. "Not as long as that somebody doesn't flaunt himself on my block. Mercer didn't want to talk about such things—or anything, actually.

"So then I dropped by Fred Thomas's firm where I found a lawyer too chickenshit to even say hello unless he has another lawyer with him. Thomas's mouthpiece said he had nothing to say either."

"Why did you go see them?"

"Now they know we know. Pressure. If they take off or destroy any evidence, they can't plead innocent ignorance."

"Do you have men watching them?"

"Our police department doesn't have one of those TV fantasy budgets. The only guy being baby-sat is Senator Robert Woodson out in Washington state. That's not the kind of delicate job left to an unsophisticated street cop like me. Yesterday morning the good senator was advised that there were definite problems with his number one boy and his legal eagle, and that he was sort of in the shit stew too. His hands are being held by his campaign manager and the FBI's Special Agent in Charge of Washington state."

"What happens now?"

"Unless something pops out of the parking lot manager we're squeezing or the pictures of Mercer we're showing around, nothing. Not until after the election. You can't blame the feds: they're catching enough flak from ABSCAM they don't need to crucify a U.S. senator right before election when his only real crime is massive stupidity."

"He's not that stupid," I said. "He wanted not to know."

"Yeah, well, you get the crime of willful ignorance on the law books, I'll fill the jails."

Mad Dog played me a variation of the *nothing now* song that afternoon.

"Of course it's a great story!" he said. *"FBI and D.C. police investigate senator's office for corruption!"* We can confirm that, and it's only half of what you gave us. But *you* know there's a minimum four-day lag time between when we file and when the column hits the papers. We file now, it'll hit next Monday or Tuesday. We'd be smearing Woodson right before Election Day. Ned doesn't give a rat's ass about Woodson, but we don't want to look like cheap-shot artists."

Saul hesitated, softened his words: "Does Tara know?"

I shrugged. "That's not my job anymore."

"John . . ."

"She's . . . She's not in this."

"But . . ."

"I can't tell her, Saul. This is never."

He didn't understand, but he knew what I meant.

That was Friday, October 31, 1980. Halloween. The same

day the *Washington Post* headlined New Jersey senator Harrison Williams's ABSCAM indictment. The next Tuesday Ronald Reagan swept Jimmy Carter out of the White House with the confirmed results being public before the polls even closed in Washington state, where Robert Woodson won reelection to the U.S. Senate despite his mysterious disappearance act in the last days of the campaign. After two decades, the Senate changed ideological tilts; Woodson made no difference in that balance.

On the following Sunday 932 newspapers carried the first of two Ned Johnson columns detailing the FBI-police probe into Senator Robert Woodson and his associates. The senator was in the headline, though the columns noted that "all indications are that the overtrusting Woodson was duped by sophisticated schemers." That was how Saul and Joey Malletta said the senator from the great state of Washington was a fool, not a crook. The two columns had most of it: the unreported Panchax, Inc.; examples of contracts modified more than 50 percent above their awarded bid; links to campaign contributors; plus a hardball sentence: "Government investigators are most intrigued by last May's back alley beating death of one Eddie Hampton, a small-time accountant who handled Panchax's books, who received a special boondoggle 'consulting' job as a result of a suspicious contract modification, and who, according to reliable sources, was the bagman for bribery schemes concocted by Panchax kingpin and Senate aide Martin Mercer."

Nowhere in the columns were Tara or I mentioned.

The U.S. attorney had a carload of marshals at my office before I'd even finished reading that Sunday's color comics. They didn't have a warrant and acted like they didn't care. We went downtown. Their prosecutor boss screamed at me about "wrecking" his case by leaking it to Ned Johnson. After an hour of his tirade I yawned, which was the first and last time I opened my mouth to the law on that subject. The prosecutor yelled some more, then sent me home.

By Monday, a herd of reporters scrambled after the story their editors had read first in Ned Johnson's columns, which caused said editors to wonder in not so gentle terms what their own highly paid headline hunters had been doing. On

Tuesday morning, front page follow-ups appeared in both the *Washington Post* and the *New York Times*. I got a couple of calls, told the reporters there was nothing I would add to what Johnson had already published. That netted me the 17th paragraph of the *Post* story:

"Authorities have also questioned John Rankin, a local private investigator and former Ned Johnson reporter, regarding Hampton's murder. Rankin refused to comment to *Post* reporters."

Also on Tuesday one of the marshals showed up with a subpoena for a grand jury appearance two weeks away. I thought about calling Art Dillon for advice on how careful I could be, decided to wait.

That decision saved me legal fees. Thursday morning, Martin Mercer, who'd been besieged by reporters, served with a similar grand jury subpoena, and hit with a stonewall every time he tried to talk to his senator boss, showed up at the prosecutor's office with a couple hotshot criminal lawyers. Fred Thomas's lawyer—who didn't come from the same firm as his client—had previously arranged for Thomas and the prosecutor "to have a little off-the-record chat." All of which eventually preempted my grand jury gig.

"They wanted to nail it down fast," Nick told me later, "and copping a plea is the best way. They probably talked to half the big-time crooks on the East Coast, any and everybody they ever did business with. The question became how much they needed to suffer for their sins—and I'm not talking just about jail. Thomas cracked first, which behooved Mercer to jump while he could still have a hand in making his own catch net. They're going to take some other guys with them, but not many and nobody too big."

"That stinks," I said.

"Sure it does," he said. "But *we're* the winners if you consider what probably would have happened. Ain't nobody too excited about how the law got all its evidence."

"Meaning me," I said.

"Meaning you. I don't want to say you done bad, but you stepped over a whole lot of lines. That makes it hard for the good guys to call you buddy or even talk to you and still walk into court."

"*Good guys* could have gotten it all if they'd looked."

"The law doesn't function on could-haves and you know it. If the law pushed these guys to trial, they might walk. The murder case would never make it. Most of the racketeering and bribery stuff is shaky, especially for a jury of our peers to understand. If the judge ruled against the prosecutor enough times, the jury would be so confused it wouldn't know what it was hearing. The tax-fraud stuff looks good. That ain't a whole lot, and if the prosecutor coughs at the wrong time, he might build an appeal for the bad guys, who could win just by hanging in there. There's a chance they could even be acquitted outright. It's happened before in this town."

"So why are they willing to cop?"

Nick smiled. "If we knew that, we wouldn't let them. Probably there's pressure on them from guys who don't want us stirring up more muck while we build the case. Probably they done something we don't know about that they're afraid we'll discover, something we could nail them hard for. Probably they don't want to gamble. White collar crooks aren't famous for their courage."

"Will the prosecutor go for it?"

"If he can get enough." Nick shrugged. "A plea is a cheap, sure thing."

The cheap, sure thing came together late that Saturday.

Martin Mercer agreed to plead guilty to tax fraud, racketeering, and two bribery-public corruption charges. He also agreed to "cooperate with federal and local investigators whenever possible in the course of their ongoing work." In February, a judge sentenced him to a minimum of five years plus fine plus probation. He went to the federal prison facility at Lompoc, California, where former Nixon White House Chief of Staff H.R. Haldeman, former Deputy Assistant to the President Dwight Chapin, attorney-and-Watergate-"ratfucking" expert Donald H. Segretti and a couple of my journalism sources also went "through the university." Last time Nick Sherman checked, Mercer had given FBI agents 1,200 pages of secret testimony on how Washington works: *everybody* knew that Mercer told what wouldn't get him whacked, not everything he knew.

Fred Thomas agreed to plead guilty to tax fraud, civil fraud (he manipulated Woodson's assets entrusted to him in the blind trust to set up Panchax, Inc., with criminal intent) and one count of racketeering. He resigned from the Bar before his fellow barristers threw him out. He got a fine, plus three years at the federal prison in Allenwood, Pennsylvania, the *alma mater* of Watergate warriors CIA-White House consultant E. Howard Hunt, White House-CREEP (Committee to Re-Elect the President) aide G. Gordon Liddy, Deputy Assistant to the President for Domestic Affairs Egil "Bud" Krogh, Jr., and Deputy Director of White House Communications Jeb Stuart Magruder.

Robert Woodson, senator from the great state of Washington, had immediately agreed to cooperate in whatever way he could. Nobody charged him with anything, nobody sentenced him to anything. He talked at great length to the FBI and federal prosecutors, to Nick and the D.C. police. He knew little of value. His nervous colleagues in the Senate "agreed" to his "request" for a "full public hearing" before the Ethics committee "as soon as possible"—which turned out to be March of 1981 (everyone wanted to be sure all the ducks were in a proper row). Mercer and Thomas made carefully orchestrated cameo appearances in which they absolved Woodson of all evil. Woodson read a long and noble speech written for him by his new lawyers and new Administrative Assistant apologizing for letting his concern with the greater issues of the day overshadow his responsibilities for effective administration of his senatorial duties. Woodson then announced that as soon as the committee had concluded its work and the proper authorities no longer needed him, he would resign from the Senate.

The committee praised his candor, his conscience, his long years of faithful service. There were solemn pronouncements about the need for better staff oversight, fewer pressures on public servants, more efficiency in government. The hearing record and report was printed and bound along with a thousand other congressional reports and, if it's still in stock, is available to the public free of charge from the Senate Document Room, U.S. Capitol, Washington, D.C. 20510.

Nobody mentioned me. Nobody mentioned Tara. Later in

1981, half a dozen contractors were indicted on the corruption charges copped to by Mercer and Thomas. Five of them went to jail for a few months, paid fines; one of them got off when he stalled the law until the third prosecutor to get the case tripped and the judge declared a mistrial. The government never bothered to ask for a retrial. The parking lot manager who'd subcontracted my beating also walked: "We decided not to charge him," Nick said. "Shaky case. He feels my hand on his ass. He'll go inside soon enough." By November, 1981, the manager had copped to an unrelated receiving stolen property charge. The three guys he'd hired continued shuffling in and out of prison on various charges.

Eddie Hampton stayed dead and buried.

Tara came to see me that Sunday, November 16, 1980. The papers that had been full of her father during the week now reported other matters:

Saturday's *Post* described the extradition fight between Guyana and the United States over a Peoples Temple cult member accused of murdering former congressman Leo Ryan.

Sunday's *Post* bannered the story of Union Station, the depot at the base of Capitol Hill that Congress had turned into a pitiful disaster by trying to graft a "National Visitors Center" on what was once a great place to catch a train. When the plan for the visitors center was announced in 1967, its legislative father, Congressman Kenneth Gray (D-Ill.), proclaimed in his Floor speech that "the proposal we bring to you today will not cost one cent of taxpayers' money." By that November, 1980, Sunday, Congress had spent or committed $117 million of taxpayers' money and destroyed Union Station. The main building would soon be closed as a safety hazard. The debacle's end was nowhere in sight. Congressman Gray had retired amidst the storm of a sex-and-influence scandal precipitated by Liz Ray, a blond, busty secretary he'd hired in 1972 even though she claimed she couldn't type. Liz Ray's revelations of sexual and political hijinks forced another of her bosses, powerful committee chairman Wayne Hays, to resign from Congress.

"I can't stay," Tara said as she stood in my office doorway.

She moved further in. "My father . . ." She shook her head. "I didn't come just because he wanted me to. And before, I . . . that was never why . . . before."

"I know," I said.

She gazed around the office as if to see what had changed.

"I'm sorry," I said.

"You're sorry!" Her eyes overflowed as they so often had. She looked away, paced nervously, stopped. "What do you have to be sorry for?"

"That anything bad happened." She wiped her face as I spoke. Her hair was still golden, her form lithe. "That it happened to you.

"My father . . . My father said to tell you he's sorry."

I said nothing.

"He's not bad!" she insisted. "Not really. He's not . . . He's just . . . He's my father. He tries."

"I suppose he does."

She shook her head, searched my face with her blue iceberg eyes: "You know that I'm sorry too, don't you?"

Make me answer the question, I thought. "Everybody's sorry."

"You don't sound like you believe me."

"You're wrong."

"God I hate this!" There seemed nothing worth saying, so I waited. She became as businesslike as she could. "My father owes you."

"I never signed on with him."

"That's not the point."

"It is for me."

"Will you please listen?!" The tears started again, stopped.

"It's not what you did, it's what he did, what he let happen. He and I . . . we talked about it. We had no other choice. He . . . You went through a lot, lost a lot."

"That's my job."

"No it's not," she whispered.

There was nothing I could say to that.

"He . . . He wants to reimburse you."

"I won't take his money."

"We figured that." She smiled. "He worked something out

with his lawyers—his new lawyers, not . . . not Fred Thomas's bunch. He even cleared it with the U.S. Attorney.

"They did a good job," she said as she laid a bulky manila envelope on my desk. "Since it's reimbursement, you won't need to pay income taxes on it. Some forms, even an opinion from the U.S. attorney which should help convince the IRS, all that's in there. Along with the keys, new license plates and title in your name, all the transfer documents, three years' insurance policy.

"It's the Porsche," she said.

Before I could refuse, she continued:

"I'm leaving it parked out front. Fair trade: my car for yours. It was legally his. I never wanted it. I won't take it back, neither will he. You can let it sit there and rust or get towed away or stolen or whatever." Her smile was weak as she mimicked our old Watergate joke routine: "You could do that, but it would be wrong.

"My father . . ." She shook her head: "He never meant to do anything wrong!"

I'd stayed behind my desk when she showed up. That seemed no longer necessary or right, so I moved close to her. She must have felt my nearness as much as I felt hers.

"It's going to get rough again," I said, not knowing if she knew about the scheduled Ethics Committee hearings, about the inevitable and insatiable press analyses, about the pointing fingers and stares and whispers that would dance around her like shadows in a lightning storm. She might not know those details, but she was smart enough to predict their plot. "Not just for him. For you."

"So what?" Her words were steel. Tara wouldn't shirk *or* answer her own brutal questions; she clung to them because they kept her from falling back inside those iceberg blue eyes where all the tears came from. She was as careful not to show anything deep in there as she was afraid to see it.

"I'm sorry," I said again. She nodded. Her chin, her swollen lips trembled, a new stream trickled down her cheek.

"Thanks," I said.

"Oh God!" she whispered, closed her eyes, leaned into me. Her sobs shook my frame, her tears soaked through my shirt.

Carefully, deliberately, I cupped her tense, thin shoulders in my hands: Again I smelled the salt of her tears, the damp warmth of her face buried in my neck. Her golden hair brushed my cheek.

For a moment, maybe more. Then she leaned away and I let go. She looked up, but her eyes never quite met mine.

"Only you," she whispered, "all the others . . . It was only you. You know that, don't you?"

Not too many days before I would have bet my life that I knew exactly what she meant. But I didn't, and I knew *that*. It would have served no good to tell her, so I nodded politely.

Her lips trembled a smile and those iceberg eyes met mine. She nodded, another tear fell. Then she walked out the door.

Nobody called me on the phone, nobody came for me as I stood there, a quarter hour or more. God didn't write the answer on my wall. I went out to the street.

The Porsche waited at a parking meter smack in front of The Eclectic. I stared at the car, stared up Pennsylvania Avenue, searched above the Sunday strollers and the nearly naked trees, but couldn't see the Capitol's dome.

"I thought she was gone," said Rich as he came up behind me. He nodded to the Porsche. I'd explain it to him later.

"She is," I said. He stood with me, waiting, worried.

"I thought she was the one," I said, still looking up the Avenue.

"She was," he said. Smiled. "You just didn't get to choose *which* one."

That week I took a couple days off, ran the Porsche on the highway, ended up in Asbury Park, New Jersey, a seedy American beach town made famous by everyone from F. Scott Fitzgerald to Bruce Springsteen. There are cheap motels and pizza parlors and beer joints where rock bands play during "the season." There's a fortune teller's booth. An indoor merry-go-round with brightly painted horses. There's a boardwalk with a civic convention center at one end and a huge arcade building at the other with the white-lettered word "CASINO" high up on dirty brown bricks. The sand is tan, the sea gunmetal gray. Black boulder jetties stick far out into the inlet to sap the waves' strength before they hit the shore. Nobody goes there in November.

All through the ride I thought I could smell Tara's musky scent mixed in with the steel and leather of the car. Many days were like that, many nights worse. I'd go to a party, and in the crowded kitchen I'd see a strawberry blond halo surrounding a face obscured by some man's shoulder, taste my heart in my throat; he'd move and it wouldn't be her. My telephone would ring in a quiet moment and I'd wonder/hope/fear. I'd sit alone in a dark movie theater, eat popcorn and remember when I used to bounce kernels off her forehead to tease her. I saw her once walking along Pennsylvania Avenue's flat face near where we met. Once Joey Malletta cautiously told me he'd seen her at a party of *Washington Post* types. Joey said she'd been with a *Post* reporter named Cliff something-or-other. They were laughing. Joey said maybe he was working on a story about her father or something. I said no, he was just a nice guy. In the spring of 1981, Katie told me Tara moved to Paris, finagled a job as a script girl on a Truffaut movie. I've never been to Paris. For too many heartbeats Tara was wrapped around me like a dark and harsh shroud I couldn't shake.

And then one day the shroud was gone, the harshness vanished. It didn't hurt anymore, like the pain in my knees as I ran down the Mall then turned the Reflecting Pool's corner in front of the Lincoln Memorial, started back home *suddenly* without hurt, *suddenly* with full and easy breaths, *suddenly* with sunlight all around and the buildings life sized and where they belonged. The pain lost no significance, it just lost its power.

The beach at Asbury Park was deserted. A few prisoners of a retirement home shuffled over the boardwalk on a day-trip furlough, but most of the stands and stores, even the fortune telling booth, were closed. The wind whipped spray off the sea, tingled my face and cut through my leather jacket as I walked far out on a jetty, churning water to each side, granite boulders slippery beneath my sneakers. I stood out at the end until the chill filled my body. No thoughts, just being there was sufficient. Inside my flap pocket was the plastic bag of cocaine. About a third of the load was left. I used my car key, risked the wind and spray to hit each nostril twice with huge white mounds. The rush burned through me. So sweet. So extreme. The bag still held more cocaine than the average American consumer ever sees at one time. Crystal magic, dangerous and delightful. It either meant a great deal or not a lot; maybe too much and maybe nothing. Whatever, merely holding it put me where choices were ultimate and unavoidable, no matter what *the whole truth* was. I'd spent too much time trapped between extremes. I flicked my wrist: the bag sailed over the rocks, fell into the waves.

One week after Tara came to see me, Bruce Springsteen stormed Washington. Katie and I went to his Sunday night show. Her husband, Saul "Mad Dog" Lazarian, was *busy* and didn't have a ticket anyway. She talked a lot about Saul, but I was either too deaf or too distracted to understand. They divorced eight months later, as swiftly as they'd married. She told me: *"Suddenly it became clear that I'd misjudged time."* He told me: *"She expected me to change."* That night Springsteen played my heart out. My eyes searched the crowd for Tara but didn't find her. I didn't get home until 1:30 A.M., but was up at 7, at the D.C. Courthouse at 7:30, bleary and blown out but ready for the sentencing of Herbert Jerome (aka "Magic") Murphy, who'd pled guilty to one count of simple assault and one count of pandering.

Court convened at 8:00 sharp. While I waited I read the *Post* story on 1960s rebel rock 'n' roll leader Bob Dylan, who had announced that—like the now lame duck president who once quoted him—he'd become a born-again Christian, forsaking the fire for faith. Magic was the fifth case up, following a sentencing for nonsupport, a sentencing for drunk driving, a no-show for whom the judge issued a bench warrant, and a burglary case that started out as an arraignment and, after a quick conference between client and attorney (who had just met), ended up as a guilty plea with a date set for sentencing.

Maybe it was his uptown attorney who'd arranged for Magic to walk through the holding-cell door at 8:34 in a three-piece blue pinstripe suit, white shirt and dark tie instead of a jail-issue gray pants and work shirt. Magic was shorter than I expected, five-foot-ten, stocky, with a smooth, nicely featured face. Ebony hue. Cobra eyes. He moved like a dancer supremely confident of a winning performance. After reading the charges, the summation by the prosecutor of his case and his announcement of acceptance of defendant's guilty plea bargain, after defense counsel's lengthy rambling about how they'd accepted the government's offers and wished the court to remember that Mr. Murphy had been languishing in jail for over a year facing an unjust, unsubstantiated and untrue murder charge which took a grievous toll on an innocent man who'd been fully cooperative with authorities (despite a slight misunderstanding when he "technically" jumped bail and needed to be caught and then extradited back to D.C.), the judge took over. He started to read aloud parts of the presentencing probation on "Mr. Murphy," got as far as "seems to be a confirmed member of a subculture and is ultimately unlikely to deviate from it or from the generally recognizable, exploitative patterns of pimps . . ."

When Magic boomed out: "Excuse me, Your Honor, but that isn't true!"

Even the whispering attorneys who'd been killing time in the back rows fell silent. I saw Magic's attorney close his eyes, pale.

"I beg your pardon, Mr. Murphy?" said the judge.

"What it says there, it's just not true!" Magic's attorney put a hand on his client's arm. The defendant's voice was indignant, angry. "Your Honor, can I say something?"

"Certainly, Mr. Murphy," said the judge. He was more curious than angry about the interruption. Not often will a defendant jeopardize his fate by antagonizing the man with the gavel.

"What that says there," said Magic, a worldly leer clear in his tone, "about me being a *pimp*. Exploiting people. That's not true. I never used my magic to get anybody to do anything they weren't already doin' or fixin' to do."

"Really? Am I to understand you are changing your plea?"

Magic's attorney grabbed his arm, whispered frantically in his ear. Seconds later, the defendant said, "Um, ah, no sir, Your Honor."

"Then do you mind if we continue?"

Magic shook his head.

"If you voice no objection, let the record show you agreed to my continuing." Magic kept silent and the judge continued, flipping through pages about Magic's high school drop-out career, about petty theft probations, about a downgraded drug charge, about time he'd spent in a French jail for possession of a handgun and attempted murder, about several unindicted arrests.

"The prosecution has asked me to send a message to the streets with your case, Mr. Murphy," said the judge. "I think it is obvious to everyone in this courtroom that whatever you claim to be, what you do is faithfully represented in these documents and by your own admission through your plea. To my knowledge—and I had my clerk check—you are only the fourth person charged with pandering or pimping in this city this year. Given the hundreds, perhaps thousands of such potential defendants the court has been made aware of over the years, I am particularly pleased to see you standing before me today, and I am most heartened by your plea and the chance it gives me to 'send' that 'message to the streets,' for what little good it will do."

With that, the judge gave Herbert Jerome "Magic" Murphy the maximum sentence he could: five years in prison. With credit due for the time he'd served awaiting trial, plus "good time" he earned in prison, Magic was released 14 months later.

Almost all the leaves had fallen from the trees as I walked back to my office that morning. The sky was gray with thick clouds, rain was expected. The wind pushed against my leather jacket. Nick said he would tell Tom Armstrong in Eugene, Oregon (where there's a river and it's green all year round), what happened to the man who killed his daughter. "I'll handle the *whats*, friend," Nick told me. "You've got enough problems handling the *why*."

He was right. I had piles of transcripts, letters, grand jury and police reports, tapes of conversations, my own notes, the knowledge of how I'd been fooled by her trick book and where it had taken me. What I saw there was a woman no one ever really knew who turned out like no one ever expected. She was who she was. Maybe she believed she'd find her life's redemption in someone else, in Magic. The truth is that never works, even if you call it love. In 1980 I paid a lot less for that lesson than she did.

That wouldn't help a good man who was her father make sense of her life, or his own. He hoped I'd found an ultimate force behind this death in America's city of power. There were a thousand things I could tell him, none of which added up to the cathartic breakthrough he so desperately wanted. I suppose I could have bundled up all those "cold, hard facts," the tapes and transcripts and photocopied reports of blood and degradation, dropped them in the mail with a wordy dissertation cross-referencing this statement with that assumption to this pretentious theory, all of which wouldn't boil down to a *why* answer any better than the one I typed out that morning, mailed to him along with a bill marked "Paid in Full by Eddie Hampton" and the hope that a good man in Eugene, Oregon, would accept the simple sense I found in Janet's life:

"She betrayed herself."

There was a lot of that that year.

Maybe simple truth like *you are who you are* creates its own sense. I don't know. I'm just a guy working a job.

The rest of 1980 kept challenging America's ability to make sense out of life's turmoil. On a bitter December Monday night, a man gunned down ex-Beatle John Lennon outside his New York apartment building because the killer had delusions about being John Lennon and promoting the 1950s American novel of adolescence *Catcher in the Rye*. No one is assassinated in *Catcher in the Rye;* it was written when the Beatles were English schoolchildren. In 1972 the FBI secretly shadowed Lennon, hoping to find a way to "neutralize" him because they feared his political influence would embarrass then-President Richard Nixon. On that cold December Monday night of 1980 there were no angels of law and order to stop an assassination. The next night in Philadelphia, Bruce Springsteen stood center stage, looked out over the crowd, and, as *Time* magazine's cover story (Bruce once had a *Time* cover story of his own) on Lennon noted:

> Instead of ripping right into the first song, Springsteen simply said, "If it wasn't for John Lennon, a lot of us would be some place much different tonight. It's a hard

world that asks you to live with a lot of things that are unlivable. And it's hard to come out here and play tonight, but there's nothing else to do."

Then Bruce and the E Street Band tore into Springsteen's own anthem, "Born to Run," . . . Guitarist [Miami] Steve Van Zandt let the tears roll down his face, and organist Danny Federici hit the board so hard he broke a key.

"In the day we sweat it out on the streets of a runaway American dream . . ."

Life was no more comprehensible in the next year, 1981. The 52 American diplomat hostages came home from Iran after 444 days in captivity, and a 26-year-old drifter "from a good family" with a John Lennon button in his pocket, method stolen from the movie *Taxi Driver,* and a hunger to forge his name in fame to the woman who played a prostitute in that movie, shot actor-turned-president Ronald Reagan, his press secretary, a Secret Service agent and a D.C. policeman. The would-be assassin fired his pistol barrage about three blocks from Martin Mercer's apartment. President Reagan was rushed to George Washington University hospital where both Janet Armstrong and I had been treated for criminal-assault wounds.

Sometimes all the people I knew in those days seem like strange ghosts to me; what we did seems like a movie I watch and am part of, too. I see the crowd of faces—Eddie Hampton, Nick Sherman, Janet Armstrong from her newspaper clippings, Saul and Katie. Rich and Maggie and Paul, Art and Cheryl, Joey Malletta and Martin Mercer. Tara. Everyone else. Some human form in sneakers glides through them and then is gone. I look and he's me; look again and he's all of us; look a third time and he's just another runner in the street.

114

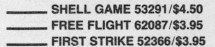

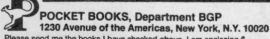

Outstanding Bestsellers!